Praise for C
Christmas C

"'Tis the season for hunky cowboys, and Brown has delivered one right to us… a holiday treat to be savored."
—*RT Book Reviews*, 4 Stars

"Cowboys, Christmas, love, mistletoe, and lots of humor—a great combination for a steamy read you won't be able to put down."

—*Thoughts in Progress*

"This story of very quiet holiday 'miracles' [is] full of color and caring… Written with the verve and sense of liveliness that marks all [Carolyn Brown's] books."
—*The Book Binge*

"A deliciously sexy tale… Packed with humor, adorable pets, a vicious snowstorm, sexy situations, Christmas, steamy hot romance, and true love, this story is a winner."
—*Romance Junkies*

"Carolyn Brown hits it outta the park once again with *Mistletoe Cowboy*… a sweet story of love, family, and community."

—*Guilty Pleasures Book Reviews*

"A sweet, erotic romance… Creed Riley is the epitome of the rugged Texas cowboy—tall, dark, and handsome; and yet he's also sweet and gentle. I felt like I was right there in the Texas Panhandle."

—*Fresh Fiction*

"Sassy and quirky and peopled with an abundance of engaging characters, this fast-paced holiday romp brims with music, laughter… and plenty of Texas flavor."

—*Library Journal*

"A sweet romance that really stresses the chemistry that builds between two highly likable characters… Readers will enjoy this cozy bright contemporary romance."

—*RT Book Reviews*, 4 Stars

"Carolyn Brown is a master storyteller! A love between two people that will enrapture and capture your heart."

—*Wendy's Minding Spot*

"Sassy contemporary romance… with all the local color and humorous repartee her fans adore."

—*Booklist*

"Full of sizzling chemistry and razor-sharp dialogue."

—*Night Owl Reviews* Reviewer Top Pick, 4.5 Stars

"This book makes me believe in Christmas miracles and long slow kisses under the mistletoe."

—*The Romance Studio*

"Carolyn Brown creates some handsomefied, hunkified, HOT cowboys! A fun, enjoyable four-star-Christmas-to-remember novel."

—*The Romance Reviews*

THE COWBOY'S CHRISTMAS BABY

CAROLYN BROWN

sourcebooks
casablanca

Published by Sourcebooks Casablanca, an imprint of Sourcebooks, Inc.
P.O. Box 4410, Naperville, Illinois 60567-4410
(630) 961-3900
FAX: (630) 961-2168
www.sourcebooks.com

Printed and bound in Canada
MBP 10 9 8 7 6 5 4 3 2 1

To Danielle Jackson,
in appreciation for all you do!

Chapter 1

THERE SHE STOOD WITH A DEAD COYOTE AT HER FEET, a pink pistol in her right hand, three bluetick hound pups cowering behind her, and cradling a baby in her left arm.

"Natalie?" He raised an eyebrow and blinked sleet from his eyelashes. Yesterday he had awakened to overbearing heat in Kuwait, and today Texas was colder than a mother-in-law's kiss on the North Pole. Maybe he was seeing things due to the abrupt change in weather. She looked like the woman he'd been talking to via the Internet for the past eleven months, but he hadn't expected her to be so tall, and he damn sure had not expected her to be holding a baby or a pistol.

She whipped around and raised the gun until it was aimed straight at his chest. "Who the hell... oh, my God... you are early, Lucas. Surprise!" she said.

"Yes, ma'am," he drawled. "I guess I am, but you aren't supposed to be here for two more days."

"We were working on a big surprise for your homecoming. Hazel was going to make your favorite foods and we had a banner made and I heard a noise and the coyote had the puppies cornered and..." She stopped and stared at him as if she expected him to disappear.

She caught her breath and went on. "Why in the hell didn't you tell us you were coming home early? You've ruined everything."

"It's my ranch. It's my house and I can come home when I damn well please," he said.

Lucas looked from the baby to the dead coyote, to the puppies, finally meeting Natalie's big blue eyes staring at him across the six feet separating them. There'd been more warmth in her face when there were oceans and deserts separating them than he felt with only six feet between them.

The whole scenario he'd played out in his mind was shot to hell and back. She wouldn't take two steps forward, hug him, and then share an intimate, passionate kiss that said that yes, they had become more than Internet friends.

A whimper came from the blue bundle and she looked down at it. "I know you are hungry, son. We'll go inside in just a second."

Dammit!

He'd thought he'd found the right woman. Hell, he'd even entertained notions that she was *the one*. He'd been right all along: people were crazy to believe what they saw on the Net or to trust anyone they met on there, either.

"Joshua is hungry. Can you put these pups back in the pen? Sorry little critters dug out from under the fence and the coyote cornered them up by the porch," she said.

She damn sure looked different in real life with curves and legs that went from earth all the way to heaven. She was stunning in those snug-fitting jeans, red flannel shirt, and thick brown hair floating in gentle waves down past her shoulders. How could he have not known she was pregnant?

Because you only saw her from the waist up and in

pictures that she posted. Man, you got duped real good this time. Sucker!

"Well?" She shoved the pistol into the waistband of her jeans, shifted the baby to a more comfortable position, and headed toward the porch.

He dropped his canvas duffel on the icy ground. "I'll take care of the coyote and the pups. Then we've got some serious talking to do. Where are Grady and Gramps and Dad?"

"Grady took Henry home after supper. You hungry?"

Yes, he was hungry. He'd foregone supper until he got home because he couldn't wait to have Hazel's home-cooked food. But the way his stomach was churning around he wouldn't be able to swallow. A baby boy, for God's sake! And she never mentioned him one time.

"Hazel in the house?" he asked stiffly.

She stopped and turned. "No, she is not. I've got to get Joshua inside, though. He's cold. Just take care of those pups."

"Don't boss me, Natalie," he barked.

"I'm going inside. You can stay out here and freeze to death if you want, Lucas. The way you are acting, I don't reckon it'll be much warmer in the house when you get there anyway," she said.

He folded his arms across his chest. "And that is supposed to mean what?"

"Figure it out for yourself."

"Shit!" he mumbled under his breath.

He gathered up three wiggling bluetick hound pups and stomped toward the dog pens. What in the hell did she expect—a big old passionate kiss with a pistol and a baby between them?

He opened the gate and set the puppies down inside the chain-link fence, where they made a beeline toward the hole they'd dug. One by one they scampered out of the pen and into the yard and ran helter-skelter back to the dead coyote. One grabbed its tail and the other went to work on its ears, all the while growling like vicious, mean hunting dogs.

Lucas grabbed a piece of two-by-four and chinked up the hole, fought them away from the coyote, and put them back in the pen.

"Whole bunch of you haven't got the brains that one of you should have. That coyote could have killed all three of you if it hadn't been for Natalie." He could hear their whining all the way across the backyard.

He thought about carrying his duffel bag to the bunkhouse, hooking up his laptop, and telling her via Internet to get the hell off his ranch. It would serve her right for not telling him that she was pregnant most of the eleven months they'd been cyber-friends or even mentioning that she'd had a baby. Hell, they'd shared everything over the Internet, so why shouldn't they break up over it too?

He was supposed to be waiting anxiously on the porch for her to arrive in a couple of days and they'd fall right into a wonderful relationship that ended in a trip down the aisle to the altar. Well that damn sure wasn't going to happen now.

He'd been right all along. He'd never believed in all the Internet shit the guys talked about. Not until Drew Camp pulled out his laptop on the first night and there was Natalie on the computer screen with her big smile and twinkling eyes. He'd always been a sucker for blue eyes, and if it had blue eyes, it had brought him nothing but heartache in the past. So why did he expect anything different with Natalie?

He threw his duffel bag over his shoulder and started toward the bunkhouse. He'd almost made it to the back-yard fence when that damned niggling voice in the back of his head told him he was a coward. Lucas kicked the trunk of a pecan tree so hard that it jarred his leg all the way to the hip as he murmured cuss words under his breath. He wasn't afraid to face Natalie or to have it out with her. But he damn sure didn't want to do it in front of Hazel.

Still, it had to be done, and Hazel could just sit there and be quiet.

"Yeah right," he said.

Hazel was never quiet. She spoke her mind and didn't spare the cussing when she did. He whipped around and the north wind blew little sleet pellets in his face that stung every bit as bad as a sandstorm in Kuwait, maybe even more so because his jaws were set so tightly.

"Might as well get it over with," he grumbled as he stormed back across the yard.

Two puppies had figured out how to get out of the pen already and beat him back to the yard. They were fight-ing over the dead coyote when he reached the porch.

"Babies! Pups or kids, ain't nothin' but trouble!" Lucas tossed his duffel bag back on the ground and picked up the coyote by the tail. "You want to show him that you are big mean huntin' dogs, you can do it closer to your pen."

They followed behind him, growling and nipping at the carcass while he dragged it back to their pen and dropped it right in front of the new hole where they'd dug out again. "If another coyote comes sniffing around, you'd best have enough sense to use your get-out hole as a get-back door to protect your sorry little asses."

He left big boot prints in the snow-and-sleet mixture and started to open the door into the utility room, but he wasn't ready for the fight just yet. He sat down on the back steps and stared at the duffel bag so long that his muscles tensed up from the cold and his jaws ached from clenching them. Maybe he should just get in his truck and go to a motel until morning, then hit the recruiting office and enlist in the regular army. They'd send him back to Kuwait tomorrow morning if he asked, and God only knew that he'd damn sure rather be over there than on his ranch in Texas right at that minute.

The back door opened and Natalie poked her head out. "You intendin' on sitting out there all night?"

"I might," he said.

"Suit yourself. I'll tell Grady to bury your stubborn old carcass with the coyote in the morning." She slammed the door shut.

"What a homecoming," he mumbled.

———————

Natalie Clark's hands shook, more in anger and frustration than in nervousness, as she made her way across the utility room and into the kitchen. Why hadn't Lucas told her the night before when they talked via cyberspace that he was coming home early? It was his rotten fault that they met in such a crazy, mixed-up way, and he could sit out there and fume until he grew a damn Santa Claus beard.

Well, you didn't tell him that you were already at the ranch. Her conscience pricked at her soul.

"Hush," she snapped.

She paced the floor, checked on Joshua in his port-a-crib beside the table at one end of the loop, and peeked out the kitchen window at Lucas still sitting on the porch on the other end.

"Lucas, you are as stubborn as a cross-eyed Texas mule," she mumbled. "It's just a baby, for God's sake, and he's a good baby at that."

She'd promised Hazel that she'd stay to keep the old girl from having a heart attack in addition to hurting her hip. Now that Lucas was home, he could hire another cook and housekeeper. Surely the guys could fend for themselves until they could rustle up someone to take on the job. It was evident that he'd changed his mind about wanting to meet her in person and get to know her better. Forget the long, hot kisses he'd promised or the real bedroom scenes he'd hinted at during cybersex.

She made Joshua a bottle and tried to remember the nearest motel that she'd passed on her way to Savoy, Texas. It had to be back in Sherman, so that's where she'd land for the night. She'd be on the road early the next morning and reach her Aunt Leah's by suppertime. But she was not leaving until Lucas came in the house and they had it out. That would be closure in more ways than one.

You always did have a healthy dose of impulsiveness, didn't you? She'd already told her inner voice to hush. Evidently, it didn't realize she had a pistol.

"I'm not in the mood to fight with you. I've got to feed this baby and then put my stuff in my truck," she said.

She sat down at the kitchen table with Joshua in her lap. The only noise in the whole room was the slurping sucking noises of the baby having his six o'clock bottle, but her thoughts pounded so loud in her ears that she couldn't hear anything else. That cleft in his chin, his dark brown eyes, and all that gorgeous black hair came from his father and her best friend, Drew Camp.

The first time Drew went to Kuwait she'd cried for days after he left, just sure that they'd ship him home in a flag-covered casket. At the end of a year he came home and it wasn't so hard the next time he was deployed. By the third time, she wasn't a bit anxious; maybe a little awkward after that night of tequila shots and waking up in bed with him, but not nervous. He'd come home twice and he would again. When he got home, they would have both forgotten about that one crazy night when they were both drunk out of their minds—the night that they broke the vow to never let romance interfere with their friendship.

In Kuwait the sun was just coming up when she talked to Drew, and he always woke up chipper and full of bullshit. Her day was just ending and that evening when Lucas told her that he hated to be the one to inform her that Drew was dead, she'd thought he was playing a horrible prank.

Just like that. Her best friend was gone from her life. Her heart had shattered right there in front of Lucas, who was packing up Drew's belongings to send home to his oldest sister.

After that evening, they'd become friends and then it developed into something more.

"Shit! Shit! Shit! Cover your little ears, Joshua! Your momma deserves to cuss," she whispered to the baby.

She clamped her mouth shut when she heard Lucas coming into the house. He tossed his duffel bag into the kitchen ahead of him and kicked it out of the way after he slammed the door shut. Inside the house, in good light and in uniform, he looked ten feet tall instead of six feet four inches. His blue-black hair was cut military short, and his brown eyes darted from her to the mesh-sided crib.

She inhaled deeply and got ready for the questions.

"Where is Hazel?" he asked.

She'd expected something other than that. Something about what, where, and why there was a baby in his house.

"Hazel is in the hospital. She fell and hurt her hip last night. Jack is at the hospital in Denison with her," she answered. "Go ahead and spit it out. We might as well get it over with before I point my truck west and get the hell out of Dodge and out of your life."

He slumped down in a kitchen chair and crossed his legs at the ankles. He looked absolutely miserable, and that part of her heart that wanted to fix every broken thing yearned to reach out and comfort him. When she looked at him a second time he looked more pissed than uncomfortable and the anger boiled up inside her even hotter.

"How much of what we shared was real and how much were lies?" he growled.

"It was all real. I'm really from Silverton, Texas. I really was a basketball coach. I really did grow up on a ranch, and my name is really Natalie Clark. I really had this baby nine weeks ago and his name is Joshua and I'm really for damn sure leaving as soon as I get up from this table. You are a jackass, Lucas Allen, for acting like this over a baby."

"You should have told me. Why didn't you?"

She shrugged. "Because I was in denial."

He still looked like he could chew up full-grown cedar trees and spit out Tinkertoys.

She went on, "So what are you most pissed about? That I didn't tell you or that your homecoming wasn't perfect?"

He shot a dirty look across the table. "I'm pissed because I thought we were close enough you could tell me anything."

"I don't suppose you've got any secrets that you didn't tell me, do you?" she asked.

"I don't have any kids, if that's what you are asking. Why'd you arrive here early anyway? I had things planned out a helluva lot different."

"So did I! I'm part of the surprise. Hazel called me last week and we've talked every day since. She wanted me to be here when you got home and together we were going to cook up all your favorite foods and fix a banner across the front porch posts welcoming you home."

"I don't believe you. I talked about you to Hazel, but I never gave her your phone number or email address or anything like that."

"FYI, honey, there is only one Natalie Clark in Silverton, Texas, and my home phone number is in the telephone directory." Her phone rang and she jerked it out of her pocket. She didn't even check the ID before she put it to her ear and said, "Hello."

"Natalie, you sound like shit," Hazel said.

"Is your hip broken?"

"Hell, no! I'm too mean to break a hip. My daughter

says I'm going home with her for a month to get well. You've got to promise me that…"

"He's home, Hazel. He came early to surprise everyone," she said.

"Well, shit! Guess it can't be helped. Is he pissed about the baby or happy?"

"Pissed as hell," Natalie said.

"You are staying or I'm not going, and if I fall again, this old hip will break. So he can damn sure get over it. If you don't stay, they'll burn down the house trying to cook and the bathroom will go to mildew and ruin, and I don't even want to think about the laundry. Promise me right now, damn it!" Hazel said.

Natalie looked across the table, her blue eyes locking with Lucas's brown ones. It would serve him right for being such a self-righteous son of a bitch.

"Promise!" Hazel yelled.

"I'll think about it until tomorrow morning," she said.

"Fair enough. I'm supposed to go home with Willa Ruth tomorrow morning. If you go, I'm comin' home and he ain't seen pissed if I have to come home," she said. "Now give him the phone."

Natalie put it on the table and gave it a shove. "Hazel wants to talk to you."

"Well, shit, Hazel, what was I supposed to think?" he said after a full minute of listening.

"Okay, okay! I will, but I don't have to like it." He shoved the phone back toward her. "She says that you are staying until she comes home in a month."

"What do you say?"

"Doesn't look like my opinion on anything means much around here anymore."

She raised a shoulder. "That'll teach you not to leave."

"Hazel—was she surprised when you showed up with a baby?"

"I told her about Joshua before I came. She said that you had always loved babies and that you wouldn't have a problem with him. Guess she didn't know you as well as she thought," Natalie said.

"How'd she fall, anyway? I told her not to get up on that step stool. She gets light-headed."

Natalie set the bottle to one side and repositioned Joshua to burp him. She gently patted his back. "She wasn't climbing on a step stool. We were talking, and she remembered a cake she had in the oven for supper. She hurried out to the kitchen, tripped over a chair, and fell. We called the hospital and they sent an ambulance. It took twenty minutes for them to get here and the whole time she begged me to stay."

Grady pushed his way in the back door. "There's a dead coyote out by the dog pens and them pesky pups are carryin' on like they killed it."

"I shot it," Natalie said.

"Good for you." Grady noticed Lucas and his blue eyes widened.

Lucas stood up and they met in the middle of the kitchen like two big grizzly bears in a fierce hug. Finally, Grady pushed back but kept his hands on Lucas's shoulders and looked at him from toe to forehead.

"Don't look too worse for the wear. You're early. We had a big welcome home all planned out. Did you sign the papers sayin' you are finished with all that soldier shit?"

A big grin covered Lucas's face.

That was her Lucas.

Not the brooding one who'd scared the bejesus out of her in the backyard.

"Yes, they are signed, sealed, and delivered. My guard time is officially over. I won't be reenlisting this time," Lucas said.

"Well hot damn! I'm too old to run this ranch for a whole year by myself." Grady was near six feet tall, slim as a rail fence, and gray-haired. His face was a study in wrinkles of every length and depth with bright blue eyes set deep in a bed of crow's-feet.

"You didn't run it by yourself. Dad and Gramps helped. But you could run it standing on your head and cross-eyed."

Grady looked over at Natalie. "Surprised you, did he?"

Natalie nodded. "Yes, he certainly did."

Grady went to the cabinet and poured a mug of coffee. "What'd Josh think of him? Lucas has always been good with babies and animals."

"He's being pissy," Natalie said.

Grady's smile got bigger. "Lucas or Josh?"

"Lucas."

"Stop tattling," Lucas said.

"I'm not tattling. I'm stating facts. You *are* pissy."

Lucas threw up both palms. "Well, Jesus, I've got a right to be, don't I? Come home and no one is here and you got a baby you didn't tell me about."

"Trouble in paradise." Grady chuckled.

"Trouble in hell. She's a she-devil," Lucas said.

"Well, darlin' you are definitely not an angel," Natalie said. "So stop pouting."

"I do not pout." He accentuated each word with a poke of his forefinger toward her.

She slapped his hand and heat radiated from her fingers all the way to the core of her being. Shit fire! It was a damn good thing he hadn't kissed her or the whole ranch would have gone up in instant blazes.

"Don't you slap me," Lucas said.

"Quit acting like a child," she said.

Grady clapped his hands. "My turn if you two can stop carryin' on like teenagers. Jack called a few minutes ago. Hazel is bossing everyone in the hospital, so he's coming on home before the snowstorm hits big-time. You hungry, Lucas? He gets real touchy when he's hungry, Natalie. All us Allen men are like that. We ain't fit to live with if you don't keep us fed. That's probably why he's so irritable."

"I'm starving because I didn't eat supper. I wanted home-cooked Hazel-type food," he said.

"Well, it ain't Hazel food but it's damn sure good. This little lady made lasagna for supper and let me tell you, cowboy, it's better than that stuff you buy in a restaurant," Grady told him. "Come on over here and take a look."

Lucas followed him.

Grady reached up into the cabinet and handed him a plate. "We're lucky she was here when Hazel fell. Reach over there under that towel and get a chunk of that Italian bread she stirred up from scratch. Did she tell you that she's been cookin' since she was a little girl?"

"She mentioned it." He dug a slab of lasagna out from the dish sitting on the back of the stove.

Of course she'd mentioned it! They'd shared all kinds of information about each other in the past months. She knew what kind of food he liked, that he woke up grouchy every morning, that he liked strawberries but hated blueberries, and that he loved basketball but wasn't a big football fan.

Grady carried his coffee to the table and sat down. "So y'all have met each other now. You going to work through this first shock or what?"

—⁓—

Lucas couldn't tell Grady how disappointed he was.

"Well?" Grady asked.

"We're *still* in shock." Natalie bent to pick up the baby and there was a perfectly rounded bottom staring right at Lucas. The way she filled out those jeans created a stirring both physically and emotionally. He could have worked past the surprise if it hadn't been for that baby. "I'm going to take Joshua back to the bedroom and settle him down for the night."

Grady set his coffee cup on the table and hurried over to her side. "I'll take the crib back there for you. Lucas needs to eat before that lasagna gets cold. Got to admit though, it's good enough that I'd eat it right out of the fridge."

Lucas had only taken two bites when Grady was back at the other side of the table. "What in the hell is the matter with you? I've never seen you so rude or seen you pout before in your whole life."

"I am not pouting, Grady. Eleven months that woman and I have been talking almost every day and she didn't say a word about that baby. Now she says she was in denial, whatever the hell that means. Maybe she doesn't even know who the kid belongs to and that's why she didn't tell me." The words spewed out like hot lava.

One of Grady's shoulders hiked up a few inches. "You'll have to ask her that for yourself. I figured you two told each other everything the way you talked about her all the time."

"I thought we had. Now I wonder if it was all just a bunch of lies."

"She don't strike me as the type to tell a pack of lies, and there might be a reason she didn't tell you about Joshua. Ask her and stop your brooding," Grady said.

"I don't pout and I can't think of a single reason that she'd keep something as big as a baby secret."

He looked up to see her standing in the doorway. A good strong machete couldn't have sliced through the tension between them. Her cobalt blue eyes flashed and her jaw worked like she was chewing gum. He checked to see if she had that pistol still stuck in her waistband, but it was gone, thank God.

"I've got something to say," she said through clenched teeth.

He pushed back his plate and followed her into the dark den just beyond the big country kitchen. She stopped in the middle of the floor and turned around so quick that he plowed right into her. Her hands went instinctively to his chest and electricity lit up the room as sparks sizzled around them like lightning streaks. His hands wrapped around her waist, but as soon as they were both steady he took two steps back.

"So?" he asked.

She shut him up when she shoved one finger under his nose and said, "I'm not a liar. Everything we shared was the gospel, honest truth. The only sin of omission I have to repent for is Joshua. And I couldn't tell you because I didn't believe it myself. Then I didn't know how to tell you. There I was six months pregnant and you damn sure wouldn't believe me when I told you that I'd been in denial about it. You'd have thought I was one of those cyber bimbos that lie about everything."

"And you're not?" he asked.

Natalie really did not like him right then. He'd been such a sweetheart the past eleven months. Lord, she'd have curled up and died without him to talk her through the tough times. How in the devil could a man as sensitive and kind as Lucas change because of a little baby?

"I am not, and I do know who Joshua belongs to. Believe me, I know very well," she said in a high voice. "It takes a big man to accept a single mother and a baby. I'd hoped you'd be that big. I was wrong. I'm going to call Hazel and tell her to come home instead of going with her daughter. I won't live under the same roof with you for a whole month."

Her finger annoyed him worse than all the sand in Kuwait. He pushed it away. "Grow up. We don't have to like each other for you to take on the job of cook and housekeeper. And who is the father?"

She whispered, "After the comment you made, you don't deserve to know. You really are a jackass, but I couldn't have made it through this past eleven months without you. You were my stability. Even when times got tough, I could depend on you to be there just before I went to bed at night. Without that I don't know that I could have ever lived through Drew's death or losing my job. He'd been my best friend since we were toddlers and I still miss him so much. Good night." She brushed the flowing tears from her cheeks with the back of her hand and headed out of the room in long strides.

He watched her go and knew exactly how she felt. Drew had been his best friend from the time that the man settled into the bunk right above his. The camaraderie over there was something that civilians could never understand. Drew talked about Silverton, Texas, a little town up on the edge of the Palo Duro Canyon and being able to see nothing but cotton fields and sky in that part of the country. But mostly he'd talked about his best friend, Natalie Clark, those next two weeks. He'd told them stories about her that sounded outrageous, but after the pistol, the coyote, and the way that she didn't back down an inch from him, Lucas believed every one of them now.

Lucas eased down into his favorite recliner and for the first time he felt like he'd come home. What in the hell was he going to do? The attraction was there just like he'd thought it would be, but he could fight that until Hazel came back home.

He shut his eyes. Damn, that woman was a spitfire!

"Overwhelmed?" Grady asked from the doorway.

"Yes," he said softly.

Natalie curled up in a ball on the bed and wept into a pillow. She needed Drew to tell her what to do and he wasn't there. He was buried at Arlington and his oldest sister had gotten the medal they gave him posthumously.

Lucas had filled the boots Drew left behind. Lucas had been the one whom she told about her basketball team winning the regional tournament. He'd been the one that she whined to that spring after the first track meet, and he'd laughed at her sunburn around Hollywood-type sunglasses. Lucas had been there for her when the school did not renew her contract late in the summer. He'd listened to her talk about weariness after long hours of supervising the cotton crew that fall. He'd been out on a weeklong mission when she had Joshua and she meant to tell him about the baby, but down deep she must've known that he would react just the way he did. She'd wanted to see him in person so badly, then Hazel called and swore that he'd be fine with the baby.

Now it was all gone.

Her contract to coach and teach science at the high school in Silverton had not been renewed. They'd said it was because they were combining the girls and boys coaching duties and hiring a full-time science teacher for the junior high and high school. That was just to cover their asses. They weren't hiring her because she was pregnant with Drew Camp's baby, but they damn sure didn't want a lawsuit brought against them if they admitted it. Drew Camp had gotten the title of resident bad boy after they'd gotten to high school. That was the year that her parents did everything including telling her that she couldn't hang out with him anymore, but the bond between them was so strong that it hadn't worked. Then, in the blink of an eye, he was gone. But at least she had Lucas to keep her from going crazy and now he was gone, too.

For the first time in her life, she was totally alone and it hurt so bad that she thought she'd die.

"What would Drew tell me to do?" she whispered.

He would tell you that you'd whined enough. Get up and wash your face and quit that carrying on. He'd tell you that come light of day, things just might look a helluva lot different, the inner voice reminded her softly.

She threw the pillow against the far wall and wiped her eyes dry with the tail of her shirt. She was a strong woman. She'd lived through the vicious gossip in Silverton when folks figured out she was pregnant. She'd held her head up when she told her folks and her three younger brothers that the baby belonged to Drew and she was keeping it. She'd settled down on the back of the cotton farm in her single-wide trailer house and worked for her father, taking only minimum wage like the rest of the hired hands. Two weeks after Joshua was born she helped bring in the cotton crop with him settled into a sling like a little Indian papoose.

She could endure Lucas's rejection even if it did hurt like hell. But it would take a miracle to change things come daybreak. Some things couldn't be changed and Lucas would never accept Joshua, which meant that she wouldn't accept Lucas.

Joshua made sucking noises in his sleep. She gently touched his chubby cheeks with her fingertips. There was no denying that those dark brown eyes and thick lashes had come from the Camp side of the family. She wanted to pick him up and hug him close to her chest, but if he woke up, it would take a band of angels to get him back to sleep.

Chapter 2

JACK POPPED THE HANDLE ON THE SIDE OF THE RECLINER and leaned back. His salt-and-pepper-colored hair was too long again, but he only went to the barber once a month no matter how shaggy it got. His eyes were brown but not as dark as Lucas's. He was built on the same frame as Lucas, only a couple of inches shorter: tall, broad-shouldered, big muscles, and an angular face that was beginning to show signs of rough and rugged work.

Grady followed his lead and claimed the recliner next to his. "Get comfortable, Lucas. You are home."

"Spit it out, son. There's something gnawin' at you," Jack said.

Lucas paced from one end of the oversized den to the other. Four recliners—two on each end of a long brown leather sofa—a sturdy wooden coffee table, entertainment system with a large plasma screen television, and end tables scattered among the recliners, and still the room looked half-empty.

Back when Gramps built the place, there was supposed to be a dozen boys romping through the house, so he'd oversized the living room, kitchen, dining room, and den to accommodate them and their friends. But Jack was the only child that Henry and Ella Jo could ever have, and the house was lonely until they brought Grady to live with them too, after his mother and dad died.

Lucas settled into the recliner again, but he couldn't find the words to spit out anything. He was glad to be home, but he wished he was back in Kuwait so he didn't have to face all the crazy emotions wound up inside him like a string of last year's Christmas lights.

He had just finished the last of his supper when Jack barreled into the house telling all about the weather and Hazel in one breath. He'd stopped in his tracks and quit talking when he saw Lucas sitting at the table.

"Well, I'll be damned. You made it home early. It's a good thing Hazel is laid up in the hospital. She's been planning your homecoming for a month. It's all she's talked about. What she was going to make for you to eat, the banner she'd ordered to string out on the porch, whether this storm would keep your plane from landing—I could go on and on." He'd crossed the floor and hugged his son.

Now they were lined up like three tired old cowboys in the recliners they'd used for years. Grady's and Lucas's on one end of the sofa, Jack's and Henry's on the other end.

"He's all upset because Natalie didn't tell him about Joshua," Grady said.

Jack looked down the length of the sofa. "That so?"

Lucas nodded.

"Even with your problem? I'd think it would be a good thing. But that's your call. You're the one who's been doin' that Internet dating shit with her for almost a year. But hey, you don't have to like her or the baby. It's up to you, but I promised Hazel I'd do anything in my power to keep her here on the ranch until Christmas, so that's what I'm going to do. You got a problem with that?" Jack asked.

Lucas nodded again. "Yes, I do, but I'm not going to fight with Hazel when she's sick. Why would Hazel want her to stay?"

"You caused it. You told her all about how that you'd found a woman who could cook for the harvest crew, take a tractor engine down to bare bones and put it back together, and who loved basketball as much as you do. It's come back to bite you square on the ass, son. Hazel thinks she's just the woman for this ranch and if she hadn't fallen and hurt her hip, she'd be matchmaking."

Grady picked up the remote and then laid it back down. "Hazel is way past eighty, Lucas. She's been telling me and your dad all year that as soon as she got you home she was going to go live with her daughter in Memphis. Don't none of us believe it. She's just fussing and fuming about wanting you to get married to the right woman."

Lucas slapped a hand over his eyes. It was too much for one night. First Natalie and a baby, for God's sake, and now Hazel talking about leaving Cedar Hill. It damn sure wasn't the homecoming that he'd thought he'd have.

Hazel had been there when his dad was born. She was older than Henry and was the very fiber of the ranch. She could not leave. He'd hire someone else to do the work, but the ranch needed Hazel. He'd wait on her hand and foot until her hip healed if he had to.

"Humor her," Grady said. "It's just until Christmas. Hell, you could live with any woman in the world that long and it'll make the transition from here to Memphis easier on her if she stays. I'd bet hundred-dollar bills to wooden nickels that she's bitchin' to come home in less than a week. But just in case she doesn't, she'll think she had a little bit to do with her replacement."

"No one could ever replace Hazel. She's been like a mother," Lucas said.

Jack set his mouth in a firm line and his head bobbed up and down as much as possible from a reclining position. "We all know that and it's not like she's leaving forever. She'll probably get tired of that Memphis shit and come back to the ranch. I give her six weeks at the most. Soon as she gets done with therapy on that hip, she'll see that she needs somebody to boss bad as we need bossin'."

"How's she gettin' to Memphis?" Lucas asked.

"Willa Ruth has a friend who has a little charter plane. He's flying into Denison to get them soon as they are released. Doctor said he'd let her go tomorrow since Willa Ruth is a retired nurse and knows how to take care of her mother," Jack said.

Lucas loved Willa Ruth. She visited Cedar Hill twice a year, at Easter and at Christmas. When her children were young she brought them with her. Two girls just a little older than Lucas, but they were always up for a four-wheeler ride or playing games with him. He looked forward to seeing them every year until they both grew up and got married. Nowadays, they came to see Hazel at least once a year and brought their own kids.

Grady touched a button on the remote and the weather channel popped up on the television. A cute little woman in a short skirt waved her hands around telling them what to expect as the winter storm really hit north central Texas. Sleet and ice could cause power failures. Roads would be slick and travel was discouraged.

"And it's stalling out right over Grayson and Fannin counties, so don't look for any changes for at least a week. More sleet, intermittent freezing rain, and up to four inches of snow. It's too early to tell at this time, but we could be in for a white Christmas, folks," she said.

"I'm going to the hospital tomorrow. I don't care how slick the roads are," Lucas said.

"Pickup has four-wheel drive, and we got chains in the barn if it gets too deep," Jack said.

Lucas uncovered his eyes. "I can't let her leave without seeing her."

"I'm not going to fight with you," Jack said. "She'd never stop bitchin' if she didn't get to see you before she leaves, anyway."

The house phone rang beside him and he jumped. Because Hazel said it wasn't healthy to walk around with a phone stuck to the ear, they'd kept the old rotary phone in the living room just for her. And when her hearing got bad, they'd turned up the volume. When it rang, it could rival a storm siren.

Lucas reached for it. "Hello."

"Is that you, Lucas? Did you talk Natalie into staying? Don't you be paying her no minimum wage. You give her what it's worth to have a woman in the house to do your cookin' and wash your clothes," Hazel said. "There is gingerbread in the big tin can out in the pantry. I didn't tell Grady and Jack I made it or they'd eat every damn bit of it up from you."

"Thank you."

"What's the matter with you? You sound like hell. Don't tell me that you are still mad over Natalie not telling you about the baby."

"Yes, ma'am, I am and it's going to be a long time before I'm over it. Aren't you supposed to be in pain and getting doped up real good?" he asked.

"Don't be trying to change the subject. I'm in pain and Willa Ruth went to tell them to bring me another pain pill, but I got to take care of you before that shit knocks me on my ass."

Lucas tried to chuckle but it came out a cough. "You don't worry about me. You take care of you."

Hazel moaned. "If you don't convince her to stay, I'm not going anywhere, and the doctor says if I don't stay off this hip for a month, it'll mean surgery and they don't want to do it at my age. If you don't talk her into staying, then I'll die and it'll be your fault."

"Dammit, Hazel!"

"I'm an old woman layin' here on what could be her deathbed with only two wishes. One is that I see you before I die and the only other one is that you talk Natalie into staying at Cedar Hill. I've taken care of your dad and you all your lives. You can't even give me my last dying wish? Come on, Lucas, I'd move hell into heaven to give you your last wish. Oh, shit, the pain is coming back. I'm not sure I'll make it through the night." Hazel groaned again.

"I'll be there in thirty minutes," he said.

Her voice was instantly stronger. "Don't you dare. It's sleeting and you could wreck. You wait until morning."

"What if she doesn't want to stay?"

"Convince her."

Lucas covered his eyes again. God Almighty, what in the hell had he come home to face?

"Promise me you will," Hazel whined.

"Okay, okay. Y'all all win." His tone was filled to the brim with exasperation.

Willa Ruth's voice came through the line. "Lucas! Welcome home. I had to fight this tough old broad for the phone so they could give her a pain shot."

"Tell me the truth. How bad is it?"

"It's not broken but it's bruised all the way to the bone. She won't be able to walk on it for a few weeks and they suggest therapy. I'm just glad she didn't break it. It would have been tough on her to endure that kind of surgery at her age. She needs to slow down, Lucas," Willa Ruth said.

"You try to slow her down if you think you are big enough," Lucas said.

He could hear Hazel in the background. "I'm not old, dammit, and if either one of you think you can tell me what to do, you've both got cow shit for brains."

Lucas chuckled.

"Guess you heard that," Willa Ruth said.

"Oh, yeah, and it's music to my ears. You take care of her for a few weeks and then we'll see what she wants to do."

"Momma says she won't get in the airplane until she's got your word that Natalie can stay on at Cedar Hill."

"I have offered her a job for a month. If she refuses, it won't be my fault."

"Fair enough." Willa Ruth lowered her voice to a whisper. "And if she doesn't, don't tell Momma, okay?"

"You got it, darlin'."

Men folks in Natalie's part of the world liked a big breakfast served before the sun came up. She'd slept

poorly the night before and dreaded facing Lucas the
next morning. Even worse, she hated the idea of the
drive to Conway in bad weather with a baby in the
truck. And right up top on the dread list was the next few
weeks of withdrawal. She'd talked to Drew every day
of her life, or at least since she could remember, right
up until he died, and then Lucas had been there. Like an
alcoholic, she was drawn to the computer every night at
ten o'clock. In Lucas's world it was six in the morning
and he was just getting out of bed. It was going to be
a long, long time before she broke the habit of saying
good night to someone.

Joshua had awakened at two and she'd made him a
bottle with him cradled in her arms to keep him from
waking up the whole house with his hungry squalls.
From then on, she'd flipped and flopped from one side
of the four-poster bed to the other. She'd balled her pillow up, fluffed it out, and wadded it up again a dozen
times from then until five o'clock. Finally, she crawled
out of bed, picked up the baby monitor, and carried it to
the kitchen.

She got the iron skillets out of the cabinets and set
them on the stovetop, turned on the oven for biscuits,
and started breakfast. Cooking always calmed her. In
that respect she was more like her Aunt Leah than her
mother. The few times Debra had to cook, it looked like
the kitchen had been hit by a tornado and her mother had
been in a horrible mood for a week.

Hazel had set up the kitchen pretty close to the way
the cook at the Clark ranch kept hers. Skillets and cooking pots were under the cabinets to the right of the stove.
Spices and cookbooks were in the upper cabinets on that

side. Cups and mugs of every description and size were above the coffeepot. Silverware was in the drawer to the left of the sink with the dishwasher on the right.

Sausage was sizzling for gravy and she was cutting biscuits with a glass that had been dipped in flour when Jack reached the kitchen. Without a word he went straight for the coffee, poured a cup, and carried it to the table on the other side of the bar.

A full three minutes passed and the biscuits were in the oven before he said, "Good mornin', Miz Natalie."

She glanced at him and kept working. "Good mornin', Jack."

Grady did exactly the same thing. He poured a mug of coffee, carried it to the table, and drank a fourth of it before he spoke. "Smells good in here. Hazel don't have nothin' to worry about, does she, Jack?"

"Morning, everyone," Lucas said from the doorway.

His expression said that he'd just as soon not wish her a good anything, but the gentleman in him had to include her in the mix. He couldn't feel the wiggling sensation like a bunch of fishing worms in a tin can in his stomach like she did in hers.

Natalie looked up from the other side of the bar and inhaled deeply. She hoped that no one heard her sudden intake of breath or if they did, hopefully they thought she was sniffing the sausage.

Why did he have to be so damn sexy? His tight jeans were faded, but they bunched up perfectly over the tops of his boots. Muscles stretched the fabric of a light brown and black plaid flannel shirt. His boots were scuffed and well worn, proof that he was more cowboy than soldier.

His face registered that he was still on Kuwait time. Over there it would be getting on toward evening. She blinked and looked away before they made eye contact.

"Jet lag," he answered before anyone asked. He poured a cup of coffee and added a heaping teaspoon of instant coffee granules to it.

"Like it a little strong, do you?" Natalie asked.

"I'll need it to get through this day," he answered. He looked at Jack. "Heard from Gramps this morning?"

"He says wild horses or wild women couldn't drag his old bones out in this kind of weather. Not even for a look at Natalie or to eat her good cookin'. Says he don't reckon you'll be going anywhere, so he'll see you when this thaws or when you drive back to his place." Jack chuckled.

Natalie pulled biscuits from the oven. "Y'all want this on the table or you want to serve yourselves off the bar?"

"Bar is fine," Jack said.

Lucas's jaw set so tight that it was a wonder it didn't pop out of place. Evidently he didn't like breakfast on the bar. Then she looked at Jack, who was shifting his eyes from Lucas to her, and a cold shiver chased down her spine. Her father did that when he wanted one of his children to do something without saying it.

Jack and Grady were both waiting, plates in hand, when she set the bowl of gravy and the biscuits on the bar. When she turned around to get the scrambled eggs and bacon, Lucas cleared his throat.

"Hazel says I'm supposed to convince you to stay on the ranch until Christmas," he said.

"You don't have to convince me of jack shit, cowboy.

I'm staying. I made up my mind, but it's not for you. It's for the guys and for Hazel. I can endure you for a month to make them all happy," she said.

"I'll pay you good," Lucas said.

"Yes, you will," she said.

Drew's voice popped into her head again. *One month won't kill you or Joshua, and evidently these folks really want you to stay. Don't slam the door of opportunity, Nat.*

She wasn't used to looking up at a man. She stood five feet ten inches in her stocking feet, and lots of men she'd dated had been shorter. She cocked her head to one side and thought of those gorgeous red three-inch high-heeled shoes that she'd bought last Christmas.

"How much is this going to cost me?" Lucas asked.

"Sorry. I was woolgathering. Minimum wage," she said.

A grin tickled the corners of his mouth.

"At twenty-four hours a day, seven days a week," she said.

He groaned.

Jack threw back his head and laughed. "We'll be getting a bargain, son. Sign her on."

"God Almighty, Dad!" Lucas said.

"Yep, He is Almighty, but He ain't your dad," Grady said. "Sounds like you've met your match, Lucas, my boy."

"Okay, okay, but it'll break the bank," Lucas said.

"Hell if it will." Jack laughed harder. "Only man in the north part of Texas that's richer than you is Colton Nelson and that's because he won the damn lottery."

Lucas would not be a good poker player. His expression gave away what he was thinking and right then it wasn't showing good things. Evidently, he thought she was out to take him for a financial roller coaster ride. Hell, she came from a spread that was bigger than Cedar Hill, so she knew it took money to run a ranch.

"Can't none of us cook. Grady would burn water if he tried to make oatmeal," Jack said.

Grady motioned toward Jack. "And Jack can't even make coffee with the directions written on the pot. I tell you we'll all three starve if you don't stay on the ranch and cook for us."

"You can't leave anyway for a couple of days because the roads are too bad. The ice ain't melting until the temperatures rise above freezin', which won't happen for a while. The storm has stalled out right above us and it'll be days before the roads are cleared off. In this part of the world, as you know, snow and sleet cripple us," Lucas said.

She thought of her father and her brothers and she couldn't say no. Lord, they couldn't even make a bologna and cheese sandwich. And they'd run around in God only knew what color underbritches if they had to do laundry.

"I told Hazel last night that I'd stay and she's already called four times this morning to make sure I hadn't changed my mind," she said.

"Thank you, sweet Jesus!" Grady looked toward the ceiling. "This ain't our last decent meal, Jack!"

"Hey, I know how to make toast, and Jesus didn't have a thing to do with Natalie staying or going," Lucas protested.

"Not without burnin' the hell out of it, and the way you've been acting, it took intervention by Jesus Himself to get her to stay," Grady argued.

Joshua's whimpers came through the monitor on the cabinet and all three men stopped arguing and stared at the equipment as if it were a real baby. Natalie quickly turned off all the burners and the oven and made Joshua a bottle. On her way out of the kitchen she snagged a biscuit. She'd signed on to cook and clean and last time she checked, the hired help didn't eat with the ranch owners.

Whimpers had turned into demands by the time she reached the bedroom. He was chewing on his fist and kicking his legs in protest.

"Mommy is here, baby boy," Natalie crooned as she picked him up out of the portable crib. "Do you feel like you are in prison in that thing? Well, it's only for a few weeks, sweet baby boy."

She unzipped the footed pajamas and changed his diaper. "Your granny would have a fit if she knew we are on a ranch with four men, so we aren't going to tell her. Now be still and let me get your feet back inside this thing."

Joshua smiled at her for the first time and her heart went all gushy inside her chest. "Would you look at that? You remind me of your daddy with a grin like that."

She picked up the phone on her way to the rocking chair and called home. When her mother, Debra, answered she squealed. "Joshua just smiled and I'm sure it wasn't gas this time. I could see it in his eyes. They twinkled just like Shawn's do when he's about to get into big trouble."

Debra sighed. "And I missed it. Did Leah see it? She'll gloat and brag and carry on awful if she saw him do something before I did."

"Aunt Leah didn't see it. We're in the bedroom and

he's having his breakfast bottle right now," Natalie said. "Aha! There it is again. He's grinning around the bottle nipple. He's going to charm the boots right off all the cowgirls in Texas."

"You got to keep him on the ranch if he's going to be a cowboy. And a cowgirl won't fall for anything other than a real, bona fide cowboy, so bring him home where he belongs. He can't grow up to be a cowboy at Leah's place. Lord, that yard ain't no bigger than a postage stamp. If you aren't home by Christmas, I'm sending your brothers to get you," Debra said.

They said a few more things about the baby and then Natalie snapped her phone shut and laid it aside. Being raised on a ranch did not necessarily produce a cowboy. Drew was proof of that. He hated cotton farming, hated cattle raisin', and most of all he hated Silverton. That's why he joined the army in December of their senior hear of high school. Two days after they'd graduated he was on a bus headed for Lawton, Oklahoma. He finished basic training the same week that she started college.

She looked down at the two-month-old baby in her arms. "Granny says you are going to be a cowboy. I hope so, Joshua. I don't want you to be a soldier. The war took my best friend and your daddy. I couldn't bear for it to take you away from me." She hugged him close and hummed an old country music tune. The clock said that it was time for the morning sunrise, which was her favorite part of the day, but the view out the bedroom window presented a solid gray sky spitting sleet, snow, and freezing rain.

Not totally unlike the feeling in her heart.

She carried him up the hall in one arm with his infant

seat in the other hand. Lucas ignored the baby and made his way across the kitchen to the utility room. He pulled on a work coat, removed the gloves from the pockets, and shoved his hands down into them.

"I'm going to see Hazel," he said.

He opened the door and three puppies bounded into the room, stuck their noses to the ground like they were following the scent of a coyote or a coon, and headed straight for Joshua. The runt of the litter even threw back his head and howled at the ceiling when they found the baby. The biggest one licked the baby's cheek and Joshua smiled like he had in the bedroom. The runt crawled right up in the carrier with him and laid down, head on the baby's lap. Joshua wiggled his legs and smiled even bigger. The middle-sized hound settled down on one side of the carrier as if he was guarding Joshua.

"Well, would you look at that? Guess they're afraid that a coyote might get at him," Jack said.

"Bluetick hounds don't belong in the house." Lucas gathered them up, but the runt squirmed out of his arms and took off running down the hall.

"Help me," he said.

"I'm still eating," Jack said. "You was big enough to fight a war and you can't control three little old hounds?"

With a pup under each arm, Lucas set his jaw and headed down the hall. He stopped at the open bedroom door. That was Natalie's private space as long as she stayed at the ranch, and he hadn't been invited inside. Still yet, there was that pesky pup, chewing on one of the baby's teething rings.

Natalie brushed past him and picked up the puppy.

"You can keep it, sweetheart. You need something to teethe on too."

When they reached the kitchen, Grady held out his arms. "I'll take him and help Lucas shore up the pen. You don't need to be gettin' out in the cold unless you have to."

———

Hazel looked up from the hospital bed and held out both arms.

Lucas crossed the room in a few long, easy strides and hugged her. "I missed you most of all this past year," he whispered.

"Bullshit!" Hazel laughed.

He kissed her on the forehead and sat down in a chair beside her bed. "I did! Why are you laid up in this bed anyway? If that hip ain't broke, then you could hobble around in the kitchen and rustle up food."

Her black eyes twinkled. "I told you not to join that reserve shit. I told you that the wars would just keep coming. Now you got three choices. You can cook in my kitchen, which means you'll all four starve to death. You can go out to the bunkhouse and eat with the hired hands, which means you'll bitch yourselves to death. Or you can keep that woman you been flirtin' with all year."

She was just over five feet tall and her dark hair had just begun to sport a sprinkling of gray. Her eyes were black as coal and set into a round face that did not look like it could have been barking out orders for more than sixty years. She was eighty-five on her last birthday and she'd helped raise Jack and Grady along with Willa Ruth and her son that had died in Vietnam. When it came to

Lucas there was one rule and he could recite it from the time he was three years old: what Gramps or Jack said was to be obeyed without question, but what Hazel said was the law.

That was the year that his mother left the ranch in her rearview mirror and never returned. Hazel stepped into the maternal role and they'd formed a bond made of pure steel. The world would have come to an end if she hadn't met him on the porch every day when he got out of the school bus. Joining the Army Reserve unit had been their compromise. He'd wanted a few years off the ranch right out of high school and had talked to a recruiter. Hazel threw a hissy. She'd given one son to the damned war and she wasn't giving up another one. So he'd joined the reserves and gone to vet school.

"So did you talk her into staying on, or did you take one look at that baby and start backpedaling?" Hazel asked.

"Did you know she had a baby?"

"Hell, no! I only knew what you told me. I was so happy when she come bringing that baby in that I almost did a dance right there in front of God and everyone. It was like buying a heifer at the sale and finding out when you got her home that a calf came with her."

"Natalie is not a cow," he protested.

"I didn't say she was." Hazel giggled.

"That child can't be very old, which means she was pregnant most of the time we were getting to know each other," he said.

"So?"

"She should have told me."

Hazel reached through the bars on the side of the bed and touched his arm. "Tell me about your first impression of her. What did you feel when you first laid eyes on her for real?"

His forehead drew down in a frown as he told Hazel about the dead coyote, the pups, and the pink gun. "She saved those three pups by shooting the coyote, I'm sure, but there she was with a baby in her arms. How much of what we shared was lies and what was the truth?"

"You aren't stupid, Lucas. You did intelligence work for the guards."

"What's that got to do with Natalie and that baby?"

"Can you tell if one of them prisoners is lying?"

He nodded.

"Do I have to spell it out for you? You wouldn't have fallen for her if she'd been a lyin' bitch, now would you?"

Lucas's first knee-jerk reaction was to take up for Natalie and tell Hazel not to call her a bitch or a cow. Then he realized that Hazel had played him into the position where she wanted him.

"But why didn't she tell me?"

"She's got her reasons. Get to know her for real. Damned old computers anyway. They'll be the death of the country, I swear they will. Some things is private but them damned things has opened up the lives of everyone to the whole damned world. Internet dating. Don't even get me started on that shit. Man needs to go out in the world and find a wife, not look at some picture on the Internet and fall in love."

"I'm not in love. I just wanted to meet her in person," he protested.

Willa Ruth poked her head in the door. "Well, look who is here to see us off this morning. Doctor just released Momma and by the time the nurses get the paperwork all done, the plane will be here to take us home."

"You'll be ready to bring her back in two days. A hurt hip didn't take a bit of the cantankerous out of her." He chuckled.

Hazel narrowed her eyes at him. "Natalie leaves the ranch and I won't come back, not even for Christmas, and me and you only missed one Christmas together in your life. And that was because you wouldn't listen to me. I told you not to join that shit."

"She hasn't changed a bit, has she?" Lucas teased.

"And I ain't plannin' on changing. You remember the rule." Hazel raised a hand and pointed at him.

"What Hazel says is the law," he said.

"That's right! Did you bring everything Willa Ruth told you to put in my suitcase?"

"Yes, ma'am," Lucas said.

"Okay, then you get on out of here and drive slow on the way home. The roads are slick."

Lucas shook the legs of his jeans down over his boots when he stood up. He kissed Hazel on the forehead once more and hugged Willa Ruth. When he reached the door, he looked over his shoulder and said, "See you around, crocodile."

Hazel smiled. "Later, gator."

They'd never said good-bye in their lives. Not his first day of school when she put him on the bus and waved from the porch. Not when he left to go to college or when he went to Kuwait.

Hazel hated good-byes.

Besides, this wasn't good-bye. It was just until Christmas. Hazel wouldn't be away from the ranch at the holidays. Lucas just had to be patient.

Chapter 3

THE CHICKENS HAD ENOUGH SENSE IN THEIR PEA-SIZED brains to stay inside the coop and not venture out into the sleet and cold wind. But somehow the eggs wouldn't grow legs and walk up to the back door, and Natalie needed an even dozen to make a pound cake for dinner. There were four in the egg basket inside the refrigerator. She could make a chocolate sheet cake instead, but Lucas liked almond cream cheese pound cake.

She shouldn't want to make his favorite food after the way he'd acted, but Hazel had called earlier that morning and told her exactly what she was going to cook for dinner the first day he was home. Roast, cooked long and slow in the oven, not the Crock-Pot. Noodles made in the beef broth instead of potatoes. Lima beans, which were in the freezer in the utility room. Hot yeast bread and almond cream cheese pound cake for dessert. She could also thaw out a container of frozen peaches to serve with it.

"And how is he adjusting now that he's had time to sleep on the idea of a baby in the house?" Hazel asked.

"Slowly," Natalie had answered.

She put on her mustard-colored canvas work coat and bundled Joshua up in a thick bunting with a snug-fitting hood. He gave her a big toothless grin when she slipped him into the sling that had been his home-away-from-home since the day he was born.

"You like going outside, don't you? Rain, sleet, hail, or boiling hot sunshine, a rancher has to take care of business, right, son?"

He cooed and wiggled deeper into the folds of the sling.

She picked up a galvanized milk bucket from the back porch, tossed the sleet pebbles out of it onto the ground, and started toward the hen house. Henry had taken her and Joshua on a very short walking tour of the backyard, pointing out the hen house, the dog pens, and the nearest barn after Jack left to follow the ambulance to the hospital. It wasn't set up so very different than the farm she'd grown up on south of Silverton. There were more trees in north central Texas and fewer crops and more Black Angus cattle, but ranchin' was pretty much the same no matter where it was located.

"I'll hurry so you don't turn into a Popsicle," she told Joshua.

The bitter north wind stung her face, and her boots made a crunching sound with each step. The trees were covered in a thick layer of ice, and there wasn't a single peep coming from the chicken house. Yes, sir, she should have made the sheet cake and not taken her baby boy out in the horrible weather. If he came down with a cold, she was going to blame Hazel.

The door squeaked in protest when she opened it and a dozen beady little eyes looked up to see who the intruder was. Thank God they hadn't all frozen to death. Two old speckled hens tucked their heads back under their wings when they realized it was a human and not a coyote.

She removed a leather glove and tucked it up under her arm. The first hen didn't even cluck when she shoved her hand under the warm feathers and found two eggs. The second one didn't appreciate a cold hand and let out a high-pitched squeak.

"Sorry, old girl, but thank you for the egg." Natalie giggled.

She had thirteen eggs in the bucket when she left the hen house and hurried across the yard. She was more than halfway back to the house when Lucas rounded the end of the house, stopped in his tracks, and crossed his arms over his chest. She stopped just as fast and almost dropped the bucket with the eggs inside.

"You scared the bejesus out of me," she snapped.

"Well, you damn sure didn't do anything for my blood pressure either," he shot right back.

He'd been sexy as hell as a soldier, but as a cowboy— Lord, women would stand in line just to get to gawk at him for five minutes. They'd pay good money for the privilege of touching the merchandise. Hell, she could probably get a thousand dollars a night from any blue-blooded woman if she could shuck her clothes and crawl into bed with him.

Lucas wanted to take another step toward her, but his feet were glued to the ground just as surely as if every drop of sleet was coated in superglue. He opened his mouth to say something but then clamped it shut.

He could see eggs in the galvanized bucket, but what was inside that plaid thing around her neck? Surely to God she didn't carry around a baby in that thing. And why in the hell would she go gather eggs with a pink pistol strapped to one of her long, long legs?

"What?" she asked without breaking stride.

"Why would you take a pistol to the hen house?"

"Varmints. Things like coyotes or snakes or rats the size of house cats. I don't take too kindly to any of those things messin' around the hen house."

He pointed to the sling. "What is that thing?"

"It's a baby. He is not a thing. He's a tiny human being. His name is Joshua and he's two months old. And before you ask, there are thirteen eggs in the basket, the hens are all doing well, and there is a roast in the oven for dinner."

She breezed past him, leaving him still stuck to the ground.

Warm air filled with the aroma of food in the oven, bread rising on the counter, and a crackling blaze in the fireplace met him when he opened the back door. He stomped the sleet from his boots, hung his hat and coat on hooks, and scanned the kitchen. The bucket of eggs was on the counter, but Natalie had disappeared. He poured a mug of coffee and held it in his hands to warm them.

He had just taken the first sip when she was back in the kitchen. She wore a sweatshirt with Santa Claus riding a bull on the front, faded jeans, socks but no shoes or boots, and her hair was braided in two ropes that hung to her shoulders.

He had to swallow fast to keep from spewing coffee all over the place. The hot liquid burned all the way from throat to stomach, but it wasn't steaming coffee that set him on fire. It was the sexual attraction he'd had for Natalie from the first time he'd laid eyes on her smiling face on the computer screen.

She'd put that ridiculous sling away and now the baby was in a conventional baby carrier. He looked cute in a green sweat suit with a basketball hoop on the front of the shirt. If he grew up to be as tall as his momma, he would probably make a good basketball player. With her coaching savvy, he might even go on to play some college ball.

"I appreciate you sticking around until Hazel gets settled in Memphis. Once she's there she won't know if you are here or not," he said.

"You got more nerve than I've got if you are plannin' to lie to Hazel. I told her that I'd stay until Christmas. You offered me a job and I set a price. You can't fire me because if you do, I'm calling her." She set the bucket on the kitchen table and talked to the baby. "There you go. You practice that new smile and I'll get the pound cake in the oven." She touched Joshua's cheek and he graced her with his most brilliant grin yet.

"He's a good-lookin' kid. Why didn't you tell me you were pregnant and seeing someone else?" Lucas asked.

"I couldn't. I wasn't seeing anyone else," she stammered.

He sat down in a kitchen chair and looked at the baby. He looked vaguely familiar, but he couldn't put a finger on why. "You want to explain that?"

Natalie busied herself at the kitchen bar, measuring flour and then sugar, and putting ingredients into Hazel's big crock mixing bowl. He thought she didn't hear him and had his mouth open to ask again when she started to talk.

"Drew and I were best friends before we could even remember. His daddy worked for my father on the ranch. They lived in one of the trailers out at the back of the property that Daddy brought in for hired help families. He was the baby and the only son after four daughters. They were all grown and married and had kids of their own when Drew was born. Looking back, I think his mother must have been over forty that year that he was born. I was the oldest with three little brothers. He was used to being bossed around with all those older sisters and his mom and dad and I was used to bossing." She added baking powder to the stuff in the bowl and then brought out a sifter. It made a scratchy noise as she ran all the dry ingredients through it several times, from one bowl to the other.

"I didn't ask for your life story. I asked why you didn't tell me you were sleeping with someone while we were talking online." Lucas stuck his finger in the palm of Joshua's hand and the baby grasped it tightly.

"That's what I'm telling you right now if you'll be patient."

"You are bossy, aren't you? Drew said that you were a firecracker, but I didn't see that side of you this past year."

"Do you want to hear this story or not? And believe me, Drew knew me better than anyone in this world ever did or ever will. If he said I was a firecracker, he was paying me a compliment. I'm more like an overloaded stick of dynamite."

Lucas pulled his finger away from Joshua when the baby tried to put it in his mouth. "Go on."

"Drew and I made a vow in junior high school that we would never ever date. We were best friends and we didn't want to ruin that."

Lucas nodded. "He told us that when we teased him about being stupid for not dating you."

She stopped sifting and their gaze met in the middle of the kitchen. "You did?"

"Sure we did. Damn, Natalie! You looked like a million bucks on that computer and he declared that you were just his best friend. We wondered for a while there if he was straight."

Her laughter didn't belong to a full-grown woman but a little girl and sounded so innocent that he jerked his head around to see if there was another child in the kitchen.

"Why is that so funny?"

"Drew never had a bit of problem finding a woman. Another day, you remind me to tell you the story of the quilt he carried in the trunk of his car," she said.

"We found that out pretty quick. They flocked to him like starved women lookin' at an all-you-can-eat buffet. Tell me about the quilt now," Lucas said.

She set the sifter aside and picked up the mixer. "Not today. I've got another story to tell you right now. I cried my eyes out the first time he was deployed. It wasn't so rough the second time because we talked every night no matter where he was. At least it was night in my world. In Drew's he was just waking up. The third time we had a party and…"

He waited.

And waited some more.

"Well? You had a party and what?" he asked.

"We drank too much. Way, way too much. The drunker we got, the crazier we got. I made him promise that he'd come home again just like he had the past two times he'd been deployed. He made me promise that I wouldn't get married while he was gone."

"Why?"

"Because Drew was my person. The one I went to for advice on relationships and who told me I was bitchy when I was and who told me when a man was a bastard and I shouldn't be dating him."

"And you listened to him?"

"Most of the time. When I didn't and my relationships went sour, he crowed around like a rooster and told me 'I told you so' until I wanted to use that pistol in my room and shoot him."

"But you did get into a relationship without him knowing, didn't you? And that's why…"

Natalie held up both palms. "Let me finish. We were throwing back tequila shots and then the clock struck two in the morning and we had to leave because the bar was shutting down. He drove me home and I kissed him good-bye. Remember I said that we were very drunk. Well, he kissed back and it wasn't like a best friend kiss. And the next morning we woke up in my bed. We'd broken our vow and we were both miserable. Hangovers. Headaches. And I felt like I'd just slept with my brother, which was nauseating as hell. I loved Drew but I damn sure did not intend to have sex with him. He apologized a dozen times, got dressed, and had barely driven away when Momma knocked on my door to tell me to get up for church."

"Bet that was the last place you wanted to be that morning," Lucas said.

"They sang louder than they'd ever sang before and every coin that dropped into that silver offering plate sounded like a rock band in my head," she said.

Lucas looked back at Joshua. It was the cleft in the chin that looked so much like Drew.

"Did he know?"

She shook her head. "I didn't know until two months after his funeral. Thought my body was messed up from all the stress of losing him."

"You could have told me."

"I couldn't even tell my mother. I was past six months pregnant when she figured it out on her own. When the news hit the gossip queens in Silverton, it was awful. How could I have ever let myself get mixed up with that horrible bad boy? My mother should have put a stop to our friendship years before, and so forth and so on. I held my head up, but even going to the café was a chore. Thank goodness school was out for the summer or they'd have probably fired me on the spot."

"Drew was a good man and a great soldier. They shouldn't have held grudges against him. He was over there protecting their right to gossip," Lucas said.

"I'm sorry that I didn't tell you, but I'm not sorry that I have Joshua. A little piece of my best friend lives on in him. Now your turn… what secrets did you keep from me?"

Lucas brushed imaginary dirt from the legs of his jeans. "What makes you think I have any secrets? I told you all about Hazel raising me after my mother left, my dad and Grady being cousins, and Gramps."

"Is that a picture of your dad and mother on the dresser in the room where I'm staying?"

He nodded. "Yes, it is. The only one ever taken, probably. I've never seen any other ones. Granny died when Daddy was a little boy. Hazel was already keeping house and working on the ranch, so she finished helping Gramps raise him. Dad waited until he was almost thirty to get married, but age doesn't seem to matter much. He married my mother and she hated country life so bad that when I was two she left it and me both, so Hazel raised another kid for the ranch. Our luck ain't too good when it comes to women in this family."

Natalie cracked an egg on the side of the bowl and turned on the mixer. It required a full minute of high beating after each egg or the pound cake would be heavy and soggy.

She couldn't imagine walking away from Joshua and she'd only had him two months. "Why didn't she take you with her?"

"She had aspirations about being an actress and a two-year-old doesn't fit with that image, and besides, Dad said that she was free to go but if she took me away from Cedar Hill, he'd tie up the courts so bad, she'd never even see a settlement. He made her a one-time very generous offer to leave me with him and she took it," Lucas said.

"Did she become an actress?"

"No, but she did find a high-powered business executive and married him a couple of years after she left the ranch," he said.

"You ever see her again?"

"Oh, yes. She comes at Christmas every year. Her folks live over in Bells and she comes home for a couple of days. When I was a little kid, Grady would take me over there for an afternoon. She hasn't set foot back on the ranch since she left. Nowadays, we usually meet for lunch somewhere in Denison and spend an awkward hour together."

What kind of mother only saw her child on Christmas? And why didn't she come back to the ranch?

Natalie finished beating the cake mixture and poured it into a loaf pan, slid it into the oven, and refreshed his coffee cup before she sat down at the table. The tension had eased slightly and the feeling between them loosely resembled what they'd had on the Internet.

"Jack never remarried? Is Grady married?"

He shook his head. "Neither one. Dad said he learned his lesson and Grady swears he learned from Dad's mistake. Besides, he always said it took two of them workin' full time to raise me. An Allen man only gives his heart away one time. Gramps told me that a long time ago along with the lecture that I'd best be damn sure I was giving it to the right woman before I let go of it."

His cell phone rang and he dug it out of his shirt pocket.

"Sure thing. I'll be right there." He paused and listened some more, nodding when he agreed and shaking his head when he didn't.

"No, sir! She ran me off and they should be in the air by now, maybe even part of the way to Memphis. Give me five minutes to get my coat on and drive down there."

He pushed back the chair. "Hold down the fort, Josh. I've got to go check on a couple of cows that aren't acting right. Probably just need warming up in the barn, but if they are ailin', we'll need to separate them from the herd."

Natalie held in the excitement, but it wasn't easy. He'd actually talked to the baby. It was one tiny step in the right direction, and it hadn't even grated on her nerves that he called the baby Josh instead of Joshua. When she'd had him, she'd declared to her parents and her brothers that he was to be called by his full name, not Josh or a nickname like Buddy or Little Man.

Lucas opened the back door and two cows were right there. One was on the porch and immediately stuck her head in the door and looked around until she caught sight of Joshua, then be damned if that critter didn't smile.

Natalie shooed at it with a tea towel. "What the hell? Do you let cows in the house?"

"Never known them to do that before." Lucas grabbed the heifer by the ears and pushed, but the other cow had her head up and was telling the whole world that she was not moving.

"First dogs and now cows. Are you sure these animals aren't used to coming in the house?" Natalie asked.

"Hell, no! Shit, I don't know what's wrong with them. Move along now, you stupid…" Lucas yelled.

He couldn't get the cows out, but somehow three puppies ran through their legs and into the house, headed straight for Josh, tumbling over their big paws and growling at each other on the way.

The baby kicked and cooed at them just like the last time, but this time the runt grabbed the toes of one of his socks and pulled until it came off. Joshua wiggled his toes and thought the whole fiasco was something funny.

Natalie picked up the baby and the puppies stayed so close to her that she had to be careful or she would have tripped.

"Damn dogs and cows," Lucas growled. "I wish I was back in Kuwait."

"Temper, temper!" Natalie scolded. "Are those old cows that maybe missed you while you were gone? Or else they got into the yard and think this is the barn. And these puppies have taken up with me since I've been here. That's why they keep running toward the house. You just need to get their pen fixed better."

"They're just cows, Natalie. I don't know why they're trying to get in the house, but there's no way they can get any more than their heads through the door. And I may give every one of those pups away to the nearest neighbor whether he wants them or not."

Natalie finally reached the door. "Look, baby boy. Grandma never let a cow in the house, but they do here."

"I told you…" Lucas started but stopped when the cow sniffed at Joshua and then backed out of the door. She swiftly traded places with the other heifer, which poked her head in the door, sniffed the baby, and then contentedly backed down the steps.

"I'll be damned." Lucas scratched his head.

"It made Joshua smile and coo. I think he liked the cows. I know he likes the puppies, but you better get them out of here because they're stealing toys and socks."

"Come on, you mangy rascals." Lucas gathered them all up in his big arms and disappeared out into the snow. "I've still got to go see what's going on in the north pasture. We'll be in at dinner if not before. Must be this storm that's got everything spooked," he said.

She was folding a load of baby clothes that she'd tossed in the washer after the men had all cleared out that morning when her phone rang. The ring tone said that it was her Aunt Leah, and she answered on the second ring.

"Are you on the way? Are the roads slick?" Leah asked.

"No, I'm not on the way. The roads are slick and it's still coming down. He came home last night." Natalie put a cup of water into the microwave for hot tea as she talked.

"And?"

"It was very awkward."

"I told you to tell him about Joshua."

"I know, and he was very angry, but we've talked today and I'm staying. I promised Hazel that I'd stay until Christmas. How long can you hold off the army?"

"I don't know. Debra called all worked up because Joshua really smiled and she didn't get to see it and she asked me if I'd seen it yet and made me promise to take pictures of the two of you and send to her. Now how are we going to handle that one? If you send photos, she'll be able to tell from the background that they damn sure aren't in my house," Leah said.

Debra and Leah were twin sisters, born in Goodnight, Texas, and looked the same up until Debra had four kids. Now she was twenty pounds heavier than her sister who'd opted for a career instead of a family. Leah kept her brown hair dyed a rich chestnut. Debra let the tendency toward early graying shine right on through. Leah worked as an economics professor at the college in Conway and lived in a gated community on the south side of town in a new modern home. Debra still lived on the ranch where Jimmy Clark took her as a bride almost thirty years before. And Leah knew all about Lucas and the relationship that had budded over the Internet. Debra didn't even know that Lucas existed.

"I'll handle it," Natalie said.

"You'd better tell her pretty soon, girl. She's going to know something isn't right and I'll be the one in the crosshairs."

Natalie giggled. "And she don't waste ammo."

"Never has before, so I don't expect her to start now. So now tell me about him. Is he as handsome as you thought?"

Natalie swallowed hard. "Yes, he is."

She told Leah the whole story about him coming home and finding her with a pistol in her hand and how he had reacted to Joshua. When she hung up, it seemed like she'd talked for an hour, but the clock said it had only been a few minutes.

She wasn't sure about the dinner schedule on Cedar Hill compared to the one at her father's ranch, but at a quarter to noon, Jack, Grady, and Lucas all pushed inside the house. Evidently, they did things the same way her family did. Breakfast by six in the morning. Dinner at noon. Supper at six in the evening.

"Man, this place smells good," Grady said. "Is that yeast bread I smell?"

"Pot roast isn't worth much if you haven't got hot bread to eat with it." She smiled.

"Give us a few minutes to get washed up," Jack said.

When they took their places around the table, Grady and Jack's hair had been combed back and their faces were shiny clean. Lucas's big hands were still semiwet like he'd washed them well and barely touched the towel. He looked at the dinner table like he could hardly believe all the food in front of him.

Joshua was content in the portable swing she'd set up close to the table. Everything fascinated him and he brought out his big toothless grin when he heard male voices.

"If the click of the swing is bothersome…" she started.

"Hey, that ain't nothing to complain about," Grady

butted in. "Kind of nice to have a baby in the house again. We ain't had that since Lucas was little. They've sure enough come up with fancy things since then. When he was that size, we ate dinner with him sittin' on Jack's or my knee."

"He going to be smart." Jack helped his plate and passed bowls to Lucas. "You can tell by his bright eyes. I bet he's walkin' a long time before he's a year old."

"I see a pound cake back there on the cabinet," Grady said.

Jack nudged Lucas with his elbow. "Had a dinner like this since you left home?"

Lucas shook his head and piled potatoes and carrots on his plate. "No, and I'm hungry."

"You eat all that, you won't have room for pound cake and peaches," Jack teased.

"That means I get his cake, right?" Grady asked.

"You got that pistol handy, Natalie?" Lucas asked.

"Keep it ready," she answered.

"Anyone touches my cake, you shoot to kill."

He had no idea that he had just handed her the moon, the stars, and maybe even the sun. The man that had comforted her after Drew's death and who'd carried on an Internet relationship with her was back.

"Momma taught me not to waste ammo. I could just break their arms," she said.

Jack threw back his head and guffawed. "If that didn't sound just like Hazel."

"Well, thank you," Natalie said. "I didn't get to know her, but what little time we visited, I got the impression that she was a pistol."

"Oh, honey," Lucas looked across the table and locked

gazes with her, "Hazel ain't a pistol. She's a big-assed double-barreled shotgun."

The energy between them sizzled so loudly that she wondered if Jack and Grady could hear it too. It had that strange eerie feeling that came five minutes before a tornado hit. Noise was all around them, but they were in a vacuum with no sounds but the flutter of their hearts. His eyes bored into hers and she could hear the storm coming closer and closer. She'd never had a man strip her totally naked just by looking into her eyes.

She blinked and looked at Joshua. When she chanced a look back at Lucas, he was loading his plate with roast and potatoes.

Chapter 4

THE HARDWOOD FLOOR IN THE HALLWAY WAS COLD enough to make Natalie wish she'd dug a pair of socks out of her suitcase. She reached for the old-fashioned glass knob on the bathroom door, but it was locked. She whipped around to do a fast tiptoe back to her room and the door flew open.

"Next," Lucas drawled.

She stopped and looked over her shoulder. The scent of men's soap, musky shaving lotion, and minty toothpaste all combined and again created that crazy feeling of a storm on the way. Moist, warm air flowed out of the room, but it did little to warm her chilled feet. She had to remember to drag out the fuzzy house shoes or at least put on socks in the morning.

"Good mornin'," she said. "I'll only be a minute."

"Doesn't matter how long you take. Dad's already been in here and he's out with Grady doing some early morning chores. So it's all yours."

She shoved her hand into her pocket. Touching the baby monitor should have grounded her back into reality and taken her mind off that dark red towel slung low around his waist and what was beneath it. She should be thinking of Joshua and not wondering what it would be like to run her hands over that acre of bulging muscles on his chest.

He propped an arm against the doorjamb and looked at her. "Did you sleep well?"

Her hair probably looked like it had been combed with a hay rake. She hadn't brushed her teeth yet and her nightshirt was five years old and faded. Was he truly being nice or was he telling her that she looked like hell?

"Joshua was only up once through the night, so it was a good one," she answered.

"That's good," he said.

Holy shit! She was blocking the door and the hallway. He probably felt like a bull penned up in a cattle trailer. She stood to the side to let him pass and his shoulder brushed against her breasts. A flannel nightshirt separated soft skin from hard muscles, but the air in the hallway still crackled and fizzled around them like embers in a red-hot fireplace.

Mother Nature was a bitch.

It wasn't fair for her to turn all the pheromones on the whole planet of Venus loose in the small confines of a hallway in a ranch house in Savoy, Texas. Or that Mother Nature had dropped a man with all the testosterone of Mars right there in the same place. There was sure to be a war of the planets. Would the house be standing when it was finished, or would the bed sheets be on fire?

It was only four weeks and she could get through the days by reminding herself that when Christmas came, he was going to owe her one helluva paycheck.

His back was to her when she took the next step into the bathroom. Her cold foot got tangled up in a throw rug in front of the vanity. One second she was thinking about what it would be like to kiss him, the next she hoped that the fall didn't break her nose when she hit the edge of the claw-foot tub as she fell forward.

Shit! Momma will kill me if I die in this place. She doesn't even know about Lucas!

She was suddenly jerked to an upright position. She hit his chest with a force that reminded her of the first time she shot her dad's thirty-caliber Argentine Mauser rifle. It kicked the shit out of her shoulder. Slamming against Lucas's chest came close to knocking the breath right out of her just like the rifle had that first time.

She looked up and noticed there were gold flecks in his brown eyes. Her hands were on his chest. Her gut twisted up in a pretzel and those pesky pheromones began to dance around a bonfire right there in the middle of her stomach. Mother Nature had not redeemed herself at all. She'd just shown Natalie what she could never have.

She was about to thank him for saving her and wiggle free of his embrace when she realized that his eyes were going all fuzzy and closing very slowly, leaving heavy black lashes to rest against his high cheekbones. She barely had time to moisten her lips and then boom! The whole earth spun around like a merry-go-round. She couldn't think or breathe; she could only feel. And the passion was blistering hot!

She'd known it would be. There had never been a doubt in all those months that she was drawn to the computer screen every night that if they met, the attraction would be strong and the heat sizzling. But in her imaginary world, he would feel the same way.

Yes, ma'am, Mother Nature was a coldhearted bitch. And Fate was her mean old sister.

Natalie did not want to open her eyes when the kiss ended. She wanted to stay in that make-believe world where he would pick her up and carry her off to bed. But the whimpering on the monitor in her pocket brought her back to reality with a thump.

"I'll put the coffee on," he drawled.

She barely nodded. Her brain was still in a mushy state, so words were not possible anyway. If she'd had to speak or eat dirt, she'd have gone to the kitchen and gotten a spoon.

He stepped out of the bathroom and was gone. She shut the door, put the lid down on the potty, and sat down. She'd only come close to fainting one time in her entire life and that was the day she looked at the pregnancy stick and it showed positive. She put her head between her knees and inhaled deeply several times. The walls stopped weaving and the floor settled back down where it belonged.

Hellfire! If one kiss could do that, what would happen if they ever…

She didn't let herself finish the thought.

———

Lucas's hands shook when he pulled on his jeans and snowy white T-shirt. He wasn't going to ever acknowledge that baby or even talk to him. But hell, he was Drew's kid, and Drew was dead and he owed his old buddy that much. Besides, he was so damn stinkin' cute that no one could resist him. Not totally unlike his mother, who had just turned every testosterone jet loose in his body with that kiss. Lucas had figured kissing her would be pretty damn great; he hadn't expected to hear bells and whistles and see stars.

His hands were still trembling when he buttoned the plaid flannel shirt he had dug out of his closet. Sex had never brought on such turmoil in his body, much less a single kiss. Granted, it had been a year since he'd touched a woman. Maybe that was the problem. He just needed a good rousing bout of sex so that a kiss wouldn't turn him into a jiggling mess of nerves.

He'd been born and raised in the house, so he knew his way around every piece of furniture without turning on a light. The hallway opened into the living room of that end of the house. A doorway to the left took him into the kitchen. He rounded the end of the table and stumbled over the baby swing, knocking it over and almost sending him into a headlong fall toward the stove.

"Dammit!" he swore as he set it up again.

He'd endure the swing and even learn to walk around it, but if he stepped on one of those slimy teething things on his way to the bathroom in the middle of the night, he'd fire Natalie on the spot. He didn't care what the family said or how hard they begged.

He flipped on a light to be sure there wasn't anything else between him and the coffeepot. Cussing must be good for the soul, because his hands were steady as a rock when he turned on the water for coffee and stared out the kitchen window.

The sky was still gray, but there was nothing falling. The thermometer outside the window fluttered around the twenty-degree mark, which meant what was on the ground wasn't melting off that day.

The coffeepot gurgled to a stop as Natalie and Joshua made it to the kitchen. She smothered the baby's face with kisses and put him in the swing, wound it up, and kissed him one more time. "See, I told you if you ate all your green eggs and hams, you could go to Six Flags this morning."

"What in the hell are you talking about?" Lucas pulled two cups out of the cabinet and filled both. "I don't cook, but I make a mean pot of coffee."

"Strong?" she asked.

He held a steaming mug out toward her. "Oh, yeah. It has to make your eyes flash tilt to be good coffee. Green eggs and ham? Oh, you read Dr. Seuss to him, right? And the swing is like an amusement park ride. I get it now."

"That's pretty close to what Daddy says about good strong coffee."

Their fingertips brushed in the transfer and his hand was hotter than the steaming coffee in the mug she held. Her touch hadn't produced as much blistering fire as there had been in that scorching kiss that came near to blowing that red towel right off his body. But it was going to be a long, long month if every time he accidentally touched her, he was aroused to the point of pain.

He was a rough cowboy and a soldier. He had nerves of steel. He could do his job in the desert or on a ranch, and he was good at both.

"Got a preference for breakfast this morning?" Natalie busied herself getting stuff out of the refrigerator.

"Omelets and waffles," he said quickly to take his mind off her lips.

Her head bobbed once.

"So you like to cook?"

He stopped by the swing and touched the baby's cheek. He expected a grin, but Josh latched on to his finger and stared right at him as if sizing him up. Did babies know more than adults thought they did? The boy's eyes didn't blink for several seconds, and Lucas wondered what he really thought of the folks at Cedar Hill Ranch.

Natalie took bowls from the cabinet and turned on the oven. "Momma can't boil water. Aunt Leah, her twin sister, is the cook in the family. There were just the two of them, and Aunt Leah hated getting her hands dirty, so she learned to cook when she was young so she could stay out of the fields. You know what folks say about it taking both twins to make a whole. I believe it. They are as different as night and day and yet when one of them is in trouble or sick, the other one knows before anyone says a word. Aunt Leah never married, but she's a gourmet cook. Momma married, had four kids, and Daddy hired a cook and housekeeper instead of a field hand. She can work all day outside the house and supervise a crew both inside and out, but she doesn't cook or clean."

"And you?"

She plugged in the waffle iron and the red light on top came on. "Daddy said I had to learn both worlds."

"Which one do you like best?"

She pulled the egg basket from the refrigerator. "Neither when I was younger. All I wanted to do was coach basketball and teach. But after three years of that, I decided farming wasn't so bad. When I wasn't rehired at the school, Daddy hired me to work on the ranch. But Momma stole me to help our cook pretty often."

"And your brothers?"

"You've got one up on them. They can't even make coffee, but they're all married to women who are hell on wheels in the kitchen."

He smiled. "You are the oldest, though, right?"

"Yes, I am. Momma had me and two years later she

had Isaac, then the next year Jarrett came along, and Shawn the year after that. Four kids in five years. They're all married and ranchin' with Daddy. Shawn just got married last week."

"I remember you telling me that. How was the wedding?"

She cracked eggs in the bowl, added a splash of milk, then salt and pepper. "Beautiful. His bride comes from the next cotton farm up the road. She had a Christmas wedding even though it's still a month away."

Jack rounded the doorjamb and zeroed in on the coffeepot. He poured a cup, took several sips, and then sat down at the end of the table close to the baby's swing.

"Good mornin', sunshine! Did you sleep well last night or did you keep your pretty mommy up? Did you know that today me and your Uncle Grady are going to bring the Christmas tree in out of the barn and set it up? You'll love the lights, I betcha. And if you could reach those shiny ornaments, you'd be trying to put them in your mouth."

Joshua cooed and waved his hands around.

"Yes, sir, with those very hands. It won't be long until your hands will be big enough to hang on to a pony's reins. By then you won't care as much about Christmas tree stuff."

"You're putting up a tree today?" Natalie asked.

"We usually get it out of the box the day after Thanksgiving, but Hazel said we had to wait until Lucas got home. We're already a week late and this blasted weather is keeping us from doing much else, so this is the day."

Lucas had never shared the ritual of putting up the tree with anyone but his dad, Grady, and Hazel.

"But," he started.

Jack held up a palm and shot a look that said *enough* across the table. "Can't have a party without a tree, can we?"

A rooster crowed and something hit the kitchen window. Lucas looked up just in time to see the rooster try to light on the casing, fail, and flop back to the ground.

"What the hell?" Lucas headed for the door. "Did you leave the hen house door open, Natalie?"

She popped both hands on her hips. "I'm a ranchin' woman. I double-check things like that."

He opened the door and more than a dozen big Rhode Island Red hens flocked into the house. He slammed the door shut, but not before the three puppies rushed inside with the rooster right behind them, squawking when he left a few tail feathers behind.

"Holy shit!" Henry yelled. "What did you do, Lucas?"

Chickens were everywhere. Puppies chased them, biting at their tails and spitting feathers out in their wake. Grady and Jack jumped up and chased the dogs, but they were wet from the snow and no one could get a grip on the slick little devils. Men, chickens, and dogs all in a blur with Natalie trying to get to Joshua before a stupid chicken flew at him and hurt her baby.

The rooster flew over everyone and roosted right there on top of Joshua's swing, like the king of the mountain daring the puppies to try to get him. He fluffed up his feathers, threw back his head, and crowed in his loudest voice. One hen followed his lead, settled down in Joshua's lap, wiggled around until she was comfortable, tucked her head under her wing, and shut her eyes.

Lucas was closer to the swing than Natalie, so he

rushed over to get the dumb chicken out of Josh's lap. If that critter pecked at his little chubby cheeks or worse yet, at his eyeball, Natalie would shoot first and ask questions later, and she'd be aiming at Lucas Allen's heart.

He grabbed the hen and Natalie grabbed Josh at the same time. A freshly laid egg rolled out of the baby's lap and splattered on the floor between them. Three puppies ran over to lick up the mess and Grady picked up two while Jack got hold of the other one.

"We'll get them out, and by damn, I'll fix that pen myself," Jack said.

"And what's that supposed to mean?" Lucas asked.

"It means that I bet they don't get out again. Shoo them damn chickens out of the house. Must be this storm that's got them all crazy. Never knew chickens to do that," Grady said.

That's when Natalie buried her face in Josh's hair and giggled like a little girl. Lucas stopped in the middle of a whole flock of chickens and stared at her. Was she laughing or crying?

Natalie looked up and shook her head. "That was the funniest sight I've seen. Men, dogs, and chickens. Feathers flying and rooster crowing. I wish I'd had my video camera out here."

The rooster crowed once more and then flew down the hall. "Hold on to Josh and don't move. I'll be back to get that rooster soon as I get all these damned chickens back out to the coop."

When the hens were all out of the house, Lucas raised an eyebrow at Natalie. "I bet that cantankerous old boy is in your bedroom. You got a problem with me going in after him?"

She shook her head and smiled. "The whole scene would have been a hoot to send in for *America's Funniest Home Videos*."

A grin tickled the edges of his mouth and finally he just gave in and let it materialize. "Well, let's hope the rooster goes without too much trouble."

The damned old bird was roosting on the edge of the portable crib, crowing like he'd just found a brand-new harem of hens. Lucas reached out to pick him up, and the rooster flogged him, pecking and tearing at his arms.

"You rotten old bastard, I swear to God, we'll have you with dumplings tonight," Lucas yelled.

Natalie stepped inside out of the hallway, still holding Josh in one arm.

The rooster flew away from Lucas and lit on her shoulder.

"What are you, a damn animal whisperer?" he asked.

"Never have been before. If you'd quit inviting them inside, this wouldn't happen. Be quiet. I'll see if I can simply walk him out to the coop."

"You can't take that baby out there like that. One of his socks is even missing," Lucas said. "Give him to me."

The rooster flogged Lucas again when he reached for Josh. Lucas backed off and the old boy flew back up and sat on Natalie's shoulder.

"Okay, I'm going to pick up Josh's blanket and wrap him in it. And I'll hurry," Natalie said. "This bird does not like you!"

"Isn't too fond of you either, or he wouldn't have just left his calling card running down your back," Lucas said.

"One more time, you rascal, and I'll be the one who wrings your neck and puts you in the boiling pot," Natalie growled.

Lucas went ahead of her and told Grady and Jack not to make a sound. Grady held up two eggs. "Found these on the back porch. Feels like they're probably frozen solid."

Natalie came through the kitchen, baby in her arms fighting against the blanket, rooster on her shoulder, crowing away. He rode there all the way to the coop, hopped off, flapped his wings, and strutted into the coop like the king of the whole world.

Lucas lined up with Grady and Henry, noses pressed against the window as they watched her hurry back to the house.

"That has got to be the damnedest thing I've ever seen," Grady said.

"Your grandpa ain't goin' to believe a word of it," Jack said.

"I'm not sure I do," Lucas said.

―――――

Natalie had planned on meatloaf for dinner, but she changed her mind. If they were going to put up a tree, then she'd make a big pot of vegetable beef soup, corn bread, and a pan of brownies for dessert. Supper could be leftovers with a side dish of cheese and crackers.

Grady came inside from the cold and went to the coffeepot. "If them pups crawl out again, I'll swear they are magic. When do y'all put up the tree?"

Evidently, the folks at Cedar Hill were a lot like those over at the Circle A in Silverton. The front door was used for company, not family.

"Usually two weeks before Christmas. Daddy and Momma have had their own tradition since before they had kids. They go out on a Saturday afternoon hunting just the right cedar tree, and believe me, that's not easy in a land where there's little but plowed pasture and sky. But they always bring one home and then on Sunday we all are there to help decorate after church and dinner. Momma don't abide excuses on that day. Her boys and their wives are expected to be home. Only sickness nigh unto death or maybe the birth of a grandchild is reason not to be home."

"We ain't put up a real tree in years. Henry put up a fuss about it at first, but he still cuts a real one for the cabin and he's finally accepted a fake one in this house," Grady said. "But we got us the biggest, realest-looking fake one we could and Josh is going to love it. Christmas is always better if there's a kid in the mix."

Natalie opened her mouth to say she was sure Hazel would be home by Christmas and that she wouldn't even be there. Then a whoosh of cold air blew Henry into the kitchen before she could get anything out. He quickly kicked it shut with his boot and hung his black felt hat on a hook and his coat on the rack. His thick gray hair had a ring around it where his hat had set and his sharp nose was as red as Rudolph's.

"Got lonesome as hell down at my place and I'm tired of them damn things you put in a toaster in the morning. Where's the baby? Good Lord, he's done grown a foot since Jack took me home on Sunday. I'm waitin', Lucas! You ain't too big or too old to hug your Gramps. If Kuwait did that to you, I'll buy the whole damn country, plow it under, and spread cow shit all over it."

Lucas met Henry halfway across the floor in a fierce hug. "Might be a good idea, but where would we put all those people?"

"Texas is a big state." Henry patted him on the shoulder. "Good mornin', Miz Natalie. Looks like we're havin' omelets. I want onions in mine and a thin layer of picante. Rest of this crew ain't got the stomach for jalapeño, but I like it. And I see the waffle iron too. Lord, I knew I was coming to the right place even if the path down to my place is slick as Jell-O on a glass doorknob."

His voice was gruff, but he had tears in his eyes when he hugged Lucas. "It's an answer to an old man's prayers to see you sittin' in this kitchen. I prayed every day that God would bring you home safe. Grady says you've done your enlistment and you ain't signin' up for another one. Tell me that's right."

"It's right." Lucas threw an arm around Henry's shoulders and walked with him to the table.

Henry looked up at the ceiling and said, "Thank you, sweet Jesus."

"You remind me of my grandpa," Natalie said.

Henry took the coffee that she poured for him. "Is that a good thing?"

"Oh, yes," she answered.

Henry took one sip of coffee and set the mug on the table. "Then thank you. Now I need to see Josh. I like his name. It's a good strong name like Lucas. Nowadays, girls are namin' their kids such weird names it looks like they just throwed the whole alphabet up in the sky and whatever fell on the table, that's what they named their kid."

He grabbed the back of a chair and dragged it to the swing. "Now me and you are going to visit. Won't be long until you get some of them eggs with picante sauce on them and I betcha you like it as well as I do."

Natalie and Lucas exchanged a look across the tops of the three men's various shades of gray hair. In a couple of easy strides he was in front of the refrigerator. He pushed things around and brought out a pint of picante sauce and set it on the cabinet beside the stove.

"They're having such a good time with a baby in the house. It's like they've got a brand-new toy," he whispered.

She nodded. "They *are* happy, aren't they?"

"They like you and there are a couple of things that we haven't discussed that I will pay you extra for."

"Cooking, cleaning, and what else?"

"Couple of parties. One to arrange, but Hazel has notes. And one to attend with me at the local Angus Association."

"The *what else* will cost extra," she said.

"Give me a bill before you leave. I can afford it. Look at them. Lord, they're more excited about that child than they are me coming home."

She slapped at his arm, missing it by a few inches. "Are you pouting?"

"Hell, no! I don't pout. I'm just stating facts."

"I promise when we're gone you can be the glory child again." She poured egg mixture into a cast-iron skillet and deftly whipped up a gorgeous omelet for Henry. She'd timed it perfectly so that the waffle iron blinked to the green light right after the omelet was on the plate.

"Still not pouting," he whispered.

She ignored him. "Serving up breakfast for Henry. Putting in breakfast for Jack now. What does he want on his omelet?"

"Make Lucas's first. I'm not through talking to Josh and it'd be a bad example to talk to him with food in my mouth. Way Gramps has been pushin' ahead of me, he won't even know my voice if I don't put in some time with him," Jack said.

"I'll have sausage and cheese in mine. No onions," Lucas said.

"Warm strawberry syrup on the waffles, right?" she asked.

His brown eyes sparkled. "You remembered."

"Of course she remembered. Them computers is good for something. We didn't have to pay to talk to you and we could see you even if your nose did look too big in the picture on the screen," Grady said. "I expect Natalie was shocked when she saw that your nose didn't look like Jimmy Durante's."

"Or Pinocchio's." Henry laughed. "This is some good breakfast. Worth every bit of the sleet that fell off that tree right down my shirt collar when I was getting in my truck."

―――⁓―――

Natalie would put up with Josh instead of Joshua because it seemed to make the old guys happy, but she'd draw the line on Hoss or Buddy or Jay-Man! God, she hated nicknames. She didn't even like it when Drew called her Nat, and he only did it when they argued.

The phone rang while she was loading the breakfast dishes. She recognized the ring tone and said, "Good morning, Aunt Leah."

"Your mother is on the warpath. The shit is about to hit the fan, girl, and I'll be damned if I'm in front of it when it does. If you are going to stay in that place with your Internet boyfriend, then honey, it's time to call her. I can't fend her off any longer," Leah said.

"But she's going to have a fit," Natalie whined.

"Yes, she is, and she is entitled to a real old-time hissy," Leah told her. "You should have told her 'bout Lucas in the beginning."

"I know, but it's complicated. I mean with the Internet thing. Lord, she would have had a heart attack. Everyone here is in love with Joshua and they're all excited about Christmas with a baby in the house. They call him Josh and I haven't even fussed at them for it. They'd be so disappointed if I left and..."

"And you kissed that cyber cowboy and you liked it, right?"

Natalie gasped. "How'd you know?"

"It's in your voice. It's high-pitched and squeaky like when you called and told me that you were pregnant and the baby belonged to Drew. Only thing that would make it go shrill like that is if you'd kissed Lucas. That's all you did, right? I mean, you've only been there a couple of days."

"Settle down. I inherited my squeaky voice from you, and I only kissed him a little while ago."

"Call your mother. I'm going to be out of the house all day and I'm turning my phone off with the excuse that my students are taking final exams today. Lord, I don't want to deal with the fallout!"

"I promise I will. But by night you'd better have it turned back on or she'll be on your doorstep as soon as she can get there. It'll be easier to talk her down on the phone than in person," Natalie said. "Got to go! We are putting up the Christmas tree today."

"God help us all!" Leah said and the line went dead.

Four men brought in an enormous box with a picture

of a Christmas tree on the outside before she could get the phone back in her pocket.

"I smell"—Henry raised his eyebrows—"vegetable soup, right?"

"No, you don't. You're getting old. That's chocolate cake, isn't it?" Grady said.

"Don't be calling me old. I know what I smell. Ella Jo made it once a week even in the summertime because it's my favorite," Henry argued.

"It's both," Natalie said.

"See, I told you it was chocolate," Grady said.

"I'll never get them raised," Lucas whispered and headed across the den and dining room toward the back door.

The front of the house was an enormous square. Two doors opened from the wide porch. One into the living room that was as big as a hotel lobby. Two archways opened up to the left off the living room. One led into the den, the other into the dining room, with a third arch separating those two. The kitchen was at the back of the dining room with a normal-sized door opening into the living room and one into the dining room.

The whole effect created by so much openness was spacious and intimidating to Natalie. The guys set the biggest box she'd ever seen on the floor of the living room, just to the left of the fireplace. The picture on the box reminded her of the one they put up at the Opryland hotel in Nashville, Tennessee. She'd been mesmerized by that tree when she was a little girl and they'd gone there in December for a week.

"Hey, you come on back here, Lucas. Your job is right here. You're the tallest one of us and you can do this without getting a ladder. We'll go on out and get the rest of the boxes. You can put this thing together," Jack said.

"Sir, yes, sir!" Lucas returned and saluted sharply.

Henry slapped him on the arm. "That's enough of that shit. You ain't in the army no more."

"You'd never know that he's an ordained preacher the way he talks, would you, Natalie?" Lucas said.

"Don't you be tattlin' on me while I'm gone," Henry said.

Natalie picked up Joshua from the swing. "I'll take him back to the bedroom and change him. It's time for his morning bottle. Shall we sit on the sofa and watch or what is my job in all this?"

Lucas opened the box and picked up the base. "Your job is to make those old farts happy, and it don't matter what you do, if Josh smiles at them, they are happy. So I guess your biggest job is to make sure they can see the baby and talk to him. Never knew three old dogs to get so excited over a new pup."

Lucas was glad she was staying, but it could never work between them, not with a baby involved—no matter how much the family liked having a child in the house.

Natalie hadn't been honest with him, but then he hadn't been up-front with her, either. Still, it seemed like her secret was bigger than his... or was it?

"Okay, this box says lights and garland. Jack is bringing the one that says ornaments, and we're letting Henry carry the one that says skirt and tree topper. He's pitchin' a shit fit, so don't tease him about not being able to carry anything heavier," Grady whispered to Lucas as Henry appeared in the living room.

Natalie was back by the time Henry set down his box and was about to sit down in a rocking chair when Henry reached for the baby.

"I'll feed the baby while you young people decorate the tree. Me and him are already good friends. Been a while since I burped a baby, though. Is it still two ounces and then throw 'im over the shoulder?"

She draped a burp towel over Henry's shoulder and handed him the baby and the bottle. "It's like riding a bicycle. It all comes right back. I think he does like you."

He put the bottle nipple into the baby's mouth and eased down into his favorite rocker/recliner. "Babies always like me. Jack liked me better than his momma and that used to just bug the shit out of her. Now Mr. Josh, we are going to get real comfortable and you can take a little nap after you get your belly filled up. Don't you worry none, son. I'll wake you up when they plug in the lights. You won't miss the good part, I promise."

"And you, missy, are going to help Lucas put the lights and the garland on the tree while I watch and make sure it's all on there just right," Henry told Natalie.

"You mean while you boss us all around like hired hands," Lucas said.

"It's a tough job, but I'm up for it," Henry teased.

Chapter 5

LUCAS CAREFULLY SLIPPED THE CARDBOARD CENTER out of the first strand of lights and looped them over his arms. Natalie didn't have to be told what to do next. She'd seen her mother and father do this dance her whole life. Her father slowly walked around the tree and her mother placed the lights in the right spots. When she was a little kid it took forever. She and her brothers bounced around the room impatiently waiting for their turn to put ornaments on the low branches.

She could visualize Lucas as a little boy doing the same thing while Jack and Hazel draped the lights and the garland. Until that moment, she'd never thought of him as a child. He'd come into her shattered world as a full-grown adult. Had he been a quiet, brooding child or a busy, loud boy that kept Hazel on her toes?

"Starting at the bottom," she said.

Lucas held out his arms. "Is that a question or a demand?"

"It's a statement," she shot back.

"Don't be too rough on him. This is his first year to do this job. Usually Jack and Hazel put the lights on the tree, and he's the impatient one waiting to hang the ornaments," Henry said.

So he hadn't been a dark introvert but a normal kid like her and her brothers.

Grady pointed at Lucas. "And you don't antagonize her."

"Hey, don't take up for her. She's already sassy enough," Lucas said.

"And don't you forget it." She picked up the end of the string of lights and squatted to clip the first one on a bottom branch. When they'd finished that strand and started on the second, she realized why it took so long and why her mother and father giggled so much while they walked around and around the tree.

Every time she and Lucas moved they brushed against each other. His arm against her breast. His hip against her belly. Her bare hands on his forearms as she unwound another length. His eyes so close that she could count the gold flecks in them. It might be humorous to a couple of married people who'd been in love for nearly thirty years, but it wasn't a bit funny to her that morning.

Her whole body hummed like a bumblebee when they clipped the final light at the top of the tree. She should write a self-help book about relationships, and the first test would be decorating a Christmas tree. If the two parties involved didn't want to fall into the nearest bed after they'd put the lights on a tree and tear each other's clothing off, then they should shake hands and walk away.

"And now the garland," Henry said.

"Joshua ain't asleep and he didn't put up a fuss when you held him, so it's my turn." Jack took the baby from Henry before he could protest.

It was normal for elderly women to rush around after church to get their hands on babies or young teenage girls to hurry over to her side to be the first to hold Joshua. But most normally, old men looked from afar at babies and kept a good safe distance from them. Yet there was Jack and Henry fighting over him and Grady keeping a close watch to swoop in for a turn at holding Joshua.

Natalie squatted again to begin placing the gold tinsel ropes.

It was her first tree ever to decorate without Drew. Damn the army. Damn the war. Damn the IED that blew him up. Damn all of them. Why did he have to go to the army anyway?

He should have gone to college. He should have been born to parents who were young enough to keep up with him instead of a couple who already had grandchildren and were too tired to care where he was or what he was doing. Maybe then he wouldn't have been in such a big hurry to get the hell out of west Texas.

His father and mother had both passed during his first tour of duty. He came home for each of the funerals but only for a couple of days. When he died, his sisters came to the funeral and one of them tried to comfort her by saying that Natalie had been more like his sister and they were like his aunts. It hadn't helped much.

"That loop is too droopy," Lucas said.

His deep drawl jerked her back into reality. She re-adjusted it and glanced over at the three men. Jack and Grady were on opposite ends of a long leather sofa and Henry was still in the rocker/recliner. Drew would have liked all of the Allen men, but he'd have really liked Henry with his twinkling eyes and sense of humor.

"See that, baby boy? Folks are going to think it's the prettiest tree in the whole state come Saturday night, aren't they?" Henry said.

Natalie stood back a ways and looked at the tree.

"This thing is huge. It might take until Saturday night to get it decorated."

Grady chuckled. "Honey, you're doin' just fine. Y'all will have this done by dinnertime and then we'll eat that chocolate cake and start the rest of the decorations. The tree ain't even half of what we got to do."

"Oh my Lord! The cake!" She dropped the garland and dashed off toward the kitchen in a long-legged blur.

She ran with the grace of a gazelle, all legs and no wasted motions. Lucas wondered what it would be like to have those legs wrapped around him. The room was already ninety degrees hotter than hell from all the accidental touches and bumps, and thinking of her in bed, in a hayloft, or even in the cab of his truck jacked it up another ten degrees.

Her voice floated back to the living room. "It's burned black. I'm opening a window to air out this kitchen. Then I'm going to whip up another one. It only takes thirty minutes and y'all can eat it warm with ice cream on top."

"I thought I saw a pecan pie on the counter. We'll make do with that," Jack said.

"Henry likes chocolate. I'll just be a few minutes."

Lucas carefully laid the garland on the floor. His mouth was parched worse than it had been during a Kuwaiti sandstorm. "Y'all want a glass of tea?" he asked. "I'm going to get one. This is some tough business."

"I want cake and she's making one just for me. I'm special," Henry said.

"Evidently, but I'm having pecan pie," Jack told him.

"I'm glad the first one burned because I like chocolate cake when it's still warm and the icing is all gooey," Henry said.

"You old rascal. I bet you knew it was burnin', didn't you?" Grady said.

Henry smiled and tilted his chin up. "Me and Josh don't tell everything we know."

"You want tea or not?" Lucas asked.

"Yes, thank you. One for each of us," Grady said.

Natalie was already putting ice in five glasses when he reached the kitchen. The aroma of burned cake mixed with simmering soup filled the kitchen, but the smell of coconut shampoo and some kind of floral perfume caused him to shove his hands in his pockets to keep from circling her waist from behind and sinking his face into her hair.

He'd been determined that first night not to like her, but the heart wanted what it wanted and his had wanted Natalie since the first time her bright blue eyes popped up on Drew Camp's laptop screen.

She looked up at him. "I heard you ask. Henry must be hungry. I'll put some cookies on a plate for them too."

"You're spoiling the whole bunch of them. This tree trimming business is hard work no matter which side you are on. Decoratin' or watchin', either one," he said.

"But it's so much fun. I love Christmas. I love the decorating, the cooking, the shopping, the presents, all of it. It's my favorite holiday of the whole year," she said.

"Gramps says that Granny did too. He says that her spirit comes home to roost every year during the month of December." Lucas filled the glasses with tea. The ice cracked but the sparks between him and Natalie were making more noise than frozen cubes splitting apart as they melted. He wanted to kiss her again to see if every kiss would come close to dropping him to his knees like the first one had.

As if she could read his mind, her cold hands snaked up around his neck and she rolled up just slightly on her toes. Her blue eyes closed and their lips locked together in a flaming kiss that shot desire through him like an IV dripping hundred-proof moonshine.

She took a step backward. "I promised you a kiss when you got home. My promise is now paid in full."

"Oh, no! You promised a kiss on the first day I got home, within minutes of getting home. The interest has accumulated on that debt and that little old kiss isn't going to do the job. I will have another one to take care of the vig."

"That sounded like loan shark talk," she said.

"Interest is building even as we speak. It might take two or more to cover your promise," he teased.

"I thought we didn't have to like each other," she said.

"We don't have to like each other to like kissing each other, do we?"

"Don't know about you, but I don't go around kissing men that I don't like," she said.

"I can truthfully say that I've never kissed a man I didn't like." He chuckled.

A loud slurping noise made them both turn at the same time. A big black horse had stretched his head through the open window and was busy eating her pecan pie. Half of it was already gone.

She squealed and fanned a towel toward the horse, but he grabbed the rest of the pie in one big bite, tossed his head back, and chewed.

"What the hell is going on out here? It's just a burned cake, for goodness… oh, my God! Where did that horse come from? We don't own a black one!" Henry said.

He had Joshua in his arms. The horse stopped chewing, letting pieces of the sticky pie filling fall on the floor.

Natalie expected to see three puppies come wiggling through the window at any minute and gobble up the leftovers from the floor.

"Did I hear a horse?" Grady asked.

"That's old man William's horse. How'd it get on our ranch? That man lives two miles up the main road. I'd better call him and tell him to come get the animal," Jack said.

"We could take it home," Henry said.

"Hell, no! We're decoratin' our tree today," Jack said. "He let the horse out. He can come get it."

The horse neighed and stretched his neck out farther.

"You are a bad horse. You could have eaten the burned cake," Natalie grumbled.

Joshua kicked and squirmed in Henry's arms.

Henry took a step forward, and it was as if Joshua had control of his hands and movements. He reached out and touched the horse between the ears and the old boy lowered his head.

"It's not Natalie that is the animal whisperer, it's Josh." Lucas laughed.

Jack said a few words into the phone, put it away, and said, "Tommy Williams said that he'd be here in about three minutes. He was transporting the horse from his place to his daughter's, and the critter kicked his way out of the trailer when he stopped at a stop sign about a quarter of a mile up the road."

Tommy drove up in the backyard, and the horse let him lead him right out to the truck. "Don't know what got into him. Must've been a mouse in the trailer. I swear he's scared of mice worse he is of snakes. Hope he didn't ruin anything."

"Everything is fine," Henry called out. "He had himself a pecan pie, so if he goes to bloatin', that's the reason."

Tommy chuckled. "I'll bring one to the party to replace it."

"You got a deal," Henry yelled and then turned to whisper to his son, "Shut this window, Jack. That damned animal comes up here and eats my cake, Tommy will have a dead horse on his hands. Come on, Josh, we've got a tree to decorate."

"We'll bring tea and then I'll get the second cake in the oven. The smell is pretty well cleared out," Natalie said.

Her Aunt Leah wasn't going to believe all the stories she had to tell next time they talked.

"You stir cake and I'll take tea to the guys. Want me to make a glass for you and take it out there too?" Lucas asked.

"Just leave mine on the counter, and thank you," she said.

He put four glasses on a tray and was glad that he hadn't tucked his flannel shirt in that morning. Even after the horse incident, the ice tea would probably be put to better use if he poured it in his lap rather than down his throat.

—⁓—

Natalie had argued with her friends that things like weak knees, light-headedness, and trembling hands were all just propaganda generated by the romance book business. Women read that stuff and were disappointed when real life wasn't just like it. Sure, she enjoyed romance books and she could fall into the world of happy-ever-after quite happily. But she was wise enough to know that it didn't happen in reality.

At least until that morning. Both times that they'd kissed, her knees had gone weak and butterflies invaded her stomach. There was something between them that rocked the world right off the axis. His eyes said that he felt it too. But there was also a dark cloud hovering above them shouting that it would never work.

Lucas picked up the tray like a restaurant waiter and carried it to the guys in the living room. Natalie checked her reflection in the microwave door. Her lips didn't look too bee-stung and her face wasn't totally scarlet. She balanced a plate of cookies on top of her tea glass and carried it to the living room. It seemed like they'd been in the kitchen half an hour but the clock on the wall above Henry's head testified that it had only been a few minutes since she'd remembered that there was a cake in the oven.

"Is it one of them flat cakes with icing as thick as the cake?" Henry asked.

She set the plate of cookies on the table beside Henry's recliner and her tea on the coffee table.

"Yes, it is. Momma's sister gave me the recipe. And your job is to watch the clock and tell me when thirty minutes is up." Natalie's voice was surprisingly calm. She figured it would sound like she'd sucked all the air from a helium balloon. Her insides surely felt all jittery like she had.

"I can do that, but why is it your aunt's recipe? Don't your momma cook?" Henry cocked his head to one side.

"Aunt Leah is the cook. Remember I told you about her," Natalie said.

"Yep, you did. Ella Jo used to make that kind of cake and sometimes I can talk Hazel into making one. She says anything that takes three fourths of a pound of butter is too rich for my old heart." Henry chuckled.

Natalie went back to putting tinsel on the tree. "Aunt Leah says the same thing. That's why we don't get it very often either. She used to live close to us but now she is in Conway, Arkansas. Momma married a rancher and raised me and my three younger brothers. Aunt Leah married a career."

"I see. Looks like maybe you got the best of both worlds," Henry said. "Damn, this tea is good. Ain't nothin' like sweet tea, don't matter if it's winter or summer. Unless it's a shot of Jack Daniel's after supper on a cold night. Don't you give me that look, Lucas. The Bible says not to get drunk. It don't say I can't have a sip of Jack to warm my old bones."

"Ain't nothin' like an icy cold beer in the summer when the day's work is done," Grady said.

Jack chuckled. "Or a bottle of cold watermelon wine chilled in a cold creek."

"Guess there will be an open bar like always at the party?" Lucas asked.

"Oh, yes there will," Jack said. "I even ordered a few bottles of watermelon wine and a couple of strawberry wine just for you."

"Tell me about this party," Natalie whispered to Lucas.

"Dad, tell Natalie about the Christmas open house," Lucas said loudly.

"We always have a little get-together for the neighbors and our business friends at Christmas. You don't have to do much. Caterers come in with the food, and the hired help moves the furniture out of the living room and helps set up the tables and all. Folks filter in and out from about six to midnight. Mostly they stay about an hour and go on to the next party and then some more come in. Usually ain't no more than thirty or forty in here at one time. Y'all probably have something like it out there in Silverton, right?" Jack asked.

She nodded. "Lawton Pierce has a big Christmas party down in the Palo Duro Canyon every year. Last year it had to be postponed a couple of weeks because of that snowstorm we got out there. We began to think it wasn't going to stop until it filled the whole canyon. Momma has a New Year's party in the big sale barn and everyone in the whole county is invited. Unless the weather is bad, we have a barn full."

They'd finished the second roll of tinsel and the tree was beginning to look decorated. Lucas stood back and eyed it, walking all the way around to the back before he nodded. "I believe we've got it. It's ready for the ornaments. You guys have to do those since we did the hard part. And we get to sit in the chairs and boss you."

"Josh here is nodding off. I'd better sit right here and hold him," Jack said.

Natalie shook her head. "No, sir! It's your turn, and besides, I'm thirsty. So I'm going to hold Joshua and enjoy that glass of tea before it gets so watered down that it's tasteless."

"Sassy bit of baggage, ain't you?" Jack smiled.

"That's the understatement of the whole year. I'm sassy. I'm bossy. I pitch fits. And I'm more stubborn than a cross-eyed mule. I see the sun is trying to peek through the clouds out there"—she pointed out the window—"which means it'll be thawing in a couple of days. You sure you want me to stay on until Hazel comes back?"

"Yes, he's sure. I'm not about to eat his cookin' for a whole month. I'd rather spend eternity on the backside of hell sittin' on a barbed wire fence. And honey, you got a long, long way to go before you ever get as bossy as Hazel," Henry said.

"Gramps!" Lucas said.

"Well, I would. Jack can barely make a pot of coffee. His momma never could teach him the ways of the kitchen. I'm putting the ornaments in the middle. I'm too old to bend and too mean to stretch," Henry declared.

Jack handed Joshua off to Natalie, and the three old men talked about every ornament they picked up. This one was from the first years that Henry was married to Ella Jo; that one was what Lucas made in school in the second grade. It sounded like home, which reminded her that she had to call her mother.

When every one of the ornaments was dangling from a tree branch, Henry stood back like Lucas had earlier and cocked his head to one side. "It's time to put the top up there. Josh is the youngest, so he gets to do it."

"Good grief! He's two months old and he just learned to smile. There's no way he can put the top on the tree," Natalie said.

"Sure he can if we help him. Lucas, you hold this and I'll hold the baby up there. Grady, you got the camera?"

"Right here," Grady said.

Lucas reached up and set the angel on top of the tree and Jack braced Joshua with one hand under his bottom and one at his back. "Right now, snap it while he's got a hold of one of her wings."

"He thinks it's edible." Henry laughed.

"If he wants to slobber on it, that's just fine. Angels love babies as much as we do." Grady chuckled.

After half a dozen pictures were taken, Jack handed Joshua back to Natalie and said, "Turn that baby boy around here, Natalie. He's got to see his first Christmas tree the minute that it lights up."

Sharp guilt hit Natalie in the heart. It should have been her momma's tree that he saw first or even hers, not one that he'd probably never see again. Two steaming hot scorching kisses did not mean there was something permanent at Cedar Hill for her and Joshua. It just meant that her hormones were out of control and that Lucas Allen was one very sexy cowboy.

She turned him around and propped him upright in her lap, and Jack kept his eyes on Joshua while he stuck the lights into the plug.

"Look at his eyes!" Henry said. "They're big as cow patties."

"He's smiling and it ain't none of that gas stuff," Grady said.

Jack stood up, folding his arms over his chest. A smile tickled the corners of his mouth. "I knew he'd like it. Wait until Saturday night when all the neighbors come. He's going to be the star of the show."

―――

Natalie figured the rest of the decorations would be a few candles, maybe some extra lights to go around the window behind the tree, and a wreath for the door.

Boy, was she wrong! Just when she thought they couldn't get another box stacked in the living room, they brought in a dozen more.

"Well, that does it for the house decorations," Henry said. "Grady, you can have the hired help get all the yard stuff out of the barn and put it out there close to the porch. Lucas can decide how he wants it put up, but the blow-up things are going up close to the house so Josh can see them when I hold him up to the window."

Lucas winked at Natalie. "You want me to go outside or put up stuff inside first, Gramps?"

"I want that train put up around the bottom of the tree. I want to see the baby's face when he sees and hears that train," Henry said.

"We haven't put that up in years," Lucas said.

Jack slit the packing tape on a big box that had TRAIN written on the side in three-inch letters. "Not since you was a kid. But we got a baby in the house now, and he's going to love it just like you did when you were little. That was your favorite part of Christmas."

Natalie had seen Lionel trains in pictures but never had seen one in action. She had trouble keeping her eyes off of those tight jeans stretched across Lucas's butt while he crawled around and obeyed the orders that all three of the older guys barked at him. She needed a long walk outside in the freezing cold weather by the time he got that blasted train running in circles around the tree.

Joshua blessed them with his biggest smile of the day when Henry propped him on his knee and the train whistled.

"See, I knew he'd love it," Henry said. "We'll sit right here in this big old recliner and watch it go round and round a few times."

"It's going to take days to empty all these boxes y'all have brought inside," Natalie said.

"Naw, honey. We'll have it done by the time we go to bed tonight with your help," Jack said. "We got a system. First, we'll do the tinsel around the walls. I'll have to get out the ladder for that. Even Lucas can't reach the ceiling."

By midafternoon tinsel was looped around the top of the walls with a Christmas ornament hanging in the middle of each loop. A Nativity scene was set up on a table at the far end of the living room and a Santa scene on a table on the other end. Family pictures had been cleared off the mantel and replaced with an assortment of beautiful angels in cut crystal, china, and even a gorgeous one carved from wood.

"Look at Josh," Henry beamed. "He likes the shiny angel with the gold wings the best. That was Lucas's favorite one when he was a little boy."

"I like the wooden one," Natalie said.

"Gramps, tell her about that one," Lucas said.

Henry picked up the figurine from the mantel. "Well, when me and Ella Jo was first married, we had bought the ranch and we was living in the little cabin. It was tough those first years until we got on our feet, so we made each other a Christmas present. That first year I got a good warm wool scarf and hat that she knitted special for me. And I carved that angel out of an old cedar stump for her because she was my own special angel. Look at this, Josh." Henry held the angel out to him.

"When you get to be a grown man, you find someone who just takes your breath away and looks just like an angel to you. When you do, you chase her until she says that she'll be yours forever."

Tears welled up in Natalie's eyes, but she kept them at bay with several blinks.

"And now for the crowning glory," Jack said. "I searched everywhere to find a bunch big enough to hang pretty this year." He held up a ball of mistletoe as big as Lucas's head. "The hook is still there from last time, and I tied a pretty red ribbon on it. It ain't holidays without mistletoe."

"Hell, you wouldn't ever get a kiss if you didn't put that up there for the holidays." Grady laughed.

"Don't I know it, and just think, Saturday night is the night." Jack laughed with him.

Lucas was standing under it when Jack hung it on the hook. He looked down at his son and motioned toward Natalie. "He's in the right spot, girl."

"Dad!" Lucas exclaimed.

Natalie walked right up to him, smacked a kiss on his cheek, and looked up at Jack. "Is that the way it's done?"

"It'll do for starters." He nodded seriously, but his expression was anything but serious.

"And now it's about Josh's nap time, so Natalie can put him to sleep while we take care of the lawn stuff," Henry said.

She and Joshua watched from the window for a while, but he got fussy, so she gave him a bottle and he went right to sleep. He didn't even wiggle when she laid him in the crib. While the guys argued about the outside lights and the right place to put the blow-up decorations, she cleaned up the kitchen and put a load of laundry in the washer.

She'd never had a problem throwing her underpants in the same washer with her brothers', but that day she blushed when her things and Lucas's all went into the washer together. It seemed far too personal even though they had shared kisses and bumped into each other dozens of times.

She thought about leaving and not looking back. Then she thought about staying. The work wasn't any more or less than what she did at her folks' ranch and the pay was a hell of a lot better. She and Joshua had a single-wide trailer on the back of the cotton farm out there; here they had a bedroom with a rocking chair and a nice view of trees and cows at Cedar Hill. The only con about the setup was that they had to share a bathroom with everyone else in the house whereas they had their very own in their small trailer.

She fished her phone from her shirt pocket and slowly poked in the numbers rather than hitting speed dial. It barely finished the first ring when Debra said, "Did I miss something else? I don't think you should stay at Leah's all week. The weatherman says that it's clearing off tomorrow, and if Joshua does something else that Leah gets to see before I do, she'll never shut up about it."

"Are you sitting down, Momma?" Natalie asked.

"Yes, I've spent the morning cleaning up the tack room and I just now made a pot of coffee," Debra rattled on.

"Get a cup of coffee and don't say a word until I'm finished," Natalie said.

"You are scaring me. Are you all right? Has something

happened to Leah or to Joshua?" Debra's voice was filled with panic.

"Everyone is fine. I should have said that first. I'm sorry," she said.

"You scared the hell out of me. What could be so damned important that I have to sit down? You didn't take a job out there in Arkansas, did you? I swear, I won't have it! I wasn't happy that you had a baby without a husband, but I got over it and I love Joshua. Please don't tell me you found a coaching job and you are moving in with Leah. All you have to do is wait a couple of years until the stink dies down around here and you'll have a job at the school again."

"Momma! I said you couldn't say anything until I finished telling you what I have to say. I did not take a job in Arkansas, and I have no intention of living with Aunt Leah."

"Well, halle-damn-freakin'-lujah!"

"But I'm not coming home next week." She went on to tell her mother the whole story, from the time that Lucas first appeared on the computer screen with Drew and how that it was Lucas who'd kept her sane after Drew died.

She ended with, "I'm staying here until Hazel comes home."

A long, pregnant silence made her wonder if her mother had fallen off the stool in front of the worktable in the tack room. She could be lying dead on the barn floor with the phone stuck to her ear and an expression on her face even the mortician couldn't erase.

"Well?" Natalie asked.

"You'll be home by midnight or I'm sending your

father and all three of your brothers to get you," Debra whispered.

Natalie was twenty-six years old. She was a grown woman who could make her own decisions, but cold chills chased down her spine as if someone had filled her shirt with sleet. Debra could yell, rant, and cuss, but when she whispered, the devil covered his ears and whimpered.

"Mother, I have been talking to him every night for almost a year. I know him as well as I knew Drew. And I know Hazel, Henry, Jack, and Grady as well as I know Lawton Pierce and Widow Presley. They've become my friends, and I'm not going to a motel."

"The hell you do! The folks around here are real. Those people could be fakes. He could have told you anything over that damn computer. I read every day where some woman goes to meet a man she met on one of those dating sites and is never seen again. You go pack your things back in that truck and get to the nearest motel right now. And call me as soon as you check in."

"Momma, I'm going to hang up, but I want you to look at the pictures I just sent you. You'll see that Henry Allen is not a serial killer and that Lucas Allen is just a cowboy on a ranch. It's just candid shots of them while we were decorating the tree this morning. Call me back as soon as you look at them."

"Shit!" Debra yelled as Natalie hit the end button.

Natalie watched the second hand inch its way around the clock three times before her phone rang. She answered on the first ring.

"Well?"

"Shit!" Debra said again.

"Does that mean you don't think they're going to steal Joshua and sell me into slavery?"

"It means that I know those folks. My dad and Henry were friends a long, long time ago. They were in the Lone Star Angus Association together when I was a little girl. He and his wife came to Goodnight and bought a bull from my dad just about the time that I got engaged. I remember showing my ring to his wife. After your dad and I married, we joined the Panhandle Angus Association, so I didn't see Henry again. I recognized him by that mop of white hair. I'm not afraid of that family, but I damn sure don't have to like the idea of you being there."

"Small world, ain't it?"

"Hell, no! It's a huge world and a bigger state when I think about you and Joshua that far away. Girl, you will be home for the New Year's Eve party. You can bring your Internet boyfriend with you, but by damn you will be here," Debra said. "I ought to make you tell your dad."

"But Momma," she whined.

"Oh, hush! I'll tell him because I can ease into it gently. He'd have a heart attack if you told him like you did me."

Joshua was still sleeping soundly when Natalie finished talking to her mother, so she called her Aunt Leah to tell her that the fan was turned on high speed, and if she didn't want to get covered up, she should duck.

"Hmmmph," Natalie all but snorted. "I thought you were turning off your phone, Aunt Leah!"

Chapter 6

A FEW SNOWFLAKES HAD SURVIVED JOSHUA'S WARM little cheeks by sticking to his thick dark eyelashes while he snuggled down in the sling around Natalie's body. He'd fallen asleep as she'd gathered eggs that morning, which was unusual. Most of the time, she could set her clock by when he wanted a bottle and when he took his nap. Natalie hoped he wasn't coming down with something. She tiptoed into the house, set the basket of eggs on the counter, and held her breath all the way to the bedroom.

She carefully laid the baby in the middle of the bed, unzipped his bunting, and removed it. His body was toasty but his face was still cold from the trip to the chicken house. He didn't look like he had a fever, but just to be sure she got out the thermometer and gently rolled it across his forehead.

"Normal," she whispered after a few seconds.

He made sucking noises in his sleep but didn't open his eyes when she transferred him from bed to crib. She touched his mouth with his favorite pacifier and he latched right on to it.

She was tiptoeing down the hall when she heard a ruckus out in the front yard. She rushed to the front door, threw it open, and stepped out on the porch.

A tall, lanky man with a rim of brown hair circling a bald head had a shotgun trained on Lucas's chest. "I swear to God, Lucas, you better not…"

"And I swear to God, Mr. Crankston, that I don't want these damned goats. They've already eaten my blown-up Santa Claus, and Gramps is going to have a fit when he sees what they've done to Frosty the Snowman. So shoot 'em or take 'em home."

"I'll shoot your sorry ass instead. My grandson will whine and carry on like a little girl if one of them is hurt. And my wife will have a fit and burn my biscuits for the rest of my life. I didn't know I was going to have to keep every damn goat born for five years when I bought that old ram and them two females. So they are yours," Mr. Crankston said. "I'll tell them that they ran off and I couldn't find the sorry critters."

The puppies came dashing around the house, falling over their feet and yelping at each other. Natalie sighed. She should have shot those damn dogs and kissed the coyote right on his sharp nose.

She whistled for the dogs and they looked her way but only momentarily. They took off after the goats, nipping at all that gorgeous winter wool on their underbellies. One goat ran right through Frosty, hooking one of its horns in the thin fabric that was filled with a warm air pump inside the thing. The torn black and white material flew out behind the goat like Batman's cape. One of the puppies grabbed it and hung on with his teeth, the goat pulling him along on the slick surface like the hound dog was skiing.

The second goat tried to climb Mrs. Claus, knocking the hot air right out of her and making her collapse in a heap in the snow.

"Damn Pashmina varmints. I wish I'd never bought a damn one of them. I planned to shoot every one that had jumped the fence, but I couldn't when I got here. My wife would leave me for sure." Mr. Crankston yelled as he chased goats around the yard behind Lucas who was busy chasing puppies.

The noise woke Joshua and he set up a howl that Natalie could hear even without the monitor. She rushed back in the house, picked him up, and threw a blanket around his little body. When she got back to the porch, the scene hadn't changed much. Men were still cussing. Dogs were still running after goats, and goats were trying to climb anything in sight to get away from the dogs.

But wait. There were three goats and now there were only two. She heard a noise above her and stepped out into the yard and looked up. Evidently goats could climb ladders because that's the only way that critter could have gotten up there and he was feasting upon the Christmas bunting that Grady had hung.

What did roasted goat taste like? Was it pretty good with barbecue or did she need to cook it in a soy-based sauce and serve it with rice?

"Hey, Lucas," she yelled.

When he looked back over his shoulder, she pointed up.

He threw up his hands and sat down on the porch step. "You should have shot the dogs instead of the coyote," he huffed.

"I already thought of that."

Mr. Crankston fired into the air and the puppies stopped in their tracks, peed in the snow, and slunk over to Lucas. Then they saw Natalie, bounded up the stairs, and pawed at her legs until she stooped down. One of them grabbed the edge of the baby blanket and the others licked Joshua's hands.

The goat on the roof came down the ladder in a flash and all three goats—one with red and green bunting still hanging from his mouth, one with a limp cape, and the last one with a bit of Mrs. Claus's apron fabric stuck to his horns—cowered on the porch with the puppies.

Mr. Crankston looped a rope around each of them and led them to his truck. "I'll have to remember to fire next time before they tear up everything in sight. I'll be replacing those before the party, but I swear, Lucas, I'm going to hold a grudge against you for not taking these critters off my hands. Clearly they like it over here."

Natalie almost offered to trade the puppies for the goats, but puppies couldn't climb ladders.

Lucas put the pups back again, but he could not find the place where they were digging under the fence. He'd had an acute case of severe conscience all day and he'd decided it was time to tell her his secret. It wasn't going to be easy after the fit he thrown there at first over Joshua, but better he tell her than it slip from one of the old guys' lips over supper sometime.

He pushed into the kitchen and said quickly before he changed his mind, "Hey, I have a confession."

"What? Did you let those mutts out again? If Josh is cranky all day because he didn't get a nap, it's going to be your fault."

"I have a secret, but it's a hell of a lot bigger than those damn pups. I believe that they could crawl their way up from hell if I shot them and buried them ten feet deep," he said.

"Oh, ho! So you kept something from me, did you?

You aren't as innocent as you pretended. Well, I'm not so sure I want to know your secret."

Their gaze met in the middle of the living room. Sparks hit the walls and fizzled out as they landed on the hardwood floor. The sizzle sounded like fireworks and the heat put a crimson glow on her cheeks.

He leaned against the kitchen cabinets. "I'm going to explain whether you like it or not."

It took several seconds before he spoke, and when he did, it came out in a hoarse drawl. "I had a girlfriend, actually a very serious girlfriend, before I went to Kuwait, but a year over there can clear up the mind real good."

He pulled out a kitchen chair and sat down. "We split up for several reasons. One was that I was going to Kuwait. The second was that she was determined we would not live on the ranch. And the third is my confession. She has a brother with a mental disorder and we went for genetic testing before we set a date. She was fine but I…" He paused.

God, it was hard to say the words out loud even after a year.

"What?" Natalie asked.

"I can't have children. Well, maybe that's not the way I should say it. There's a one chance in ten million, the doctor said, that I could make a baby. I just thought you should know."

"So you could have adopted if you'd really loved each other," Natalie said.

"She didn't want any children at all and that's what really split us up," he said.

Natalie busied herself cutting shortening into flour for piecrusts.

He shoved his hands into his pockets. "Her name is

Sonia and she's engaged now to one of our ranch hands, Noah. She is very high-maintenance and she will be at the party. You should know the background."

Natalie stopped what she was doing. "Will Noah be here too?"

He sighed. "Yes, he will."

"Well, then I guess we'll worry with that when the time comes. We've got to tell Henry about those things the goats ate before we have to worry about that."

"I was devastated because I've always wanted children. Gramps built this house for a dozen. I wouldn't care if I had that many."

Natalie stopped what she was doing and sat down at the table with him.

She covered his hand with hers. "I'm so sorry. That had to have been a shock."

The sound of her voice was soothing and her blue eyes floated in tears. Finally, one got loose and rolled down her cheeks. He brushed it away with his free hand.

"I've accepted it. The line ends with me. Don't cry."

She pulled her hand back and wiped away the free flow of tears dripping off her cheekbone. "I never cry, not even when I'm angry or sad, but I've gotten emotional since Joshua's birth."

"I got the news about Kuwait the same day we got the test results. She said she wasn't giving up a year of her life to wait for me to come home and that she wasn't ever going to live out in the boonies with bawling cows, anyway," he said.

Natalie stood up and went back to the pie dough. "If she's going to marry Noah, then I guess she might be living on a ranch whether she likes it or not."

"Maybe so. Are all our secrets covered now?" he asked.

"I don't have any more. Do you?"

He shook his head. "Don't know if it's a secret, but a bunch of guys will show up at the party that I played basketball with in high school. Some of them kind of got stuck in that era, so I'm forewarning you."

"And Sonia's cheerleader friends?" Natalie asked.

"They'll all be here too. It's a small community. Most of them didn't stray far from the place where they were raised," he answered with a shrug. "How did you know she was a cheerleader?"

"I came from a small town too. I bet she was the head cheerleader, wasn't she? And you were the star basketball player," Natalie answered.

Baby sounds came from the monitor sitting on the cabinet.

She wiped her hands on a towel and hurried down the hallway.

When she returned with Joshua, Lucas was gone.

She pulled the baby's swing into the kitchen and put him in it. "There we go, cowboy. Now you ride this pony all the way to the back forty and back while I make a pecan pie and a peach cobbler. Tonight you get rice cereal. Your granny said that you are ready for it and that's why you are fussy at night. You aren't full. So yum-yum. Get ready for something brand-new."

Joshua looked intently at her, as if he was waiting for her to say something more.

"The books say you aren't supposed to laugh out loud for another month. You be working on that for my

Christmas present. I want to hear a big baby belly laugh on Christmas morning," she said.

He cooed and waved one chubby hand in the air.

"Aha, you're going to be a bronc buster, are you? One hand on the rope and one in the air."

"Who's going to be a bronc rider? I told Lucas that he's a rancher, not one of them rodeo cowboys." Henry hung his coat and hat on the rack beside the back door and slipped his boots off, leaving them on the rug. "Snowin' still, but it won't last long. Big flakes like that are just for show. It's them little ones that don't swirl around that you got to be fearful of. It'll be sunny and thawin' out come morning."

"You heard the weather, did you?" Natalie stirred up the filling for the pecan pie, filled the shell, and put it in the oven.

Henry warmed his hands with the escaping heat. "No, I can tell by looking at the sky. And I'm gettin' Jack's gun from the safe in his room and shootin' any horse that steals that pie away from me."

Natalie shut the oven and went to work layering the peach cobbler. "We missed you at breakfast."

"Went up to the doughnut shop and had coffee with the guys this morning. Sonia, Lucas's old girlfriend, came in. She's goin' to come to the party. Just thought I'd tell you about that before she gets here." Henry blew on his hands to finish the job. "Got to get them warm. Can't touch Josh's cheeks if they're cold."

Natalie finished the cobbler and shoved it in the oven with the pie.

"Why do you call him that? His name is Joshua," she said.

"Cowboys all have nicknames. Joshua sounds like a preacher, not a cowboy. Now Josh, that sounds like a bull ridin', calf ropin', ranchin' man with a swagger in his walk. Even Lucas had a nickname, darlin'."

"What was it?" she asked.

"Hoss. Boy could ride that stick horse a million miles a day before he put him in the barn at night. And I mean in the barn. He'd take the horse out there and put him in a stable before suppertime, put a few oats in a bag that Hazel made special, and right after breakfast, he'd go get the horse out again." Henry chuckled.

Natalie bit her lip to keep from laughing out loud.

"So?" Henry asked.

"What?" Natalie asked.

"I just told you that Lucas's old girlfriend was at the doughnut shop, and you didn't even flinch. I thought maybe you liked him enough to get a little jealous." Henry grinned.

Natalie poured a cup of coffee and handed it to him. "We all have a past, Henry. I have a son and no husband or boyfriend either one. I'm not innocent, so I can't be throwing stones."

He wrapped his hands around the mug. "You are a good woman, Natalie Clark."

She leaned in and whispered, "He told me about her today, and I have to admit I was a little jealous."

He set the coffee on the table and reached out to touch the baby's cheek. He got a grin for his efforts and the snort quickly turned to a chuckle.

"And now maybe I'd better tell you about your neighbor's goats and how they've destroyed the hot-air decorations. But Mr. Crankston said that he'd replace them by the party time on Saturday night, so don't worry. But I expect Grady better find one more piece of that bunting for around the house because one crawled up on the ladder and ate it," she said.

Henry threw back his head and roared. Joshua cooed and giggled at him rather than crying at the sudden noise. "God, I wish I'd have been here to see that. Old Crankston hates them goats, but his wife makes fancy yarn out of the wool and his grandson names every one of them."

———

On Thursday morning, just like Henry predicted, the sun came out bright and shiny. By midmorning the crackle of melting ice filled the countryside. Natalie bundled Joshua up and took him out for a walk so he could hear the noises.

"This is your first ice storm. You won't remember it, but I want you to hear what the sun can do to the ice. See how warm it is on your face. It's that warmth that melts the ice."

Lucas rounded the corner of the house and said, "He's pretty young for a science lesson. You can tell that you are a teacher."

"A child is never too young to talk to. If you don't start early, then how do you expect them to understand your tones and voice?"

Lucas stopped so close to her that she got a whiff of his aftershave. "Aren't you afraid you'll make him sick bringing him outside in the weather?"

She shook her head slightly. "It's good for him."

Two raging fires burned within her. Newly acquired

motherhood complete with all the mood swings took first place. But the second blaze belonged to Lucas, and the idea of him putting it out was both exhilarating and scary.

Sunlight created deep blue highlights in his jet-black hair, and his jeans stacked up over his old rough work boots. His jacket was unzipped and hanging open. Her fingers longed to unbutton his shirt like Sonia had done and run her hands up the toned and rippled chest underneath.

She'd never been so physically attracted to anyone in her entire life. And there was every possibility that he was still in love with Sonia—immature or not. The heart wanted what it wanted. It didn't matter if her heart wanted Lucas. If his heart wanted Sonia, then they could never be happy together. Lord, what a tangled mess life could get to be.

"How do you know so much about babies?" he asked.

"I had three younger brothers."

"Walk with me out to the barn. I want to show you and Josh the new calf that was born this morning."

His legs were long but her stride matched his well enough that they could walk beside each other without one slowing down or the other speeding up. A breeze had picked up and coming off all the ice, it was cool in spite of the sun's warmth.

"Has he seen a new baby calf yet?" Lucas asked.

"No. Calves are born in the spring, not December."

"You got that right, but a couple of our prize heifers went visiting the bull pen at the wrong season. We had no idea they were in heat until it was too late to do anything about it. We aren't even sure which bull bred them."

"Which means this one goes with the calf crop to the sale next fall, right?" she asked.

He chuckled.

"What in the hell is so funny?" she asked.

"Nothing. I just never knew a woman who knew so much about ranchin'. I thought you were a basketball coach."

"Well, I was a rancher before I was a coach. I can grow cotton or pull a calf just as well as I can take a basketball team to state play-offs. And I can do it with a baby on my hip," she smarted off.

"Kind of like Gretchen Wilson's 'Redneck Woman'?"

"That's right. Oh, Joshua, would you look at that pretty baby? He's beautiful, Lucas. Which bulls were in the pen? Can't you tell by lookin' at him who his daddy is?" she asked.

Lucas shrugged. "They were both Angus. One is my best bull and the other one is a good bull but not prize stock. I use him for sale calves."

He looked like a cowboy out of an old Western movie with a shoulder propped against the doorjamb. She could picture him costarring in something about rustlers or maybe range wars with Tom Selleck or Sam Elliott.

The calf came over to the stall door, and she squatted so that Joshua could see it better. He cooed and the new baby stuck out his tongue and licked Joshua on the hand.

She shook her head to erase the vision and said, "I want to buy that calf from you, Lucas."

"Why?"

"Because it's the first baby calf Joshua has seen and he needs to own him. Instead of a paycheck for this month's work, I want that calf. By the time I leave he'll be old enough that I can finish raising him with a bucket."

"Okay, but that's pretty cheap work for a whole month," Lucas said.

"Depends on how you look at it. Could be that his bloodline is good and he'll throw some of the best calves we've seen out in Silverton. Now it's time to get back in the house. Henry asked for cinnamon rolls for dinner and the dough is probably ready to roll out."

Lucas reached out and wrapped his fingers around her arm. He ran a gloved hand down the length of her jawbone and she could feel the heat building from deep inside her through the leather of his gloves. Instinctively, she looked up and their eyes locked over the top of the baby in the sling between them. He bent his broad chest around Joshua and kissed her gently, then deepened it into more and more. His tongue rimmed her upper lip and eased its way inside her mouth to do a slow, easy country waltz with hers.

Joshua squirmed and whimpered when Lucas's arms drew her closer.

"Oops. Sorry about that, feller. I got carried away. Did I squish you too badly?" Lucas asked.

"I'll see you at dinner." Natalie blushed.

She spun around and hurried across the yard.

She expected Drew to spout off something in her conscience and was disappointed when he didn't say a single word.

"Shit!" she said when she was in the kitchen. "Don't you repeat that word when you get older, Joshua."

Chapter 7

"GOOD GRIEF, LUCAS HAS BEEN MY 'DEAR DIARY,' AND I didn't even realize it," she told Joshua as she changed him from pajamas into clothes for the day.

The baby kicked his legs and waved his arms about, cooing the whole time at his mother's voice. As fast as he was growing, it wouldn't be long until he could control those arms and legs and his cooing would become real words. She wondered what his first word would be.

"You are a boy, so you won't ever have a little pink diary to write all your secrets in. Boys don't do that. But I did until I was about thirteen and then I just told Drew everything and forgot about my diary. When he was gone, I shifted my diary mode over to Lucas. I wonder if you can even buy them anymore. I'll need one to start the year off if we are back in Silverton."

Joshua looked up at her and drew his eyes down in a frown.

"Okay, enough talk about the future. But let's get something straight about tonight. There'll be strangers in and out all day and a big party tonight. Don't you get too friendly with them, and other than Henry, Jack, and Grady, you aren't to smile at them. Those are my smiles, and I'm not sharing your precious smiles with anyone."

Natalie kissed him between the eyes. "Yes, you can smile at Lucas, but that's the whole list."

She carried him to the kitchen, settled him into the

swing, and was busy winding it up before she realized that the smell of coffee filled the kitchen. She quickly looked around and there was Henry, pouring two cups full.

"Good mornin'," he said brightly.

"What are you doing up and about so early?" Natalie asked.

"It's party weekend. Ella Jo, that would be my wife and the other half of my heart, loved Christmas and her spirit comes back the month of December every year to visit with me. Folks probably think I'm crazy, but I can hear her voice in my head and she talks to me," he said.

"I don't think you are a bit crazy."

Henry flashed his brightest smile. "I don't want to miss a minute of time with her." He handed Natalie a mug. "If I get here early today and tomorrow, I get to look at the tree a little while with her before all the noise starts. She tells me if I need to change an ornament, and we visit about the old days when we first settled on this ranch. Is that an old man losing his mind?"

Natalie shook her head. "That is the sweetest thing I've ever heard."

"She said I was an old hopeless romantic. When we first bought this ranch back in the forties we started off in a one-room cabin. I promised her a decent house and a yard full of kids. She lived to see the house, but she only got Jack before she died. I miss her even after fifty years. I told her about Josh this morning and I could feel her smiling."

Natalie swallowed twice before she got the lump out of her throat. "What did Ella Jo make for breakfast on party day?"

Henry smiled. "Sausage gravy and biscuits. She only got to have one party in the house before she died. I remember our first Christmas together though in the little cabin. We went out in the woods and I chopped down a cedar tree. We strung cranberries and popcorn in the evenings to put on that tree, and the ornaments were made out of paper and what few I could carve out of scrap wood. They looked more like Easter eggs than ornaments, but we thought they were beautiful. I made a star for the top out of an old pie pan that had a hole in the bottom."

Natalie crumbled sausage into a skillet. When that finished browning, she pulled a bowl down from the cabinet and sifted flour into it.

"It sounds beautiful," she said.

"It was. I thought she was going to throw me out in the barn for cutting up that tin pan though. She said that if she made the crust thick enough that the hole didn't matter." Henry chuckled. "Look! Josh likes that story. He's smiling. Let me tell you, feller, a man can know everything in the world about ranchin' and cattle, but that don't mean jack squat when it comes to understandin' a woman. When I put that star up on the tree, Ella Jo just stood there and cried. And I never did hear another word about cuttin' up her pie pan."

"Where is the topper now?" Natalie asked.

Henry cleared his throat and blushed. "When she died, I planted a cedar at the foot of her grave and every year I decorate it and put that pie pan on the top. It's gettin' rusty, but so am I."

"Bullshit!" Lucas said from the doorway. "You could work circles around any of the young hired hands on the ranch. Ain't nothing rusty about you."

"That's because I get up and around in the mornin'. I don't sleep until noon," Henry said.

Lucas brushed against Natalie's thigh as he crossed the kitchen floor. "Noon! The sun isn't even up and the rooster hasn't started crowing."

"You might check the back porch. He might be waitin' to do his crowin' in the house." Henry chuckled.

Natalie inhaled sharply.

Lucas was damn sure more than a "dear diary" because she'd had a little pink diary as a child. It even had a lock on it, and she wrote all kinds of things about her brothers and her friends. Not one time had that diary made her want to throw her dough-covered hands around it and kiss it with so much passion that it would melt all the snow in north Texas.

Lucas held the mug of coffee tightly in his hands to steady them. Just touching her hip had stirred him into semi-arousal. A man would have to be stone-cold dead not to be affected by Natalie Clark. She was more than just a tall, beautiful woman. So much sexual energy surrounded her when she walked into a room that even Sonia, who had always been the prettiest girl in Savoy, was relegated to the backseat.

It wasn't right to compare the two women, but he couldn't help it. Sonia had been the love of his life for so many years that she was the yardstick to measure all women. Short, vivacious, always ready for a good time, every man's dream of a trophy wife, and Natalie was none of those things. She was beautiful, could talk basketball and cows in the same evening, run a house with a baby on her hip, and killed coyotes with her own pink pistol.

"What's got your mind wrapped up in barbed wire this morning? Thoughts of seeing all your old buddies?" Henry asked.

Lucas heard his grandfather's voice, but it didn't register until Henry yelled, "Lucas, are you awake?"

He nodded. "Barely. I'm sorry. What did you ask me?"

"I asked you what had your brain all wrapped up in barbed wire. It's plain as day that you was way off thinkin' about something that put a frown on your face. That stuff over there still on your mind at times?"

Lucas carried a cup of coffee to the table. "It was a big cultural shock when I got to Kuwait, but Drew helped me settle in. He'd been there two times already, so he knew the ropes."

"Talk to me about it," Henry said.

Lucas shrugged. "Drew had the upper bunk and I had the bottom one in the tent where we were assigned. He taught me how to hang sheets over the sides and my wet towels over the end for some privacy. He showed me where the phone room was so I could call y'all and talk when we didn't use the computer. Twenty-five men in one tent. Bathroom outside in a portable toilet. Showers in another building. Everything is a luxury here and sometimes I think about the guys still over there. Or those on their way." He paused.

Henry waited.

"Just being home doesn't knock the place out of your head. You wake up in a cold sweat not knowing where you are and the dead silence is scary. It feels like the middle of a tornado. Like a vacuum that will disappear any minute and be replaced by chaos," Natalie said.

Henry looked away from Joshua at her.

Lucas raised an eyebrow. "How did you know that?"

She went on as she put a pan of biscuits in the oven. "Then you realize you are home and you worry about those you left over there. The friendships you make in those times are even deeper than the ones you've made your whole life at home. That's because you are so dependent on each other for your lives."

"You been over there, Natalie?" Henry asked.

"No, but Drew told me about it. We'd be watching a movie in the living room at my folks' place and he'd drift off only to wake up with a jerk and a crazy look in his eyes. I'd make him talk about it, so I know what you are saying, Lucas," she answered. "I can't imagine the shock of that place. Just the physical heat and sand in everything would drive me insane. Then you come home in the middle of winter with snow falling and utter quiet at night with none of the noise of twenty-five other men in the same tent with you. It's got to be tough."

"It is," Lucas said hoarsely.

"Drew said it takes a couple of weeks before you adjust. You want eggs with your sausage gravy and biscuits?" she asked.

"Omelet?" he asked.

Natalie nodded. "Henry?"

"Honey, I'll eat anything you put on this table. I love a big breakfast. That kind of food sticks to the ribs so a man can work all morning without listenin' to a grumblin' stomach. How about you, Josh? You want an omelet this morning?" Henry said.

Natalie's soft laugh sounded like tinkling Christmas bells in Lucas's ears. It was honest and real, totally unlike Sonia's high-pitched giggle. There he went comparing apples and oranges again.

"I don't think Joshua is ready for an omelet. Baby rice cereal is his buffet of choice for a few more weeks. Momma says on Christmas morning he can have a jar of baby food bananas or pears. He gets to choose," she said.

Henry turned his attention back to Joshua. "Well, son, next Christmas I promise you can have an omelet. You'll be a full year old by then, and we'll sit right up here at this table and we'll have us an omelet and bites of biscuit. By then you'll have a mouth full of teeth. Way you are slobbering I'd say the first two are already on their way."

"Really?" Natalie asked.

"Oh, yeah. Probably have them by Christmas. Reminds me of that old song about all I want for Christmas is my two front teeth. Josh here, he just might get two by then." Henry chuckled.

"What's so funny?" Lucas asked.

"Your granny always said that when a baby cuts teeth early then the next one is on the way," Henry answered.

"Bite your tongue," Natalie raised her voice.

Lucas opened his mouth to tell his grandfather that by the next Christmas, Josh would be back in Silverton, but he clamped it shut. Arguing with the old fellow wouldn't accomplish a thing, and upsetting him during the holidays was just plain wrong. He looked forward to their Christmas party kicking off the whole season in and around Savoy. No way in hell would Lucas ever ruin one bit of the holidays for Henry. He lived and breathed Christmas because that's when he felt closer to his precious Ella Jo's spirit and felt as though she came back to visit with him every year.

The ring tone of his cell phone said that Hazel was calling. Lucas fished it out of his shirt pocket and said, "You need to be home, not laid up in a bed playing sick."

"I can plan that party from here, so don't give me none of your sass," Hazel said.

Lucas shook his head. "Always did say that you barked orders like a five star general. I'm putting you on speaker so everyone can hear you including the baby, so watch your language."

"The hell I will," she said. "I didn't watch my language with your dad or you and I'll be damned if I watch it with another generation on the ranch. Now Lucas, you and Jack, make sure all the lights are working right. If one of them old bulbs is shot, it'll throw the whole line out of whack."

"Yes, ma'am," Lucas said.

"Grady will oversee moving the furniture out to the barn, and there'd better not be one scratch on it. And Henry's job is to take care of the crew bringing in the tables and party ware. You got that?" Hazel asked.

"I do," Henry said.

"Who else is in the room?" Hazel asked.

"Natalie, me, Gramps, and the baby," Lucas said.

"And what's my job?" Natalie asked.

"You are to make cookies all morning and keep the coffeepot and tea pitcher filled for the folks who are working at setting up. Fix sandwiches for dinner, and tonight those men are taking you out to eat because the kitchen belongs to the catering crew in the middle of the afternoon," Hazel said.

"It's snowing again," Henry said. "We might not be able to get out to be going to a café, and besides, Natalie's cookin' is better'n what they'd serve up anyway. The caterers can just move over and give her some room or hell, she can cook at my place and we'll all eat there."

"If the caterers can get in, you can get out. Lucas, you make reservations over at the Red Lobster in Sherman," Hazel said.

"Why there? Maybe we want to go to a steak house like Texas Roadhouse," Lucas said.

"Don't you argue with me. You can eat steak any day of the week, and besides, they serve steak and lobster specials over there all the time. Do you like seafood, Natalie?" she asked.

"Yes, ma'am. Love it," Natalie said.

"Then that's where you are going tonight for all your hard work, cooking and putting up with them cantankerous old farts while I'm laid up. You'll take lots of pictures and send them to me over this computer thing that Willa Ruth has set up, right? Jack has her address for it," Hazel said.

"I'll be sure you have some by morning," Natalie answered.

"Then it's all covered. Y'all have fun. I got to go. Willa Ruth has my breakfast ready. It tastes like shit, but she says it doesn't have too much fat or carbohydrates in it, whatever to hell that last thing is. I tell her to let me eat what I want and die when I'm supposed to. Seems like in this house if it tastes like shit, it goes on the table and if it tastes good, it stays in the grocery store. Bye now."

The line went quiet. Lucas picked up his phone and

shoved it back into his shirt pocket. "She ain't changed any at all."

"I'd say she's callin' it like it is," Grady said from the doorway.

"It ain't fair to the baby to have to watch us eat like that and all he gets is that stuff that looks like wallpaper paste," Henry said.

Natalie laughed again. "He thinks it tastes just like an Angus T-bone. He told me so when I shoved it into his mouth."

The sound of her voice and laughter stayed with Lucas all morning as he helped his dad tighten every light bulb around the roof, fix the bunting where the goat had eaten his dinner, and string lights down the fence on either side of the lane leading from road to house. Snow fell steadily through the morning, leaving almost two inches on the ground and settling on the brim of his old work hat.

A dusting of white covered the ice that had accumulated on the tree limbs, but the gray skies didn't let a glimmer of sun rays through. Unless something drastic changed, the guys would drink too much and the women would flirt too much and there would be rolling in the snow before the night was done. It didn't sound like fun to Lucas. He'd rather take a four-wheeler ride across the ranch with Natalie snuggled up against his back.

Like that would happen! There was no way in hell that she'd leave Joshua and go for a ride with him. Besides, he was the soldier home from the big bad war and he had to stay at the party until the last dog went home. He fingered his dog tags. He should take them off, but it didn't seem right, not yet. Not when Drew had died over there. Maybe his death wouldn't have affected Lucas so much if there had been others or if they hadn't gotten to be such close friends, but until it felt right, he would wear the dog tags to honor his fallen friend.

He checked the final four strands of lights around the porch posts.

"All done," Jack said.

"We put up lights in our tent and several of the guys had a little fake tree, but it wasn't home. We saved our packages until Christmas morning and those that didn't have one, the rest of us shared with them. Hazel's cookies were the biggest hit in the tent," Lucas said.

"I'm glad the boys enjoyed them. She got a big kick out of fixing boxes to send to you. Was Drew there then?"

"He was there when we got there, then he went home for about six weeks over the holidays and came right back. It was his third tour," Lucas answered.

"And he was Natalie's best friend. We haven't had much time alone since you got home. I know that baby was a big shock, but we thought you'd be excited. Seems like a blessing after those tests," Jack said.

Lucas removed his hat and shook a layer of snow from it. "I wanted my own kids, Dad."

"Everything happens for a reason. Some women aren't mother material. Your mother, Marilyn, wasn't. Your grandpa tried to make me see some light, but I had on blinders where that woman was concerned. She was so pretty and had so much energy. I thought she'd channel all that into raising you, but it didn't work that way. Sonia is a lot like her. Besides, that doctor didn't say it was impossible. He said it would take a miracle. I believe in miracles, especially at Christmas," Jack said.

Lucas shoved his hat back down on his head. "I'm not sure that even God has a miracle that big up His sleeve. Here comes the first truckload of stuff, and I smell chocolate chip cookies coming from the house. Let's get in out of the cold and grab them while they are hot right out of the oven."

———

Furniture, except for the kitchen table, had been carried out while Natalie was busy baking. She was removing another dozen cookies from the pan to cool when a tall, blond-haired cowboy reached out and grabbed one.

"I'm Noah Call and these look like some fine cookies, ma'am," he said.

"I'm Natalie Clark and thank you." She smiled.

"This'd be your baby, the one that everyone is talking about?" He nodded toward Joshua.

"Yes, it is. His name is Joshua."

Noah reached for another cookie. "Good strong name. Momma says that a man needs a good name. All her eight boys are named after boys in the Bible."

Noah Call—if she'd gone to school with him, he would have sat between her and Drew Camp when the teachers put them in alphabetical order. Would one little change like that have put her life on a different course?

"So you from around here?" she asked.

"Yep, grew up right here on this ranch. My daddy was a hired hand until last year when he and Momma retired and moved down to Waco to be around my oldest brother and his wife. Lucas is two years older than me, but we went to school together. Played a couple of

games of basketball on the same team before he graduated. I hear you was a coach for a while," Noah said.

Mercy! The gossip vine had surely done its job.

The burst of cold wind brought Lucas, Jack, and a
dozen more people into the living room before she could
reply to Noah's comment. Lucas made a beeline for the
table and snagged two cookies.

"They're every bit as good as Hazel's," Noah said.
"You don't want to keep her around, kick her over the
pasture fence and we'll hire her out in the bunkhouse to
cook for us. Might be fun to have a baby boy out there."

Lucas clapped a hand on the cowboy's shoulder.
"Noah, where have you been keepin' yourself? I been
home a whole week and you haven't come by."

"Grady sent me and Emmett to the old line shack for
a few days. He was afraid the storm was going to be
worse than it was. Weatherman was talkin' blizzard and
a foot of snow for a while there. We're just glad to get
back to the bunkhouse in time for the party. Glad you
are home, but I'm sorry to hear that Hazel is laid up for a
few weeks." Noah picked up two more cookies. "I got to
run. See y'all tomorrow night. Natalie, honey, you got a
real pretty little boy there, and I really do like his name."

"Thank you." Natalie smiled.

He settled his hat on his blond hair and disappeared
out the back door. She looked across the room at Lucas
and asked, "Is the line shack the cabin that Henry and
Ella Jo lived in at first?"

Lucas shook his head, "No, it's even smaller than the
cabin. Dad and Grady built it before I was born, and it's
at the very back side of the ranch."

"Just how big is Cedar Hill?" she asked.

"Just under nine sections. Gramps started with one section and bought up land when he could. The shack is four miles from here back into the woods. Only way to get to it is by four-wheeler or a horse."

She did the math in her head. Nine sections at six hundred forty acres per section came up to about five and a half thousand acres. Pretty nice little spread they had carved out of the mesquite and scrub oak.

"And your ranch?" he asked.

"Twenty acres," she answered as she took more cookies from the oven.

"That's not a ranch," he said.

"You asked about my ranch. It's twenty acres. I bought a corner of land from Daddy and I have a trailer on it. That's my ranch. If you want to know about Daddy's ranch, it's about twice the size of Cedar Hill. We put in six thousand acres of cotton a year and the rest we use for pasture to raise Angus."

His smile was so bright that it lit up the whole kitchen. Hell, it might have run the sun some competition if it had been out. For the life of her, Natalie couldn't think of a single reason the size of her dad's place was so amusing.

Chapter 8

NATALIE DRESSED IN HER BEST DESIGNER JEANS, Western shirt, and boots. She'd twisted her brown hair up into what she called a messy French twist and held it with a big crystal-encrusted clamp that matched her belt buckle. On most days she didn't take time to put on makeup, but that night she did. A little dark eyeliner and pale blue eye shadow, some mascara, a touch of blush, and a bit of lip gloss.

"Don't know why I bother with all this. No one will even see me anyway. You will be the center of attention," she told Joshua as she dressed him.

Natalie's dad, Jimmy, declared from the day that they found out Natalie was having a boy that his first grandson would leave the hospital in boots and jeans. The jeans were soft denim and the legs had to be rolled that day. The boots were made of kid leather with soft soles, but by golly, they had pointed toes and the tops were detailed.

Now Joshua's feet fit into the boots like they should and the legs of his jeans didn't need to be rolled anymore. In another month both would be too small. She had already bought the shadow box to frame them. It was made of rough cedar and had barbed wire strung around the outside edge.

"If the basketball players can frame their jerseys, then we can do the same with your first jeans and boots.

Someday you are going to be a famous bull rider, yes, you are." She talked in a high-pitched voice that brought out Joshua's biggest grins.

When he was dressed and his dark hair parted and combed to one side, she placed him inside his car seat. "The ladies are all going to flock around you wanting to dance. You be careful and don't lead none of them on."

His brown eyes sparkled.

"I'd love to know what you are thinking." She picked the seat up and carried it to the living room.

"Would you look at that?" Henry exclaimed. "There's a rancher for sure. I didn't even know they made boots that little."

Grady took the car seat from Natalie and the three older men flocked around it. "Look at that hair. Now that's a boy's haircut. I hate it when the women folks put that jelly stuff in a little boy's hair and make it look like he stuck his fingers in a light socket."

Jack touched his hand. "All you need is a cowboy hat and you'll be right up there with the big boys, Josh."

Henry chuckled. "See, I told you he was a Josh, just like I told all y'all that Lucas was a Hoss."

Natalie giggled.

"I hate nicknames," Lucas said.

"Me too," Natalie whispered.

"Are you old women about through carryin' on?" Lucas asked.

"Don't be callin' us old women," Jack said.

"You'll embarrass Josh," Lucas said.

"No, we won't. He likes us," Henry said.

Natalie was glad that they were doing all the talking and didn't ask her anything that required an answer, because she was totally speechless. Lucas wore starched jeans that bunched up just right over the tops of shiny black boots, a tooled belt with a silver buckle with what had to be the Cedar Hill brand engraved on it, and a brown Western-cut shirt that matched his eyes perfectly. The top two snaps were undone and his dog tags were tucked down inside. He held a black Stetson against his thigh, and her eyes strayed in that direction. She quickly blinked and was looking toward the dog tags when she opened her eyes again.

"You look very nice," he said.

"Thank you. You clean up pretty damn good yourself." She was surprised that words actually came forth when she opened her mouth. She figured she'd sputter and stutter around like a teenager meeting Blake Shelton after a concert at the state fair.

"Can Josh ride with us?" Henry asked.

"I'd better take him," Natalie said.

"Next time it's our turn, right?" Henry said.

"Hazel says that time about is fair play," Jack said.

"And we'd keep him so entertained that he wouldn't cry," Grady put in his two cents.

"Next time." Natalie nodded.

She hadn't thought about riding all the way to Sherman alone in a truck with Lucas. She'd figured she and Joshua would go in her club cab truck and the guys would all go together. Suddenly, she was as nervous as a virgin bride on her wedding night.

Grady handed the seat to Lucas. "You carry him out for Miz Natalie. This boy has been puttin' away some groceries. He's too heavy for his momma to tote around when there's a bunch of us cowboys to help out."

"No puppies," Lucas whispered when they were on the porch. "I told you I'd make that pen air tight after the goats."

In the yard, she looked up to the roof. "No goats and no... huh, oh!"

Mr. Crankston's old blue truck came to a sliding stop in front of the house and he bailed out, shotgun in hand. "I tried to give you them damn goats and you wouldn't have them and now you steal my jackass. What's the matter with you, Lucas Allen? Did your brains get scrambled over there?"

Henry pointed at a dappled donkey coming around the side of the house straight toward Lucas and Natalie.

"See there! You stole my donkey to keep the coyotes away. I heard that your new woman killed one right up in the backyard. Chester, he don't like nobody but me. Onliest animal on my ranch that is mine. He can't even stand the grandson, and you been tamin' him since you been home so you could steal him," Crankston said. "I've a mind to just shoot you this time for real."

The donkey stopped a couple of feet from Lucas and shook his head. Joshua fought his way out of the blanket and cooed at the donkey.

"Ain't nobody going to be shootin' no one. We're on our way to town to have supper. Your donkey should be safe right here in the yard fence until you bring over the decorations tomorrow. You can get him then," Henry said.

"The hell I will. By then, he won't let me near him. He's a jackass that takes up with only one person at a time, I'm tellin' you. By tomorrow he might decide to take up with one of y'all instead of me. Come on, Chester."

Crankston looped a rope around his neck and tied him to the back of the pickup truck. "Y'all go on ahead of me. I'm going to drive real slow and take him back home. It ain't but a little over a mile back to my place."

Joshua spit out his pacifier and cooed around it when Natalie reached over the seat and put it back in his mouth. She told him he was a good boy and that was the extent of their conversation on the twenty-minute drive from Savoy to Sherman.

"I wonder what all this is with the animals," Natalie asked.

"Fluke or coincidence. Or all this weird weather. Take your pick," Lucas answered.

He stole looks at her while he drove. She wore her jeans and boots like a woman who was comfortable with the ranching life. He could hardly believe that she'd given birth to Joshua just a couple of months before. Her waist nipped in above rounded hips and below a chest that filled out that shirt right well.

He parked, got out, and opened the door for Natalie and waited for her to unbuckle Josh from his seat. "You sure look pretty tonight."

Her smile lit up the whole parking lot. "Thank you, so do you."

"Pretty?" He cocked his head to one side.

"You know what I mean."

"What exactly do you mean?" he asked.

"I mean that you are sexy as hell, look good in those jeans, and I like the shirt. It's the same color as your eyes. Oh, and I like the way your butt looks too," she said.

The grin got wider. "You don't have any trouble saying what's on your mind, do you?"

"I call it like I see it," she said.

And all you said was pretty. You want to amend that? Drew was back visiting Lucas.

"Well, darlin', there aren't enough words in an unabridged dictionary to say how stunning you are tonight," he said.

"There's a lot of words in that dictionary I hope you aren't thinking. Like fat, ugly, hateful…"

"Okay, okay. You take my breath away. When I stepped into the living room tonight, my mouth felt like it did in the middle of a sandstorm over there in Kuwait. If I'd have had to speak or drop dead, I'd have just crossed my arms over my chest and fell down graveyard dead."

"Very, very good pickup line," she said.

"It's the God's honest truth," he protested.

"Then thank you." She wrapped a blanket around Joshua and didn't waste any time getting into the restaurant. Lucas was just glad she didn't bring out that denim rag thing that she slung around her shoulder and carried him in at the ranch. That thing was just plain ugly.

Henry, Jack, and Grady waited for them right inside the door of the restaurant. Jack reached toward Natalie. "I'll take the baby. I'm glad you left that bucket thing in the car. Babies need to be held, not toted around like a basket full of eggs."

Joshua promptly spit out his pacifier and cooed at Jack.

Grady caught it before it hit the floor. "Good try, son. But I'm faster than you are." He hooked it on his little finger and touched Joshua's cheek. "Did you have a good ride? I bet those two didn't give you nearly as much attention as we would have."

"Y'all really are as bad as old women at church when a new baby is brought in for the first time," Lucas said.

"We are not. Just wait until tomorrow morning and you'll see that we can't hold a candle for those old gals to go by," Henry said.

Church! In Savoy the whole family went every Sunday and sat on the same pew. Natalie went to church with her family in Silverton, and even if she hadn't, she'd have to come up with a damn good excuse, like death, to get out of going. Jack and Henry would insist on it. That meant Lucas, Natalie, and Joshua would drive to the little white church in town together. And they'd all sit on the same pew and the gossip vines would produce an abundant crop that week!

The waitress showed them to a table for six and Jack kept Joshua in his arms. He propped the baby up on his lap and said, "Next year you can eat with us. You'll have teeth and I bet you will order a beefsteak as big as a platter," he said.

Lucas seated Natalie and sat beside her. He picked up the menu and immediately the hair on his neck stood straight up. Someone was definitely staring at him or sneaking up on his blind side. That sensation never failed him and kept him out of trouble lots of times. He glanced sideways at Natalie, but she was busy looking at her menu. His gaze went one by one around the table. Jack was talking to the baby, and Henry and Grady were arguing over whether to choose the steak and shrimp special or to go for the lobster.

Jack stopped telling Josh how it wouldn't be long

until he could sit in one of those kiddie chairs and asked Natalie, "So how does Fannin County compare to your part of Texas?"

She laid the menu to one side and bit her lower lip. It drew Lucas's attention to her lips and he wanted to kiss them, which brought on a red-hot desire for more than a kiss. Now he had a full-fledged arousal and the hair on his neck was still prickling.

"Well," she said slowly.

The waitress appeared at the table before she could say another word. "What are you folks having to drink?"

"Bud Light, please," Natalie said.

"Same," Lucas said.

"I'll have sweet tea, but we also want a bottle of your best champagne and five of those fancy glasses," Henry said. "Our boy has come home from Kuwait and we are celebrating with a toast before we have supper."

"Congratulations on making it home in one piece and thanks for serving our country," the waitress said. "Your son looks just like you. Bet you were glad to get home to see him while he's still little. Y'all ready to order or do you want me to bring your drinks first?"

"We're ready," Henry beamed.

Something just flat out wasn't right. The last time Lucas had been spooked so badly was the last morning Drew left the tent. Something hadn't been right that morning either, but he couldn't put his finger on it until he heard the explosion. He looked at Natalie again, but she was sipping her beer. Jack, Henry, and Grady all looked like the old proverbial cat that had found its way into the cream.

Was someone about to bomb the restaurant? Was there

a terrorist sitting somewhere close? Something horrible was about to happen because his nerves were getting more uptight by the second.

They ordered and the waitress left and then he heard something like the scraping of a chair on tile floor. He looked at Natalie, and they both glanced over their shoulder just in time to see Sonia walking toward their table. Her high heels sounded like gunshots on the tile floor and he had to hold his hands tightly to keep from throwing them over his ears.

She stopped between Lucas and Jack and slung a hip against Lucas's shoulder. "Well, hello! I'd forgotten that y'all always go out to eat on the night before the big party. Got everything all decorated? Remember that year that you and I strung the lights, Lucas? It was so warm that we were out there without jackets and in our shorts. This is more like Christmas, isn't it?"

"Sonia, I'd like to introduce you to Natalie Clark. Natalie, this is Sonia," Lucas said.

"It's nice to meet you. You are engaged to Noah, right?"

"Yes, I am. We're planning a big beautiful Christmas wedding." Sonia barely glanced Natalie's way.

"Oh, there are my girls!" She waved to a group of women coming toward her. "We're having a girls' night out to talk about what we are wearing to your party tomorrow night. It kicks off the whole season in Savoy, Miss Clampton, and even the hired help is invited. You'll have a good time."

Natalie smiled brightly. "I'm sure I will, and it's Clark, not Clampton."

She brushed a quick kiss across Lucas's cheek. "Save me one dance for old time's sake, Lucas."

"I'm not sure that's a good idea. Noah is my friend," he said.

She flipped her hair over her shoulder and sashayed back to the table where her girls were gathered.

"Well, now you've met Sonia," Henry whispered.

"Yes, I have. Now what do I want to order?" Natalie looked at the menu.

The heat radiating from Natalie's back to his arm was about to burn holes in his skin. His brain flashed pictures of her long legs tangled up with his in soft sheets. "Blue Christmas" was playing in the restaurant and suddenly the bedsheets in his mind were the color of her eyes. He heard the words about her being gone and how that he'd have a blue Christmas without her, but he didn't want to think about that.

"Would Noah be mad if you danced with her?" Natalie whispered.

"I just don't think it would be right. You will dance the midnight dance with me, won't you?"

"That's a pretty important dance at any Texas party. You sure you want to fire up that gossip vine?"

Lucas dropped his hand from the back of the chair and wrapped his fingers around Natalie's shoulder. He leaned toward her and whispered softly, "I'm very sure, and thank you."

—◦◦◦—

Lord, his breath was like pure fire on her skin and he smelled like heaven and hell mixed up together. If there ever was a devil in blue jeans, he was sitting beside her and his name was Lucas Allen. He wasn't playing fair, touching her arm like that and whispering seductively in her ear.

Well, as her mother said, "What's good for the goose is good for the gander."

She reached under the table and laid a hand on his thigh. She felt his quick intake of breath and knew that he was feeling every bit of the heat that she was. She squeezed gently and ran her hand up another two inches.

"Now, before we were interrupted, I was askin' about your county out there in the Panhandle," Jack said.

"It's a small world. Momma remembers Henry and his wife coming to her ranch over by Goodnight when she was just getting engaged to my dad," she said.

Henry's gray eyebrows drew down until they were a solid line. "What was her maiden name?"

"Adams. My grandparents are Dollie and Walter Adams," Natalie said.

Henry's eyebrows returned to their proper place and he chuckled. "Knew them well. Was in the same Angus Association with them for years until we split the state up so we all didn't have to travel so far. Haven't seen them since that time, probably because that was the year that Ella Jo died. That'd be out in Briscoe County, right?"

"Silverton is. We only have two towns in the whole county," she said.

"That's because your dad owns half the county," Lucas said.

Natalie saw a quick movement at the table behind them and glanced over her shoulder. It would be asking too much for Sonia to fall out of her chair and die, but surely God could make her choke almost to death. Or even give her a bad stomachache so she'd have to go home early. But the woman's expression said that she'd like to use that bottle of wine in the middle of the table as a weapon on her, instead of drinking it. Natalie smiled and wiggled her fingers in a girlish wave toward her.

"Not quite half but a big chunk." Natalie looked back at the guys. "With what Momma owns, it might be more than half, though."

"So what's the other town?" Grady asked.

"Quitaque," she said.

"I remember that place. It's not spelled like it sounds. Thank goodness the way you say it, kit-a-key, is out there on the welcome sign or me and Ella Jo would have never figured it out."

"How's it spelled?" Lucas asked.

She said the letters slowly. "Most folks want to say quit-ick or quit-ache. Silverton is the county capitol and the courthouse is on the square. Not much town but we get by. We've got an implement company, a grain and gin company, and a place to buy gas and milk. The rest we drive into town for kind of like y'all do."

"What's the population?" Grady asked.

"Somewhere close to eight hundred last time they took count. Not much different than Savoy. Big enough to be a town and have a post office. Small enough that everyone knows their neighbor's business." She smiled.

Lucas's hand on her arm got hotter and hotter. She wanted to pick up the menu and fan with it, but it was the middle of the winter and the restaurant wasn't overly warm. She'd be glad when their food arrived so he'd have to remove his arm to cut up the steak he'd ordered.

"Y'all got coyotes out there? Look, the baby has gone to sleep."

Natalie moved her hand on his thigh up another inch.

Dammit! Touching his leg was making her every bit as hot as him touching her arm.

"I can hold him," Natalie said. That would give her a logical reason to stand up and walk around the table to take the baby. That way she wouldn't lose the fight.

Jack shook his head and made a cradle for Joshua by crossing one leg over the other. "See there, I can eat and take care of him. It's like riding a bicycle, darlin'. I used to hold Lucas like this at meal times."

"If he gets too heavy, I'll hold him and yes, we do have trouble with coyotes. But we fight the lobo wolves too. A pack of them will take down a calf in seconds," she answered.

"And that's why you have a pink pistol?" Lucas squeezed her shoulder gently and then settled his hand closer to her neck. Bare skin against bare skin. Her insides were boiling hot. Another inch or two up his thigh and she'd know for sure if he was having problems too.

"I have a pink pistol because I wanted it and I have a license to carry it concealed. I have a twenty-two rifle that takes care of wolves and coyotes. Momma taught me two things. Shoot straight and don't waste ammunition."

"Your momma is a good woman," Jack said.

Their drinks and the bottle of champagne arrived and Henry asked the waitress to pour the chilled champagne for them. He stood and raised his glass.

Lucas had to move his hand to hold the glass.

Natalie had to move hers for the same reason.

Tie, she thought. *Neither of us backed down a bit, but thank God for champagne or who knows what might have happened.*

"To Lucas for making it back home," Henry said.

Five glasses clinked together and they all sipped the bubbly champagne.

Jack raised his glass and said, "To my son. Not a day went by that I didn't worry about you, and I'm glad you are home. And to Natalie for being here to help us through this tough time without Hazel."

"Thank you," she said and held up her glass again when she saw Grady standing up.

Grady stood and held his glass out toward Lucas and Natalie. "Put them together, kids. This is to you both for bringing a baby into our lives. We didn't realize how much we were missing. And I'm sure glad you're home too, Lucas."

From the look on Sonia's face, not one single word was wasted. If Fannin County was anything like Briscoe County, by tomorrow morning the whole place would think that Joshua belonged to Lucas. Just how that could have happened when he was in Kuwait and she was in Texas was a mystery. But hey, rumors could make miracles and perform magic, and they had wings that carried them faster than the wind in a tornado.

Chapter 9

NATALIE CHECKED EVERYTHING ONE MORE TIME BEFORE she carried Joshua back to the bedroom to get him ready for the evening. Tables for six were set up along the walls in the living room, den, and dining room. Miniature Christmas trees decorated with flickering lights and tiny ornaments were set in the middle of the tables covered with red and green plaid tablecloths. Finger foods and festive desserts including pecan tarts and miniature cherry cheesecakes were displayed on long tables against the far wall in the dining room. The portable bar was right inside the den. A gray-haired bartender wearing a white shirt, black pants, and red vest waited to pour, shake, or blend whatever the guests wanted.

The catering staff would keep the tables refreshed and pass among the guests with pretty silver trays with flutes of champagne and hors d'oeuvres. On a much smaller scale, it reminded Natalie of the barn party that would be taking place on New Year's Eve at the Clark ranch and suddenly she was homesick.

"We'll probably be home for that party, Joshua." She talked to the baby lying in the middle of her bed. "Your grandma might forgive us for Christmas, but never for the New Year's party."

Her phone set up a ring tone that said Debra was calling. "Hello, Momma. I was just telling Joshua about the New Year's party. You must have ESP."

"I've got more than ESP, Natalie. What's wrong with that cowboy and all those men?"

"Momma, I'm getting ready for the Christmas open house party thing here at Cedar Hill. What are you talking about?"

"We'll start with Henry. What's wrong with him?"

"Nothing. He's a sweet grandpa who loves Joshua and is lonely for his wife. Christmas was her favorite holiday, so he imagines that she's here with him all month. He's not deranged. I hear Drew's voice in my head too."

"You and Drew were two peas in a pod. You were almost as connected as me and Leah, so I'm not surprised. Now tell me about Jack," Debra said.

"Jack reminds me of Daddy. Only without you. His wife left him to raise Lucas all alone. Well, not alone but with the help of Grady and Henry and Hazel. Why are you asking all these questions right now?"

Debra did one of her humphhhs. The one that lasted through a couple of breaths and that irritated the hell out of Natalie. "You've always wanted to fix everything. If we would have allowed it, you would have taken in every stray in the whole damn state. It was like you had a sixth sense that beckoned to them. And we won't even talk about Drew and how you took him under your wings."

"These are not strays, Momma. Not a one of them is broken. It's me that's broke this time, and they are all putting me back together again," she said.

Was that why animals kept showing up all the time? Was she unwittingly drawing them to her side? Well, if she was, she needed to break the spell because goats on the roof and chickens in the kitchen were not a good thing.

"I should be doing that," Debra said.

"Sometimes God works in mysterious ways, Momma."

"Go enjoy your party and promise me again you'll be home for New Year's."

"I promise and I love you, Momma," Natalie said.

She laid the phone down and looked at her reflection in the cheval mirror in the corner. She'd dressed in her best jeans, boots, and a festive blue Christmas sweater that dipped low in the front. She added a small sapphire pendant on a gold chain that Drew had given her when he came home from Kuwait the first time.

"Oh, Drew, if only you hadn't been so eager to go back over there. You didn't have to volunteer for a third tour," she said.

The living room was buzzing with conversation and no one even noticed when she and Joshua made their appearance. She stayed in the shadows beside the Nativity scene and looked over the crowd. Henry was talking to an older fellow about the wooden angel on the mantel. Jack and Grady were evidently talking bulls by their hand gestures.

Lucas was sitting all alone at the table shoved up in a corner. He caught her eye and patted the chair next to him. She nodded and started that way. She'd only taken two steps when the front door opened and Sonia swept into the room like a prom queen in a bright red velvet dress that stopped at mid-thigh. It had a high neckline with a tight-fitting collar encrusted with big stones of every color ornament on the tree. The flowing chiffon sleeves were gathered up at her wrist with tight cuffs of the same stones. Her blond hair was done up in a crown of curls so that not one sparkle of her dangling diamond earrings would be wasted.

She sent a tight-lipped smile toward Natalie and headed straight for Lucas. Natalie felt underdressed, tall, gangly, and downright plain in all the glitter and glam that paraded into the room.

"Shit!" Natalie mumbled. "Lucas didn't tell me we were having a prom."

Sonia leaned down and dropped a quick kiss on Lucas's forehead. "Lucas, everything is absolutely beautiful. I ordered the snow just for you because I knew that you'd need it after all those months over there in the sand."

"Well, thank you for doing that. Where is Noah?" Lucas drawled.

"He's on his way. I told him the girls and I would be arriving together."

"Okay. Well, if you will excuse me, ladies. Natalie and Joshua have just arrived."

"Can you believe snow in Savoy?" one of her friends said. "Remember our senior year. It snowed that year for the party, but it hasn't since then."

Another giggled. "That was the year that y'all boys took us outside in our pretty dresses and rolled us in the snow. My momma had a fit when I came home in a wet dress."

"I'm sure we've grown up past that," Lucas said.

The front door opened and half a dozen big cowboys pushed their way inside. They took off their hats, hung them on a long, narrow rack right inside the door, and headed straight for Lucas, circling him and all talking at once.

Sonia sighed. "I wish we didn't have to. Girls, y'all come over here and let me introduce you to Miss Clampett," her thin voice singsonged across the room.

Natalie heard her and gritted her teeth, but she made a beeline for the bar instead of even acknowledging the woman. Poor little thing; she didn't even know how to catfight.

"Miss Clampett, I want you to meet my friends," Sonia said a few feet to her left.

Natalie turned slightly and smiled. "Well, hello. I didn't realize you were talking to me. My name is Natalie Clark. Y'all can just call me Natalie since I'm probably younger than any of you. Don't y'all all look lovely tonight. It's like prom, isn't it?"

"We like to dress up for the parties." Sonia's gaze dropped to Natalie's boots and traveled from there up to her hair. "God, you really are tall. You were sitting down last night and I didn't realize how tall you are."

"Don't know how tall God is, but if you are talking about me, I'm probably right at six feet tall with these boots on."

"Don't be a smart-ass," Sonia whispered so low that only Natalie heard it.

Natalie chose to ignore the remark. "What are you drinking? Marvin here can make you whatever you want."

Sonia snarled her nose at the beer in Natalie's hand. "We are champagne, chocolate, and roses girls, not beer, bait, and ammo women. We heard you shot a coyote."

Natalie propped a hip on one of the dozen bar stools. "Got him with one bullet. I'll take a beer anytime over champagne, love to fish and I bait my own hook, and if I get out my gun, you'd best be runnin' or sayin' your prayers."

Sonia didn't back down a bit. "Must be why you are so big. You've done man things all your life and God just let you keep growing and growing."

Natalie smiled sweetly. "Never thought of it like that. I just figured God made me tall because both my parents are tall and that He gave me a momma who could teach me to shoot the eyes out of a rattlesnake at fifty yards. You sure have big eyes, Sonia."

Sonia shivered. "Changing the subject now because I want to talk about Lucas. When did you meet him?" Sonia popped a hip up on a bar stool and the rest of the girls followed her lead.

"About eleven months ago. Did you all graduate with Lucas or go to college with him?" Natalie asked.

As if on cue, Lucas appeared by her side. "I see that Sonia is introducing you to the old cheerleading squad from Savoy High School. You want me to take Josh for a little while, honey? I'd like to introduce him to the guys. Soon as they say hi to Dad, Gramps, and Grady they'll be heading for the bar." He reached out and slipped Joshua from her arm into his.

She wondered what he felt like when he carried the baby across the room to introduce him to his friends. Rumor had it that Joshua belonged to him. Would the guys over there think that he looked like Lucas?

"Where did you meet Lucas?" Sonia asked.

"That's not important. Let's get you girls something to drink and then you can tell me your names while we find a table." Natalie motioned for Marvin. "Drinks first and then names. Again, I'm Natalie Clark, not Clampett.

Sonia must think I look like Daisy Mae. She's tall like me, but she's got blond hair and a helluva lot better build. Lord, I'd kill for that waistline she's got."

Sonia flashed another dirty look her way. The woman was crazy if she thought she could scare Natalie with evil looks. Evidently, the way her "girls" adored her, she had one side for the people she liked and another for those that she didn't.

Natalie smiled. "Sonia doesn't need to introduce herself, but the rest of you I haven't met."

Natalie used word association and put an animal with each woman. Lisa was a fox with her sharp nose. Melody was a cardinal with all that red hair. Cassie reminded her of a golden retriever puppy the way she clung to Sonia's every word. Jolene was definitely a coyote with that hungry look in her eyes. And Franny was a Persian cat with that pug nose. When she got to the end of the line, Natalie realized that the only animal she could think of to put Sonia with was a possum. It pretended to be asleep when all along it was plotting its next move.

"I want an apple martini," Sonia told the bartender after the introductions. "And I want to know this story about you and Lucas."

Natalie led them to a table, held up her beer when they were seated, and waved. "It's nice to meet you all. We'll have to get together for lunch sometime and you can tell me stories on Lucas. And Sonia, good luck on your wedding. Christmas weddings are so lovely and sweet. I hear a fussy baby. That's my cue to leave you ladies with your drinks."

She met Lucas halfway across the room, but he didn't

hold Joshua out to her. He motioned with a nod of his head down the hallway. She followed him, wondering what in the hell he was up to now. He opened the door to the bedroom where she'd been sleeping and closed it when she was inside. He pulled Joshua's pacifier from his shirt pocket and stuck it in the baby's mouth. He instantly stopped fretting and made angry sucking noises.

Natalie sat down on the edge of the bed. "He just wanted that thing. Why'd you let him fuss?"

He slumped into a rocking chair, laid the baby on his chest, and set the chair in motion with his boot heel. "Because I had to get out of there for a few minutes. I felt like the walls were closing in on me and all that noise rattled in my head. Even the music grated on my nerves and I love Marty Stuart, but the drums sounded like gunfire. Just a little more than a week ago I was in Kuwait, Natalie. The adjustment is harder than I thought it would be. Drew said that coming back wasn't as easy as leaving. I wasn't ready for a crowd, but I couldn't disappoint Dad and Gramps."

She sat down on the side of the bed. "Drew had trouble like that too. He didn't want to go to the movies or anywhere that might have loud noises or too much talking. He said that even the debriefing didn't get him ready for the home front that first time. He thought it would be easier the second time around, but it wasn't."

Lucas nodded.

"Sonia is a piece of work," she said.

He leaned his head back and shut his eyes. "Always has been."

She kicked off her boots and stretched out on the bed. "Want to talk?"

"Nope, just want to enjoy the peace. Josh was a big hit with the guys. They all said that he looks just like me. Amazing what a rumor can create and how fast it can travel, isn't it?" He yawned.

"Are you sure you should let that rumor keep spreading?" she asked.

He didn't answer because he and Joshua were both asleep.

———

Drew's job was driving the brass around the base. That morning Lucas was supposed to accompany them and Drew was pushing him to hurry. "Come on, man! Get the lead out of your ass. I'm the driver, so it's my ass that gets chewed if we're not on time. And on time means five minutes before the set time," Drew had said.

Then the lieutenant poked his head in the door and yelled that Allen was to report to the commander's tent on the double.

"I'm supposed to go out this morning," Lucas said.

"Not anymore. There's a big problem and the commander says that he needs you right now," the lieutenant said.

Drew squeezed his shoulder and jogged out of the tent. Lucas finished tying his boots and had just stepped outside when he heard the explosion. He shaded his eyes with the back of his hand and saw black smoke billowing from light brown sand to pale blue sky.

In his dream, Lucas ran in slow motion in that direction. His feet were like lead, but he had to get to Drew to pull him out of all that smoke. He screamed but nothing came out of his mouth. He kept yelling, "No, no! I can't tell Natalie!"

He awoke with tears in his eyes and holding a baby in his arms instead of Drew.

"Your dad was a hero," Lucas whispered to the sleeping baby.

Natalie slept. Her dark hair created a halo around her head and black eyelashes fanned out on her high cheekbones. He laid Joshua in the crib, removed his little boots, and covered him with a light blanket then stared at Natalie.

He reached out to push an errant strand of hair from her cheek, but her eyes popped open before he touched her. She sat up in one fluid movement.

"Good Lord, how long did I sleep? Some hostess I am!"

"Ten minutes at the most. Look at the clock. We came in here at nine and it's only a quarter past. Not bad at all to get a fussy baby to sleep, is it? You ready to go back out there and face the monsters?"

She raised her hands above her head and rolled the kinks out of her neck. "No, but I suppose it can't be helped. I feel somewhat like the ugly duckling with all that glam and glitter around me. I'd just as soon stay in here and read a good book, but that would disappoint the guys."

He leaned forward and brushed a kiss across her lips. "You, darlin', are the prettiest woman out there. Don't let Sonia get to you. She's all fluff and no heart. Most people don't ever figure that out or if they do, like I finally did, it takes a long time."

He straightened up to his full height and held out a

hand. She put hers into his and picked up the baby monitor with the other one.

"Leave the door ajar. I've got the monitor, but I'm more comfortable if the door isn't shut," she said.

They'd only taken one step into the noisy party again when Sonia and Noah crossed the room, coming right at them. Poor old Noah looked like he was being pulled by a mule.

"I've got a question, darlin'. Is that really your son?"

"Good grief, Sonia!" Noah rolled his eyes. "I'm sorry, Lucas. She has trouble holding her liquor, and she's already had three martinis."

"I want to know, darlin'." Sonia weaved slightly and hung on to Noah for support.

Lucas untangled his fingers from Natalie's and threw his arm around her shoulder. "That's okay, Noah. And to answer your question, Sonia, that's mine and Natalie's business."

"Going over there changed you, Lucas," she said.

"Yes, it did," Lucas said.

"I'm going to the dessert table. My girls are trying to decide between cheesecake and pecan tarts. I may have both." She winked at Lucas and teetered that way on her spike heels.

Lucas frowned. "She's trouble, Noah."

Noah nodded. "The heart wants what it wants and mine wants Sonia."

"It ain't goin' to be easy," Lucas said.

"Nope, but that's okay. Easy ain't never been mine to have anyway. Daddy always said that in our family a man only gives his heart away one time."

Lucas clamped a hand on Noah's shoulder. "Gramps says the same thing about a man giving his heart away."

Noah nodded seriously and left by the front door.

Lucas turned to look at Natalie. "I hate drama. Want to dance?"

"It's not midnight."

"There's more than one dance in the night, darlin'."

"I'll be honey, sweet cheeks, or even baby, but I'm not a darlin'. Not after hearing Sonia call you that tonight," Natalie said.

"Then, sweet cheeks, can I have this dance?" He asked.

She set her beer down and slid off the bar stool. He took a long swig of the one the bartender had just uncapped before he took her hand in his.

———

They were on their way to the dance floor when someone opened the front door to step out on the porch for a breath of air, and three puppies rushed inside like a hurricane, dashing under tables and around chair legs.

One ran past Sonia's chair and stopped long enough to slurp a tongue from her knee to her hip, then grabbed the tail of her dress and pulled at it. She slapped at the dog, spilled her martini, and squealed like a cat with its tail caught in a buzz saw.

Her girls ran to her rescue, but the puppy had quickly lapped up the martini and hiked a leg to pee on her shoe.

Natalie bit back a giggle and helped Lucas corral them into the hallway.

So much for an airtight pen, but the whole bunch of pups had redeemed themselves for the chickens and the goats when the feisty one hiked his leg on Sonia. He had just covered a multitude of puppy sins, and she hoped that the martini didn't make him sick.

Noah came out of the bathroom in time to see what was happening and scooped one pup up in his arms. He grabbed for the second one, but it squirmed out of his hands and pushed right into Natalie's room.

"I'll take that critter on outside." Grady reached for the pup.

Noah shook his head. "I got a good firm grip on him. I'll meet you at the pens when you catch the other two."

If that runt woke Joshua, Natalie intended to take back all the redemption she'd given him. And if she really had some kind of sonar brainpower that drew animals to her and disrupted her life, she wished someone would flip the switch and turn the damn thing off. She was missing a sexy dance with Lucas.

She and Lucas tiptoed into the room to find the last two puppies sitting beside the portable crib, wagging their tails and whining. Joshua was smiling even though he was sound asleep.

She and Lucas each picked up a puppy and stared at the baby for a few seconds longer. The smile faded and he slept peacefully.

"Do you think he was dreaming of the future when he can run in the yard and play with puppies? Maybe it was some kind of baby and puppy telepathy that called them in here," Lucas said.

"Who knows? I think they are just feisty hound dogs who like people."

Natalie Clark never did believe that stuff her mother said about animals. Still yet, there was that crazy thing with the chickens.

Grady reached for both dogs when they were out of the room. "Y'all go on back and have a dance or two.

Me and Noah will take care of these critters. I swear if I could find the way they're getting out of that pen, I'd concrete it shut."

As they passed the bathroom door, Natalie could hear Sonia's girls reassuring her that her dress wasn't even torn and that they'd washed all the dog slobbers and dog pee from her leg.

"But my shoe?" Sonia yelped.

"It's only one spot and it's already dry," Melody said.

"Could we try this one more time?" Lucas asked. "May I have this dance?"

Natalie put her hand in his. "My pleasure, sir."

Chapter 10

JOSHUA FRETTED AND CHEWED AT HIS FIST THE WHOLE time that Natalie changed his diaper and dressed him in zip-up pajamas. When she sat down in the rocking chair and touched the bottle nipple to his lips, he latched onto it with a sigh and shut his eyes.

"Some party cowboy you are." She laughed.

He snuggled down deeper into her arms.

"You fall asleep before it's in full swing, forget about your ten o'clock snack, and now at eleven you want to eat."

He grinned around the nipple, but he didn't open his eyes.

The noise of the party filtered down the hall and she heard the deep timbre of Lucas's laughter. Henry said something but she couldn't make out words, only distinct and separate tones. Boots on hardwood sounded like drumbeats at the beginning of a county song. They stopped one door short of her bedroom and the bathroom door opened. How in the world they'd managed to get through the night with only one bathroom in the house was a miracle. The barn where they held the party in Silverton had cowboys and a cowgirls restrooms and each one could accommodate three people at a time.

Joshua finished his bottle, burped one last time, and went limp in her arms. That meant he was fully asleep and she could put him back in the crib, but she held him a few minutes longer.

Lucas scanned the room every few seconds to see if Natalie had returned. He hadn't expected to be mesmerized by Josh's brown eyes staring intently into his when he took him from Natalie's arms that evening. Hell, a week ago, he hadn't even planned on ever touching that kid. Now, he wanted to tiptoe into their bedroom and tell him good night. And that was just after toting him around the room for a little while. How would he feel at Christmas when Hazel came back and Natalie left?

When he'd drawn her close to dance and had buried his face in her hair, the whole room disappeared. They were on a cloud with nothing but the sounds of a tinkling country piano in the background. And he'd felt complete for the first time in his life.

He'd had his first date at fourteen when he'd asked Melody to the Valentine's dance at school. There had been three fairly serious relationships before Sonia. And then the next several years, he'd thought he was in love with her.

He checked the clock on the mantel above the blazing fireplace: eleven thirty. So many nights he'd shut his eyes in the unbearable heat over there and thought about a cold winter night with the sound of a wood fire crackling. He could visualize each and every ornament on the tree, hear all the stories about them, and Natalie was always there beside him.

Then I see her for the first time with a pistol in one hand and a baby in the other. That's reality, folks. He scanned the room one more time.

Each click of the clock's second hand lasted hours,

and minutes were eternity plus four days. He'd given up on seeing her again that night when she touched his elbow and said, "I believe it's midnight and this is our dance."

He barely heard the music go from country music Christmas songs to a slow waltz when he she wrapped both her arms around his neck. The world disappeared as he drew Natalie close with his arms around her waist. They fit together so well that he didn't even have to bend to whisper in her ear or smell the sweet fragrance of her perfume.

"Look at those three guys in the corner. They're watching every move we make," she whispered.

"We both know they are playing matchmakers, Natalie. What we have to do is ignore them and make up our own minds about our relationship," he said.

"I wouldn't be surprised if they didn't have a plan worked out with the DJ tonight."

"Is that Anne Murray?" he asked. "I remember this song. Dad used to play it when I was a kid."

"Yes, it's Anne, and the song is from the early eighties. It's Momma and Daddy's song. They've been dancing to it since before I was born. When I ask Momma about it, she just smiles and says I'll dance to it someday and understand," Natalie said.

Anne sang that she would always remember the song they were playing the first time that they danced and she knew that she had fallen in love. She asked if she could have this dance and if he would be her partner for the rest of her life.

"Listen to those words. They are meddling big-time, aren't they?" Lucas said.

"Oh, yeah!"

"They're grinnin' like a bunch of possums eatin' grapes through a barbed wire fence," Lucas whispered.

"It's cute, isn't it?"

"What? Them or the picture of the possums?" He held her closer.

"Both. My granddad says things like that about possums. Sometimes he gets a helluva lot more graphic." Natalie toyed with his hair. "We might as well give them something to grin about."

He brushed a kiss across her lips when they were under the mistletoe. "Grinnin' like a possum pickin' seeds out of a fresh cow patty?"

She giggled and planted her feet firmly.

"What?" he asked.

She pressed her body so close to his that she could feel his racing pulse and drew his lips to hers for a longer kiss.

"Do you know what you are doing to me?" he drawled.

"I know what you are doing to me. If it's the same thing, then it's a wonder the heat isn't melting those little white berries on the mistletoe," she said.

He chuckled. "You got that right."

The song ended way too soon. He could have held Natalie in his arms all night right there in the middle of the living room floor. He wouldn't care if the same song played over and over for hours. And he'd gladly dance with her the rest of his life.

Whoa, hoss! His thoughts came to an abrupt halt. *You're not ready for that kind of commitment.*

—⁓—

The guests were all gone. The caterers had packed up and left. Like cowboys in a Wild West bar, Henry, Jack, and Grady each had a beer in their hand and their boots propped up on the bare table nearest the Christmas tree.

"Whew, doggies, I believe that's the most people we've ever had at a party. I'll be glad when they bring my recliner back in the house tomorrow," Grady said.

Jack nodded. "Food is all gone. Bar is almost wiped out. And we got church tomorrow mornin', so we better guzzle these beers and catch a few hours of rest."

"Yep, we should or we're going to be the most wore out lookin' old wise men in the church play," Henry said.

Natalie didn't mean to groan but she did.

"Sorry," she said sheepishly.

"We don't have to go. I expect these wise men can worship baby Jesus without us there." Lucas yawned.

"Ain't happenin'." Jack shook his head from side-to-side. "If we're goin' to be wise men, then Joshua is coming to church to see us."

The hair on Natalie's arms prickled. Somehow she knew by the way Henry was beaming what was coming.

"Who is playing baby Jesus?" Lucas said.

"Some little girl's doll baby. Mary Alice and Jake got a girl and she's one of them fussy kind, so they're playin' Mary and Joseph, but the baby is going to the nursery. Little girl's name is Ziva and that don't seem right for a baby Jesus no way," Grady said.

"It is an Israeli name," Natalie said defensively.

"I don't care what kind of name it is. It's a girl baby. God might send lightnin' down through the church ceiling. Jesus was a boy baby, a king, not a queen," Henry said.

Henry yawned and said, "Now it's time for me to go home. Jack, you can drive me. It's just a little way farther down the road than your place, and I don't see none too good at night. Natalie, honey, don't bother with breakfast. We'll just all meet up at the church at eleven sharp."

"I'm ready for bed too. I'm glad that bunkhouse ain't a mile away. Been a long couple of days, but the party was worth it," Grady said.

Jack slung his boots off the table, finished his beer, and stood up. "Forgot to tell y'all that I had the crew put my stuff back in my house while they were moving things around. House is all yours again, son. Natalie, you can spread out across the hall if you want to. I'm all moved out."

Natalie covered a yawn with her hand. "Good night. I'll see you all tomorrow morning."

She was halfway to her room when the music started playing again and Lucas tapped her on the shoulder. She turned around at the same time he took another step forward and they collided. The only thing that kept her from falling was his arms tightly around her. Fall or burn with desire: both choices would make for a long, long night.

"Looks like I'm fated to keep falling into your arms," she said.

"May I have this dance, ma'am? One without an audience and music of our choosing," he drawled.

He two-stepped backward with her into the living room as Randy Travis sang "Honky Tonk Moon." He sang about pool table, cue balls, and troubles seeming to melt away through the smoky haze. A country piano player tickled the keys as the lyrics said that his arms were around his baby shuffling on the floor with the honky tonk moon shining and everything was all right.

"You telling me that you want to play pool?" Natalie teased.

"You play?"

"Oh, yeah, I play. You got a table hiding somewhere?"

"No, but I know a little bar just like Randy is singing about and I betcha we could find a honky tonk moon. We'll have to go some time."

"Why, Lucas Allen, are you askin' me for a date?" she flirted.

"I am. I bet the three wise men will watch Joshua for us to go shoot a few games and have a beer or two," he said.

She giggled. "Where is this honky tonk?"

"Between Savoy and Bells. We'll try to go on a Friday night since that is karaoke night. You going to sing?"

"Hell, no!" she said. "Are you?"

"I bet you I can whip your ass at pool and if I do you have to sing," he whispered.

"If you beat me, I will. If I beat you, you have to sing, so you'd best be practicing all week in the shower. Momma taught me how to shoot a mean game, and I'm damn good, cowboy," she said.

"Your momma must be a pistol," Lucas said.

"Yes, she is, but Granny is the boss. She can handle a rope, work cattle, cook a meal fit for a king, and believe me, she can outshoot either me or Momma," Natalie said.

She looked up to see what kind of reaction that brought from him. His eyes were half-shut with dark lashes fluttering toward his cheeks. She moistened her lips and got ready for the kiss but nothing prepared her for the sizzle when his mouth found hers and the song started all over again.

She listened to the words about a blue smoky haze. She wondered if the singer had experienced the same kind of emotional roller coaster she'd been on for two weeks. Was the smoke a result of the fire in his kiss? Did the honky tonk moon bring out the scorching desire in the people in the song?

The first kiss was sweet. The second one was hungry and hard. His tongue teased her lips apart and he made love to her with his lips and tongue as they clung to each other in a darkened living room.

She leaned into his hard chest and God help her, but she wished they were lying down rather than standing up. Their feet stopped moving to the beat of the music. His hand cupped the back of her neck, and his fingertips gently massaged that soft skin right below her ear. She leaned in to get the full effect and his mouth left hers and went to the soft part of her long, slender neck. He could have set up shop right there for the rest of the night because his lips sent bursts of heat through her body with every kiss. But just when she thought she'd explode, he trailed hot, steamy kisses up to her ear, across her eyelids, and back down to her mouth.

He sat down in a chair and drew her into his lap. Travis had started singing "Forever and Ever, Amen."

Yes, oh yes, keep this up forever and ever, she thought.

He pulled her shirttail out of her jeans and then his hands were on her bare rib cage, skimming them like butterfly wings. They circled around to the back when they hit the band of her lacy bra and went to the hooks in the back. She leaned back and looked up at him.

The question didn't need words. If she shook her head or said "no," he'd kiss her good night. Like a gentleman he would lead her to her room door and kiss her again. But without blinking, she reached up and unfastened the top button of his shirt and worked her way down, one button at a time. Between buttons she kissed that broad, hard chest, teasing his nipples into taut little knots. When the last button was undone, she laid her cheek against his chest.

"Your heart is pounding," she whispered.

"It's just keeping time with yours," he said.

He scooped her up in his arms and carried her down the hall and laid her gently on a king-sized bed covered with a soft brown comforter the same color as his eyes.

"You are so damn beautiful," he whispered hoarsely.

"Still got five pounds of baby fat."

He drew his hands back and said, "Oh my God! Is it too soon for this?"

She shook her head. "Joshua is almost three months old. I could've done this three weeks ago. It's not too early."

He stretched out beside her and pulled her close again. He took his time removing her shirt and bra, teasing her skin with strings of kisses on her ribs, her breasts, and that tender part of the neck right below her ear. She trembled and arched toward him, and he hadn't even gotten around to taking her belt off.

"I feel like I could catch on fire any minute," she said.

"Darlin', I mean sweet cheeks, I'm already on fire," he said.

She straddled his waist and quickly stripped his shirt off his body then tasted every inch of his skin from the waist up. His belt wouldn't pull from the loops when she got the buckle open, so she left it hanging and unzipped his jeans. He was erect and ready when she slipped her hand inside.

"Commando?" she asked.

"It's a hell of a lot more comfortable. Now my turn again. It's been a long, long time, Natalie. I'd like to play a lot longer, honey, but I'm already about to explode," he groaned.

"Me too on the exploding issue," she whispered softly. "And it's been a long time for me too. I was too wiped out to even remember much about the last time."

He shifted enough to finish undressing her but not so much that she had to remove her hand. He tossed her jeans to one side and brought her underpants down an inch at a time, caressing and tasting as he did. He kissed her toes and then worked his way back up. By the time he got to her lips, she had wrapped her long legs around his waist and their tongues were doing a mating dance.

"First time might not last long," he warned her.

"I can count to ten," she panted.

"What does that mean?"

"I bet the tenth time lasts a long, long time." It came out of her mouth a word at a time between more hungry, demanding kisses.

He slid into her with a long hard thrust. She groaned and worked with him, rocking at the right time to bring them both the most pleasure. He took her to breathtaking heights half a dozen times and then backed off before the thrusts finally became shorter and faster.

"God, that feels so good," she said.

"I know," he panted.

"I'm going to fall off this cliff and die," she moaned.

"Ready?" he panted.

Lord, the man even drawled when he was having sex. She managed to nod, but she didn't have the breath to say another word.

He slipped his hands under her bottom and with a dozen fast and furious thrusts, he brought her right up to the biggest climax she'd ever known before he said something that sounded like her name and collapsed on top of her.

"Holy hell!" The words came out in a deep throaty grown when he could breathe again.

"Mmmm!" She tightened her legs but there were no words to describe the weightlessness that she felt. She didn't want him to leave. Never, not in any experience, had she felt such passion, and she didn't want it to ever end.

"That was… wow!" she finally said.

"It's because it's been so long," he said.

"No, it was awesome. I've never…" she panted.

"Never what?" He toyed with an errant strand of hair that had fallen across one eye.

"Never ever felt like my body and soul separated and I was floating." She inhaled deeply and straightened her legs. He rolled to one side and gathered her tightly in his arms. She was reminded of a scene on a television show where the couple fell back on the pillows, stared at the ceiling, and panted. The viewer knew what had gone on before that big moment even if they hadn't seen it. Until that night she'd figured those times really only existed in scripts for actresses and actors.

She shivered.

He wrapped the side of the comforter around them and kissed her on the forehead. "Well, sweet cheeks, it might take me a few minutes to build up to a second round after that."

"Who needs ten when one is perfect?" she mumbled sleepily.

Having sex with a man that much taller was a brand-new experience. She could bury her face into his neck instead of looking him right in the eye.

"Lucas, this isn't going to make it all awkward between us, is it?"

He propped up on an elbow and studied her face by the light of the moon, drifting through the mini-blind slats on the window across the room. "Why would you ask that?"

"It did between me and Drew. Crazy thing is we were both so drunk that we weren't even sure what had happened."

"No, it's not going to be awkward. We didn't take a vow to be just friends forever and after what we just had, wild horses or hellfire couldn't force a vow like that out of me." He chuckled.

He plopped back down and she settled back into the curve of his muscular body. The flickering colors of the afterglow dimmed as she shut her eyes and fell asleep.

Chapter 11

NATALIE DRESSED FOR CHURCH IN A LONG DENIM SKIRT, bright blue sweater, and boots. She made a pan of quick cinnamon rolls from sweet biscuit dough that morning since she only had to cook for two. They were almost ready to take out of the oven when a blast of winter wind blew Lucas in the back door.

"Better bundle up good before we go this morning... wow! You look gorgeous, and is that cinnamon rolls? You didn't have to go to so much trouble," he said.

"It's no trouble. About last night," she said.

She'd never been one to sit on the fence or worry about something for days. Like an old Angus bull set loose in a fancy China shop, she dealt with problems head-on.

He hung his coat and hat on a rack and raised an eyebrow. "What about last night? I thought I was pretty awesome considering that I haven't had sex in almost a year."

"I don't want it to make us awkward," she said.

Lucas poured a cup of coffee and sat down at the table with it. "I missed you this morning. I thought you were cuddled up to my back, but when I turned over it was the pillow. If it was going to be weird between us, I wouldn't have wanted you to still be there in bed with me."

"Joshua woke up at two o'clock for his bottle," she explained.

"I figured as much. You could have come back to bed afterward. You've got that monitor thing," he said.

She set the pan of cinnamon rolls on the table and sat down across from him. "I started to but I thought I might be pushing my luck."

"I thought guys got lucky." A big sexy grin split Lucas's face, and there was laughter in his eyes.

"You know what I mean. We've been such good friends and…"

"Like I told you last night, I'm not Drew. I liked him. He was my friend and I miss him. But I'm not just your friend, Natalie. Haven't been in a long time. Now pass those cinnamon rolls. My mouth is watering," he said.

Joshua's swing made a clicking noise. He looked from one to the other, as if trying to decide who to grace with his smile that morning.

Lucas changed the subject as he shifted three rolls onto his plate. "Joshua woke up in a good mood."

Natalie appreciated that more than he'd ever realize, but she had to know where she stood. "What am I at this point, Lucas? Housekeeper, cook, friend, lover?"

Lucas pushed back his chair and rounded the table. He put a hand on each of her shoulders and leaned in for a kiss. He tasted like hot coffee and sweet, sweet cinnamon rolls.

When he pulled back, he said, "I want more than a friendship with you, Natalie."

"Okay, I can live with that," she said.

He kissed her again and ran a hand down her arm. Her hormones started humming and begging for more.

"Lucas, Joshua is…"

He put a finger over her lips before she could finish. "I don't think he minds if we share a kiss."

"That's not what I meant."

"I know what you meant." He sat down on his side of the table and finished off his cinnamon rolls. "You should have told me about him, Natalie. He's a good kid and I like him a lot."

"I wanted to meet you so bad. Your visits were all that kept me going most days right after Drew died. And then when we started talking on the phone on weekends and things were going from friendship to something more, I really wanted to tell you. But I was afraid you'd tell me to stay away from you. So I came and then Hazel fell and why would she make me promise to stay here anyway?"

He reached across the table and covered her hands with his. "I talked to you every morning before I went to work. I talked to Hazel and Dad and whoever else was in the house every evening before I went to sleep. Guess I told them all about you, so they knew how much you meant to me. Didn't you tell your folks about me?"

"Hell, no!" she said so loud that Joshua jumped.

His dark eyebrows shot so high that they looked like they'd touch the ceiling. "You didn't?"

"Not until last week."

"Why?"

She shrugged. "Fallout."

"Which means? Are you ashamed of me?" He frowned.

She shook her head emphatically. "Hell, no! My folks and my brothers don't believe in the Internet dating thing. They'd have a fit if they knew I'd met you that way and was coming halfway across Texas to meet you. They'd think that you should come to Silverton if you wanted to meet me and we should date the proper way. And that means without the Internet or late-night phone calls. And then there was the Drew thing, and we'd talked it to death, but I was afraid that you had just stepped into his shoes and what if that's all we had. Oh, hell, Lucas, we don't have time to pick this thing to the bare bones right now."

The grin returned. "Maybe this evening we'll take a ride over to Sherman. Joshua is probably getting stir-crazy. And we'll pick it apart then. What do you think?"

"That sounds fine. We've got half an hour to get to the church. And you still have to get dressed," she answered.

He downed the last of his coffee. "I'll be ready in ten minutes. You can go ahead and get Joshua into his seat and I'll carry him out to the truck. Oh, and you really do look beautiful this morning. Maybe not as gorgeous as you were last night with nothing but a sheet pulled up over you, but beautiful all the same."

Natalie blushed from her toenails to her eyebrows. When Joshua had begun to fuss in the middle of the night, she'd been so deep into sleep that she hadn't even heard the monitor until he set up a real howl. She'd scuttled out of Lucas's bedroom without a stitch of clothing on her body. When she stepped out into the hallway, she glanced at Jack's bedroom door and was glad that he'd moved out into his own house.

She'd jerked on a nightshirt that barely came to her knees and fresh underpants before she did anything. Joshua was already mad as hell. Thirty more seconds wasn't going to make bit of difference. She carried him to the kitchen and prepared a bottle. There'd been no grins or cooing when she put the nipple in his mouth.

He'd latched onto it like it was the last thing he'd ever get to eat and glared at her.

"You are like your father when you are hungry, little boy. He was an old bear too when he was hungry, but when you get older, you won't get away with throwing fits." She smiled as she settled him into his car seat that morning. "Hopefully, you've gotten the temper all out of you and you'll be good this morning. We're going to church, and I don't want to see one of those temper fits. You've had your bottle and even a bit of rice cereal, so you shouldn't want to eat again until noon. Church should be over by then." She talked as she fastened all the straps.

Lucas's boots on the hardwood floor announced that he was on the way. "Make sure he's bundled up good. It's sixteen degrees out there and spittin' sleet again. We don't usually get this much bad weather until February in these parts."

"We don't either, out in the Panhandle."

She didn't want to think about snow or even Christmas. She wanted to stare at Lucas all morning instead of going to church. He was so sexy in those black jeans and light tan Western-cut shirt. Not as sexy as he'd been all wrapped around her in the bed the night before, but still enough that she talked too much to cover up the effect he had on her.

"Dad talked about that storm. He got prepared for it to hit the ranch, but it weakened and bypassed us on the north. Oklahoma got it worse than we did. Where's your coat?"

She nodded toward a chair in the living room where she'd draped her coat earlier. The place still looked like it had when the party ended the night before. The folks who owned the tables and chairs would be back that afternoon to pick them up and the crew would return the furniture to its rightful place. She glanced at the big open space in the middle of the living room floor and remembered the dances. Then she looked at the Nativity scene. From dancing to the honky tonk moon song to going to church to hear the Christmas story, all in less than ten hours. Talk about cultural shock!

His fingertips brushing against her arms as he helped her with her coat sure enough made her wish she was still dancing beneath the honky tonk moon rather than going to church.

Savoy, like Silverton, might be small, but by golly, they celebrated Christmas. Windows glittered with lights from Christmas trees and yards were filled with decorations. The sleet and snow lent the perfect touch to the season.

Well, that and the mistletoe, Natalie thought. Could that stuff really have magic in it? Ever since that first kiss under the mistletoe, he'd been different and it had been very, very good. But still, Natalie kept her guard up. Sometimes when the magic show was over, all that remained was fairy dust and a puff of wind.

Lucas parked on the west side of the church. "We all dreamed about having a white Christmas when I was a kid. This is real Christmas weather even if it is a bitch to work in."

"I remember some holidays that we played football out in the yard without a coat, but we always dreamed about white Christmases too. I think it was because we thought Santa Claus could fly better in the snow," she said.

"I deserve this kind of Christmas after the last one. We had a sandstorm that was the mother of them all. I swear we even limited our intake of fluids so we wouldn't have to go outside to the bathrooms," he said.

She unbuckled her seat belt and pulled the collar of her coat up around her ears. "Well, you'd best keep your mouth shut about that today."

He cocked his head to one side. "Why's that?"

"You reckon these little elderly folks like this kind of messy weather, or the mailman or the folks who are running around the country fixing all the power lines ice breaks down? If they find out that God just froze up this part of Texas for you, they'll haul your sexy ass out into the road and stone you to death," she said.

He bailed out of the truck, jogged around the front side, and opened the door for her. "Oh, you think my ass is sexy, do you?"

Everything about him was sexy—from his grin to his fingertips. And the way he looked at her made her feel sexy.

"You going to answer me?"

"Not today. I have to be nice because the three wise men will glare at me if I'm not," she said.

"I bet Mary told Joseph his ass was sexy," Lucas said.

"If she did, she was talking about the donkey he rode into town on, and she didn't use the word sexy. She said the jackass was cute." Natalie slid out of the seat and helped unfasten the harness holding Joshua in the seat. She scooped him up into her arms, slung his diaper bag over her shoulder, and bent her head against the wind as she headed toward the front door.

She looked up at the gray sky just before she climbed up the three porch steps.

Lucas held the door open for her. "What are you looking at?"

"Checking to see if the clouds have parted enough for lightning bolts. You were edging up on sacrilege right talking about the Virgin Mary like that," she said.

He ushered her inside with his hand on her back. The second she walked inside the warm church, Sonia and Melody grabbed her arm.

"You need to put the baby in the nursery. We need both of y'all to sing in the choir, and we've got to get you in choir robes. Weather has kept some folks at home and we're short," Melody said.

"No, ma'am. I'm not singing in a choir because I promised the three wise men who are Grady, Dad, and Gramps that Joshua would be sitting right up front and he could see them," Lucas declared.

Sonia frowned and tapped her foot. "We need choir members. You sure that kid can't go to the nursery?"

Natalie nodded. "I'm very sure. He stays with me."

"I took my boys to the choir with me when they were little. I can hold a baby and sing, and I bet Natalie can too," Melody said. "And a front row seat right there by the Nativity scene will give the baby a lot better view of the three wise men."

"Thank you," Henry whispered to her left.

Lucas winked as he followed Grady, Jack, and Henry to a different room. "Boys and girls don't get to dress in the same room," he threw over his shoulder.

The ladies' choir robes were stored in a closet in the Sunday school room meant for preschoolers because all the chairs were small and the tables low. She damn sure didn't intend to lay Joshua on one of those tables. Lord, he could wiggle off there and land on his head. The floor wasn't even carpeted to break the fall if he did.

"Hello, I'm Mary Alice," a small dark-haired woman said. "What a cute little boy. He looks just like Lucas. My baby girl, Ziva, looks like my husband's mother. Red hair and blue eyes. We'll have to get together and have a play date when they are a little older."

"That would be nice." Natalie picked out the longest robe in the closet.

"Here, I'm already dressed. I'll hold the baby while you get the robe on." Mary said.

Natalie hesitated.

"I won't break him, I promise. Ziva is my first girl but she's my third child. I know how to hold a little boy," Melody said.

Natalie shifted the baby into her arms and set the diaper bag on a nearby table.

"He's just adorable with that dark hair, and I like the way you comb it like a cowboy's hair. I bet the guys at the ranch are just crazy about him," Mary said.

"Not as crazy as he is already about them." Natalie adjusted the white collar and pinned it down.

"Your robe is the longest one we have in the church and it is still too short. I'm glad that the banister will keep everyone from seeing your legs. You'll be sitting on the back row so…" Sonia said.

"No, I will not. I'll sit on the front row. You can put me at the far end and leave the chairs behind me empty if my height is a big problem, but Joshua will see the three wise men, and he can't from the back row," Natalie said.

"Sounds like a doable plan to me," Mary said.

"Oh, all right," Sonia said coldly.

Lord, why didn't she pack her pistol in the diaper bag instead of a hairbrush and compact mirror? She'd known that Sonia would be there that morning. That wild night of sex had addled her brain and kept her from using the good old common sense that she'd been blessed with.

She turned around and there was Sonia in a flowing white angel robe. It nipped into her tiny waist with gold Christmas tree tinsel that matched the halo floating three inches above all that big blond hair. Big white fluffy wings shot out from her back and it took a trained eye to see the elastic bands holding them onto Sonia's petite body.

"Well?" Sonia did a slow three-hundred-and-sixty-degree turn.

"You look lovely just like you do every year," Melody said from the doorway.

Sonia looked at Natalie.

Natalie smiled sweetly. "Your black bra strap is showing and I can see a fine black line where your thong rests. When the lights come on, it'll shine. I used to tell my basketball girls to never wear black underwear under their white uniforms."

"Shit!" Sonia gasped. "Melody, trade with me."

"Honey, I wear granny panties and my bra would go around you twice. You are on your own this time." Melody laughed.

"Don't you dare laugh at me. Go out there and tell Noah to hurry back to his house and get a white set," Sonia hissed.

"Sure thing. Be right back. Good thing that we got here early, isn't it?"

"If I undo the belt, I think I can make the change

without taking everything off," Sonia said. "What is Hawaii like anyway?"

Natalie frowned. "Why are you asking?"

"That is where you got pregnant with that kid, isn't it? Noah said that Lucas got a couple of days of R and R in Hawaii. You met Lucas there, right? So what's it like at Christmastime? I heard it never snows there." Sonia checked her reflection in the mirror and applied more pale pink lipstick while she waited.

"It's complicated," Natalie said.

"I imagine it is." Sonia laughed. "I bet he told you he couldn't make babies, didn't he?"

"That's personal," Natalie said.

Melody rushed back inside and tossed a white bra and pair of silk bikinis on a table. "Noah said that you left these in the pickup last night, so he didn't have to go all the way home."

Sonia did a half giggle, but she didn't blush.

Melody tossed her blue velvet dress over the back of a chair and donned her angel robe. She was a bottle blond just like Sonia, but her hair was cut in a bob that brushed her jawbones. She was a couple of inches taller and several pounds heavier than Sonia.

"Why would he tell her he couldn't make babies? You know Lucas has always said he was going to outdo me when it came to kids." She adjusted the robe, belted it, and then set the halo on her head.

"It's complicated." Sonia's laugh was brittle.

Cold chill bumps played hopscotch down Natalie's backbone.

"Well, I ain't got time to listen to a long-winded story right now. I've got to go take care of Tommy. His daddy won't ever get him lookin' right. That's my oldest son who is playing the little drummer boy today. I've got four boys," she explained to Natalie as she slipped out the door.

"Bad as I hate to do it, I'll give this pretty boy back to you. I've got to go get ready for my place." Mary Alice handed Joshua off and left Sonia and Natalie alone in the room.

"I kind of lied to him one time." Sonia did another turn and looked at Natalie. "Can you see my under-wear now?"

"No, you look like an angel, but then looks can be deceiving. What did you lie to him about? I can't believe you are an angel, but that doesn't have anything to do with you lying, does it?"

Sonia shrugged and then had to adjust one of her wings. "I didn't want kids. My brother has this mental issue and I told Lucas that I didn't want to take a chance on bringing a baby into the world like that. We went to have tests run and when they came back, I lied to him about the results. He didn't ask to see them, so it…" Sonia waved her hands in the air as she talked.

"What did you tell him?" Natalie asked.

"I hated the idea of my waist getting all fat like Melody's and my boobs sagging and those horrible marks on my stomach," Sonia said.

Angels weren't supposed to lie. But then a woman who had a child without a marriage license and who had had sex the night before with a man who wasn't the baby's father didn't have much room to judge wayward angels.

"I might as well come clean about it all since you already know," Sonia said.

"Know what?"

"That he *can* make babies. I told him that the test said his swimmers were weak and that the doctor said it would take a miracle for him to ever produce a child. I was afraid he'd ask to see the report or want to go to the doctor with me, but I lucked out on that," she said.

"My God," Natalie whispered. She was as fertile as a bunny rabbit if she got pregnant from that one time with Drew. And the night before was right in the middle of her cycle when ovulation would be at the highest.

Was it a mortal sin to kill an angel in the Sunday school room? Maybe God would even give her a medal for strangling a lying angel so that He wouldn't have to kick the bitch out of heaven.

"Guess you done figured that out, right?" Sonia looked at Joshua.

Natalie couldn't even nod.

"I hear the music. That's the cue for the choir to take your places and for me to get into my place too." Sonia disappeared out of the room in a whirlwind of white.

Complicated just shot up to a whole new level. Surely she wouldn't get pregnant a second time as the result of a one-night stand. She held Joshua tightly to her chest and looked up to see Lucas standing in the doorway.

"I told Sonia that I was sitting beside you so I can help with Joshua. Here, I'll carry him. Just think, this is his first time to sing in the church choir," Lucas said.

He carried the baby with one arm and held Natalie's hand. They filed into the choir loft and sat down together on the far end of the first row. Joshua's bright eyes took in everything and he smiled at two live white lambs tied to the wooden manger.

There was a tense moment when Sonia picked up the microphone and led the choir in "Silent Night." The loud music made him jump and for a second Natalie thought he was going to set up a howl, but the music quieted and he went back to staring at the lights.

Would Sonia's horns pop out of that blond hair if Natalie choked her skinny neck until she turned blue? Knowing that Lucas could produce his own children changed everything. Jack, Grady, and Henry would not be so hell-bent on pushing them together if they were aware that he could populate Cedar Hill with little dark-haired real Allen boys or even girls.

When the song ended, Noah stepped up to the pulpit and read a scripture verse about the wise men coming from afar. He was dressed in a robe just like the rest of the choir. Evidently at the church in Savoy, Texas, all real angels were female and there were only three of them.

His voice was deep and booming and commanded attention. He and Sonia would make pretty babies. Both of them were blond and had gorgeous eyes, but Natalie was glad that Sonia didn't want kids. It would just be her luck that Joshua would grow up and fall in love with their daughter.

She felt a movement and glanced up to see Henry wink at her from beneath a tinsel crown. His cape was scarlet and no matter how he tried to keep it pulled together, his boots and jeans still showed. Jack wore a brilliant blue robe and Grady's was gold. They bowed to the baby doll and laid their brightly wrapped presents beside the manger.

Noah led the men in the choir in "We Three Kings." All during the song, Joshua cooed and smiled at the wise men and from the expressions on their faces, they were not only wise but very happy.

The two live lambs moved as far as their ropes would allow and kept their heads turned toward Joshua. If they'd thought to put some lamb feed in the manger, maybe the congregation would have seen more than their little short wiggling tails during the whole production.

Natalie wondered how Mary and Joseph handled the issue of Jesus not really belonging to Joseph when they had other children. They should've let a woman write at least one book in the New Testament so that important details would have been recorded.

Another man from the choir read more scripture and then Sonia and Melody sang "What Child Is This?" with no background music and with only a few choir members humming along. It was a breathtakingly beautiful sound, but Natalie still wanted to snatch the woman bald headed and then slap her for not having hair.

Then the preacher took the pulpit and reminded everyone that there was a potluck dinner in the reception hall. Other than the angels removing their wings, everyone who'd played a part should stay in costume.

"Yes, you choir members can hang your robes back up." He smiled.

He made a few more announcements. Two different families had added a baby to their families during the past week. One elderly lady from the nursing home had passed and her funeral would be held Tuesday.

The Hanging of the Green ceremony would take place on the next Sunday morning. "And I'm reminding everyone again that Sonia and Noah will be married right here in this church on Christmas Day at eight o'clock in the evening. Most of the festivities surrounding your family affairs will be over by then, so plan to wind up the day by attending their wedding. Now if Henry will dismiss us in a word of prayer, we'll all go on to the fellowship hall."

Natalie decided that the place to tell Lucas about the big fat lie Sonia had told him was not in church.

Lucas talked to Joshua when the prayer ended. "You were a good boy for a whole hour, but I see that your fist is about to be chewed plumb off. You think we'd best hurry on to the Sunday school room and get a bottle made up for you?"

People stopped them every two steps to get a glimpse of the baby. They didn't fool Natalie one bit. Silverton wasn't much bigger than Savoy and the reason they were flocking to their sides was more than just welcoming Lucas home. They wanted to see if Joshua looked like Lucas.

One elderly man poked Lucas in the ribs. "You kinda snuck that little fellow in on us, didn't you?"

Lucas smiled down at the old guy. "Guess I did. And now I'm going to have to sneak him on out of here or you're going to see him throw a real Allen fit."

He laced his fingers in Natalie's. She hadn't been blessed with tiny, little delicate hands. Not at her height. But they felt small in his as they left the sanctuary.

"The truth will come out," she whispered.

"Maybe I don't want it to come out," he said from the side of his mouth.

Henry came up behind them and laid a hand on Natalie's shoulder. "Mighty fine job y'all did."

"All we did was sing. It was y'all who did a fantastic job," she said.

"Well, that's all we did too, but Joshua made it worthwhile. He grinned right at me. Did you see it?" Henry asked.

"Joshua thought the gold you gave baby Jesus was shiny and pretty," Natalie teased.

"Gold-covered chocolates." Henry chuckled. "I got so hungry standin' up there like a statue while Noah sang that song. Lord, it went on forever, didn't it? Anyway, I started to sneak a couple of them chocolates out and eat them right there. But I didn't want to go temptin' God."

Henry took a breath and went on, "Now we can go eat brisket and ribs. If I'd had your big breakfast instead of one of them cardboard things that pop up out of the toaster, my stomach wouldn't have thought my throat had been cut."

"Well, don't be goin' without a good breakfast again," Natalie said.

"I won't. Believe me, after wonderin' if I'd pass plumb out from hunger up there when I was a wise man, you can bet I won't. I'll be there every morning from now on, darlin'. Now y'all get whatever you need for Josh, and we'll meet you in there." He left them in the hall and disappeared inside the door where all the good smells were coming from.

Natalie changed Joshua's diaper while Lucas added scoops of dry powder to the water already in the bottle. He put the cap on and shook it well then grimaced.

"What?" Natalie asked..

"Poor little fellow. All he gets is old dried milk shook up in water and we're about to dine on the best beef brisket and ribs that Cedar Hill can produce."

"He thinks he's getting steak and potatoes. Don't tell him any different," she whispered.

She redressed him in a navy blue knit outfit with feet built into it, put a bib around his neck, and held him close to her face. "You did so good on your choir singing, sweet boy. Someday you can be the little drummer boy. I feel bad, Lucas. I didn't know there was going to be a potluck or I would've brought something. Hey, I didn't think boys and girls could be in the same choir room?"

He shook his head slowly. "No, ma'am. You can't feel bad. We supply all the meat for this shindig every year. The ranch hands smoke it a few days before and freeze it, then all the ladies heat it up in the oven. I could smell it while we were out there in the sanctuary. And about being in the same choir room, I'll just leave my robe hangin' on the outside of the door. They'll all know I wanted to help with the baby."

Natalie had caught a whiff of the smoke too, but she'd figured it was the devil scorching Sonia's wings. Natalie would gladly fan the blazes if he had.

Noah was the first person they passed when they opened the doors into the long dining room. He stuck out a hand toward Lucas and said, "The little fellow did good in the choir. I remember when Melody used to hold her babies while she sang. It does them good to grow up in church. Y'all will come to the wedding, right?"

Lucas shook his hand. "Wouldn't miss it."

"Thank you, Lucas. That means a lot to me, comin' from you," he said.

Sonia joined him from across the room. "And the girls are so excited about a Christmas wedding."

Noah threw his arm around her shoulders, but she

looked right at Lucas when she talked. "All his brothers are coming home for Christmas, so his whole big family will be here. And my sister and brother will be at Granny's, so they'll be here. It's going to be the prettiest wedding this town has ever seen."

Lucas kept his eyes on Joshua who slurped down his dinner. "Want me to burp him… Natalie?"

She caught the hesitation before he said her name. She owed him one for not calling her sweet cheeks right there in front of Noah and Sonia.

"You hold the bottle and I'll do it. So how many kids are you two plannin' on?" Natalie smiled at Sonia.

Sonia looked like a cornered rabbit with her eyes darting from one side of the room to the other and back at Noah. It was good enough for her after the stunt she'd pulled on Lucas.

"What do you think, Noah?" Sonia finally asked.

"I grew up in a big family and loved it," he said. "But I sure don't want that many. Maybe some ornery boys like Melody and Jake have."

Natalie smiled at Sonia. "Well, four is a good round number. I always thought I'd like to have four like my momma had."

"Sounds good to me," Sonia said.

Did the woman ever tell the truth? She'd lied to Lucas and now poor old Noah thought he was getting a family out of the marriage.

"I must go help get the spoons put in the food. We sure can't eat it with our fingers." Sonia giggled nervously. "Why don't you guys take the baby so Natalie can help me? I'll introduce her to the church ladies."

Natalie shifted Joshua into Lucas's arms before he

could even reach for him. The catfight had barely begun and she was more than willing to take it to the next level. Hell, she'd even take it outside in the street. She would borrow two butcher knives from the kitchen. Whoever came back inside after the fight could have a second helping of that chocolate layer cake on the table.

"That was hateful and mean," Sonia hissed on the way across the room.

"And what you did to Lucas wasn't bitchy?" Natalie asked.

"I was protecting my waistline, and besides, no man stays in love with a woman when she's puking up her guts every morning and her ankles are swollen like she's got the gout," Sonia said.

"Do you love Noah?" Natalie asked.

"Of course I love him or I wouldn't be marrying him. But just for your information, I will always have feelings for Lucas. We were together for a long time, but I guess I screwed myself out of that, didn't I? If he'd known he could make babies, he would have used protection and you wouldn't be here today, so I wouldn't have a chance at him again even if I did want it, which I don't. But, darlin', you can be damn sure every time he's in bed with you, he's thinking about me."

Natalie stopped so fast that Sonia had taken two more steps before she realized she was alone. She turned so quickly that her halo fell to the floor and she stumbled on the tail of her angel robe. Natalie reached out and grabbed her shoulder to keep her from falling.

"Whoa! Can't have you all bruised up for your wedding," she said.

"You tripped me," Sonia said.

"You were five feet ahead of me, girl. I did not trip you. Noah is a good man. Why would you marry him if you still have a thing in your heart for another man?"

"I'm almost thirty. It's time for me to be married." Sonia stomped off toward the tables where the ladies were putting out casserole after casserole and too many desserts to count.

Lucas was suddenly at Natalie's side. "What was that all about?"

"Just a little friendly catfight."

"But you're going to tell me before nightfall, aren't you?"

She looped her arm in his. "Ladies do not catfight and then tell."

Sonia cornered Melody and they were whispering and shooting looks toward Natalie that would get a real angel kicked off her cloud. A vision of Sonia hitting earth with a thump so hard that it would knock her halo sideways put a smile on Natalie's face.

"If I wasn't so hungry, we'd leave right now," he said.

"But the little ladies wouldn't get to fuss over Joshua," Natalie teased.

She wasn't ready for the long talk she and Lucas needed to have. First of all, they had to address the sex. No more unprotected sex.

She needed some time to process the last twenty-four hours. A week would be wonderful, but even two hours would help. Her Aunt Leah had always said that she was too nice for her own good. Trusting came easy, but she'd just found out that there were people that couldn't be trusted.

"And right in church," she mumbled.

"What was that?" Lucas asked.

"Nothing. I'm hungry. Do we have to wait much longer?"

Jack waved from the other side of the room and motioned them over. "Willie here wants to take a look at Joshua. He says that we should've let Josh be baby Jesus. I told him that Josh wanted to sing in the choir, not lay there with nothing to do."

Lucas steered Natalie in that direction with his hand on her lower back. A simple touch of a gentleman's hand shouldn't have a woman thinking about sex on the front pew of the sanctuary.

But it did!

Chapter 12

"THIS LITTLE ANGUS WENT TO MARKET. THIS LITTLE Angus stayed home. This little Angus had smoked ham. This little Angus had none. And this little Angus, this little Angus, this one right here cried moo, moo, moo all the way home." Henry chuckled when he got a grin from the baby.

"I thought it was piggies," Natalie said.

"Not in a beef rancher's house," Jack said. "It's my turn to hold him, Henry. All them people at the church this afternoon come damn nigh to stealin' him away from us."

"You'll have to wait until later, Dad. I'm going to give Natalie and Josh a tour of the ranch before it gets dark," Lucas said.

"You can't take Josh to the cabin without me being there. I want to see his face when he sees it the first time. You and Natalie go on and look but Josh has to stay with us. Get my keys from my coat pocket so you can get into the church while you are driving around," Henry said.

"Josh would rather stay here and play with us as get back in that car seat anyway," Grady said.

"That's right," Henry said. "Baby's been passed around enough for one day."

"That don't mean you get to hold him the whole time they're gone," Jack said.

"His little bones will get sore if too many people hold

him," Henry said. "Besides, we need to talk some more about Angus cattle, don't we, Joshua?"

"Wise men?" Natalie mumbled.

"Or not so wise," Lucas whispered.

"Go on. Get out of here. Take your time," Henry said.

Lucas helped Natalie into her coat. "Can't fight 'em."

"He has a bottle in an hour. We'll be back by then," she said.

"We can read directions and we'll figure out how to make him another one if he gets hungry," Jack said.

"His diaper bag is stocked with everything," she said.

"Go. Shoo! Get on out of here. We'll take care of this baby and enjoy every minute we get with him," Henry said.

The sleet had stopped and now big beautiful snow-flakes floated from the sky in a lazy fashion. The wind had completely died, so they drifted straight down from heaven and landed on a solid layer of sleet and ice coating the ground.

Grass blades, covered with a thin layer of ice, reached up to grab the flakes and hold on to them like a mother protecting her child. Natalie shook the snow from her hair when she got into Lucas's truck.

"It's still a couple of weeks from now, but if it doesn't warm up, Josh's first Christmas could be a white one." Lucas backed the truck up and then started down a path that was nothing but two ruts leading around the yard fence and toward the back side of the ranch.

"We'll have to take pictures no matter what kind of Christmas it is. Momma is having a hard time with us being gone as it is. She'd never forgive me if I didn't have pictures to show her," she said.

"What's on your mind? Josh will be fine with them. Only thing that they might do is spoil him so much that you have to hold him all the time," Lucas said.

"What makes you think something is on my mind?"

"I have known you for almost a year and I recognize that expression. You are worried about something. Are you sorry about last night?" he asked.

"No," she said. "It's those three wise men back there. They're getting awfully attached to Joshua. It'll break their hearts when I take him back to Silverton."

He reached across the bench seat and laid a hand on her thigh. "Confession time," he said.

"I'm not a priest and this truck doesn't look like a confessional," she said.

"You might not be, but I need to tell you all the same. I really did talk about you a lot and I showed them pictures of you and they know chances are slim to none that I can ever have a child." He paused.

"And they thought we were getting serious before I ever came to Savoy, right?" she finished for him.

"Oh, yeah! And Dad was worried that you'd want kids and I couldn't produce them and…" Another pause.

"Joshua is like icing on the cupcake for them, and I'm all right with that rumor that Sonia got started with her smart-ass remarks."

The truck tires crunched on the icy lawn as he stopped in front of a cabin. Two big cedar trees on either side of the porch were covered in twinkling lights and dusted with newly fallen snowflakes. The cabin had been built of hewn logs and the roof was corrugated sheet metal that had years and years of rust peeking through the light layer of snow settling in the valleys. A fully decorated

Christmas tree shining in the window sent an array of colors out to settle on the white ground.

"He sure did it up good this year. He'll make sure Josh sees it sometime during the season." Lucas got out of the truck and hurried around to open the door for Natalie.

"But it's so far away from everything that no one sees it," Natalie said.

"Granny does. Gramps is convinced that her spirit comes to the ranch every December and lingers through until New Year's. She loved the holidays and he does all this just for her. That's the reason the place is named Cedar Hill Ranch. Gramps would have named it Christmas Tree Hill, but Granny said that didn't sound like a ranch. They went out to get their first tree and found it on a little rise, so she named it Cedar Hill. It reminded them both of Christmas trees." Lucas threw an arm around Natalie's shoulders.

The inside was warm and cozy with the heat from gas logs blazing brightly. One big room contained an iron bed that had been painted white against the wall away from the fire. A kitchen had been set up against the other wall that consisted of a long cabinet, a tiny stove with only two burners, and a small refrigerator. A crocheted doily topped a table that had been painted bright yellow. A poinsettia sat in the middle of the doilies and the two chairs beside the table were pulled out as if someone had just left. Two rockers in front of the fireplace were painted the same color.

Natalie took in the whole cabin in one glance. "Isn't he afraid to leave an open fire burning?"

"He says Granny would tell him if it caught on fire

and he'd come put it out." Lucas removed his coat, hung it over the back of a chair, and then helped Natalie remove hers. He motioned toward the table. "Have a seat. I'll make us a cup of coffee. Gramps says that this is the same furniture that they started out with. It was four years before he could scrape up enough money to build her a real house. And even after they'd moved into it, she'd sneak off down here on Sundays. Gramps called it her playhouse."

Natalie sat down in a chair and watched Lucas put together a pot of coffee.

"So how many girls did you bring here?" she asked.

He slapped a hand over his heart. "I'm hurt that you'd even think such a thing. Granny wouldn't abide me bringing women in here with no supervision."

"I'm here," Natalie said.

"But…"

Natalie had never seen a grown man blush like that before. Something way more than just bringing a girl to the cabin was going on.

"And?" she said.

"Gramps would have my hide if I ever brought a girl to the cabin or to the church with intentions of making out with them. But it's okay if you are here because I told them that I thought you were the one and that this month would tell the tale."

"And it all blew to hell when you saw Joshua, right?"

His dark eyebrows drew down so far that they became one line. "Dammit, Natalie! If the situation were reversed, what would you have thought? And didn't you think that I might be the one? Why else would you have come all the way across the state to meet me?"

She was busted and speechless both.

Lucas raked his fingers through his hair. "Well?"

"You didn't tell me about the tests that you and Sonia had done," she whispered.

"That's a little different than a flesh-and-blood baby."

"Aunt Leah said this Internet friendship and dating thing was why so many people are disillusioned about relationships."

Lucas poured coffee in two mugs and set them on the table before he sat down. "I never believed in them either. Some of the guys around here were meeting women on there, and I told them they were crazy."

"Why?" Natalie asked.

"Because to really know someone, you've got to live close enough to her to know her family, her way of life, and what kind of snow cone she likes," he said.

"And yet, here I am."

"You are a rancher. You come from a long line of ranchers and you like white coconut snow cones. Ours is an unusual circumstance," he argued.

She sipped the coffee. Black and strong enough to open a woman's eyes. That's what she'd told him when he asked how she liked her coffee. He'd remembered the little details like Drew always did.

Was Lucas the one for her?

Lucas's warm hand covered hers. "We've still got some time. We don't have to dot all the i's and cross all the t's tonight."

The touch of his hand hushed the argument going on in her head.

He gently squeezed and abruptly changed the subject. "I haven't done any Christmas shopping yet. After supper tomorrow night, I thought we might go to Sherman and work on that. Santa Claus is usually at the mall all month. We could get Joshua's picture taken with him and maybe have ice cream at Braum's afterward."

"I know where I stand now. What about Joshua?" she asked.

"He might be my best friend someday." Lucas smiled.

She could live with that for the time being.

"Let's take our coffee to the rocking chairs. Have you ever sat in a tall woman's chair?"

He led her to the other side of the room but didn't let go of her hand.

"I didn't know they made them in tall or short."

Using his boot, he pushed the chairs close enough together that he didn't have to let go of her hand.

She eased down and sighed.

"Pretty neat, isn't it? Granny was as tall as Gramps, which would make her about your height. She said that she felt like she was biting her knees in most chairs, so Gramps made this set of chairs for her wedding gift. The seat and legs are both longer than normal," Lucas explained.

"I could rock Joshua all night in this. But why didn't she take them to the big house when they moved?"

"She did but when she died, Gramps brought them back down here. He said her spirit never left this house and that he wanted her to have her special things when she came back to visit."

A single tear found its way down her cheek. She couldn't let go of the coffee cup or his hand, so she did her damnedest to ignore it.

"That is the sweetest thing I've ever heard. That's

what I want, Lucas. A relationship like they had," she said hoarsely.

"Me too," he whispered.

He set his cup on the floor and reached for hers. Without a word she handed it to him and didn't protest when he pulled on her hand. She shifted from her chair into his lap and curled up like a child in his arms. Lucas Allen had a good strong heart, one that he'd only give away one time in his life, and she wanted it for Christmas.

She looked up into his eyes just in time to see them flutter shut. She barely had time to moisten her lips when his mouth covered hers in a hard, hungry kiss. Her hands snaked up around his neck and she snuggled in closer to his body.

"Ever had sex in a rocking chair?" he asked.

"Bite your tongue, Lucas! Your granny might be in this room right now," she whispered.

"If she was, she'd have already upset the chair. I think she likes you."

She studied his face again. She'd always been a sucker for brown-eyed cowboys, but not a one had ever affected her like Lucas Allen did. The tree lights flickered in his eyes, creating a soft, dreamy effect. Then they closed and his lips found hers in another blistering hot kiss.

One minute they were rocking, the next he was carrying her across the room toward the bed. She felt tiny in his arms, a first for her because at almost six feet, not many men had the strength to pick her up like a bag of feathers and carry her like a bride. He laid her on top of a gorgeous wedding ring quilt and stretched out beside her.

"Oh, my!" she gasped.

"What?" he asked.

She propped up on an elbow and ran a finger down his cheekbone. "What if your granny comes home and finds us in her bed?"

"Granny is gone, Natalie. Gramps just keeps her memory alive this way."

"I don't believe it. If Henry says that she comes home for the holidays, I believe him."

Lucas kissed her on the forehead.

She traced Lucas's lip line with the tip of her finger.

"That is making me so damn hot." He slipped his hand under her shirt and rested it on her ribs. "Your skin feels like satin sheets. I could spend the whole day here and do nothing but touch you."

She moved closer to him and changed the subject before things went a step further. "Did you go to the doctor's office with Sonia when she got the results from that test?"

He forgot the bra, grabbed her hand, and kissed each finger. "No. One time at that place was enough for me. Why are we talking about this? I'd rather tell you how beautiful you are and talk about us."

"Did you see the papers with the results printed on them?" she asked.

He frowned and dropped her hand. "Where are you going with this, Natalie?"

"Did you?"

"No, I did not. She told me what they were. We had a hellacious fight because she acted happy about it and I was heartbroken. We broke up and I left two weeks later for Kuwait and didn't see her again until last week," he said.

She pushed away from him and sat on the edge of the bed. "We might be in big trouble, Lucas. We had unprotected sex last night."

"Remember what the doctor said. A miracle. One chance in ten million. I'd say we got a lot of chances left before ten million."

"Maybe not," she said.

His jumped up from the bed. "Did Sonia lie to me about those tests?"

"She says that she did. Who knows with that woman? I suppose she thought the cat was out of the bag since we have Joshua, so she might as well 'fess up. She doesn't carry that gene for whatever her brother has either. You were both given a good bill of genetic health according to what she told me at the church today," Natalie said.

"I'd better go for another test, right?" he asked.

She shrugged. "Or anytime we have sex, we'll have to use protection. Are there any babies that might pop up from your Kuwait tour?"

"Hell, no! I could strangle Sonia! For the lie and for the fact that I don't carry protection in my hip pocket anymore."

"Want to borrow my pink pistol? It's loaded."

"Don't tempt me." He swore under his breath.

"Kind of changes everything, doesn't it?" she said.

"Gramps says never say never. Guess I'll call the doctor tomorrow and see which time she was lying. Dammit! I thought I knew that woman."

She patted the bed. "Sit down. If the test says that she was lying to you from the first, then it changes more than just us having sex, Lucas. The old guys can have their own blood kin babies to play with."

He plopped down so hard that the old metal springs

squeaked in protest. "They already love Joshua. More would just be another layer of icing on the cake."

Another tear hung on Natalie's thick lashes. Saying it didn't make it so. Blood was always thicker than water. She slipped her hand under his and he laced his fingers with hers. Together they faced their demons for several minutes before either of them spoke.

"We'd best be going," he said finally. "You've got to see the church before we go home. Please don't tell them about this until I call the doctor tomorrow."

She shook her head. "I won't tell them anything. That's your job, Lucas. And we saw the church this morning, so we can just go on home, can't we?"

Home!

Where did that come from? Home wasn't on Cedar Hill. Home was in Silverton. Or was it?

"That's not the church I'm talking about. When Gramps and Granny bought this place, they also bought the little country church on the land with it. It hasn't been used as a church for years, even though Gramps is an ordained minister. He preaches sometimes when the minister of our church is gone. But every so often there's a wedding in the little church," Lucas explained.

Words lightened the heavy fog hanging over their heads.

"That's where Granny and Gramps got married, so that makes it a very special place," Lucas went on.

She stood up and put her coat on without his help. "I can't wait to see it."

She'd be willing to look at the snow falling outside or the grass growing to keep from talking about what might have happened in the passion of the night before.

The church was tiny, with eight pews on each side of a center aisle and an old oak pulpit in the front. In the days that it was built, the whole congregation sang together and there was no choir. They didn't need a baptismal because, come spring, all new converts could be baptized in the creek or a pond.

It was cold inside but Natalie noticed an old potbellied stove in the corner. "So is that thing operational?"

"Gramps fires it up if there's going to be a winter wedding," Lucas answered.

"Doesn't the water freeze up?"

Lucas laughed. "No water in here. Bathrooms were out back in the days when services were held here all the time. They did have two. The half-moon on the door was for the men and the star was for the ladies."

Natalie sat down on the front pew. "It would never pass code for a gathering today, but it sure is peaceful."

Lucas sat down beside her and took her hand in his. "Gramps says if you sit here real quiet during Christmas that you can hear the ghosts of all the folks who used to attend services here singing Christmas carols."

"Shhh." She shut her eyes.

Lucas began to hum "Silent Night."

And she could imagine the church filled with people a hundred years before, all singing that song. Little children's innocent voices blended with old folks' quivering voices. She opened her eyes just as Lucas stopped humming. "If these walls could talk, they'd tell us some interesting stories, I bet."

He leaned over and kissed her on the cheek. "Oh, yes, they could. You ready for the rest of the tour?"

They drove past Henry's place, a small white house

with a wide front porch. Rocking chairs set back in the shadows and pansies shot little purple flowers up through the snow in the flower beds beside the walkway.

Jack's place was bigger, but the porch wasn't quite as wide. In the spring the roses would be beautiful on each side of the house, but that evening they were just sticks covered in ice and snow.

"When Dad built his own place, he wanted to make it a duplex and move Hazel into the other side, but she wasn't having any part of it. Said that she'd lived in the same little frame house since she set foot on the ranch before Willa Ruth was even born and that she wasn't moving out of it. Besides, it's only a little ways from Dad's place." He drove down a path to a white house with a picket fence around it.

"Does she still drive?"

"Oh, yeah! Lord help the person who tries to take her license. That's her truck sitting in the driveway. She takes it to Savoy and drives to the women's meetings at the church and funeral dinners. We try to make sure one of us takes her any farther than that when she wants to go," he said.

"No wonder she's so homesick. If I had a place back in the woods like this, I'd be homesick too," Natalie said.

Lucas raised an eyebrow. "Did she say she was homesick?"

"I haven't talked to her since she went to Memphis, but I know she's homesick because I would be if I'd lived in one place all those years and then got yanked away from it. She'll be home, Lucas. There's no doubt about that. But she's too old to be takin' on the whole house and cooking, too. You've got to hire her some help."

"I did," he said.

Chapter 13

NATALIE HAD THROWN A LOAD OF TOWELS INTO THE washer and was in the process of cooking breakfast when her phone rang. She fished it out of her hip pocket and held it to one ear and stirred scrambled eggs with the other.

"Hello," she said cautiously.

"Natalie, is that you? So you did stay? I was afraid you'd light a shuck out of there after the reception Lucas gave you there at the first. Boy ought to be whipped coming home like that before we had his surprise all ready," Hazel said.

"I'm still here," Natalie said.

"I've been meanin' to call for days. I talk to Jack every night and he told me that story about the chickens and the puppies, and those damn goats of Crankston's gettin' loose. I swear I'm missin' all the fun. Oh, I'd have given my eyeteeth to have seen that puppy lick on Sonia's leg and when he hiked his leg on her... Shit! That was priceless. I would have let them out of the pen myself to get to see that sight. I'm so homesick I could just scream. Everything is going on there and I'm stuck out here until the week of Christmas and I can't wait to get home."

Natalie waited for her to catch her breath.

"Well?" Hazel asked impatiently.

"I'm sorry. I was setting the eggs off to one side.

Breakfast is nearly ready. They are eating my cooking, but they miss you, Hazel."

"Hummph!" she snorted. "With you and Joshua there I bet they don't even remember what I look like. Now tell me what happened after the play in the fellowship hall. Jack said that you and Sonia had a little catfight."

Holy shit! Did everyone in Savoy know? Or had Jack been close enough to hear?

"Talk, Natalie," Hazel said.

Natalie told her what had happened at the church and that Lucas was calling the clinic where he and Sonia had the tests done. "But you've got to swear to me that you won't tell anyone until we know the results and he tells his dad and Henry."

"I ain't sayin' a word. I knew that woman was trouble the first time I met her. She's one of them," she paused for several seconds, "bitches that have to have everything in the world. She's all sweet as sugar to folks that she likes and wants to please, but believe me, underneath that sugar is some sour shit. Poor old Noah don't have no idea what he's gettin' himself into. What is it you youngun's call that today? High something or other?"

"High maintenance?" Natalie asked.

"That's it. You got to have a special bank account just to keep her in shoes, hair spray, and fingernail polish," Hazel said.

"Kind of looks that way," Natalie said.

"Noah has got a hard row to hoe if he vows to love her to the end of his days. Betcha he prays for the end to come soon after he's married to her a week."

Natalie pulled the biscuits from the oven and slathered melted butter over the tops. "They're gettin' married

Christmas day. You should be here to see it happen. Maybe you can talk him out of it."

"I'm just glad she's leavin' my Lucas alone. If she comes near him again after the stunt she pulled, I'll kick her all the way to hell."

Natalie giggled. "Your hip is hurt, Hazel. I don't expect that you'll be kicking anyone very hard."

"Honey, I could kick her skinny ass to hell with a busted hip if she makes trouble. Since I can't come home for a couple of more weeks, it's your job to keep her away from him and make Noah see the error of his ways, too. I don't give a damn how you do it. Make her mad, feed her to the coyotes, just don't let her sneak her way back into Lucas's life. Promise?"

"But Hazel, what if Noah loves her down deep in his heart?" Natalie asked.

"Hmmph!" Hazel snorted. "He just thinks he loves her. Give that precious baby a hug for me. Wilma's got my breakfast ready. Damn, but I'm ready to be home."

A burst of freezing air blew Henry into the kitchen. He slammed the door and stomped the snow from his feet. "Damned storm! It's been teasin' us for a week and now I'll be damned if it ain't got down to real business. Too cold for these bones to help with chores. I'm stayin' in this warm house and playin' with Joshua. You can help with chores this morning."

"Give the phone to Henry. I need to talk to him," Hazel said.

"You promised," Natalie said.

"I won't say a word until Lucas finds out, but I still need to talk to Henry. Either hand him your phone or I'll call him on his," Hazel said.

Natalie laid the phone on the cabinet. "Hazel wants to talk to you."

"Just a minute. Got to take my coat and hat off." Henry hung his coat on the rack beside the back door and his hat on a hook beside it. "I ain't talkin' very long. I got a story I want to read to Joshua."

He picked up the telephone and carried it to the den. "Is that hip going to ever get well?"

He said a few more words and then his tone changed and Natalie realized that he was talking to the baby, not to Hazel. She stepped to the door and peeked around the corner. He'd taken Joshua out of the swing and they were sitting in a rocking chair close to the fireplace. Henry had a book in his hands and he was reading to Joshua.

"Look, Natalie, he likes *Baby Jesus Is Born*. And look what I found in Lucas's old toy box up in the attic at my place." He held up a small camel stuffy. "It's old and worn because it was Lucas's favorite toy when he was a toddler. He'd hold it when I read this book about baby Jesus to him. If this damned weather ever lets up, I've got to drive into Sherman and get him some presents. Boy needs to get up Christmas morning to presents under the tree. I'm going to look for a brand-spanking-new camel for one of his presents."

"He'll only be three months old," Natalie said.

"And when he's a big boy and we show him the pictures of his first Christmas, what will we tell him? You didn't get no presents because you were only three months old and wouldn't know what they were? I don't think so, young lady. This baby is going to have a big, big first Christmas. Jack's even talkin' about a real pony. Just one of them little ones. By this time next year

he'll be walkin' and we can hold him while he rides,"
Henry said.

"Rides where?" Lucas and Jack said in unison as they
brought another gust of cold air into the kitchen.

Jack looked at Henry. "I didn't think you'd get out in
this weather."

"I wanted to see Joshua. Natalie is going to take my
place this morning with Lucas in doin' the feeding. I'll
watch the baby. My bones are too old to be out there in a
blizzard. Hell, I might break a hip like Hazel did."

Lucas smiled at Henry. "Hazel did not break a hip,
and she's older than you. Mean and ornery as you are,
your bones would be afraid to break, Gramps."

Henry shrugged. "I'm not going out to do chores.
And Natalie is. Now let's eat breakfast. Ain't nothing
in the world worse than cold gravy, and I smelled bacon
when I came in the back door."

He put Joshua back in the swing and sat down at the
end of the table.

"Bossy old fart, isn't he?" Lucas said.

Her mouth turned up in half a grin. "He's definitely
used to getting his way."

"You don't have to get out in the cold. We can feed
without you, and I'll gather the eggs on the way back in
at noon," Lucas told her.

"Not according to Henry."

"I'm sitting right here and I can damn sure hear both
of you and Natalie is right. She's going out to help this
morning and me and Josh are going to read books and
I'm going to tell him all about Ella Jo and how much
she loved Christmas. And he's going to chew the ears
off that old camel."

—⁓—

Natalie picked up the hay hooks and sunk them deep in the ends of a small bale of hay, tossed it over into the galvanized feeder, and used the wire cutters attached to her belt loop to cut the baling wire loose. The cows were reaching around her to nibble on it before she could scatter it for them. It took six times before the feeder was completely full and by nightfall it would be empty. What little winter grass had grown was covered in snow, so they'd use a lot of hay before the month was out.

Lucas yelled over the howling wind, "We'll put out the big round bales in the far pastures."

"Henry still likes the small bales, doesn't he?" she hollered back.

"Oh, yeah! We'd put it all up in big round bales, but he says it's wasteful. Besides, we've got several hay barns around the property, so we can store the little bales without any trouble and it makes him happy," Lucas answered.

Snow had settled on his hat brim and wide shoulders. Even his eyelashes were dusted with white. If they didn't get the chores done soon, he'd look like the abominable snowman.

"We should have brought out the ski masks. Your nose looks like Rudolph's," Lucas said.

She hooked another bale and carried it to the next feeder. "I hate those things. I can't breathe in them. I'd rather be cold. We'll get warmed up in the truck on the way to the next feedlot."

The wind howled through the bare limbs, creating all kinds of different sounds. Snow had begun to drift against the fence posts. If it kept up all day, they'd be doing some shoveling to get the pickup trucks out to go anywhere.

When they finished, she hopped into the truck, jerked off her leather gloves, and rubbed her hands briskly in front of the heater vents. Her nose and cheeks prickled as the cold left them.

"Bet you are wishing you'd stayed in Kuwait until spring," she said when Lucas hurried into the passenger seat.

"It crossed my mind this morning when we were out feeding the chickens and dogs. Even the pups had enough sense to stay inside the doghouse. Guess they don't want to chase coyotes if it's cold. I called that clinic first thing this morning, but they weren't open yet. I left a message, but I figure I might have to drive down there if they can't tell me the results over the phone," Lucas said.

Natalie shrugged. "I don't know about all that privacy stuff, but I sure wouldn't trust Sonia to tell the truth after she's lied to you. Hey, Hazel called this morning and I don't think her hip is nearly as bad as we thought. I think she's playing matchmaker right along with those three wise men."

She wanted to know what the test results were, but knowing would definitely change things and she hated change.

"Probably so. But we're going to do things our way," he said.

She shrugged because she wasn't sure what the answer was.

They finished up an hour later and Lucas drove the work truck back into the barn. He bailed out and slid the door shut before more snow could blow inside. Natalie didn't need anyone to help her open a door or hold her hand while she crawled out of a truck, so she was already out and staring at a basketball hoop when he finished.

"Dad installed that for me when I was in junior high so I could practice." He slipped into the tack room and came out with two wide brooms. "If we sweep the hay stubble away we could shoot some hoops."

She took one of the brooms and started cleaning the concrete floor in a long flowing motion that matched his. They uncovered the circle for free throws and then the wider one for three-pointers. He took the broom from her and set both his and hers against a stall.

"Basketballs are in the box beside the goal. We'll take ten minutes to warm up and then I'm going to whip your ass at a game of horse," he said.

"Best two out of three has to do the dinner dishes. And be warned, I'm frying chicken, and you know how many dishes that messes up," she said.

"You are on." He winked.

The ball was at home in her hands and she had full command of it. But then so did Lucas. She watched him dribble, getting the feel of the weight, and then he put up the prettiest three-point shot she'd ever seen. Lord, if she could have gotten her girls to sink a ball like that, she would have thought she'd died and gone to coaches' heaven. She could fall in love with him just because he could make a three-point basket look as easy as breathing.

She shot and missed.

"Hands still cold?" Lucas asked.

"Hell, no! Look up there." She pointed.

A ball of mistletoe tied with a red ribbon hung on the edge of the backboard.

"Where did that come from?" she asked.

"Three wise men." He laughed. "Ready to play ball? Hey, new rules. We can't knock that mistletoe down. If we do, it's a forfeit of that game."

"You are on!" She tossed the ball she'd been using to one side. Playing in a bulky coat wouldn't be as easy as baggy sweats, but she could whip a cowboy's sexy little ass any day of the week when it came to basketball.

"Catch." He tossed the ball at her.

"We can flip for first," she said.

"Give it your best shot."

She bounced the ball on the concrete at the free throw line and it cleared the net without even wiggling the threads. The mistletoe swayed slightly, but it didn't fall.

"Not bad." He caught the ball on the rebound and dribbled all the way back to where she stood.

She moved to her next position and watched him match her shot.

They were even until the last shot and she decided to do a running layup that ended in a dunk. She did just fine until she slapped the ball into the net where it rolled around the rim three times and bounced right back out onto the floor. His grin got wider as he mimicked her shot, only his dunk slammed through the net like it had been greased.

He threw both arms into the air. "I win!"

"You win round one," she said.

"First one usually tells the tale."

But it didn't. She won the second and the third.

"You do the dishes." She giggled.

He tossed the ball to the side and ran toward her. She looked over her shoulder to see if someone had come into the barn and didn't even realize he'd scooped her up into his arms until he had fallen into a pile of hay with her on top of him.

"It was worth it." He pointed up to the mistletoe. "We can't waste it."

His lips touched hers in a soft kiss that quickly turned hungry and passionate. She rolled off to one side and he propped up on an elbow, but the kisses didn't stop. Her insides turned to hot liquid and she felt like she was burning up in the coat and long-sleeved thermal shirt. She wanted to be naked with him, not fully dressed and making out like a couple of sophomore students.

"God, you taste good. Like coffee and bacon and snow all mixed together," he murmured as he moved from her lips to her neck.

His hands were warm as they moved over her skin. One slid up under her shirt and cupped a breast and she pressed closer to him, trying to melt her entire body into his. She wanted Lucas right there in the barn with the mistletoe hanging above them and the smell of hay all around them.

"I want you, Natalie," he said.

"Here?"

"Anywhere. But we can't because I don't have protection."

His phone rang and his hand left her breast to answer it. It had better be the doctor calling, because anyone else was going straight to the top of her hit list.

Lucas's expression changed in an instant. His eyes

flashed anger and his body language said that he didn't like what he was hearing.

"No, I won't forgive you," he growled.

Whoever it was must've been talking fast and furious because he started to say something several times and then clamped his mouth shut. Finally, he said, "That is enough. Good-bye, Sonia."

He put the phone back in his hip pocket.

"Sonia, I presume," Natalie said.

"You presume right. She says she'll bring the papers over here if I will forgive her for lying to me. But that I should have figured it all out when I got you pregnant," Lucas said.

Natalie picked straw out of her hair. "We need to put an end to that rumor."

"Here, let me help you." Lucas pulled a comb from his pocket and sat with one leg on either side of Natalie as he combed her hair.

Bits of straw flew all around her, but she didn't even notice. His hands in her hair made every nerve ending on her body tingle.

"There, now you are presentable and Gramps won't suspect that we've been making out," he said seriously.

"Don't count on it. I bet he's got surveillance cameras out here."

Both of them looked up at the rafters at the same time.

She quickly stood up. "Time to make dinner. I promised Grady fried chicken today."

"I love fried chicken, but I'd give it up to stay out here and kiss you all day," Lucas said.

She giggled again. "Is that your best come-on line, cowboy?"

His head bobbed. "Best I've got right now. What about you? Cook or kiss?"

The side door opened and Grady poked his head inside. "Henry says that if you two are finished playing basketball that he's getting hungry."

Natalie looked at the rafters again for the little red dots that would signal that a camera was hidden up there. "Looks like the choice has been made and it has to do with a stove rather than a bed of hay."

Lucas hopped up and threw an arm around her shoulders. "We were shooting a few hoops. I won, so she has to wash dishes."

"You won the first round. I won the next two, so you have to wash dishes," Natalie said.

"For fried chicken, I'll wash dishes," Grady said.

Grady didn't linger. He jogged from the barn to the yard fence, put a hand on the rail, and hopped over with the agility of a man half his age.

"Can you do that?" Lucas asked.

"Oh, yeah!" She took off in a lope with him right behind her.

She cleared the fence only a scant second before he did and then suddenly he grabbed her from behind and spun her around to land against his chest. The kiss was hard, hungry, and promising. She could still feel the steam rising when he opened the back door for her and stood to one side.

Chapter 14

LUCAS ANNOUNCED AT THE SUPPER TABLE THAT EVE-
ning that he, Joshua, and Natalie were all going shopping. He looked across the table at his grandfather and
shook his head. "No, Gramps, you three cannot babysit
tonight. We are taking him with us. He needs to go
through the toy store and pick out what he wants so y'all
will know what to buy for him."

Natalie had been sitting on pins and needles all day.
She wouldn't ask if Lucas had heard from the doctor,
but that had been the foremost thing on her mind. She'd
played the old game of "what if" all day. What if she
had indeed gotten pregnant again on a first-night stand?
What if she hadn't? Every emotion possible, from tears
to laughter, had run through her mind as she prepared
homemade noodle soup and chicken salad sandwiches
using the leftover fried chicken.

"Boy don't need toys. He needs a pony and a saddle
and some boots to grow into. That's what Joshua needs,
so take him to the Western store and show him the
boots," Henry grumbled. "Roads are slick. Y'all ought
to leave him here just for safety. What if you slide off
into a ditch?"

"He'll be strapped into his car seat and we both have
cell phones. We'll call you to bring a tractor and get us
out if we have trouble," Lucas said.

"I'm not drivin' a tractor in this cold," Henry said.

"Dad can," Lucas said.

"You are a spoilsport. We might not have a baby in the house after Christmas. And you're not sharing." Henry raised his bony chin a full two inches and looked down his nose at Lucas.

Jack pushed back his plate. "Then we get to keep him Saturday night while y'all go to the Angus Christmas party. And you can't be calling home every thirty minutes, either."

Henry's chin lowered and he looked up at Lucas. "Deal?"

"Hey, I'm Joshua's momma. I'm the one who really calls the shots around here," Natalie said.

Henry rubbed his shoulder. "Be nice to an old man. I always wanted to live to see one more baby on Cedar Hill, and Joshua is my Christmas present. I just want to read to him and spend a little time with the feller before Hazel comes back and you go runnin' back to Silverton. Which reminds me, don't y'all think we should get grandparent's rights? We'd get him for a weekend a month and maybe six weeks in the summer."

Natalie smiled. "But you're not his grandparents."

"That's not the rumor I been hearin'. Them old women down at the church is plumb settin' the old ladies gossip vines on fire," Henry countered. "Y'all can take him tonight but come Saturday night, he belongs to us. We're going to watch the Christmas tree lights blink and I'm going to tell him stories about Lucas and my sweet Ella and then we might even watch one of them little kid Christmas shows on television together. And if he don't like it I'll get out one of them Scooby movies in the drawer."

Natalie nodded. Sometimes it was simply impossible to beat the opposition. "Scooby?" she asked.

"It's one of Lucas's old movie tapes. We still got a VHS player, so Joshua can watch the same funny stories about that crazy dog as Lucas watched when he was a little boy," Jack answered.

Grady cocked his head to one side and then pushed up out of his recliner. "I hear something scratching at the door. I bet it's those pesky puppies again. I'm beginning to think we might as well turn them all three into house dogs."

"Bluetick hounds don't belong in the house," Henry said.

"It's the prodigal son's fault. He was gone more than a year and all the animals in the damn county want to come see him," Grady said.

"Might as well put your coat on," Jack said. "You're goin' to have to take them pups back to the pens."

Grady opened the door, expecting a flurry of puppies, but one big yellow mama cat waltzed right in instead. At first Natalie thought the cat was carrying a mouse in her mouth and then she realized it was a kitten that still didn't have its eyes open. The mama cat went straight for Henry, hopped up in the chair, and dropped the kitten in Joshua's lap, jumped down, and went to the door.

Grady opened it and she dashed out to the porch, picked up another kitten, and brought it inside. She repeated the process until five babies were squirming in Joshua's lap, and then she laid down across his legs and purred.

"I'll be damned." Henry laughed. "I believe Grady is right. Every animal in the world is coming to see you, Lucas."

"It ain't the prodigal son," Jack said.

"No, it's kittens born out of season and the mama knows it's warm in this house," Natalie said.

"We'll put her in the utility room in a laundry basket until it warms up and then she can go back to the barn," Lucas said.

Natalie changed shirts and put on a better pair of boots, ran a brush through her hair, and applied lipstick. She dressed Joshua in a bright red flannel shirt and navy blue knit pants. Then she shoved him down into a fleece bunting and stretched a stocking hat with a Santa Claus appliqué over his head. She carried him into the living room and Henry shook his head.

"What?" she asked.

"You got too many clothes on that boy. He'll sweat and then get cold and get pneumonia. You'd better leave him with us," Henry answered.

"Ain't happenin', Gramps," Lucas said.

"Soon as the truck warms up, I'll take him out of the bunting," Natalie said.

"Put it back on before you take him out in the cold air. He'll catch pneumonia for sure if he gets chilled," Henry said.

"Yes, sir," Natalie said.

Lucas helped her into her coat and ushered her out the front door with a hand on her back. "I've already got the truck warmed up so that he wouldn't get cold."

"Henry's just giving it one last-ditch effort to make us change our mind. He's really gotten attached to Joshua." Natalie crawled into the backseat and removed the bunting before she strapped the baby into the car seat. He flashed his most brilliant toothless grin at her and she kissed him on the forehead. "Feel all better, does it, son? Well, we're going to do some serious shopping tonight. What do you think we should buy Henry?"

"Duct tape." Lucas suggested.

"Why that?" She threw one leg over the front passenger seat and gracefully slid into a seated position.

"Damn, you are flexible," Lucas said.

"Yes, I am. Years of playing basketball and hard work. Now tell me more about this Angus Association party on Saturday night."

"It's the annual Christmas dinner at the Red River Angus Association. Your folks must belong to something similar," he said.

She nodded. Every year her mother fretted about the Christmas dinner for the association for months. She made numerous trips to Amarillo to find just the right dress so that Natalie's father, Jimmy, would think she was the prettiest girl at the party.

"It's at the Denison Country Club. The food is good, and you will go with me, won't you?"

She fluttered her eyelashes at him. "Lucas Allen, are you asking me for a date?"

His brown eyes twinkled. "Yes, ma'am, I am. The ladies call it semiformal. Us guys just wear our best creased jeans and shine up our boots real good and sometimes we put on a jacket. But the ladies get all dolled up. Will you go with me?"

"I don't have much choice, do I? Henry will take me out in the yard and pay old Crankston to shoot me with his shotgun if I don't let him keep Joshua that night."

She smiled. "But I did not bring anything to get dolled up in, so we'd best hit a couple of dress stores tonight."

"Yes, ma'am. Me and Josh will sit outside however many dressing rooms that you want to use. We won't even complain, will we, cowboy?" He looked in the rearview mirror. "Well, okay, we won't complain if we can play in the toy store an extra fifteen minutes."

Natalie laughed. "And when should I be ready for the party?"

"I'll pick you up at seven. Cocktails are served at seven thirty and it's about a half-hour trip over there. We have a babysitter, so that's no problem," he said.

Natalie did not miss the *we* in that statement and her heart skipped a beat before it raced ahead.

Lucas reached across the seat and laid a hand on her shoulder. "You look like you saw a ghost."

"Didn't see one. Fought with one, though," she said.

"Who won?"

"He did."

"Drew?" Lucas asked.

She nodded.

"Sometimes I wonder what he would say about all this too. I mean, he was your friend and now you are here and it's kind of crazy the way it all came about. To all of us in Kuwait, he was king of the base. But I get the feeling from what you've said that he wasn't like that when y'all were growing up. Tell me about him," Lucas said.

"Drew was that kid that was at the bottom of every social list in the county. His parents already had grand-kids when he was born and there was never any doubt that he was a big, big accident. Then he was just a little kid and he didn't have fancy clothes or boots and the other kids were vicious toward him. To be king of the base would have been like giving him a real crown," she said.

Lucas cocked his head to one side. "But he grew out of it in high school, right? He wasn't just a little kid when we knew him. He was almost six feet tall and built like a wrestler."

Natalie smiled. "By then he'd become the resident bad boy of the whole area. He was good-lookin', funny, and had a summer job workin' for my dad. He bought his own clothes and he even bought a car. Not a truck but a car in a county where every teenage boy sees visions of pickup trucks. He drove too fast, especially when he was drinking, and that was every weekend. Mothers warned their daughters about him and my folks tried their damnedest to break up our friendship."

"Didn't work, huh?"

"No, neither one. The daughters in the county flocked to him like flies on maple syrup and my parents figured out real quick that Drew and I would always be friends no matter what his reputation was," she said.

The pickup grew silent except for the baby noises in the backseat. Natalie remembered the quilt in the back of that old souped-up car Drew raced around the whole Panhandle in those two summers after he got his driver's license. If the quilt could talk, Lord, the tales it could tell would have ruined the lives of too many women to count. Their mothers might not let them date him, but that didn't mean they couldn't meet him out in a cotton field with a six-pack of beer.

"Hey, you said something about duct tape before we

got off on the subject of Drew and ghosts," she changed the subject.

"We need to wrap up some for Gramp's Christmas present." Lucas chuckled.

"Why?"

"To slap across his mouth," Lucas answered.

"How can he read to Joshua if his mouth is taped shut?"

Lucas nosed the truck into a parking space in front of a Western-wear store and turned in his seat. "Hey, feller, I betcha if Momma gets the blanket out of the diaper bag and wraps you up, you won't have to wear that tow sack into the store."

"It's called a bunting," Natalie said.

"Looks like a tow sack with a zipper up the front."

"It's red and fuzzy and tow sacks are brown and made of burlap," she countered.

His brown eyes danced and his mouth quivered as he fought back a grin. "Are we having our first fight about a blanket or a sack?"

"I'm his mother. Sometimes all you guys forget that. And we had our first fight the night you came home, remember?"

Lucas leaned across the seat, cupped her chin in his big hand, and landed a scorching hot kiss on her lips. "You would look good in a tow sack tied up in the middle with a piece of rope. Hell, I bet you could even play some killer basketball in a getup like that. And I'd have such a good time untying the belt and pulling that tow sack up over your head."

Her insides had that crazy hot melted feeling like they always did when he kissed her or even brushed past her in the kitchen or the hallway. Shit! Shit! Shit! Why did he have to affect her like that? It wasn't fair.

"Are we going to argue, make out, or shop? If you want me all dolled up for Saturday night, it might ought to be the latter." Her voice was even hoarse in her own ears, but then it was a miracle she could even speak after a kiss like that.

He cocked his head to one side and said, "I'd rather take the make out option, but since you need to shop, we'd better get with it."

"I don't think I'm going to find a thing in a Western-wear store to wear to a fancy party," she said.

"We'll go other places. I just always start here for Dad, Grady, and Gramps. This year they are all three getting new work coats. We're in for a hard winter and theirs are lookin' pretty frayed and stained up," he said.

Natalie threw a blanket over Joshua and hurried into the store with him. The first thing she saw when she removed the blanket and threw it over her shoulder was an off-white, lace dress hanging on a mannequin to her left. Long-sleeved and with a high Victorian neckline, it had a slip liner with thin straps that let skin show through the lace. They showed it with brown dress boots that had a brown cross cut into the off-white tops.

"It's the last one. Size eight and the boots are nines. Want to try it on?" the lady behind the counter asked.

"I'll look around a little bit first," Natalie said.

"Well, hello, Lucas Allen! I heard you got home. I was workin' or I would've been over to the party Friday night." Her voice perked right up when she saw Lucas.

"Natalie, meet Diane Larkin. She and I went to school together. Diane, this is Natalie Clark." Lucas's arm went around Natalie's shoulders as he made introductions.

"Oh, I've heard about you. Let me see that baby

better," Diane said. "Oh my Lord, that pesky raccoon that hangs around the garbage cans out back just slipped inside the store with y'all. It's never done that before even if it is about half-tame. I feed it scraps because I feel sorry for it."

Natalie looked down and that was one big raccoon. He sat down at her feet and looked up at her as if he expected her to give him a half-eaten burger or some stale chips.

"You open the door, Diane, and I'll shoo him on out of here," Lucas said.

She grabbed a package of cheese crackers and slung open the door. "Come on, Coonie, you old renegade. Come get the crackers."

Lucas stomped his feet and slapped his hat against his leg. "Shoo, get on out of here."

An idea popped into Natalie's head. She squatted down so that the coon could see Joshua. It peered into the baby's smiling face and then ambled out of the store.

"You are the animal whisperer. I swear I've never had trouble with animals before this." He chuckled.

"Well, I'm just glad that y'all convinced him to leave. I'd get in big trouble if my boss knew I was feeding him. Now let me see that baby."

Natalie repositioned Joshua and removed his cap.

Diane nodded emphatically. "Yep, he's got the Allen dark hair and eyes. You pulled a real sneaky on us, Lucas. Were you in the service over there in Kuwait too?" She looked at Natalie.

"No, ma'am."

"Well, you'll have to tell me the whole story sometime. What can I do for you two today? Y'all out doin' some shoppin'. Want to see what the fellows have been looking at when they've been in the last few times?" Her eyes went back to Lucas.

Lucas shook his head. "I want you to wrap three Carhartt coats. You know their sizes."

"The best-lined ones?" she asked.

"That's right."

Natalie cradled Joshua more comfortably and said, "I'd like to see what they've looked at."

"While you are doing that, I'm going to try on a new pair of work boots," Lucas said.

Natalie loved Western-wear stores. She liked the way they smelled, the rows and rows of cowboy boots, hats, and racks of shirts, belts, and jeans. Diane came from around the counter and pointed at a shelf with folded flannel shirts.

She picked out several things for the guys and asked Diane if she could please wrap them.

"And I want that dress..." She pointed to a mannequin. She wanted the boots. Hell, she needed the boots. "And the boots too. It's fate that they and the dress are my size, so I should have them."

"Oh, I agree," Diane said. "I've got a fancy cape in the back that goes with that dress. It's the softest suede you'll ever throw around your shoulders and the buttons are covered in that same lace. Lady had it on layaway, but she changed her mind and I just haven't gotten it back out on the rack yet."

She brought it out and Natalie fell in love with it.

"Can you just put all of that in a separate bag than the presents?" she asked.

Diane winked. "You are planning on surprising Lucas, are you?"

"Yes, I am. We're going to the Angus Christmas party."

"Well, darlin', you'd better take a big stick with you to beat off all the other ranchers who will try to beat his time. Jewelry?"

"No, I've got something that will be perfect, but I do like that pearl comb right there for my hair."

"You go on and look at them boots Lucas is trying on, and I'll get all this wrapped up real pretty for y'all," Diane said.

Natalie found him in the back corner sitting on a wide wooden bench. He pointed at his feet. One boot was brown and one was black. She sat down beside him and jumped when she saw a movement to her side. The coon had snuck back in with another bunch of teenage customers.

It reared up on his haunches and looked at all three of them then ambled to the back door. Diane was right behind it with crackers in hand. "I've created a mess that's going to get me fired."

The coon followed her out the back door that time. She locked it and returned to her customers.

Lucas removed the boots. "I still got a month left in my old ones, so I'll come back and get them after Christmas. Don't want to have to break in new boots in this kind of weather. Why do you think we have this problem with animals anyway?"

"Henry says that they're coming around to see you. Mama says that I've always drug in strays. Maybe it's a combination of the two of us," she said.

"Well, it's plumb crazy. What do you want for Christmas, Natalie?"

"I want—" She blushed. She couldn't tell him that

she wanted to be a permanent part of Cedar Hill Ranch and that she wanted him to accept Joshua as a real son. Lord, that would be asking for more than Santa Claus could stuff in his sleigh.

"What?" he pressured. "For real, what do you want?"

"I'll think about it and let you know later. What do you want?"

"You," he said without taking his eyes off her. "I came home in one piece and you were waiting for me."

The moon hung in a crystal-clear sky at the top of the windshield on their way home that evening. Stars glimmered around it like subjects before their king. Natalie remembered what Lucas had said about Drew being king in their barracks. She intended to paint that picture to Joshua when she told him all about his father.

"I figured he'd be sound asleep the way we've dragged him from one store to the other." Lucas nodded toward the backseat. "But he's talking to his fist and chewing on it like it's chocolate."

"It's time for his bath and night bottle," she said.

"You've got him on a pretty good schedule."

"I didn't do it. He did. From the day he was born he ate every four hours and he's been a good baby. No colic or fussing other than when he's hungry," she said. "They're not all like that, though. I've got some friends who have walked the floor with their kids."

"Melody's first one about split their marriage. I don't think either she or her husband slept the first year. They got so cranky that we were all afraid they'd divorce over that baby. I wondered if they could even get a divorce on grounds of lack of sleep because the baby is so fussy. But after he was a year old, he did a complete turnaround and he's been a good kid ever since."

Natalie nodded slightly and looked out the side window. Since they were on the subject of babies, maybe it would be a good time to ask about the test results. She opened her mouth but words would not come out.

They drove through Savoy and he made a right-hand turn and then a left onto a dirt road. A quarter of a mile later he turned right again and drove down the lane to the house. The lights strung around the porch and house were on and the Christmas tree filled the window.

"I'll carry Joshua and then come back for the bags that you can't take," Lucas offered.

Sometimes Fate did give her a decent hand. She'd worried about getting the baby and that big bag with her dress, cape, and boots into the house at the same time. She really, really wanted to surprise Lucas when she got all dolled up for the party.

The ground was as slippery as greased piglets, but she managed to keep her balance from truck to porch and then into the warm house. She rushed to her room, tossed the bag on the bed, and then hurried back out to the living room to take Joshua from Lucas.

———

He handed the baby off to her and went right back out to bring in the rest of the packages they'd bought. He slipped on the top step but with a lot of fancy footwork kept from falling on the presents. If he broke the ornament that said *Baby's First Christmas* Natalie would never forgive him. She'd searched through four stores

before she found just the right one. It was motion acti-
vated and played "Little Drummer Boy" as it revolved.

"We've got to have this," she'd declared.

"Why that particular one?" he'd asked.

"Henry reads that to Joshua almost every day. He'll
get a big kick out of it."

Lucas had gotten such a big kick out of shopping with
her and the baby that for a whole evening he'd forgotten
that they weren't a family. It had been so easy to fall in
love with Natalie after that first evening that he couldn't
even remember when it happened.

"Whoa!" he said.

She opened the door and stood to one side. "Did you
trip? I thought I heard a thump. I slipped and almost fell
on that top step. We probably need to salt it or do some
serious scraping tomorrow morning. Henry could break
a hip on it."

"No, I just remembered that Gramps always uses the
back door. I'll take care of the steps tomorrow in case
anyone does come to the house. I got all the presents in
that load. We were only gone three hours. How did we
buy so much?"

"We worked hard," she said. "If you'll take the
wrapped ones out and put them under the tree, I'll get
this boy bathed and then fed so he can go to bed for
the night."

"Yes, ma'am. Your wish is my command," he said.

"Oh, yeah. Well, do you want to do diaper duty?"

"No, ma'am!" he said quickly.

"Then my wish is not your command. We'll be back
in a few minutes." She disappeared down the hallway.

He heard water running in the bathroom as he kicked

off his boots and stretched out in his recliner. He leaned back, shut his eyes, and visualized him and Natalie taking a long, hot shower together: running his soapy hands all over her body, feeling her pressed against him, her wet lips on his as the water sprayed down over their naked bodies. He was suddenly in semi-arousal, so he pulled his shirt out of his jeans and let it hang on the outside.

Women didn't have to worry about the whole world seeing things when they were aroused. They might get flushed or even kind of glazed eyes, but they didn't have a bulge in their jeans.

"Love?" He flipped the switch to make the train run around the tracks. Lately he felt just like that little train—running in circles and going nowhere. He was in love with Natalie and he really did like Joshua. But did he like him enough to make him equal to any children they might have of their very own?

He looked at the packages in his hands and pictured his family on Christmas morning when they ripped them open.

"Hazel!" he said. "I've got to find something extra special for Hazel this year so she'll stay on the ranch and not go back to Memphis."

He placed the packages just right up under the tree and sat back on the floor and looked at them. "Love? For real?" he whispered.

Joshua was wrapped in one of those baby towels that had a hood when she brought him back to the living room. She laid him on the sofa and dried him while he fretted and gnawed at his fist.

"No smiles for Momma tonight?" she asked.

"I wouldn't smile either if I was brought in from the cold and given a bath when all I wanted was my night snack," Lucas said. "Want me to make the bottle while you dress him?"

"Yes, and thank you. The water and powder are in the kitchen above the…"

He held up a palm. "I know where you keep them and how to make a bottle. Hold on, Josh, we'll get your chocolate cake and ice cream in a minute. Do you heat it in the microwave or in a pan?"

"Neither. Room temp is fine."

———

She rubbed lotion all over the baby and bent down to kiss him on the cheek. "So tell me, what do you want people to call you? Is Josh more of a cowboy name than Joshua?"

He smiled at her and cooed.

She kissed the bottom of his feet before putting his warm footed pajamas on him. "You are a traitor. Living in this testosterone-filled man cave has changed you."

"And here it is right on time." Lucas handed her a bottle. "It's chocolate cake and ice cream this time. Tomorrow morning it will be bacon and eggs, Josh."

The baby flashed his biggest smile yet at Lucas. Little rascal was a traitor. She bet if he had a father that he'd say Daddy long before he ever said Mommy.

"Want me to feed him while you wrap those packages?" Lucas asked. "I'm all thumbs when it comes to wrapping. I only shop in stores that wrap the presents for me," he said.

Joshua snuggled against Lucas's chest and latched

onto the bottle. Lucas eased down into a recliner and held baby and bottle both in one arm while he flipped the lever on the side. "Ah, boy, this is the life, isn't it? A recliner and food. It don't get no better than this. That shoppin' business will flat take it out of a couple of hardworking cowboys. How them women folks can shop a whole day is pure magic."

Natalie glanced at them as she wrapped the presents for Grady, Jack, and Henry and slipped them under the tree. All the guys now had presents under the tree, but there was nothing for Lucas. She made up her mind right then that she was going to buy the boots for him and a vibrating neck roll pillow for Josh to give him.

Good Lord! She'd just shortened Joshua's name in her thoughts. Her brothers would roar with laughter if they knew she was even thinking the word Josh after the fit she'd thrown at the hospital when he was born.

Suddenly Christmas music filled the room and she looked up so fast that she tore the paper. "Well, shit!"

Lucas laughed. "You got to quit saying words like that when Josh gets old enough to talk. Paper cut?"

"No, that music scared the bejesus out of me. And Hazel cusses like a sailor and she raised you all right," she said.

"You don't like Christmas music?" he asked.

"Love it. It's my favorite holiday of the year, but I was way off in la-la land thinking about something else when it came on. I can't believe the baby is already asleep."

Lucas held out his arms. "I'm good with kids. Want me to put him in his little crib thing in your room?"

"That would be great, and pick up the baby monitor from the nightstand on your way back out here," she said.

CMT was playing old Christmas videos when she looked around the Christmas tree at the television. Dolly Parton was singing "Hard Candy Christmas" and every line spoke to Natalie. Most lines in the song started with the word "maybe." Natalie could relate to that so well that evening. After Hazel came back maybe she'd drive so far that everyone would forget all about her and Joshua. Or maybe if she'd fooled around and gotten pregnant again, she'd really run far, far away and never look back. Because there was no maybe to it; she was not telling her mother that she was having another baby without a father around to help raise him or her.

The song ended and Rascal Flatts sang "I'll Be Home for Christmas." Tears welled up in Natalie's eyes. Where was home? She'd thought it was in Silverton, Texas. She'd been born there and she'd die there after a long life with some old cowboy who loved ranching as much as she did. But lately when the word came to mind she related it to Cedar Hill.

"He's down for the count. You know how they kinda sigh when they're really asleep. When I put him in the crib, he did that," Lucas whispered as he crossed the room and sat on the floor beside her.

"How did you know that?"

"I don't have nieces or nephews, but I've been around babies. Lots of my friends have families already," he answered.

She put all the wrapping supplies in a sack and pushed it back. "Think the guys will be happy to see presents?"

"Oh, yeah! They're just little boys in big boy jeans." He laughed.

Scotty McCreery had just begun to sing "First Noel"

in his deep Southern voice when Lucas picked her up and sat her down in his lap. She leaned into the kiss and parted her lips. His tongue made sweet love to her mouth and the room temperature rose twenty degrees.

She wrapped both arms around his neck and toyed with the penny chain still holding his dog tags. He groaned and inched his hands up under her shirt, traveling slowly toward her breasts. They ached for his touch but he took his time, massaging, teasing, and kissing her until she was panting.

She'd never before felt like her insides were filled with molten lava about to explode any second. She ran her hands up under his shirt and touched his bare skin. Taut muscles rippled from his waist to his shoulders. She found the chain again and slipped under it to touch his neck.

He groaned. "God, that feels so good. I love your hands on my body."

"Ditto." She panted.

He broke the kiss and leaned back. "I can see the Christmas tree lights in your blue eyes."

"Your brown eyes are shot with gold from the reflection of the dying embers in the fireplace," she whispered.

She scooted away enough that she could unfasten the buttons on his shirt. "Tell me right now if we have to stop because by the time I get to the bottom button, you are going to be in big trouble if we do."

He reached up and pulled a condom from his shirt pocket. "I ain't got a word to say."

"We need that?" she asked.

"We do," he said with a big grin on his face.

The moon didn't fall out of the sky. The Christmas

tree didn't catch on fire. Tomorrow she'd think about all the maybes in her life. Right then she wanted satisfaction and the only person who could deliver it was Lucas Allen.

"You can unbutton faster than that," he said.

"Probably, but I'm not going to. I'm going to make you every bit as hot as I am."

His lips found hers in another sizzling kiss that jacked up her inward temperature to the boiling stage.

"Oh, honey, you don't even know what hot is but you are about to find out," he whispered seductively in her ear.

She finally undid the last button and threw his shirt back to look her fill of that broad chest, ripped abdomen, and taut nipples. She kissed each one and then reached for his belt buckle.

"Oh, no!" He grabbed her hand and brought it to his lips to kiss each fingertip.

Mercy! When did fingertips become an erotic zone? They washed dishes. They scrubbed floors and did laundry. They even wrapped Christmas presents, so how in the hell could he turn her on by kissing each one?

He took just as much time undoing her buttons as she did his. When he threw back her shirt and saw the bright red lace bra, he gasped.

"Like what you see?" she asked.

"Christmas has come early in the Allen house," he answered.

His hands were like coals of fire when he reached around her rib cage and unfastened her bra. She pulled his lips to hers for another hard, steamy kiss, this time not holding back a single thing. She wiggled her shoulders to help him take the shirt off and when the bra slipped over her shoulders, she leaned backward to give him better access to her breasts.

"Oh my God!" she said when his lips and tongue toyed with each one, giving them equal attention before he returned to her lips.

"I don't think God has much to do with this," he whispered as he strung a trail of slow steamy kisses down her long, slender neck before settling back on her mouth.

"You are stunning, Natalie Clark," he said.

His eyes, his hands, his kiss all made her feel like she was the most beautiful woman on the whole planet. Being the tall, gangly kid her whole life, she'd never known such a feeling.

"Listen," he mumbled.

"To what?"

"The song that's playing," he said.

Alan Jackson was singing "I Only Want You for Christmas."

"Are you serious?" she asked.

"Yes, ma'am."

What about after Christmas?

The thought was a blur as it passed through her mind. She'd worry about after Christmas later. Right then she only wanted Lucas.

He sang the chorus softly into her ear as he undid her belt buckle. Alan said that she should tie a ribbon around herself. Which part did Lucas want that ribbon tied around?

"My room?" he asked.

"Right here!" She peeled her jeans and boots off, tossing them to one side as she did.

They went from sitting to stretched out on the throw rug in front of the fireplace, both of them as naked as the day they came into the world. God, she wanted him so damn bad, but she didn't want to rush it. She wanted to look her fill into his brown eyes and touch his body until he felt the same way she did. One of his thumbs was circling her wrist, turning the bonfire inside her into a raging Texas wildfire.

His erection pushed against her belly, so she slid a hand between their bodies and circled it, teasing it to the point that he moaned.

"I'm so ready," she whispered.

He pulled a pillow off the sofa and she raised her head. He shook his slowly. "Not for that end, sweet cheeks."

She was lying there naked, panting, wanting him, hell, begging him to have sex with her—so why was she blushing at the idea of a pillow under her butt to keep him from pounding the imprint into the hardwood floor?

When the pillow was in place, Lucas cupped her face in his hands.

Natalie wrapped her long legs firmly around his waist. Without breaking the kisses, he removed the condom from the wrapper and rolled it into place.

"Yes," she said when she figured out what he was doing.

In one firm motion he plunged inside her and she gasped.

"My God… that is… wonderful," she said.

"Yes, ma'am, it is at that," he said, punctuating each word with a harder thrust.

Nothing kinky. Nothing fancy. Just plain old hot sex and her whole body tingled from head to toe. She wanted it to last, but she wanted him to go harder and faster. He took her right to the edge of the climax three times before she became so frenzied that she clawed his back and begged.

"I'm going to die if…"

He increased the rhythm.

"Oh. My. Sweet. Lord." She could force out one word at a time and panted hard between them.

Natalie was not a virgin, but she was damn sure in strange territory because when he growled her name and settled his face into her neck, her body was totally satisfied. Satisfied in a way that it had never known before, not even the first time they'd had sex after the party.

He shifted to one side and drew her close, reached up, and pulled a throw from the sofa and wrapped it around them both.

"That was incredible!" He slipped the pillow out from beneath her and tossed it across the room. "I want to hold you all night right here."

"Until the baby monitor wakes us, that sounds like a plan," she said sleepily.

He nuzzled his face into her neck. "I dreamed about this so many times when I was over there."

"I dreamed about this when you were over there. I wonder if it was on the same nights."

She brushed a sweet kiss across his lips and shut her eyes.

Chapter 15

THE CAPTAIN CLAMPED A HAND ON LUCAS'S SHOULDER. "You will not be going out today on the reconnaissance mission. We've got a situation that you need to monitor."

"Yes, sir," Lucas saluted.

Drew gave him a thumbs-up sign as the jeep pulled out of the gates. He waved and before he got to the building where the computers were set up, he heard the blast.

"No! No!" His feet were like lead as he ran toward the gate.

"I can't tell Natalie," he screamed over and over.

Natalie sat up so fast that she pulled the cover from Lucas and the room did a couple of hard spins before she got it under control. Lucas had his hands over his eyes and kept mumbling, "I can't tell Natalie."

According to the clock on the wall it was four o'clock and the sounds coming from the baby monitor said that Joshua was fidgeting in his sleep. He'd slept right through his two o'clock feeding for the first time in his life.

She shook Lucas on the shoulder. "Tell me what?"

"Captain, he can't be dead. I can't tell Natalie."

She shook him harder. "Wake up, Lucas. It's a nightmare."

He sat up and his eyes were open but the Christmas tree wasn't what he was seeing. She could tell from the expression on his face and the tears streaming down his cheeks that he was looking right at the explosion that killed Drew.

"Two vehicles went out. I was supposed to be in the one with Drew," he said in a hollow voice.

She walked on her knees until she was in front of him. "Lucas, look at me. You are home. I'm right here. I know Drew is dead. You don't have to tell me."

He blinked rapidly half a dozen times. "Natalie? How did you get here? Drew is dead? I'm sorry."

She put her arms around him and hugged him tightly. "You are home, Lucas. It was just a nightmare. Do you have them often?"

"Almost every night," he whispered.

The baby monitor noise went from whimpers to full-fledged demands.

"Sounds like we'd better fix a bottle," he said.

"You make the bottle. I'll get him changed. Meet you in the den?"

He rubbed his eyes and nodded.

She wrapped the soft throw around her like a sari and padded barefoot down the hall to her bedroom. She hurriedly threw it on her bed, grabbed a pair of underpants and a long nightshirt from her suitcase, and put them on before she picked Joshua up.

"Sorry about that, son. We'll get a fresh diaper and then go look at the Christmas tree lights. Will that make up for me being so slow?"

He wailed out his answer, kicking and flailing his arms the whole time she changed him. She met Lucas halfway down the hall. He was dressed in brown and ecru plaid lounging pants and a thermal undershirt that stretched over his broad shoulders and looked sexy as hell. Strangely enough, the baby bottle in his hand didn't take away a bit of the sexiness.

"Sounds like he's ready for this," Lucas said.

She took it from him and they returned to the living room where she sat down in a recliner. Joshua sucked hard, eyes wide open and staring up at her. "Hey, boy." She laughed. "Don't you look at me in that tone, young man. It'll get you grounded from Henry reading to you this morning."

Lucas eased down into the rocker close to her and chuckled. "That'd be punishing Henry more than Josh."

"It probably would. Now tell me about this dream you keep having," she said.

He hesitated a full three minutes.

"It helps to talk things through, Lucas," she said.

"It's just reliving that day when Drew died. Only it happens in different ways. Sometimes it's me running out to the gate when I heard the explosion. Sometimes it's me sitting in front of that computer knowing that you are going to pop up any minute. And sometimes it's me with the other guys standing at attention when they loaded what was left of him on the plane to send him home. But it always ends the same way with me waking up in a cold sweat because I don't want to tell you that he's dead," Lucas said.

The television had been left on all night and now there was a segment of gospel videos playing. Alan Jackson was singing "I Want To Stroll Over Heaven With You."

"That song was played at his funeral," she said.

"Tell me about it."

"Not much to tell. It was closed casket. The church was packed and I wasn't the only woman weeping, even though we sobbed for different reasons when that song played at the end. It was military with full honors. I jumped every time the guns fired and felt cheated when they gave the flag to his oldest sister," she said honestly.

"He would have wanted you to have it," Lucas said seriously. "Maybe someday she'll give it to Josh."

Natalie shook her head. "Whole town of Silverton knows that Josh is Drew's son, but his sisters won't believe it. I intend to tell him that his father was a hero."

"He should know that his father was a hero," Lucas said.

Joshua's eyes shifted from Natalie to Lucas, and he smiled around the bottle nipple.

"Look at that charmer. He doesn't want to be grounded from Henry's reading sessions," she said.

Lucas reached across the space between them and touched Joshua's hand. He immediately wrapped his chubby hand around Lucas's finger and held on tightly.

"He's telling me he's sorry that he looked at you in that tone, but the cowboys on Cedar Hill are cranky when they get hungry. He says it won't happen again." Lucas said.

On Tuesday evening the guys left after the six o'clock news. Joshua had fallen asleep in his swing, and Lucas pulled Natalie down into his lap in the recliner when she walked past him. She fit well in his arms, like she was made special just for him. He tangled his hand in her hair and massaged her scalp.

She groaned. "Lord, that feels good."

"I've got ulterior motives." His found hers in a hard, steamy kiss.

"I like your motives," she whispered.

"Grab that monitor and we'll take our motives to the bedroom," he said.

She reached for it and his phone rang.

"Well, shit!" he grouched.

He fished it from his shirt pocket and looked at the caller ID. "Got to take it. It's Gramps. Hello."

"Did I interrupt anything?" Henry chuckled. "There's a cow down in the pasture out by the church. Looks to me like she's havin' trouble birthin' a calf. I swear those crazy heifers don't have a lick of sense. We know when they need to be bred so they'll throw them calves in the spring instead of in the worst storm that Texas has seen in years. But do them cows ask me before they go screwing around? No, sir, they do not!"

"I'll holler at Grady and go see about her," Lucas said.

"You and Natalie can go. I'll come back and watch Joshua."

"You stay put. We'll take care of her," Lucas said.

"Cow or woman?" Natalie asked.

"Heifer, not hussy." Lucas kissed her on the cheek. "I might just shoot her."

"Don't you dare!" Natalie said.

"Can I borrow your pink pistol?"

She shook her head. "Hell, no! Don't nobody use that gun but me. She wouldn't even shoot straight if someone else used her."

Grady was watching reruns of *NCIS* on television and grumbled about having to go back out in the cold.

"Damned old cow. Just like a woman to have a baby at the wrong time of year and at night at that."

Lucas had been doing something a whole lot more fun than watching reruns, so he had a bigger excuse to bitch, but he didn't say a word. All three of the guys were so deep into matchmaking that they didn't need an extra scrap of encouragement. He liked Josh and he really, really liked Natalie. Hell, he could see himself spending the rest of his life with her right there on the ranch. But convincing her that Josh would get a fair shake out of the deal wouldn't be easy.

—⁓—

Natalie awoke on Wednesday morning to find a note from Lucas on the pillow beside her.

> *Got in after midnight. Got a brand-new bull calf in the barn. Josh will have to see him and decide which calf he wants to claim as his own. Didn't want to wake you, so I'll see you at breakfast.*

It was signed with the letter *L.*

She smiled as she read it. Sure, the *L* stood for Lucas, but wouldn't it be something if it really was the *L*-word?

The morning drug by like a lazy old slug. At breakfast Lucas said that he and Jack had to make a trip into Sherman for tractor parts and that the hired hands were doing all the feeding that morning. She baked two extra pies and made six-dozen peanut butter cookies just to have something to do. Laundry was caught up; house was spotless; Joshua was fed; and Henry was busy entertaining him.

When the last cookies came out of the oven she still had an hour before time for dinner, so she took her pistol apart and cleaned it. She intended to show Lucas that she was a damn fine shot. Her mother didn't consider target practice wasting ammo, so it wasn't a sin to fire at something stationary instead of something dangerous or moving.

Her phone rang when she had the gun in pieces. She didn't have to look at the ID to know that it was her mother.

"Hello," she said cautiously. Surely Debra couldn't hear that she'd had sex, unprotected sex at that, over the phone, could she?

"What are you doing?"

"Cleaning my pistol," Natalie said.

"Why? Did you fire it?" Debra asked.

"Killed a coyote a few days ago and haven't had time to clean it until now. I baked two pecan pies and a bunch of cookies this morning."

"Talk to me about ranchin'. You know the kitchen ain't my thing. What's going on there?"

"Just ranchin'," Natalie answered.

"And my grandson? Is he missing me?"

"Yes, ma'am. He whines at the door for you every day. Momma, he's not even three months old yet. He don't know…"

Debra cleared her throat. "Much more of that sass and I'll be out there by dark and haul you both back here where you belong. Did you sleep with Lucas?"

Natalie dropped the grip to the pistol and had to do some fancy grabbing to keep it from hitting the floor. "Why in the hell would you ask that?"

"I hear something in your voice that's never been there before. It scares me, Natalie Joy," Debra said.

"You haven't second-named me in years," Natalie said.

"Haven't had to. Promise me you'll be careful," Debra said.

"I promise. And remember I brought my pistol."

Debra laughed. "Like I told you when you started dating, I keep two shovels all sharpened. Anybody hurts you, we'll take care of the bodies and God will look the other way."

"I love you, Momma," Natalie said.

After she talked to her mother, she finished cleaning her gun, put it all back together, and had dinner on the table when the guys wandered in the back door.

Lucas brushed his fingers across hers as he passed her in the kitchen.

She sniffed the air.

Skunk!

And it wasn't far away. She sure hoped it wasn't anywhere near those puppies. She grabbed up her gun and headed outside.

"Watch the baby and shut the door," she yelled.

Lucas ignored her orders and reached for his coat.

"Skunk," Henry said.

"Reckon we ought to go help her?" Grady asked.

"Hell, no!" Jack answered. "She told us to watch the baby. She's got a gun and if they get sprayed they can be miserable together."

"Animals again," Henry said.

"I tell you it's Lucas. They're all comin' around because

he's home. It's crazy but it's the only thing that makes sense," Grady said.

"It ain't Lucas. It's Joshua," Jack said. "We've got this precious baby with us. He's a blessing and the animals know it. Hazel is the one that put me on to the idea before you tell me I'm crazy and ask me if I'm seeing ghosts and hearing voices. It's like they all have to come see what is happening since Joshua came to the ranch. I wouldn't be surprised if that coyote that Natalie shot wasn't after the puppies at all, but he was just the first visitor to come check out Joshua."

Henry cleared his throat and wiped a stray tear away from his eyes. "I was tellin' Ella all about the crazy animals happenin's last night after I got into bed and I got the same message from her. She said that we should count our blessings and that the animals were trying to make us see that Joshua is special."

"Sounds kind of hinky, don't, it?" Grady asked.

"It is hinky. But we all got to admit that something is going on and that this little boy was destined to be raised up on this ranch. I'll prove it all come tomorrow morning," Henry said.

"How's that?" Grady asked.

"You just wait and watch. I'll prove that my Ella Jo is right."

Skunks are nocturnal. They sleep in the day and come out to feed, breed, and play at night. To see one in the day sometimes meant it was sick or rabid. It was a big old fellow and it was headed straight for the dog pens when Natalie located it.

She took aim and fired once. It dropped and didn't even quiver.

"Good shootin'," Lucas said behind her.

She jumped and spun around. "You scared the shit out of me."

"Sorry. Come on in the house. We'll let him alone until after dinner and then me and Grady will dispose of it. I reckon something was wrong with it if it was out prowling around in daylight."

"It stinks. That's enough wrong with it for me," she said.

"You sound like you are speaking from experience."

"I sure am." She laced her fingers in his and headed back toward the house. "I was target shootin' once and one got me square on the jean legs. The denim did not keep the smell from getting into my skin and Momma tried everything in the world to get it out but I stunk for a whole week. Thank goodness it was in the summertime because I would have refused to go to school. Took a bad ribbin' from my brothers, and Drew was a real son of a bitch."

"Oh, the precious Drew had a fault?" Lucas asked.

"That year he didn't know when to shut up. I used to tell him that knowing when to hush would be the hardest lesson he ever learned. I'm not sure he ever did. We've been out here amongst the smell. Think we'd best take a shower before I serve up dinner."

"It's not that bad. We can eat and shower together later."

But they didn't take a shower together or make love that night. Their closest neighbor, two miles away, slid off the road into a ditch. And all four guys left before the six o'clock news to help. Henry drove the pickup and Lucas took the biggest tractor they owned.

At ten o'clock he called her to say that the neighbor and his wife had to be taken to the hospital in Denison, so he and Jack followed the ambulance. If they were treated and released, then they'd need a ride home.

"I'm sorry," he said.

"It's all part of ranchin'," she said.

On Thursday morning she woke up to another note.

We brought them home. Wilbur has a few stitches on his head. Livvy has a twisted ankle. But it was midnight when we got home. See you at breakfast.

L

The rest of the day was a real bitch. The water to the washing machine froze up. She was busy thawing it out with her hair dryer and almost burned the chocolate chip cookies. Joshua fussed all day and wanted to be held.

"Henry has spoiled you rotten to constant attention." She rewound his swing but he still fussed.

"Oh, all right," she said as she took him out and carried him on her hip as she folded laundry with one hand.

Henry had taken a pie and two dozen cookies with him and left right after breakfast to go over to the neighbors and sit with them all morning. Natalie wished she'd sent Joshua with him by the time the day was done.

Lucas came in that evening and one look at him said that his day hadn't been a bit better. So much for a shower and wild sex that night. She was worn out from a fussy baby all day. He was tired to the bone from hard work. They ate supper in silence and then Henry brought out the whiskey bottle.

"I'm havin' a drink." His tone dared them to argue with him.

"I'll have a beer." Grady went to the refrigerator. "Jack? Lucas?"

They both nodded.

No one asked her if she wanted anything. Maybe she still smelled like skunk or maybe she was a big part of the family and they thought she'd speak up if she wanted something or maybe Lucas was pissed at her about something. Even the cute little notes, which seemed more explanatory than sweet right then, didn't make up for the fact that he'd been downright standoffish since she shot the skunk.

She whipped around to see where Lucas was to find four sour-faced men at the table, three with beers and one with a shot of whiskey.

"Pour two fingers of whiskey and join us," Henry said.

She picked up the Jack Daniel's and poured a healthy dose into a water glass.

"Livvy and Wilbur drove me crazy bitchin' about how long it took the doctor to see them at the hospital. I wished I hadn't even brought them a pie or the cookies. I even put one of them frozen dinners in the oven so Livvy could sit in her rockin' chair, and she wouldn't eat it. I bet Josh missed me, didn't he?" Henry said. "Now I'm in a pissy mood. Lucas, I want you to drive me around the ranch."

She sipped the whiskey. It was warm going down, but it didn't help her mood. It would take at least five tequila shots to chase the demons from her that evening and there wasn't anything but bourbon and beer in the house.

"Damned old tractor is about to drive us to cussin'," Grady said.

"About? I'm ready to shoot the damn thing like Natalie did the skunk," Lucas snapped.

"Buy a new one. Lord, boy, you've got enough money to buy a fleet of damn tractors," Jack said. "He's a tightwad, Natalie. Won't spend a dime unless it's so necessary he can't get out of it."

"He sounds just like my dad." She tossed back the rest of the whiskey.

"Come on, Lucas. We're going for a drive. Ain't neither one of us fit for anyone's company. Poor little old Josh would think we was both old bears," Henry declared.

Jack finished off his beer with a long gulp. "See you kids in the morning."

Grady sat there a few more minutes. "Weatherman says there's a fresh storm brewing up north and coming this way. Might as well suck it up and get ready for another blast. He says this time there'll be at least three inches."

"Well, shit! That means the coyotes will come closer because they can't find food, and we'll have to watch the young calves, and those pesky pups might crawl out of the fence again. They think they're big enough to hunt with the big dogs already," Lucas said.

"I'm leaving too. See you tomorrow morning." Grady put on his coat and hat and left.

Henry put on his coat and Natalie watched him and Lucas both leave. She turned on the television and settled into Henry's recliner with Joshua in her lap. In thirty minutes the back door slammed. From the noises, she heard Lucas hang up his coat, stop to pet and talk to the momma cat, and then pad to the living room in his socked feet.

"I'm not your dad," Lucas said.

"I didn't say you were. I said that you sounded like him. He doesn't spend money when it's not necessary either."

His chin shot up so high that she could see up his nose. "I'm not a tightwad."

"I didn't say you were. Don't take it out on me because your tractor is giving you fits. Joshua gave me fits today because your grandfather has him spoiled rotten, and I didn't take it out on you," she snapped.

"I'm not taking anything out on you," he said.

"Yes, you are, and I did not say that you were my dad," Natalie countered.

"I'm not Drew, and I'm not your dad. I'm just me. Take me or leave me, but don't be making me into someone that I'm not," he said.

"You need to get in a better mood or I'm out of here. I don't have to put up with this shit," she said.

He pushed the chair back so quick that it crashed on the hardwood floor and Joshua started to cry. "Don't you threaten me, woman!"

"Don't you call me *woman*. I've got a name. Either use it or don't even talk to me." She stood up, put Joshua in his swing, and turned around. He was standing there, arms hanging limp and anger on his face. She took two steps and her breast brushed against his chest. The heat was still there when she touched him even when they were fighting. Yes, ma'am, Mother Nature was a real bitch.

"Well, that's just what you are, a woman!" he said.

"Darlin', I am not just a woman. I'm a big cup of

sass, covered in ornery sauce, with a splash of bitch, and a dash of pure old stubbornness thrown in for good luck. You remember that next time you think you can outshoot or outargue me," she said.

Joshua set up a howl, but she ignored it and continued to stare at Lucas.

"Get your baby. He's crying," Lucas said and stormed out of the kitchen.

She heard the shower running, but she'd be stripped naked and thrown out in the snow before she opened the bathroom door. She picked up Joshua and sat down in the rocking chair. He stopped crying and stuck his thumb in his mouth.

She removed it and said, "Cowboys don't suck their thumbs. They throw fits and pout, but they don't suck their thumb."

He popped it right back in his mouth when she let go of it.

"Maybe you're going to be an artist or a ballet dancer instead of a cowboy," she said.

"The hell he is," Lucas said from the hallway.

"He's my kid, as you so recently pointed out. And he can be anything he wants to be. If he wants to wear tights, cute little ballet shoes, and dance then he damn sure will," she said.

"I'm not fighting with you about this tonight, Natalie. I'm going to bed. I'll collect on that shower later."

"And I'll collect on the lovemaking, but tonight I don't even want to look at you," she said.

"The feeling is mutual." He turned around and went back to his room.

Natalie wanted to laugh or cry but she did neither.

Instead she got her baby to sleep and took a long shower. She didn't realize how stressed she was until the hot water jets beat the tension from her muscles.

Natalie was asleep within seconds after her head hit the pillow. At two o'clock the baby woke up for his feeding and she changed him, made a bottle, and rocked him back to sleep. She'd barely gotten back in bed when she heard Lucas yelling, "No! No! I can't tell Natalie."

She bailed out of bed and ran down the hall. She threw open the door to find him sitting up in bed, glazed look in his eyes, and shivering from head to toe. She crawled into the bed with him, put a hand on each cheek, and said, "Lucas, it's a nightmare. Wake up, honey. Open your eyes for real."

"Natalie?" He blinked.

"I'm right here," she said.

He grabbed her in a tight hug and buried his face in her neck. "Don't ever leave me, Natalie. Hold me."

"I'll stay, but you hold me," she said.

He picked her up and set her to one side, pushed her back on the pillows, and slipped an arm under her. He pulled her to his side and hugged her so close that she thought she'd smother. The shivering stopped and his eyes fluttered shut.

Chapter 16

"WHEN DID YOU START HAVING THESE NIGHTMARES?" Natalie asked the next morning as they worked together in the kitchen. She browned sausage in a cast-iron skillet while he started the coffee brewing and set the plates out on the bar.

"I had a few over there, but since I've come home, they've been almost every night. I'm beginning to doubt that they'll ever go away."

Henry pushed the back door open and stomped the snow off his boots. "You doubt what?" A grin deepened the wrinkles around his eyes when he saw them hugged up together.

"Is it ever going to warm up and melt all this ice and snow?" Natalie asked to get Henry talking about something else.

"Oh, it will one of these days. In a few months we'll forget all about the snow and the mess and we'll all be bitchin' about the summer heat. I heard poppin' down at my place last night that sounded like shotgun blasts. It was limbs breakin' off and fallin' to the ground. When it does thaw out, we're going to have a lot of dead limbs layin' on the ground. It'll take the work crew a month just to get the place back in some kind of order. What's for breakfast this morning?"

"Ham and eggs, hash browns, and biscuits. Anything else you want?" Natalie asked.

"Ask me what I want. It won't have anything to do with food," Lucas whispered.

She spun out of his embrace and picked up an iron skillet.

"Looks like you might ought to sit down and stop teasing her." Henry chuckled. "Where's Josh?"

Before she could answer the baby monitor said that he was awake and hungry. "Guess he's awake now," she said.

"You go on with breakfast. I'll take care of him," Lucas said.

"Diaper?" She raised an eyebrow.

"You don't think I know how to change a baby?"

She smiled. "I'll have a bottle ready when you get back with him."

"And I'll sit in the rocking chair and feed him," Henry said. "Wouldn't want you to burn my ham and eggs."

Lucas picked Joshua up from the crib and laid him on Natalie's bed. "Good mornin', cowboy. Good grief, feller, you are wet from the hide out. No wonder you're trying to eat your fists. All that milk you had last night has run straight through you. I bet your poor little tummy thinks it's starving. Okay, now be still and I'll get you all changed and fixed up for the day. We'll show your mommy that two cowboys can take care of anything."

He unzipped Josh's pajamas and peeled them off his body, then pulled the tape on the diaper. He'd barely gotten the new one under his bottom when the baby let a fountain loose that hit Lucas right in the chest before he could get the diaper thrown up over the baby.

"Got quite an aim there, cowboy. When I get you all

changed, we'll have to change me before we go find your breakfast." Lucas laughed.

He chose a cute little outfit with a stick horse appliquéd on the front and a pair of white socks for Josh to wear that day. It bothered Lucas that Natalie and Josh were still living out of a suitcase. He made a mental note to tell her to unpack her things and hang them in the closet where they belonged. When Josh was fully dressed, Lucas picked him up and kissed him on the forehead.

Josh looked up at him. Dark brown eyes met the same color eyes as man and baby bonded in the distance from one bedroom to the other. "I see why the rumors got started. I swear you do have my eyes, but then your daddy had the same color as I do. He was a hero, Josh. You can grow up proud that he is your daddy."

Lucas laid Josh on his bed and changed shirts. "Your dad was my best friend over in Kuwait. And he was your mommy's best friend too. He would have loved to see you, but he died before you were even born."

He picked the baby back up and held him against his chest. When he reached the kitchen, Henry was grinning so big it looked like his face would split. Natalie's eyes were misty and she was biting her upper lip.

"What?" he asked.

"Guess Mister Josh sprayed you down," Henry said. "I remember the first time you did that to me."

"How did you know that?"

"Heard it all on that contraption over there on the cabinet," Henry said.

Lucas's face turned instantly hot. What he'd said to the baby wasn't supposed to be broadcast all over the house.

"We'll have to be careful when we're telling secrets, cowboy. Your momma has ears in the back of her head!"

Natalie reached for Josh and hugged him tightly against her. He wiggled, squirmed, and fussed. "Good morning, sweetheart. Henry is going to feed you breakfast. You be good and eat it all."

"That'd be Gramps to Josh," Henry said.

"Humor him," Lucas said softly.

"Then Gramps, here's the bottle and here's the baby," Natalie said.

Jack came through the back door, but before he could close it, the puppies came rushing in again. The momma cat hissed and fluffed up to twice her normal size. She stood between the laundry basket where her babies were squirming and the puppies with a wicked gleam in her eye and screaming at the pups in a language that Natalie was glad she couldn't understand.

They all took off across the kitchen floor, yelping and howling, trying to get traction and sliding on their bellies all the way to the den where they hid under the leg rest of Henry's recliner.

"Damn dogs," Jack cussed as he and Grady gathered them up again.

Henry chuckled.

"What's so funny?" Jack fussed.

"Provin' my point real good. Y'all might want to look out in the front yard. I see something out there and I believe old Crankston's goats are back too." Henry laughed.

"I'll be glad when the weather clears up," Grady declared.

"It'll all be fine," Henry said. "It'll all be just fine after this day."

"You been nippin' in that whiskey too much," Lucas said.

"Now, Ella Jo never did see me drunk and she ain't goin' to this season neither," Henry declared. "And I got a little job for you today, after y'all go out there and pen up them goats before they eat more of our decorations. You're going to take Joshua and let him see all the animals on the ranch. The puppies and the cows in the barn, and even drive him up to Crankston's place and let him look at the goats and the jackass from the fence."

"Why would I do that?" Lucas asked.

"Because I'm old and Ella Jo done told me that's what she wants you to do for Christmas. So you're going to do it," Henry said.

"Just do it if it'll make him happy," Natalie whispered.

"Okay, Gramps, if it's important to you."

"It is and y'all got to go by y'all's self. No one else can go with you. Just you and Joshua. Bundle him up real good. It's cold out there," Henry said.

"I've got plenty to do to keep me busy. I'd welcome thirty minutes without a fussy baby this morning," Natalie said.

———

After supper that evening, the guys hung around until the six o'clock news was over and then lingered until after eight before they finally left.

"For three old fellers who were pushin' so hard yesterday, they've sure managed to keep us apart today," Lucas said.

"They've got something up their sleeves. You can bet

on it. I'm going to give Josh his bath and get him ready for bed," Natalie agreed.

"Josh, not Joshua?" Lucas asked.

"Slip of the tongue," she said.

"I wondered if you'd catch it. He really is a Josh, Natalie. Joshua sounds like a preacher or a professor. Josh sounds like a rancher or a bull rider."

"That's what Henry told me," she said.

"Will you sleep with me tonight? After you crawled in with me last night, the dream stopped." He changed the subject so quickly that she was taken aback.

She hesitated.

He threw an arm around her shoulder and hugged her tightly. "I'm worn completely out, sweet cheeks. Those old codgers kept me at the grindstone all day after I took Josh for his morning zoo trip. He loves going to see the animals, and watching him smile and coo sure put me in a better mood. I agree with you. The guys have got something up their sleeves. I'm asking you to let me hold you and sleep with you and that's all for tonight."

She barely tilted her head, but that was enough to keep the grin on his face.

"When you get finished giving the baby a bath, I'll hold him and feed him while you get a shower. Then I'll take one and we'll cuddle up here on the couch and watch television until bedtime. Deal?"

"Sounds good to me," she said. "But after this day I might want a long bubble bath. I probably won't have time to do much in the way of beautification tomorrow."

Lucas looked up from the recliner. "What's tomorrow?"

"Your Angus Association party."

"Well, shit! I promised to take you shopping again

for a pretty dress. I'm sorry, Natalie. We should've done that this evening."

"No need to apologize. I'll wear something in my closet." She could hardly keep the excitement of the surprise out of her voice.

"Well, sweet cheeks, you could wear that nightshirt you had on last night and look better than anyone else there," he said.

"Okay, okay, you can call me darlin'. Sweet cheeks sounds so…" She couldn't find the right word.

"Redneck?"

"That would be high class compared to what I was thinking. I'm taking this boy to the bathtub and then it's my turn," she said.

"Take as long as you want in the bathroom. Me and Josh will be fine, but you will always be sweet cheeks to me." He yawned.

Josh screamed like she was beating him the whole bath. He kicked and yelled while she dressed him and no amount of sweet-talk or even kisses appeased him.

"Looks like you got your momma's temper," Lucas said from the doorway. "I went ahead and got the bottle ready when I heard the fit."

She handed Lucas the baby when she finished dressing him. Josh stared up into Lucas's eyes and stopped crying immediately. Lucas shoved the bottle in his mouth, and the little rascal had the nerve to grin around the nipple.

—◦—

Bubbles looked like heavy foam on a glass of cold beer when she sank down in the claw-foot tub. She leaned back on a towel and sighed. Did Hazel ever feel like she was worn to a frazzle after a day in the house?

She opened her eyes when the door hinges squeaked. Joshua wasn't crying, so what could Lucas need?

He put the lid down on the toilet and sat down. "Those teeth are worrying him to death. I rubbed a little whiskey on them. He shuddered and went right to sleep."

She sat straight up. "You put what in his mouth?"

"Whiskey. I called Gramps and he said that was better than any of the junk you buy on the market. I'm not making an alcoholic out of him just by rubbing it on his gums, so don't go all pink pistol on me," Lucas said.

He picked up the washcloth and said, "Lean forward and let me do your back."

She leaned. "Pink pistol?"

"Sounded better than going ape shit on me, didn't it?"

He massaged her back with the soapy cloth until the kinks were out and she felt like a wet spaghetti noodle. When she straightened up, he was holding a sprig of mistletoe over her head.

She stretched and he bent. Their lips met in a kiss that blended two souls together as tightly as if they'd been superglued.

"Thank you," she said.

"For the back scrubbin' or the kissin'?" he asked.

"Both," she said.

"Does television noises wake Josh up?" he asked.

"That came out of the clear blue, but nothing much bothers him after he's asleep," she said.

"I moved his crib into my room. It's on your side of the bed. Thought we'd just snuggle up and watch a movie in my bedroom until we fall asleep," he said.

Chapter 17

Natalie worried that she might have overdone the whole dolled up issue as she got dressed for the Red River Angus Association Christmas party that evening. Over on her side of Texas, dolled up might mean something altogether different than it did in the north central part of the state.

"But it's what I bought and since it's all I've got other than jeans and boots and two Sunday dresses, it's what I'll have to wear," she told Joshua as she put the finishing touches on her hair and makeup.

Someone knocked softly on the door and then it opened just a crack. "The guys are about to start a stampede back here to get Josh. Mind if I take him up front?" Lucas asked.

She swung the door the rest of the way open, started at Lucas's shiny black boots and then let her eyes slowly travel upward. Jeans creased and stacked up over his boot tops perfectly, white Western shirt starched and ironed without a single wrinkle, dress jacket with a Western-cut yoke that hugged his frame, freshly shaven, and hair long enough to slick back with a little mousse.

"Well, well, you sure do dress up real fine." She was astonished that her voice sounded normal. Her insides were humming so loudly that she figured it would affect her tone for sure.

"And you, ma'am, look like you just walked off a

model's runway. God, Natalie, you are absolutely stunning," he said.

She turned around slowly. The lace dress had a high Victorian collar and long-fitted sleeves but the back had a heart-shaped cutout that started at the collar and ended with a point just above her bra. The hanky hem flounced over the tops of her boots and when she moved the lace swayed to the sides showing off the brown crosses on her boots.

"We can't go," he said hoarsely.

"What! I bought all this for the party and we can't go? Why?"

The corners of his mouth turned up slightly. "Because I will lose you. One of those good-lookin' cowboys will sweep you off your feet and I'll be left with nothing but a broken heart and a handful of beautiful memories."

She wrapped her arms around his neck and kissed him hard. "Now that's a lovely line if I ever heard one."

"Ain't no line," he said. "It's the God's honest solid truth. Promise you won't leave me stranded and run off with one of those rich cowboys."

"Promise you won't leave me and run off with one of those cheerleaders," she shot right back.

He stuck out his hand. "Shake on it."

She put her hand in his and he pulled her to him. Her body molded against his and he gently cupped her cheeks with his palms, leaned down just slightly, and kissed her deeply, exploring her lips and her mouth.

"Keep that in mind all evening," he whispered when he broke the kiss and stepped back. "Josh, your momma will be the prettiest woman at the party. The only reason she'll come home with this ugly old cowboy is because she wouldn't want to leave you behind."

"Oh, hush. Ugly, my ass." She blushed.

"Now you are telling lies. Your ass is not ugly. Matter-of-fact, I think it's pretty damn cute," he teased.

"And yours looks so fine tonight that maybe I'd best take along my pistol to keep the women from carryin' you off to do wicked things to your body," she flirted.

Lucas chuckled. "If that's a compliment, then thank you."

He crossed the room in a couple of long strides and picked up the baby. "Smells like you've already had your bath, Josh. Don't let those old farts spoil you too much, and you tell them if you get tired of all that smothering." He cradled the baby in one arm and crooked the other one toward Natalie.

She slipped her arm through it and together they went up the hall and into the den where Henry, Grady, and Jack all waited.

Grady whistled and said, "You two look like you're goin' to a weddin', not a party."

Henry chuckled. "And Natalie could be the bride in that dress. You better strap on your six-gun so them other guys will know that you ain't going to abide no funny business, Lucas."

Jack stood up and took the baby from Lucas. "Y'all have a good time and don't hurry home. We'll have lots of fun takin' care of Josh. And Natalie, you look like a million dollars. Lucas, you'd best stick to her like glue, or you could lose her tonight."

"Yes, sir," Lucas said.

"Your coat?" Lucas looked at Natalie.

She nodded toward the back of the rocking chair. He picked up the cape and swung it around her shoulders.

"Oh my Lord!" Henry gasped. "Now she looks like a queen. She needs one of them fancy diamond things in her hair."

"No, she needs a good-lookin' buff-colored cowgirl hat," Grady said.

"With a diamond hatband. That'd be a mighty fine Christmas present for her." Henry nodded.

———

"It worked," Henry said the minute they were out of the door.

"What worked?" Jack asked.

"It's the baby just like you thought and just like Hazel said and Ella Jo told me. I made Lucas take me for a ride and them feisty hounds got out again and come runnin' right in here and hid under my chair and Crankston's goats got out of their pen and came right over here. I made him take Joshua to see the animals and not a one got out today, and Crankston's old goats and jackass stayed home too. So Hazel and Ella Jo was right. It's this precious baby that was drawin' the animals."

"It was the storm," Grady argued.

"You want to chase down dogs and goats, I can go with Lucas tomorrow and leave Joshua at home." Henry narrowed his eyes. "It's a Christmas thing, and we was just too dense to see it. We was given this special little boy to live on the ranch with us, and now we got to make sure we make them two kids see that they was made for each other."

"That much I'll agree with." Grady nodded.

—ᘏᗢᘏ—

Lucas settled Natalie into the passenger seat of his truck and whistled "I Only Want You for Christmas" as he rounded the tailgate and opened the driver's door. "Tie a ribbon around yourself," he singsonged as he started the engine.

"What color and where?" she asked.

They were flirting like teenagers and it felt even better than good—it felt right.

"Anywhere, but it really should be bright red."

"How many folks will be at this party?"

"Maybe a hundred. There's about fifty members, and the party is for member and guest. Top is one hundred, low count would be around ninety. You'll meet Colton, Greg, and Mason. The four of us joined the association at the same time. Rest of the group is quite a bit older than we are. Dad is a member, but he quit going to the social functions when I joined. He hated them anyway. He's a big voice in the association and goes to all the meetings but not the parties. Anyway, we four guys formed a friendship. Greg Adams is from over around Ravenna. Colton is the billionaire cowboy who lives up close to Ambrose, and then Mason Harper is from out east of Whitewright."

"All unmarried?"

"Until Colton married last spring. The women were chasin' him for his money, so his folks and his best friend cooked up the idea that a woman who worked on the ranch would pretend to be his girlfriend. They even went so far as to get a big gaudy engagement ring to make it look real. It backfired and he fell in love with her. I can't wait to meet her. Hazel says that she doesn't give a damn about money and can run all the equipment on the ranch as well as Colton."

"And Greg?"

"Darlin', it'll take a helluva woman to bring him to the altar. That cowboy is gun-shy when it comes to women. He lives, breathes, and eats ranchin', and there ain't many women out there who'd put up with that."

"My momma does," Natalie said.

"And so do you. That's why I intend to keep you as far away from Greg tonight as possible." He laughed.

"And who was the other one—Matthew?"

"Mason. He was married and his wife passed on when his girls were barely a year old. He's got twin girls, Lily and Gabby. I'm not sure he'll ever find a woman who would take on the raisin' of those two. Lord, they could scale a glass wall on a rainy day. What one can't think of the other can, and it's never any good. You can talk to him all you want. I'm not a bit afraid of that cowboy taking you away because you'd never trust those two little heathens around Josh."

Natalie turned in her seat. "Are you telling me who and who not to talk to tonight, Lucas Allen?"

He smiled. "I'm not that stupid. You might have that pistol strapped to the inside of your leg."

She giggled and turned back. "I'll talk to whomever I so please, but rest assured there won't be a one of them that turns my insides to a boiling pot of hormones every time they touch my skin like you do."

He reached across the console and laid a hand on her thigh. "Like this."

She picked it up and put it back on the steering wheel.

"Just like that, but you keep your eyes on the road and your hands on the wheel. I didn't buy this dress and boots to get them all nasty helping you get a truck out of the ditch."

———∿∿∿———

The country club was already buzzing when Lucas and Natalie arrived. He removed her cape and handed it to a coat lady behind a counter and ushered Natalie toward the bar with his hand on the small of her back.

She was looking ahead and not paying a bit of attention to her surroundings when his hand slipped around her waist and they came to a stop in the middle of a group of people. He introduced her to Mason Harper and Greg Adams. Both did one of those traveling looks that started at her boots and went to her face, hesitating just a second longer at breast level.

"We heard that you brought a woman and a son home from the war. We didn't expect her to be so tall or so…" Harper paused.

"Or so Texan?" Lucas finished for him.

"Where are you from, darlin'?" Greg asked.

"Silverton. Out in the Panhandle."

"Natalie Clark. Kin to Isaac Clark?"

"That would be my brother." Natalie smiled at Greg. Lucas had been right. He was a cowboy from his boots to his drawl.

"Met him at the statewide Angus meeting last fall," Greg said. "Small world. You'll have to meet my grandmother, Clarice, before the night is done."

"I'd love to," Natalie said.

"So what do you think of our part of the state?" Mason asked.

"Texas is Texas. Land changes. People, not so much. Ranchers, never," she answered.

"They ought to put that on a bumper sticker," a woman said as she and another cowboy joined the group.

"Y'all meet my wife, Laura. I'm Colton Nelson from over around Ambrose," he said.

Laura extended her hand. "I heard that Lucas brought home a bride and a baby."

Natalie shook and fought a blush. "Rumors do travel fast."

"We'll have to get together and have a visit when this weather clears off. You can bring your son. Joshua, right?"

Natalie nodded.

"We're having a baby in May. You can give me some pointers. I've never been around little babies in my whole life, but I'm looking forward to being a mother," Laura said.

"We're on our way to the bar. Can we get anyone anything?" Lucas asked.

Mason held up a beer. Greg nodded toward a glass holding whiskey sitting on the table. Colton shook his head. "We'll be drinking club soda this evening or sweet tea. Since Laura can't drink until the baby is born, I've given it up too."

"It was nice meeting y'all," Natalie said as Lucas led her away.

They had both claimed a bar stool before she realized that she'd sat down beside Sonia. That night her blond hair was twisted up into a crown of curls with red baby rose buds worked into the curls. The hem of her skintight red satin dress stopped at her ankle but the slit went all the way to her hip. The material fell to the side to reveal a muscular leg and her signature four-inch red platform high heels.

"Hello, Lucas, darlin'. Noah just left to make a trip to the little boys' room. He'll be back in a few minutes."

"What are you drinking?" the bartender asked Natalie.

"We'll have two Coors. Longneck, in the bottle please," Lucas said.

"How's the wedding coming along?" Natalie asked Sonia.

"Just fine and dandy. It's going to be the biggest thing Savoy has ever seen. All the girls from my old cheerleading squad are my bridesmaids and there will be six flower girls and six little boys to carry my train. Noah is going to be speechless," she said. "Bartender, I'll have another chocolate martini, pronto."

The bartender set two beers on paper coasters in front of Natalie and Lucas then started making Sonia's martini. Natalie took a long swig and turned her back to Sonia.

"Good and cold, just the way I like them," she said.

Lucas flashed a brilliant grin. "We talkin' beers or…"

Sonia leaned forward and looked past Natalie at Lucas. "I heard a rumor that you two were married already. Is that true?"

Lucas shrugged.

"When?" Sonia asked.

Noah sat down on the stool beside her and asked, "When what?"

"Nothing, Noah. I was just telling Lucas and his new wife about our wedding and how it's going to be the talk of the whole state."

"Wife?" Noah raised both eyebrows.

Lucas raised his left shoulder again. "Dance, Natalie?"

"Love to," she said.

He led her to the middle of the floor and drew her close, wrapping his arms loosely around her waist. They were the only couple, but Colton and Laura joined them when Alan Jackson hit the first guitar licks at the beginning of "When Somebody Loves You."

Lucas was so smooth that Natalie felt as if her new boots were floating. Alan sang that they should put aside their foolish pride because when somebody loves you, it's easy to get through those hard times.

"I love you, Natalie Clark," Lucas whispered in her ear when Alan delivered the last words of the song.

She leaned away from him and stared into his eyes. His eyes said that he was not joking. "Are you sure about that?"

"Oh, yeah." He laughed. "And you don't have to say it right now just because I did. When you get ready, it'll be the right moment. I can wait."

Someone tapped her on the shoulder and she looked around to see Sonia standing there with a big smile. "Can I cut in for one last dance with my old boyfriend before I get married?"

Natalie took a step back and Sonia shoved between her and Lucas. "I can't believe you married that woman without even telling me."

"Can I have this dance, ma'am?" Noah asked.

She looped an arm loosely around his neck and put her hand in his. "Of course."

The band kicked up the tempo with another Alan Jackson song called "Who's Cheatin' Who." Noah was a fine fast swing dancer, slinging Natalie out and then pulling her back to him in beat with the music.

"This ain't your first rodeo, is it?" he said.

"Been dancin' since I was old enough to walk," she said.

"Lucas did good when he got you. You'll be good for the ranch and for him. Some ways I wish Sonia was more like you, but I knew what I was gettin' when I fell for her. It ain't like I walked into it blind," he said.

"Do I hear some doubts?" Natalie asked.

"Heart wants what it wants."

"Child wants what he wants too, but that much chocolate will rot his teeth and give him a bellyache. I'm just sayin'." She smiled.

"Thanks for the dance, Miz Natalie." Noah nodded.

Lucas circled her waist with his arm and led her toward the bar again. "That Noah is a pretty good dancer."

"I'd rather be doing a slow dance with you," she said.

"Is that your best line?" Lucas drawled.

"No, darlin'"—she found her bar stool still empty and sat down—"my best lines aren't delivered in public."

Sonia hopped up on a bar stool next to Natalie. "I heard that y'all eloped."

"Who says it was an elopement?" Natalie asked.

"Maybe it was a beach wedding and we said our vows in our bare feet," Lucas said.

"Or maybe we tied the knot in my part of Texas before I even came out here," Natalie played along. "Could I get a double shot of Jack Daniel's, neat please?" Natalie asked the bartender as he passed their part of the bar.

"God! Whiskey!" Sonia said.

"Don't knock good Kentucky whiskey," Natalie said.

"You got that pink pistol strapped to your leg?" Lucas asked.

"Might have and might have to use it if someone starts talkin' shit about my whiskey," Natalie answered.

Sonia flounced off with a snort, grabbed Noah by the arm, and hauled him out to the dance floor.

"That was fun," Lucas said.

"I feel sorry for her, Lucas. She's such a pretty woman and her friends adore her, so she has to have some redeeming qualities. She's settin' herself up for a lot of hard knocks, but tonight I'm not worrying about Sonia. She made her bed. Now she can lay in it. And I feel real sorry for Noah. He's a good solid man. But right now I'm not worryin' about him either. I'm here with the best-lookin' cowboy in the whole state and I'm going to dance half the leather off my boots, drink enough whiskey to make me feel good, and then I'm going home to sleep with that cowboy," she said.

"Sounds like a helluva plan to me, sweet cheeks," he drawled.

They were on their way home when Natalie's phone rang. She pulled it from the inside pocket of her cape and said, "Hello. Is everything all right? Joshua isn't sick, is he?"

"Everything is fine. We just decided to take him to Jack's place for the night. You two are tired and us three have already set up our schedule. I'm going to watch him until two o'clock and give him a bottle. Then from two thirty until four, Grady has guard duty. Jack will take over at four and we'll bring him home in time for breakfast. Don't cook. Jack done picked up two dozen of them doughnuts in town and we'll have them with coffee.

We're going to take him to see the livestock in the morning before we come for doughnuts and coffee and while we eat y'all can tell us all about the party," Henry said.

"What is going on?" Lucas asked.

She held the phone out from her ear and said, "They want to keep Josh at Jack's all night. They've got a guard schedule set up."

"Did they take the monitor?" Lucas asked loudly.

"Tell him that we did, but we got his little bed set up by the sofa so we can sleep right beside him. I don't trust that radio shit," Henry said.

"You sure about this?" Natalie asked.

"Of course I'm sure. Y'all are wore out. Go home and get some rest. We'll see you long about eight tomorrow mornin'," Henry said and hung up.

Lucas parked in front of the house, rounded the front of the truck, opened her door, and scooped her into his arms like a bride. "Don't want to get those new boots all muddy," he said.

He didn't set her on the floor until they were in his bedroom. He brushed a few errant strands of hair back with his fingertips, ran a hand down her jawline and around to cup her neck, then his lips found hers in a sizzling kiss that jacked the heat up inside the house and inside them at least twenty degrees.

He carefully unhooked the collar of her dress and then skimmed his hands down her bare back to the point of the heart-shaped cutout where he undid the zipper. He kissed her again, tasting the remnants of Jack Daniel's and the black forest cheesecake they'd eaten for dessert.

He tasted her body as he peeled the dress from her curves one inch at a time. When it was lying in a puddle at her feet, he walked her backward and with a gentle push, she landed on her back right in the middle of the bed. He pulled her boots off and tossed them off to one side.

He did love her, all of her from the few stretch marks on her tummy to her long, long legs and her blue eyes. Thinking about being in love was so intoxicating that he could scarcely breathe.

She sat up, wearing nothing but an off-white lacy bra and bikini underpants, and said, "Okay, it's my turn."

That's the way it would always be with Natalie. She'd meet him toe-to-toe and give as much to the relationship as he did. He knew it in his bones and all the way to the bottom of his heart.

She quickly undid the buttons on his shirt and unbuckled his belt. Her hands were cool on his warm skin and everywhere they touched brought him into further arousal. He wanted to flip her over, take her right now, and own her forever. But no one would ever own Natalie. She would give her whole heart someday and he hoped to God that he was the one she handed it to.

He groaned, "All you have to do is touch me with your little finger and I'm ready to make love to you."

"Like this." She dragged her finger from the hollow of his throat down his chest and into his pants. "Aha, you're ready, all right. I been ready since that first shot of Jack Daniel's. I forgot to tell you that whiskey, the smell of Stetson, and slow dances turn me on."

"I'll remember that." He flipped her backward and peeled her underwear off in a couple of swift motions.

In another minute his jeans and boots were in a pile with her clothing and they were under the sheets, rocking together as he made love to her.

"It's different than sex, isn't it?" she whispered.

"What is different?" he asked.

"Making love."

"Yes, ma'am. I really do love you, Natalie," he said.

She wrapped her long legs tightly around him and quivered from head to toe. "That was fabulous, but I want more."

"Number two on the way." He increased the thrusts both in intensity and speed until they were both panting.

"Condom," she remembered.

"Too late," he groaned as he brought them both to a mind-blowing climax at the same time. "I'm sorry, Natalie. I just flat forgot."

He thought she'd throw a fit but she purred.

He rolled to one side and inhaled deeply until he could breathe again like a normal person. Life with Natalie would be just like sex with her. Wild and passionate. Sweet and loving. He wanted her forever in his world, not just until Christmas. After sharing life with her the past three weeks, he couldn't imagine living it without her—or Joshua.

He pulled her to his side and wrapped the comforter tighter around them. Her legs tangled with his and her arm crossed his chest. He could hear her heart thumping as fast as his.

"Lucas," she whispered.

He didn't answer. He was afraid that she would tell him that she didn't feel the same about him and he didn't want to hear it. He wanted her for Christmas, ribbon or not, dressed or undressed. He just wanted Natalie in his life.

"I love you too," she said.

Chapter 18

SEVERAL ELDERLY FOLKS TURNED AND SMILED AT LUCAS and Natalie when they arrived at church that Sunday morning. He carried a diaper bag on one shoulder and Joshua laid on the other one with a blue blanket thrown over him. Natalie's arm was looped through his and she was dressed in her long denim skirt, new boots, and a Western shirt with the cape she'd bought for the Angus party thrown around her shoulders.

Natalie smiled at those who caught her eye. Lord, but the rumors traveled fast in small towns. No doubt about it, by the expressions on their faces, they thought that Natalie and Lucas had eloped.

She moved down past the middle of the family pew and sat down, took the diaper bag from Lucas, and set it beside her. The four men lined up in the same order they did every Sunday: Grady at the end of the pew, Jack, Henry, and then Lucas.

The preacher took his place behind the podium and nodded right at them. Heaven help them all if he decided to bless their marriage right there in front of God and all the cheerleaders of days past.

"I'm going to tell you the story of the birth of our Lord and Savior this morning." He opened his Bible and read several verses. "Now think about Mary and the situation she was in. Married, but Jesus was not Joseph's son. And think about Joseph and the trust he had to have in Mary. Then he raised Jesus as his son, taught him his trade, and loved him as a father would love a son even though more children arrived after him. We think we have complicated lives these days, but folks, let me tell you, whatever we face wasn't one bit more complicated than that little family starting out."

Lucas propped his left knee over the right one, making a cradle for Joshua. The baby spit out his pacifier and cooed. Natalie picked it up from inside the folds of his blanket and put it back in his mouth, but not before he grabbed her with his chubby little hand. Lucas nudged her with his elbow and held up Joshua's other hand to show that Joshua was clasping his hand tightly with his right hand.

Tears welled up in Natalie's eyes, but she kept them at bay. She damn sure didn't need for Sonia to see her mascara running in black streaks down her cheeks that morning. It didn't keep her from wondering if maybe Jesus had stolen Joseph's heart in much the same way.

"And now for a few announcements," the preacher said when he'd finished his sermon.

Natalie inhaled deeply. Surely he wouldn't announce a marriage that hadn't even taken place.

"There won't be a service next Sunday morning since that day is Christmas and most of you will be spending the morning with your families. Don't forget as you are opening presents and enjoying the time that it's Jesus's birthday. And for those of you who haven't heard, Sonia has decided that the wedding on Christmas was too rushed, so they're postponing it for a few weeks so she can get everything ready. She's saying maybe by Valentine's Day she'll have it ready.

If there are no more announcements…" He paused and looked right at Lucas.

"Okay, then," he went on, "Henry Allen, will you deliver the benediction for us this morning?"

While Henry prayed, the preacher made his way to the back of the church to receive the members of the congregation as they left that morning. Two ladies who sat in the pew in front of the Allen family turned around as soon as Henry said, "Amen," and reached for the baby.

Lucas handed Joshua off to the nearest one and picked up the diaper bag, threw it over his shoulder, and grabbed Natalie's hand. A whole group of ladies gathered around the queen bee that had possession of Joshua. They all talked at once, but the general train of thought appeared to be that Joshua was the very image of Lucas when he was a baby from the color of his eyes to his hair. He must have gotten that cleft in his chin from Natalie's side because they'd never known an Allen man to have one. The charm, now that came from Henry for sure, and those ears were Jack's without a doubt.

Grady, Henry, and Jack went on ahead and were soon swallowed up in the crowd approaching the doors at the back of the church.

"You should have used that time to tell them the truth. The longer we wait, the harder it's going to be," Natalie scolded him on the way home.

"Honey, I don't care if they never know the truth. Me and Josh, we don't plan on tellin' nothing, do we?" He glanced back in the rearview at the baby. "Did you hear what the guys are saying about Josh?"

"Only that he's the smartest, cutest little cowboy since you were born." She giggled.

He told her about the animals.

"Grady told me yesterday morning while we were doing chores. What do you think of that?" he asked.

"Well, Josh sure stole my thunder if that is what is happening. I thought I had a built-in sonar radar thing that drew strays to me. Momma said that I did when I was a kid. I was always bringing home some kind of varmint."

"Skunks?"

"Oh, hell, no! After smelling like one for a week, believe me, I would not drag one of those home and feed it scraps."

"You think they are right?"

"Skunks?"

"No, the guys. You believe in stuff like that?"

"I believe in the possibility of anything. I think Fate and Mother Nature are sisters. Sometimes they are sweet and sometimes they are bitchy, but they'll use anything at their disposal to get what they want. And believe me, there's a lot at their disposal."

———

Natalie had just pulled the hot rolls from the oven when the doorbell and Natalie's phone rang at the same time. She looked across the kitchen at Lucas who'd helped her by setting the table.

"You get your phone. I'll take care of the door," he said.

"Hello, Hazel," she answered the phone.

"I heard that Sonia couldn't get the wedding arranged in time. That is a load of hog shit. Noah laid down the law and Sonia told him that she wasn't going to do no compromising. She said she wasn't about to have a bunch of snotty-nosed kids, so he said they'd better rethink the Christmas wedding." Hazel finally stopped for a breath.

"Natalie, are you still there?" Hazel asked.

"Oh, yeah! Sonia is here," Natalie whispered.

"Well, shit! Go in there and shoot her," Hazel said.

"My gun is in the bedroom." Natalie laughed nervously.

"Oh, honey, I do like you. What are they saying?" Hazel whispered.

"Sonia is asking where Noah is. She can't find him and she's been crying. Oh, Hazel, I feel sorry for her. She probably realizes she made a mistake and now she's saying something about me and Lucas getting married in Hawaii and that's what she wants."

"You are married? When were y'all going to tell me?" Hazel wasn't whispering anymore.

"We aren't. Sonia kind of started both rumors. The one that Joshua belongs to Lucas and the one that we are married. Lucas didn't dispute them. Jack just stood up. Huh-oh!"

"Dammit to hell. I'm coming home. That place is going to ruin without me," Hazel declared.

"Jack told her that she could look for Noah at the bunkhouse, but that he wasn't here, that I had dinner ready, and he was hungry."

"And?" Hazel asked.

"She left," Natalie said.

"Good. I'll call later on this afternoon and talk to Jack and to Lucas. Y'all go eat your dinner. I'm bookin' a flight home this week. I was coming on Friday anyway, but I'll be there soon as I can get from Memphis to Dallas," Hazel said.

"Guess you heard that?" Jack said as the four men filed into the kitchen.

"I did," she said.

"What did Hazel want?" Lucas asked.

"She's coming home," Natalie said.

"Joe O'Malley told me that Noah laid down the law to her and said if she didn't want no kids then by golly they were going to postpone the wedding because he wanted a family," Henry grumbled.

"Let's forget all about Sonia and eat this wonderful dinner Natalie has fixed up. What else did Hazel say?" Lucas asked.

"Just that she'll be home probably tomorrow or the next day. She said that she'd call Jack later this afternoon. She was checking on flights into Dallas as soon as she hung up."

"Good. I miss her," Jack said. "Hot rolls look great, Natalie. And that pot roast looks tender enough to melt in my mouth."

———

Natalie and Joshua went to their bedroom after the dishwasher was loaded. She called her mother and told her about the whole week, rumors, mothers, and ex-girlfriends. Every bit of it, leaving out nothing—except the sex after the party and the argument she and Lucas had had earlier in the week.

"Sounds like you got a lot on your plate," Debra said when Natalie finished. "I can't stand to see you livin' that far away. If you decide to stick with that man, then you do it right. I taught you how to take care of yourself, so don't be lettin' that two-bit bitchy cheerleader intimidate you."

"I feel sorry for Noah and Sonia both. If she would just grow up and think outside of herself, she could be a good wife. Noah loves her so much, and she could be the adored, petted wife for all her life. I can't imagine being Sonia's age and seeing the whole world like a teenager," Natalie said.

Debra laughed. "Always were a bit softhearted like your father."

"And you," Natalie said. "What if I were to stay here, Momma? Are you going to throw a fit and cry?"

"Hell, yeah! But then I'll make you promise to come see me every other month, and I'll come see you the ones when you don't come here. My grandson isn't going to grow up without knowing his grandparents. Got to go. Your dad's calling the house phone. Talk to you later. Send more pictures. Joshua will be drivin' a tractor before I see him again."

"In a month? He'll hardly be big enough to drive a tractor in just a month."

She laid the phone to the side when she realized her mother had hung up and drew her knees up in the rocking chair, wrapped her arms around them, and watched Joshua sleep. Her eyes grew heavy and she had almost nodded off when she heard a soft rap on the bedroom door.

Lucas poked his head inside. "The guys have all gone home. Could we talk?"

She motioned him inside.

He sat down on the edge of the bed. "I talked to Noah. He says that he loves her, but that they'd both be miserable living together. He's wise enough to see that they want very different things in life. He has no intentions of leaving the ranch. She'd rather live in a big city. He wants kids. She hates them."

"Maybe they'll compromise and they'll be happy."

"Sometimes it's too late to do what you should have been doing all along, Natalie. Sometimes you run out of time."

Natalie set the rocking chair into motion. "Have they known each other long?"

Lucas blushed. "Since grade school. We all grew up together. Noah is a year younger than she is and she's a year younger than I am."

He kicked his boots off and stretched out on her bed. "She always thought she could talk me off this ranch. And she probably thought the same thing about Noah. Dad says she reminds him of my mother, who, by the way, called a couple of days ago and told me very quickly that she and her husband were going to Paris this year, so she wouldn't be coming to Texas."

"Tell me about your mother."

"You want the long version or the short one?"

"I've got all afternoon." Natalie left the rocking chair and joined him on the bed. His arm went around her and she laid her head on his chest.

"I overhead Hazel and Dad talking when I was a kid or I wouldn't even know the story. Seemed that Mother hated the ranch and wanted Dad to leave it. That wasn't happening, so she threatened to divorce him every week for months and take me with her if he didn't agree to sell it or at least move away from it. Gramps insisted on a prenup before they were married, so she couldn't have half the ranch, but finally Dad offered her a settlement big enough that she signed the papers and left me behind," he said.

Natalie shivered. She couldn't imagine selling Joshua for any amount of money. "Didn't she have visitation rights?"

"Oh, yes. Dad was very generous. She could see me any time she wanted but not alone. Grady or Hazel would take me to wherever she was and stay with me, but she never asked, not one time."

"How did that affect you?" Natalie asked.

"I never thought about it. I had Hazel, and you see the way the guys dote on Joshua. It was the same with me. I never really knew her, so I didn't miss her. She came at Christmas and brought me a present. I had lunch with her in town, mostly with Hazel or Grady right there beside me until I got my driver's license."

He massaged her neck as he talked. "Dad was so nervous the first time I went by myself that Grady said he walked the floor the whole time I was gone. He never talked about her to me. Never said bad things about her or anything. It's like she just left me on the porch and disappeared out of his life. And he worried about me and Sonia winding up the same way. He was right even though I didn't see it until I went to Kuwait."

Natalie kissed him on the cheek. "Jack is a good man."

"You didn't ask for all my baggage," he said.

"Did you ask for mine?"

"You are handling mine better than I did yours." He tipped her chin up and kissed her. The first one was sweet, the second one searching, the third, devouring.

Joshua whimpered a few times and then howled when no one picked him up.

"Best birth control there is," Natalie said.

Lucas chuckled and rolled off the bed. He picked

the baby up and laid him between them on the bed. "The guys have spoiled him. He's dry and he's not chewing on his fingers, so he's not hungry. He just wants to be entertained."

"Spoiled so bad the coyotes wouldn't even nibble on those precious little toes," she crooned to him.

Joshua cooed and grinned.

"I see what you mean about not missing your mother. I bet they fought over who got to watch you sleep," she said.

"Grady says they did. I've had wonderful father role models. Triple count. And you've had wonderful maternal role models in your mother and aunt. We ought to make real good parents."

Natalie was struck speechless. Was he offering to be a father to Joshua or making a general statement?

"Would you have married Drew if he'd come home?" Lucas asked.

"No," Natalie said quickly.

Lucas leaned across the baby and brushed a kiss across her lips. "But he's Josh's father and…"

She put a finger over his lips. "And we were best friends who got drunk one night. I didn't love Drew like that. I loved him like a friend. We wouldn't be good together in a marriage."

As if Joshua knew that the attention wasn't on him, he kicked his legs and whimpered.

"You really are spoiled." Natalie grabbed his foot and removed his sock. "This little piggy went to market, this little piggy…"

"Angus, sweet cheeks, Angus. Josh is a ranchin' boy," Lucas reminded her.

She started all over again. "This little Angus went to market, this little Angus stayed home…"

Joshua laughed for the first time. It wasn't a belly laugh like Natalie had ordered for Christmas, but there was no denying that it was a giggle and not a coo or even a goo noise.

"Did you hear that?" Natalie stopped before she got to the pinky toe.

"He laughed," Lucas said. "First time, right? You look like you are about to cry. Laughing is a good thing, right?" He reached across the baby and wiped the first tear away from Natalie's cheek with his hand.

"He won't be a baby forever, Lucas," she answered.

"No, he won't, but you can't cry every time he does something new. Be happy that he's healthy and happy. Henry is going to be so disappointed that he didn't hear the first laughter. He's been doing all kinds of stupid things all week so he could brag that he got to hear it first." Lucas said.

"You'd think he was really Joshua's great-grandpa," Natalie said.

"He thinks he is."

"And what happens when you have children of your own bloodline?" she asked.

"Won't make a bit of difference to Gramps."

"How do you know?"

He picked up Joshua's smallest toe and said, "And this little Angus calf… and this little Angus calf… and this little Angus calf cried moo-moo-moo all the way home."

Joshua's eyes lit up and he chuckled again.

"How do you know?" Natalie repeated the question.

"Because it doesn't make a bit of difference to me.

Lying here with you with Josh between us, I realize that we've become a family. He's not the son of my blood, but he's the son of my heart, much like the real baby Jesus was to Joseph," Lucas said softly.

Natalie swallowed hard three times before the basketball-sized lump left her throat. All she could do was nod and wonder where the future went from there.

Chapter 19

Lucas heard a gunshot and sat straight up in bed. Surely, he'd been dreaming again. He looked at the other side of the bed and Natalie was gone.

Another shot and he bailed out of bed, grabbed a pair of pajama bottoms, and was trying to get his legs in them as he ran down the hall. When he reached the kitchen, she was taking her coat off in the utility room.

"There's a rattlesnake about the size of my arm between the porch and chicken coop. Damn thing zigzagged on me and I wasted a bullet. Don't tell Momma."

Lucas melted into a kitchen chair. "Shit, Natalie! You scared me."

"I guess I did. Your britches are on wrong side out and backward. Is the baby still asleep?"

Lucas shrugged. "I forgot to pick up the monitor, but I don't hear him. He's developed quite a set of lungs, so I reckon we would have heard him if he was awake."

"I hate snakes." She set the basket of eggs on the cabinet.

"Bad as skunks?"

"Almost. Why would one be out at this time of year? They don't come out of hibernation until spring."

"Well, I didn't take Joshua to see the animals this morning yet." He smiled.

"From now on, you get that boy out every morning. I'm tired of this shit," she said.

"It'll all stop after Christmas." He chuckled.

"Why's that?"

"Granny Ella Jo will leave. We'll…" He stopped before he said *be married.*

"We'll what?" she asked.

"We'll be over this stormy weather. Hazel will be home and everything will be back to normal, including crazy animal behavior," he told her.

"Let's go into Sherman after breakfast this morning. The guys can watch the baby for us and we'll have lunch out. We can bring carryout back to them."

"Why would we do that?"

"Because I love you."

And because I want to think about that marriage word with just you and not the whole family, and I want to think about it before Hazel gets home with her meddling, he thought.

"And because you shot a big old mean snake and you deserve a morning out away from the ranch, sweet cheeks," he said.

She laughed and he knew that he'd won her over.

———

She insisted that the shopping that day would be in the grocery store stocking up for Christmas baking, and it was noon before they finished buying everything on her list. The whole backseat of the truck was full when they started loading the two carts full of food.

"Just looking at all this makes me hungry. Are you ready to eat yet?" Lucas asked.

"I'm starving," she said.

"Then let's go down to the Catfish King and get some dinner. It's not fancy but the food is good," he said.

"Good as when you catch it and fry it at home?" Natalie asked.

"Ain't nothing can compare with that." He buckled the car seat into position while Natalie got settled in the passenger's seat of his truck. "You fish?"

"Oh, yeah! Love to fish and I've got my own secret recipe for the breading," she said.

It amazed her that they could go from sex to grocery shopping, from arguing to making love, to talking about fishing with such ease. Did that mean that they were a family? Or maybe that they could be one in the next few months?

He started the engine, adjusted the heat, and leaned across the seat before he fastened his seat belt. "I didn't realize how much I do love you until this minute. Too bad Drew isn't around so I could shake his hand for introducing us."

The kiss started slow and soft, but before it ended she had both hands tangled in his hair and could hardly catch her breath.

The next morning, eight days before Christmas, Jack drove to the airport and brought Hazel home. They arrived at noon, just as Natalie was setting the dinner on the table. Grady, Jack, and Lucas rushed to the door when they heard the truck door slam and hurried out to help her. Natalie stood back and waited as they carried her suitcase and fussed at her to use her cane rather than hanging it on her arm like a handbag.

"Dammit, Jack!" she swore as she entered the house. "I'm not an invalid. I can still walk and if Willa hadn't thrown a damn hissy, I wouldn't even have that damned cane. Now leave me alone. Where the hell is that baby?"

Natalie pointed to the swing.

"Come over here and give me a hug, lady. I deserve it after that airplane ride and then comin' home at a snail's pace because Jack was afraid to drive fast on the ice. I swear to God that I could have gotten here faster with a sleigh pulled by a couple of them Chihuahua dogs." She opened her arms and Natalie bent to hug her.

"That's better," she said. "Now let's look at the baby. Oh, my goodness! He's grown a foot and would you look at that grin. Has he laughed out loud yet?"

"Sunday afternoon." Lucas smiled.

"You didn't tell me. I missed it," Henry moaned.

"He'll laugh again. I smell lasagna and hot bread. Willa don't cook nothing that ain't good for a body, and I'm starved plumb to death for decent food, so let's set up to the table and eat," Hazel said. "And after that, me and Natalie is going into town shopping. Henry, you can keep Josh for us so he don't get drug around from store to store. I ain't got a bit of my Christmas bought, and it's goin' to get crazy in the stores."

"I'll let Josh babysit me any old time. He and I get along just fine. But Natalie done laid in enough supplies to last through till next Christmas," Henry said.

"You think maybe you ought to ask Natalie rather than bossin' her around." Lucas looked right at Hazel.

"Hell, no! My job is to boss until… never you mind how long it's going to be my job. But rest assured, Lucas, I will tell you when I pass my bossin' crown to someone else. You won't have to ask. And I'm not going for groceries. I'm going for presents."

Natalie smiled. "I'd love to take you to town, Hazel."

"I still have a few things to buy, so…" Lucas started.

Hazel held up a hand. "So, you ain't going with us! You can go in your own truck and do your own shopping. This is a ladies' only party. I'm buying for you and you ain't taggin' along with us."

After lunch Natalie changed Josh, fixed his afternoon bottle, and handed him over to Henry's care. Leaving him, even in such capable hands, still wasn't easy, but Hazel was right. It would wear him out to be dragged from store to store. She helped Hazel get her coat on, picked up the cane and handed it to her, and got a dirty look.

"What?" Natalie asked.

"I hate that stupid thing," she said.

"Well, you need it. It's still slick out there and I sure don't want you to break a hip," Natalie told her.

Lucas chuckled.

Hazel pointed a finger at him. "That's enough."

"You sure you got that bossin' crown on tight? Looks like Natalie might be takin' it away from you," he said.

"It's mine until I give it away," Hazel declared. "Now let's get out of here before I take this cane to that boy's hard head."

Hazel hopped up into the passenger seat of Natalie's pickup so spryly that Natalie wondered if she'd even hurt her hip. It could have been a big setup to keep her on the ranch when Hazel found out about Joshua.

"Truth," Natalie said as she started the engine.

"About what?" Hazel drew her dark brows down over her equally dark eyes. She tucked her salt-and-pepper chin-length hair back behind her ears and straightened her back. Standing, she barely came up to Natalie's shoulder. Sitting, she was even shorter.

"Just how bad is that hip?"

"Busted!" Hazel laughed.

"Was it even hurt?"

"You are a smart cookie, Natalie Clark." Hazel continued to giggle like a schoolgirl.

"How did you…" she asked.

"It *was* bruised, so that helped."

"Did your daughter figure it out?"

"Hell, no! She wants me to move to that godforsaken city and give up my house. That'll happen three days after hell freezes plumb over. I'm leaving the ranch feet first in a body bag and with a smile on my face."

"I want to grow up to be just like you." Natalie made all the right turns to get them to the highway into Savoy.

"You got a good start, darlin'," Hazel said. "We'll go to the Western-wear store first. All the boys need new white shirts for church. Then we're going to the bookstore. Jack reads James Lee Burke novels and Grady likes Randy Wayne White."

"Yes, ma'am," Natalie said.

"After that we'll have to hit the Walmart store for stocking stuffers. They all have a particular brand of candy that they like, and I always get them funny presents for their stockings."

"Such as?" Natalie asked.

"Oh, them fancy boxer shorts with Christmas stuff on them and a toy of some kind. Movies are always good. I'm buying Henry *The Bucket List*. I saw it when I was at Willa's place. It's a good movie."

"It's been out quite a while," Natalie said.

"But he ain't seen it because he would've talked about it if he did," Hazel said.

"What do you want for Christmas?" Natalie asked as she pulled out onto the highway leading into Sherman.

"I got what I want. There's going to be a baby in the house and Lucas is happy," Hazel said.

"What if he's just happy with the idea of being happy and in a year he wakes up wishing there wasn't a baby in the house? What if that happens?"

"What if the world is hit by a shit storm tomorrow and the gover'ment banned the production of toilet paper?" Hazel snapped. "I ain't never seen Lucas this happy. It's written all over his face. Now tell me what happened when Sonia found Noah?"

"Noah told Lucas that it was over. And Jack said he heard that she was moving to Dallas, that she got the offer of some kind of job down there in an oil firm," Natalie said and went on to tell her what happened after that.

"Well, halle-damn-lujah! Good riddance. I really didn't want her living on the ranch, not even in the hinder parts of it," Hazel said. "There's a parking spot right close to the front of the store. Snag it before anyone else can get it. Oh, and tonight you and Josh are coming to my house to help me put up my tree. We got a tradition here. First we go to Lucas's house and have Christmas presents and breakfast. Then we go to Jack's and unwrap what he's bought for us, then to Henry's and then to the bunkhouse where Grady lives. And then we finish up at my house for Christmas dinner and my presents."

So that's why the only presents under the tree were the ones that she and Lucas had bought. She'd wondered if the guys waited until the very last minute to do their shopping. Now she understood.

"It's a round-robin thing. Henry usually gets his turn in the middle of the morning, and I make sure there's a platter of Ella's favorite cookies to nibble on while we are there."

"How on earth do you have time to make Christmas dinner if you are running around all over the ranch?" Natalie asked.

"Organization." Hazel laughed. "Now let's go buy some white shirts."

"And boots," Natalie said. "I haven't bought Lucas's present, and he eyed a pair last time we were in here."

"That's about as romantic as a brick," Hazel grumbled.

"What would you suggest?"

"Something a lot sexier and more private than boots," she said.

Lucas sat in the parking lot at the mall for ten minutes. Surely a storefront would jump out and grab his attention if he pondered long enough. He didn't have a single present for Josh or for Natalie under the tree and it was only six days until Christmas morning. Josh was less than three months old and the guys had already outfitted him with a pony, a saddle, and enough toys to keep him busy until he was kindergarten age. And they all had presents for Natalie under their trees.

He wanted to do something special for the baby and for Natalie, especially the first Christmas they were all together.

He should talk to Hazel before he bought anything. She'd have some ideas. She always did.

He scanned the stores again and saw Hazel and Natalie coming out of the bookstore. Did he buy a book for her? What did she like to read?

"Big, fat, thick romance books set in castle days," he said aloud as he remembered a conversation they'd had when he was still in Kuwait.

He waited until they'd gone into another store and then opened the truck door. A blast of winter wind hit him square in the face. They were in for more bad weather for sure with a cold north wind like that whipping through the state. He turned up the collar of his work coat and accidentally hooked his little finger in his dog tags.

"Oh, yeah," he said with a broad grin.

He held onto his Stetson until he got inside the bookstore and then removed it. The lady behind the counter looked up and asked, "Mystery?"

He picked up a basket. "No, ma'am, point me in the direction of the romance section."

"Next aisle to your right," she said.

Lucas didn't have any idea which authors were Natalie's favorites, so he chose by cover and title. *When You Give a Duke a Diamond* caught his eye, so he put it in the basket along with *A Gentleman Says "I Do."* A display of coupons caught his eye and he stopped to look at a booklet filled with kissing coupons. He flipped through it and his grin got bigger with every coupon. One said that with this coupon, you get a nonstop body kiss from the top of your head to the tips of your toes. Another said that the coupon was good for a long and wonderful kiss under the stars. It was a perfect present, but he wasn't sure who'd benefit more from it—Natalie or him.

From there he went to the children's books and picked up three for Josh that had bright colors and few words. And he intended to tell Josh all about them. If Henry wanted to read something new to the boy, then he could buy his own books.

The music section of the store caught his eye next and he bought a silly CD with all the children's songs on it that he remembered from childhood. Then he went to the country music section and picked out two different CDs for Natalie. One was an instrumental of an assortment of slow love songs that made him think of long, lazy nights of slow lovemaking.

"With candles," he said aloud.

He paid for his purchases, bemoaned the fact that they did not offer gift wrapping, and put the bag in the truck before he went to the store specializing in all kinds of lotions, candles, and bath items. He smelled dozens of candles before he settled on the one that smelled sexy to him. He bought bubble bath, lotion, and bath powder all in the same fragrance.

From there he meandered through a clothing store and bought funny socks with toes in them and fuzzy slippers in black and white zebra stripes to keep her feet warm when she had to get up at night with Joshua. When he found out that they wrapped for a small fee, he added a soft blue scarf the color of her eyes and a sweater to match it.

"And now to find those fancy little gold-wrapped chocolates and some miniature Snicker bars for her stocking. After that I'll go get her big present, or is it my big present? I guess it depends on what she says when I give it to her." He loaded two more bags in the truck and drove south toward Walmart.

The toy aisle was so much fun that he bought a mobile with cute farm animals on it that played "Old MacDonald Had a Farm" when it was wound up. Josh would love that above his crib.

"Crib." Lucas slapped his thigh.

He steered his cart toward the baby section and couldn't find a thing that suited him. Then he got the bright idea that he'd take his old crib out of the storage barn and refinish it. Grady and the guys would have to help, but they'd be willing. And they could take all the furniture out of the spare bedroom and make a real nursery for Josh. Lucas's rocking horse was still out there and the chair that Hazel had rocked him to sleep in until he was in kindergarten. Plus the stick horse that Henry had carved special for him when he outgrew the rocking horse.

It wouldn't be easy to pull it all off, but with help from the guys, they could make Josh his own room by Christmas morning. He noticed a complete bed in a bag set for a crib that had the same barnyard animals on it as the mobile. He tossed it into the cart, paid out, and made one more stop on his way home for Natalie's big present.

When he got to the ranch, he kept driving down the back lane to the bunkhouse where he unloaded the baby presents. Grady was snoozing in his recliner in the living room and jumped when Lucas called his name.

"Got some shopping done, I see," he said.

Lucas nodded. "I need help. Lots of it. You and the hired hands up for some hard work?"

"What do you have in mind?" Grady asked.

The more Lucas talked, the bigger Grady's grin got. "I'd say that you mean to keep Natalie and Josh on the ranch if you're willin' to let him sleep in your bed. That was supposed to be given to your first son. Henry slept in it when he was a baby, then Jack, and then you."

Lucas nodded. "It was and it is and he is. Y'all think you can strip all that white paint off it that Hazel put on it when I was little and refinish it in brown like it was when Dad had it?"

"I reckon we could do that as well as putting a fresh coat of varnish on the rocking chair and hobbyhorse. You just worry about a way to get Natalie and Josh out of the house for a few hours the day before Christmas and we'll do the rest. Fine present for a boy, Lucas. You done good," Grady said.

"Thank you," Lucas threw over his shoulder as he disappeared out the door and headed back to the house. He wanted to get the presents wrapped and under the tree before Natalie got home. All but one, and that one he carried in his pocket.

"Hey, you beat them women back home," Henry whispered.

"Josh sleeping?" Lucas asked.

Henry pointed to the port-a-crib beside his recliner. "We both were until you and all them rattling sacks that you hauled in here woke me up."

"Sorry, Gramps. Let me tell you what I've got in mind for him while he's asleep and can't hear." He set the bags down and hauled the wrapping paper from Natalie's room into the living room. He sat down on the floor and talked as he wrapped and cussed the paper and tape all at the same time.

"Sounds like a mighty fine idea to me. I've got something special for Natalie and for you, but you can refuse them and I won't be hurt a bit. Ella Jo thought I should offer, and I never could tell her no." Henry's old eyes grew misty.

"What's that, Gramps?" Lucas asked.

"You know your grandma was a tall woman like Natalie and about the same size. Well, since you're accepting this boy, I think it's time to turn loose of these." He opened his clenched hand to reveal two gold wedding bands.

"Gramps, I couldn't."

"Wouldn't offer them if I didn't think you'd made the right choice, son. Ella Jo told me it was the right thing to do right here at Christmas and all. Said it would make her happy if you'd wear them and that she really likes Natalie but she loves Josh."

Lucas held out his hand.

Henry dropped the rings into his palm. "Love her as much as I did your grandma and don't never let no one get in the way of that love."

"I don't even know what to say," Lucas said.

"Don't say nothin', son. I'm glad to pass them on to you and Natalie. Y'all kind of remind me of me and Ella Jo. Only she didn't have a baby. You're luckier than me in that respect. Put 'em in your pocket and get to wrappin'. Them women won't stay out past suppertime."

Chapter 20

FOUR DAYS BEFORE CHRISTMAS, NATALIE AWOKE TO THE sound of pots and pans rattling in the kitchen. She sat up on the side of the bed, grabbed her pajama bottoms and underpants, and jerked them on.

"Where are you going?" Lucas rubbed his eyes.

"Hazel is here early."

"She won't ground us." Lucas chuckled.

"No, but I'd be so embarrassed that I'd go up in flames and die if she caught me in your bed," Natalie whispered. She pulled a tank top on and kissed him on the cheek on her way out of his bedroom.

Josh was waking up for his six o'clock bottle by the time she reached her room. When she picked him up, he was so wet that his pajamas were dripping and there was a ring on the sheet in his port-a-crib. The smell gagged her, but she swallowed hard. Strange that it would bother her that day since messy diapers, wet ones, or even curdled spit-up had never turned her stomach before.

In case she was coming down with a flu bug, she didn't smother his face in kisses. Instead she talked to him and reminded him that it was only a few days until Christmas and then a week after that they were going home to Silverton to the New Year's party at the ranch. "Your grandma isn't any too happy with me right now. I probably should go on home for Christmas, but I just can't break the guys' hearts. I said I loved him, Josh, and he said you were the son of his heart, but he hasn't said a word since then. Maybe he's got second thoughts about us. After Christmas we'll have a long talk with him and see where this relationship is going."

She picked him up and carried him down the hallway. Jack was already at the kitchen table and he held out his arms. She handed Josh off to him and got a big whiff of the coffee at the same time. Her stomach did a couple of flip-flops before it settled down.

Dammit all to hell on a platter! It wasn't a bit fair to get sick right at Christmas. Hopefully it was just a twenty-four-hour thing that would be over by tomorrow morning.

Oh my God! Is it, could it be morning sickness? I never had it with Josh, so I don't have any idea what it feels like, she thought.

She wasn't due to start her period until... oops! She should have started three days before, but still, that was way too soon for her body to feel nauseated, wasn't it? Besides, the doctor said sometimes after giving birth it took a while to get the time clock reset, and she'd never been real regular anyway. She could not be pregnant. She just couldn't! She'd made a mental note to look up the symptoms and time frame on her laptop as soon as breakfast was over.

"Good mornin'. I hope I'm not steppin' on your toes. I just need to get back in the groove or else I'll get old and die," Hazel said.

"Not a bit, but what's my job now that you are home?"

"You help Lucas run this ranch, and I might let you do some of the housework. Cooking will belong to me until I die, unless I'm off at a church function and then you can step in and do whatever you want," Hazel said.

"But I like to cook," she said.

"I might let you take a couple of nights a week." Hazel winked.

The aroma of sausage and eggs combined with the strong coffee scent should have made her stomach growl, but instead it rolled in protest. She made an excuse and hurried down the hall to the bathroom where she hugged the toilet and tried to bring up her toenails.

"God, if this is morning sickness, please let it be over in one day. I can't take care of Josh and do this every morning," she prayed.

After she washed her face with cold water and brushed her teeth, she waited another few minutes to be sure she was done. When she slung open the bathroom door Lucas was standing in front of her with a hand on each side of the jamb.

"You look a little pale. That business with Hazel still got you spooked?" he asked.

She did her best to smile. "Yes, it does. Breakfast is almost ready, and I've gotten my orders. I'm supposed to help you on the ranch and do a little bit of housekeeping."

Lucas chuckled. "Want me to talk to her?"

"Hell, no! We've always had a cook and housekeeper, so I'm used to the arrangement. And I wouldn't hurt her feelings for all the dirt in Texas," Natalie said.

Lucas threw his arm around her shoulder and they walked in perfect step all the way to the kitchen. One whiff of the food and her stomach did another roll. She looked at Lucas in time to see him grab his mouth with his free hand.

His boots sounded like canon blasts as he ran up the hallway and there was no doubt what was going on in the bathroom. Natalie wanted to dance a jig right there in the kitchen. She and Lucas both had a stomach bug, and she was not pregnant. She could handle a weak tummy for a couple of days. Three months of it might turn her into a really mean bitchy woman that Lucas would kick off the ranch.

"Well, hell, I didn't know my cookin' would make a problem," Hazel said.

"It's not your cookin'. I just did the same thing. We must have gotten a bug. I hope you don't get it, Hazel," Natalie said.

"She's too mean to get anything," Jack said. "You and Lucas go on in the living room and settle back in the recliners. I'll bring you some dry toast and hot tea. That'll keep your strength up without upsetting your stomach even more."

"Thank you," Natalie said weakly.

"I'll take care of Josh today in the den. We don't want him to get sick and spoil his first Christmas," Henry said.

Natalie nodded.

Grady followed her into the living room, pointed to a recliner, and covered her with a soft throw when she laid back. He looked up at Lucas when he came from the bathroom and pointed to the chair beside Natalie's. "That one belongs to you. We'll take care of chores this morning. Got to get y'all well for Christmas."

The next morning, rattling pots and pans and the aroma of coffee and bacon woke Natalie again. When she opened her eyes Lucas was propped on an elbow staring down at her.

"Feeling better?" he asked.

"I'm starving," she answered.

"Me too."

"Must've been a twenty-four-hour bug like we thought," she said.

The monitor let them know that Josh was awake and fretting for his morning bottle, so she slid out of bed, hurriedly threw a robe around her naked body, and eased the door open. The coast was clear, so she padded barefoot to her bedroom, slipped inside, and gathered Josh up from his bed.

"We've got to get you something bigger if we're staying past Christmas, son. You're about to outgrow that little thing." She stripped off his pajamas and changed his diaper. "What should you wear today? We've got to go to town this morning and do some last-minute shopping. When we go to Silverton, we're supposed to take our presents. Your grandma said not to waste postage mailing them, to just bring them with us then and she'll have ours ready at that time too. You're going to have a big Christmas and you won't even remember it. We'll take lots of pictures though and when you are older, you can look at them."

Josh spit his pacifier out and stuck his thumb in his mouth.

"Well, that's a trait from your father. He sucked his thumb until he was five years old," she said.

Lucas poked his head in the door. "Is he dressed? I'll take him to the front of the house while you get ready. The two of us can even get his bottle ready before you make it to the kitchen. You sure you're feeling better? You still look a little pale to me."

"I'm fine. After breakfast Josh and I are going to Sherman to do our last-minute shopping, though. You want to go?" she asked.

He helped by putting socks on Josh and then he picked him up. "Come on, cowboy. Your fan club is waiting for you. I'd love to go with you, but I've got too much going on here to get away until after the holiday. I'm glad I've got all my shopping done."

"So how do we do our presents? Hazel told me how y'all do all the other ones," she asked.

He stopped at the door. "It's our first Christmas together. I think we should open our presents on Christmas Eve night so that it's just us. That work for you?"

"I like that idea," she said.

The words *our first Christmas together* ran through her mind in a continuous loop. Did that mean that he was planning on a second, third, or more? He'd told her that he loved her that one time but hadn't mentioned it again. And he hadn't mentioned plans after Christmas, either.

She'd counted the presents under the tree that had her name on them. She needed to buy two more small gifts for Lucas so that he'd have the same amount, and that was the real reason she and Josh were shopping again that day.

So far, she hadn't bought him a book, so she planned to go to the bookstore first, and after that, she intended to buy the biggest bottle of Stetson that she could find. Walking past him in the hallway after he'd shaved set her hormones into something between a whine and a hum. By late evening when they crawled into bed together, sometimes for a bout of steamy hot sex, sometimes just to cuddle, she could still catch a whiff of the remnants of Stetson if she nuzzled his neck. And her reaction was always the same.

Hazel had made waffles that morning with melted butter and warmed maple syrup. Natalie didn't touch the bacon or sausage but had two helpings of waffles. She'd never had a problem with any foods when she was pregnant with Josh, so it must be the aftereffects of that violent stomach flu.

"Weatherman says that north Texas is going to have a white Christmas. We're due for about five inches of snow on Christmas Eve. But then it's supposed to warm up the day after Christmas and kick back up into the forties by New Year's Eve," Henry said.

"Then I guess it's a good thing Josh and I are going to town today. When is it supposed to start?" Natalie asked.

"It's already dumping a load out in the western part of the state," Grady said.

"Probably be here by tomorrow night and when we get up Christmas morning we'll have that five inches," Jack said.

"Well, that don't mean our plans will change. We got four-wheel drive trucks and chains," Hazel said. "I'm kind of lookin' forward to it. We ain't seen a white Christmas since Lucas was about ten years old."

"Nine," Lucas said. "Noah and I built a snowman. He was seven and we thought it was the grandest thing ever. Lookin' back, it was only about three feet tall."

"More'n twenty years ago then," Hazel said. "Natalie, I'll watch over the baby while you shop. You can do it in half the time if you don't have to get him in and out. Besides, after you and Lucas both being sick yesterday,

I don't think he ought to be out amongst sick people. They'll be coughing and sneezing on him."

It wasn't until Natalie was halfway to Sherman that she realized how much control she'd lost with Joshua when she came to Cedar Hill. Her mother didn't tell her what to do the way Hazel did. There wasn't a cowboy on the whole ranch in Silverton who could waltz into her bedroom and carry the baby out to breakfast. Even her grandpa didn't tell her that she was going to help with chores while he read books to the baby.

She slapped the steering wheel. "Dammit!"

She parked in front of the bookstore and braced herself against the bitter north wind. The sun was shining but the rays couldn't do a thing to warm her as she put her head down and jogged from the truck to the store.

The clerk looked up from straightening an aisle where children had evidently been and raised an eyebrow.

"Mysteries?"

"One aisle over from romance." She pointed.

She picked up the newest James Lee Burke and a John Sandford and wandered into the romance section. Several caught her eye but she never bought for herself in December. Her brothers, her Aunt Leah, and her mother always put them in her stocking. She picked up one with a bright yellow cover and hoped one of them bought it. She loved Shana Galen's writing and that one looked so good.

Then she saw the display with the little coupon books and stopped in her tracks. The one about kisses would be a wonderful present for Lucas. She especially liked the coupon that said they'd spend the day together and no matter what they were doing or where they were they would stop to kiss each other every thirty minutes.

"What a wonderful way to watch the clock," she muttered. "But this would make too many presents."

"Put them all in one box," the sales clerk said behind her. "I gave my boyfriend one of those coupon books for his birthday last week. We can't wait until this bad weather goes away so we can see the stars. Look at the next one in the book. It says it's good for a long and wonderful kiss under the stars."

"Great idea," Natalie said.

She made a quick trip through the Western-wear store and picked up a big bottle of Stetson and was blowing warm air on her hands in her truck when her phone rang. She looked at the ID and took a deep breath.

"Hello, Daddy," she said.

"Are you in love with that cowboy? Really, really in love with him?" Jimmy Clark's deep voice boomed.

She took a deep breath.

"Yes or no? It's not a discussion, just a question, Natalie."

"Yes, I am," she said.

"I don't like that you didn't tell us about him, but I can live with it. With all this damn tomfoolery technology these days…"

"Daddy, if it wasn't for technology we'd still be picking cotton by hand and sowing wheat by broadcasting," she reminded him.

"Don't you interrupt me, young lady," he said. "I've thought about this a lot these past few days. I was mad as hell at first, but your momma said I couldn't come out there and get you and Joshua. I had to let you stand or fall on your face all by yourself since you made the decision without talkin' to us about it."

She waited.

"Well?" Jimmy asked.

"You said not to interrupt you."

"Now you can talk," he said.

She smiled. "I loved him before I even came out here, but I just didn't know how much. He's my soul mate, Daddy."

"Did he ask you to marry him?"

"Not yet," she said.

"Well, if he doesn't by Christmas then you come on home and he can court you by coming out here. Will you promise me you'll do that?"

"I promise," she said.

"Okay, then, I'll see you at New Year's, and I miss you, kiddo!"

Tears welled up in her eyes when he called her that. To him she'd always be his little girl just like to her, Josh would always be her baby boy.

"Miss you too, Daddy."

"Where are you? I don't hear Joshua."

"Sitting in my truck. I came to Sherman to finish up some shopping. I'm on my way to…"

"Walmart," he finished for her. "Woman ain't been to town unless she goes to Walmart."

"You got that right," she said. She didn't have the heart to tell him that she was going to buy a pregnancy test.

"Love you, kiddo," he said.

"Love you too, Daddy. And you're really going to like Lucas. He's rancher from the heart out."

"Thought he was a soldier."

"Not anymore. He's all rancher."

"Well, that makes me feel a little bit better, but I'll save judgment until I meet the fellow. He comes from good stock, I'll give him that much. His granddaddy and my folks were good friends when they were all young. Now I got to go. Your momma don't know I'm calling you. We might keep it that way."

"Why?"

"When you have a daughter, you'll understand." He chuckled. "Bye, now!"

The parking lot was so full that she had to park halfway to Dallas. At least it seemed that way when she ducked her head against the north wind that tried to push her all the way to Houston. Finally, she made it into the Walmart store and snagged the last shopping cart available. She braced herself for the crowd and headed straight for the side with the cosmetics, vitamins, and beauty supplies.

She tossed a pregnancy test in the cart along with two cans of hair spray, a bottle of shampoo and one of conditioner, and a big bottle of baby lotion for Josh. When she reached the end of the aisle she saw a display of lotions and bubble bath and remembered that she hadn't gotten Hazel anything. So she picked out a complete set that smelled like warm vanilla sugar and headed back through the store to look for a pretty scarf and maybe a nice brooch from the jewelry section.

She decided on a brooch in the shape of a star encrusted in tiny seed pearls with a tiny diamond in the middle, but the scarf that took her eye was bright green and red Christmas plaid. She contemplated going back to the jewelry counter and buying Hazel an initial brooch with red stones.

"Well, hello," Melody said at her elbow.

Natalie looked down at the pregnancy kit shining right there for the whole world to see and flipped the scarf over it without a second thought.

"Are you out doing some last-minute shopping too? My oldest son, the little drummer boy from the Christmas program, told Santa at school that he wanted a red wagon for Christmas, but he didn't tell me until this morning." She smiled.

Natalie smiled back. "I always think I've got it covered and then remember one more thing."

"Me too. Hey, us girls are getting together for a girls' lunch to celebrate still having our sanity sometime between Christmas and New Year's. Nothing fancy. Maybe at my house for sandwiches and soup. You should come," Melody said. "Oh, did you hear about Sonia? She took a job in Dallas and she's not even coming home for Christmas. She said that seeing Noah would hurt too bad, but—" Melody smiled and whispered, "I think she's already dating someone."

"Well, I hope she's happy in her new place," Natalie said. "Can I get back with you on that lunch?"

"Sure. Just give me a call, and if you can't make it this time, we'll do it again. I'm kind of glad that she and Noah didn't get married. We love Sonia because she's our friend, but they made the most unlikely pair in the whole state," Melody said. "Well, I'm off to find a red wagon. Santa better dang sure appreciate me for doing his work."

Natalie pushed her cart around the next corner and checked to make sure that the pregnancy box was covered.

—•—

Lucas took advantage of Natalie being gone and helped the guys move all the furniture out of the new nursery room. They'd stripped all the paint from the bed the day before and had stained the oak a rich brown. Grady worked at putting a coat of urethane on it that was guaranteed to be all right for baby furniture while Jack touched up the rocking horse and the chair.

When the room was totally empty, he locked the outside door. Natalie seldom ever went in there, but he had the perfect excuse if she tried to open it. He'd simply tell her that her Christmas present was too big to wrap and he was hiding it in the bedroom until Christmas Eve. It wasn't really a lie because there wasn't a box big enough in the whole world to wrap up the future.

She opened the back door at exactly noon and went straight to her room with a couple of bags. When she returned she'd changed clothes and wore a pair of faded jeans, a plaid flannel shirt, and her work boots. He thought she was absolutely stunning.

"Get it all done?" Hazel asked.

"I did. I'll set the table and pour the tea. That soup smells wonderful. What is it?" Natalie asked.

"Kidney bean soup. It's a good heavy soup that goes well with crusty bread and sliced sharp cheese on a cold day," Hazel said. "So get bowls and saucers. We won't need big plates."

Lucas walked up behind her and slipped his hands around her waist. "I missed you," he whispered for her ears only. "Want to go to bed and let me warm you up?"

She blushed. "Shhh…"

"You two better stop whispering or I'll think something is going on." Hazel giggled.

"I'm trying to talk her into telling me what she got you for Christmas," Lucas said.

"Boy, I don't buy that brand of bullshit," Hazel said. "Go get that baby. He might not be old enough to eat big people food, but I like it when he joins us at the table."

"Later," Lucas whispered and then kissed Natalie right below her ear. "And, sweet cheeks, you sure are cute when you blush."

Chapter 21

A THOUSAND BUTTERFLIES FLITTERED ABOUT IN NATALIE'S stomach on Christmas Eve morning. More than the usual holiday excitement had filled the house the past four days. The evening before, Hazel had insisted that she and Josh take her home to see her Christmas tree. When they got there Hazel had cookies ready and she made coffee and it was way past dark when Natalie got back home.

Home.

The word created another hundred butterflies. Was it home? Or was she fooling herself? She was so damned much in love that she wallowed in the present rather than being wise about the future.

She awoke to dead silence. Lucas wasn't even breathing on the pillow next to hers. She sat straight up and stared at the empty bed. No noise came from the kitchen, and she couldn't even smell coffee. Dear Lord, had Hazel fallen again and this time really broken her hip? She bailed out of bed, grabbed her pajama bottoms, and was pulling them up when Lucas appeared in the doorway.

"Is Hazel all right?" she asked.

"Sure, she is. It's Christmas Eve," he said.

"I know that but…" She stopped in the middle of the sentence. He was holding Josh in one hand and a camera in the other. The baby was dressed in a bright red outfit with Rudolph on the front that she'd never seen before.

"It's my first Christmas present for him," Lucas said. "And Hazel doesn't cook here on Christmas Eve. She's too busy getting dinner ready at her house for tomorrow. She usually leaves something for us to heat up for dinner and supper or we just have sandwiches."

"You could have told me," Natalie grumbled.

"It's time for Josh to see his big present. Next year he'll have to wait until Christmas morning for his Santa Claus, but I'm so damned excited, I can't wait." Lucas tried to stay serious so she wouldn't guess the surprise, but he couldn't keep a smile from covering his face.

"Dear Lord, don't tell me you brought a pony into the house." Natalie finished dressing.

Lucas motioned for her to follow him. "Didn't think of that, but I wouldn't put it past Dad to do it."

Something was missing. He was sexy as hell even in red and green plaid flannel lounging pants and a long-sleeved red thermal knit shirt, but something wasn't right. She scanned him from socks to drawstring on the pants, upward to… there it was—or wasn't. The dog tags were gone. He hadn't removed them one time since he got home, not even to shower, and now they were gone.

"Can I please make a side trip to the bathroom before Santa Claus?" she asked.

"Sure. Me and Josh will go get his morning bottle ready," he said.

She ducked into the bathroom, fished the pregnancy test out of the hiding place back behind the toilet paper on the first shelf of the cabinet behind the toilet, and read the instructions.

She simply had to know right then. She followed the instructions to the letter and paced from one end of the bathroom to the other while she waited. Every time she passed the stick lying on the cabinet she shut her eyes. Maybe she should just toss the damn thing in the trash and buy a second one after the holidays. She could go two more days without knowing, couldn't she?

The second hand on the clock dragged on like a slow-witted turtle, each click taking a full hour. Finally, it was time to look, and she couldn't make herself do it. She put the lid down on the potty and her head in her hands. She wasn't sick anymore. She couldn't eat bacon or sausage in the morning but had no trouble with ham or roast for dinner or even rigatoni for supper.

"Hey, we're waiting." Lucas knocked on the bathroom door. "You don't have to put on makeup for the pictures. You are beautiful just the way you are, sweet cheeks."

"Old MacDonald Had a Farm" started playing on the other side of the bathroom door. She opened the door just a crack and peeked out. Joshua was sitting in his infant seat in the middle of the hallway, and the bedroom door across from the bathroom was thrown wide open.

"You're pale. Are you sick again?" Lucas had a worried expression on his face.

She glanced down at the stick. Holy Mary, mother of Jesus! The line was practically screaming out the word *pregnant*.

"Are you okay? You look like you're about to faint," Lucas said.

"I'm fine. Where's that music coming from?" she asked.

Lucas pointed across the hall. "It's Josh's Christmas. I snuck in there and turned it on so it would be playing for him when we take him into his own brand-new nursery."

She swung the door open and watched Lucas proudly pick up the baby. He looped his arm around her waist and together they entered the nursery.

"Oh, my!" she gasped.

"It's old but it belonged to Gramps and then to Dad and finally to me, until today. Now it is Josh's new crib. The rocking chair is what Granny rocked Dad in and what Hazel rocked me in until I was too big to sit in her lap, and the rest of it was mine." He laid the baby in the crib.

Josh laughed out loud at the mobile going around in slow circles above his head.

"He likes it," Lucas said. "And he's got room to grow. That little old crib you brought was stunting his growth."

"It's beautiful, Lucas." Tears streaked her cheeks. "I'm pregnant," she blurted out.

He dropped down on one knee and took her hands in his. "Will you marry me, Natalie Clark? I never knew or understood happy until you came into my life."

The tears dripped from her jawbone onto the bright yellow tank top. She shook her head. "No, I cannot marry you."

"Why?" he gasped.

"Because you are only proposing to me because I'm pregnant. You don't have to do this," she said.

He handed her a folded piece of paper. "That would be a marriage license. It's good through tomorrow. I bought it several days ago with hopes that you'd say yes when I proposed this morning. I'm not asking you to marry me because you are pregnant. I'm asking because I love you. I don't want you to say yes because we are going to have another baby. I want you to say yes because you love me."

She threw her arms around him and sobbed into his chest.

He hugged her close and said, "Josh is our firstborn. My dog tags are in that little chest on his dresser. I gave them to him this morning and let him chew on them. He will know about Drew, but I want him to be my son. I want him to be proud of me for serving my country and to grow up on this ranch, which will be his legacy as much as the rest of the children we produce, Natalie."

She leaned back and looked into his soft brown eyes. The message there was clear. She could trust him with her heart, her son, and her love. "I love you, Lucas, and I want to spend the rest of my life with you. Does this mean we are getting married today or tomorrow?"

"That's your gift to me, sweet cheeks, so you decide. Gramps is an ordained preacher and the little church on the ranch is decorated for Christmas. I reckon it could be in half an hour or tomorrow, or if you want to wait a year, I can always buy a new license every ten days."

The church was decorated for Christmas with a small tree beside the old upright piano and poinsettias on either end of the altar. She wore the ivory lace dress that she'd worn to the Angus Christmas party. Lucas wore his black Wranglers, a white shirt, and carried Josh in his arms as they walked down the aisle together.

Grady, Jack, and Hazel sat on the front pew and

Henry waited at the front of the church. When they were standing before him, he reached out and took Josh from Lucas.

"Dearly beloved, we are gathered here today to join Natalie... what is your middle name, honey?"

"My full name is Natalie Joy Clark," she whispered.

"Okay, to join Natalie Joy Clark and Justin Lucas Allen in holy matrimony and to make them a family with Josh... what's his full name?" Henry asked.

"His name is Joshua Lucas Clark..."

A grin covered Henry's face. "A family with Joshua Lucas Clark, soon to be Joshua Lucas Allen. Can I have the rings please, Lucas?"

"You didn't tell me that you named him after me," Lucas said.

"You didn't ask. I named him for my best friend, Joshua Andrew Camp, and the cowboy who helped me get over his death, Justin Lucas Allen. He will also have your initials when you adopt him," Natalie said.

"You're not going to fight me on that?" Lucas asked.

"Hell, no! He's going to sleep in your crib and you gave him your dog tags. I think Drew would be happy for him to have your name," she answered.

Grady chuckled. "Is this a wedding or a discussion?"

"The rings?" Henry said.

Lucas fished them out of his pocket. She hadn't expected him to have rings, but then the day had been full of surprises.

"These rings belonged first to me and my beloved wife, Ella Jo. We are glad to share them with this couple today and it is our hope that they will be as happy as we have been all these years," Henry said.

Natalie swallowed hard as Henry blessed the rings. She hadn't even gotten over the weepy sentimental emotional roller coaster of pregnancy with Josh and now it was starting all over again.

Henry asked them to repeat the traditional vows. She didn't stutter once when she promised to love, honor, and respect Lucas until death parted them. No problem there except that even death couldn't part them any more than it had parted Henry and Ella Jo. Lucas Allen was her soul mate.

"And now you may kiss the bride," Henry said.

Lucas tipped her chin up, looked into her blue eyes, and then kissed her with so much love and passion that her knees went weak. When the kiss ended he turned around and said, "Folks, welcome Mrs. Lucas Allen to Cedar Hill Ranch."

Hazel dabbed at her eye. "And Josh. We welcome both of you."

Henry handed the baby to Lucas and hugged Natalie. "Ella Jo is so happy that she's got a granddaughter now and a great-grandson that she may stick around after Christmas."

Jack was next. "You've given us the best Christmas ever."

Grady was last in line. "Lucas sure got a good Christmas. Ain't many cowboys get a bride and a baby both for Christmas. And the rest of us are mighty happy for him. He couldn't have found a better woman to ride the river of life with."

"Thank you, all," Natalie said. "My momma says that you are all to come to Silverton with us on New Year's where she's planning a wedding reception. She's not any too happy about not being here today, so you will be going with me. No is not an option."

Hazel giggled. "I pass my bossin' crown on to you right now. And we'll all be ready to go to Silverton at whatever time you say."

―⁓―

Lucas's hand was around Natalie's waist as they carefully laid Josh in his new bed that night. He spit out his pacifier and stuck his thumb in his mouth and they both smiled.

"Are you ready for bed, Mrs. Allen?"

She leaned her head on his shoulder. "Soon as I make a trip to the bathroom."

"You are pregnant, sweet cheeks. I'm so happy about it I could scream it from the top of the barn. You don't have to check it again," he said.

She kissed him on the cheek. "I'll see you in the bedroom in a couple of minutes."

He hurried down the hall, grabbed the CD and the candle that he'd given her, and carried them to their room. He lit the candle, turned out the lights, and put the CD in the player. When he heard the bathroom door shut he pushed the right button to start the music. Alan Jackson was singing "I Only Want You For Christmas" when she walked through the door, but Lucas couldn't hear a single word of the song.

There she stood, strip stark naked, barefoot, hair all mussed up with a big red velvet bow tied around her waist and her pink pistol in her hand.

"Merry Christmas, cowboy," she whispered.

He pulled the bow and led her to the bed. "Yes,

ma'am, it surely is. You going to shoot me with that thing when I untie that ribbon?"

"No, I just keep it in the nightstand beside my bed. It goes with me. You got a problem with it?" She cocked a hip out to one side as she put the pistol in the drawer of the nightstand.

He reached out and pulled the ribbon and the bow came undone just as Alan sang that he only wanted her for Christmas, baby, that he didn't need anything else. "I don't have a problem with anything about you, sweet cheeks. Merry Christmas to me."

Dear Readers,

Merry Christmas!

This is the second book in the Cowboys & Brides series, and Lucas and Natalie would sure like to welcome all y'all to Cedar Hill Ranch in Savoy, Texas. Population less than a thousand with friendly folks, ranches, sexy cowboys, sassy ladies, and a snowstorm promising the first white Christmas in nearly twenty years.

Christmas is that time when love is in the air, as much or maybe even more than Valentine's Day. It's hustling about, cooking, and keeping secrets so that there can be surprises on Christmas day. It was the perfect time for Lucas to meet Natalie in person, the woman that he'd been visiting with via the Internet for almost a year.

He thought he'd surprise everyone when he arrived home two days early, but it was Lucas who got the surprise. Natalie had already arrived so that she and Hazel, Lucas's elderly housekeeper, could surprise him when he came home. Imagine how he felt when he rounded the back of the house and there she stood, with a dead coyote at the toes of her boots, three bluetick hound puppies at her heels, a pink pistol in one hand, and a baby cradled in her other arm.

And poor old Lucas didn't know a thing about a baby!

Folks have asked me if I plot for hours before I even start to write. This time I thought I had it all figured out, just what Natalie and Lucas would do after that first meeting—but I got the biggest surprise of all. They crawled into my head and told me exactly how to tell the story and what to say and if I did it my way, they even visited my dreams. So if you love the story, the credit goes to Natalie and Lucas and not to any plotting that I did.

And if you love the story, credit also goes a wonderful staff at Sourcebooks and my awesome editor, Deb Werksman! Writing for Sourcebooks is an amazing experience and I can't thank them enough for continuing to buy my books.

Thanks again to my agent, Erin Niumata, at Folio Literary Management, who's been steering my career for more than a decade. And thanks to Husband, bless his heart, who has lived with a loud-mouthed Rebel for more than forty years now.

And always, always big, big thanks to my readers who love my books, talk about them, pass them on to their family and friends, and continue to buy them. Y'all are simply great!

Keep your boots on because next spring, you can come back to Fannin County and read Greg and Emily's story in *The Cowboy's Mail Order Bride*. And after that, Mason Harper's twin girls get their birthday wish in *How to Marry a Cowboy*.

Happy Reading,
Carolyn Brown

Read on for a sneak peek of

The Cowboy's Mail Order Bride

Coming February 2014 from Sourcebooks Casablanca

EMILY TOOK A DEEP BREATH AND RANG THE DOORBELL.

The cold February wind swept across the wide porch of the ranch house and cut right through her lightweight denim jacket. Her heavy coat was in the pickup, but this job wouldn't take long. Hand the box of letters over to Clarice Barton and she'd be back in her truck and on her way. Then her grandfather's spirit would rest in peace. He'd said that it wouldn't until the box was put in Clarice's hands.

She heard footsteps on hardwood floors, and then something brushed against her leg. She looked down just as a big yellow cat laid a dead mouse on her boots. There were two things that Emily hated and mice were both of them. Live ones topped out the list above dead ones, but only slightly.

She kicked her foot just as the door opened and the mouse flew up like a baseball. The woman who slung open the screen door caught the animal mid-air, realized what she had in her hand, and threw it back toward Emily. She sidestepped the thing and the cat jumped up, snagged it with a paw, quickly flipped it into its mouth, and ran off the porch.

"Dammit!" The lady wiped her hand on the side of

her jeans. "God almighty, I hate them things, and that damned cat keeps bringing them up to the porch like she's haulin' gold into the house."

The woman's black hair was sprinkled with white. Bright red lipstick had run into the wrinkles around her mouth and disappeared from the middle. When she smiled, her brown eyes twinkled brightly. Sure enough, the hardwood floor to the big two-story house was so shiny that Emily could see the reflection of the woman's worn athletic shoes in it.

"I'm sorry," Emily gasped. "It was a reflex action."

The woman giggled. "Well, now that we've both decided that we hate mice, what can I do for you, honey? You lost or something?" she asked.

"Is this Lightning Ridge Ranch? Are you Clarice Barton?" Emily shivered against the cold and the idea of a mouse touching her favorite boots.

"Yes, it's Lightning Ridge, but I'm not Clarice. She's making a run out to the henhouse. We're making a chocolate cake later on and I used up all the eggs makin' hot rolls. It's cold. You better come on inside and wait for her. I'm Dotty, Clarice's best friend and helper around here. I'm going to have to wash my hands a dozen times to get the feel of dead mouse off." The lady stepped aside. "What do you need Clarice for?"

"I'm here to deliver this box."

"Your nose is red and you look chilled. Come on in the living room. We got a little blaze going in the fireplace. It'll warm you right up. This weather is plumb crazy these days. February ain't supposed to be this damned cold. Spring ain't that far away. Winter needs to step aside. What'd you say your name was?" Dotty motioned her into the living room with a flick of her wrist.

"I'm Emily, and thank you. The warmth feels good," she said.

"Well, you just wait right here. She won't be long. Go on and sit down, honey. Take that rockin' chair and pull it up next to the fireplace. Can I get you a cup of coffee or hot chocolate?"

"No, ma'am. I'm fine," Emily answered. She would have loved a cup of anything hot just to wrap her chilled fingers around, but she didn't want to stick around long enough to drink a whole cup.

"Well, I'm in the middle of stirrin' up some hot rolls. Just make yourself at home until Clarice gets here."

Dotty disappeared, leaving Emily alone in the living room. She held the ancient boot box in her lap. Her grandfather had worn out the boots that came in the box and now it held letters from a woman who was not her grandmother. His passing and her two promises to him in his final days seemed surreal, especially sitting in the house of the woman who'd written the letters more than sixty years before.

Warmth radiated out from the fireplace as she took stock of her surroundings. The room was a perfect square with furniture arranged facing the fireplace to give it a cozy feel. A framed picture of a cowboy took center stage on the mantel. She set the box on the coffee table and stepped in closer to look at the photograph. He had dark brown hair and green eyes behind wire-rimmed glasses. It had been taken in the summer because there were wildflowers in the background. One shiny black boot was propped on a rail fence, and he held a Stetson in his right hand. His left thumb was tucked into the pocket of his tight jeans, leaving the rest of his hand to draw attention to the zipper. And right there in the corner of the frame was a yellow sticky note with the words, "Miss you, Nana!" stuck to it.

The crimson flushing her cheeks had nothing to do with the heat rising from the fireplace and everything to do with the way she'd mentally undressed this man she'd never even seen in real life. *Get a grip, Em*, she thought to herself. She backed away quickly and stood by the door, but when she looked over her shoulder, the cowboy was staring at her. She moved to the other side of the room and shivers shot down her spine when she realized he was still looking at her. She tried another corner and behold, those green eyes had followed her.

She was tired. It had been a long emotional week and this was the final thing she had to do before she could really mourn for her grandfather. She'd driven since daybreak that morning, and her eyes were playing tricks on her. That must be it. Her dark brows knit together as she glanced at the picture from across the room. Did he have a wedding ring on that left hand? Determined not to let a picture intimidate her, she circled the room so she could see the photograph better, and his hand was ring free.

How old was he, and when was the picture taken? Not one thing gave away a year or a time other than it was spring or summer. He might be a fifty-year-old man with gray hair nowadays and bowed legs from riding too many horses through the years. Or he could be a lot younger than he looked in the photograph and still be in college, just coming home to work on the ranch in the summertime like she had when she was getting her degree.

Unless he came looking for a warm spot to take the chill off, she'd never meet him anyway. Her mission was to deliver letters, and studying the picture was just a diversion while she waited on Clarice.

"My grandson, Greg Adams," a woman said from the doorway.

"Fine-lookin' cowboy, isn't he? His daddy and momma wanted him to be a businessman in a big old office in Houston, but he's got his grandpa's ranchin' savvy. He's down in southern Texas at a cattle sale. Cute little sticker he left there, isn't it?"

Emily swallowed hard at the mention of a grandpa. She fought even harder to keep from blushing again. "Yes, ma'am, he is surely handsome. I'm Emily Cooper, and you are Clarice Barton?" She quickly crossed the room and held out her right hand.

Clarice's handshake was firm and her smile sincere. "Do I know you? Dotty said you had a box or something to give to me."

Her thick gray hair was cut short to frame her round face. She wore jeans and a Western-cut shirt, boots, and no makeup, and she had the same green eyes as the cowboy in the picture.

"No, ma'am, you do not know me. You *are* Clarice Barton, aren't you?"

"No, honey, I'm Clarice Adams. I haven't been Clarice Barton in more than sixty years, but I was before I got married. Let's sit down while we talk. Dotty is bringing us some hot coffee in a few minutes."

Just out of curiosity, Emily glanced at the picture and

sure enough, the cowboy followed her as she crossed the room and sat down.

She picked up the box from the coffee table and held it out to Clarice. "Marvin Cooper was my grandfather. He made me promise I'd bring these to you. They are the letters that you wrote to him when he was in Korea during the war."

Clarice laid a hand over her heart, and the color left her cheeks.

"Marvin," she whispered.

"Marvin Cooper?" Dotty set a tray holding three cups of coffee on the coffee table. "I'll be damned. Did you tell her that you were playing kickball with a damned old dead mouse?"

"No, ma'am." Emily's nostrils curled just thinking about it. She looked down at her boots. Should she simply leave them in her hotel room or try to wash the mouse from them? She could visualize the thing right there on the instep.

"Well, it took half a bar of soap to get it off my hand." Dotty went on to tell Clarice the story. "She don't like mice either, so I've decided that she's my new friend."

Clarice giggled. "I wish I'd been here to see that sight. Dotty hates mice and I hate spiders." She ran a hand down the side of the box, but she didn't take it. "I can't believe he kept them all these years or that you've brought them to me."

Emily pointed to the one that had been slipped beneath the faded red ribbon tied around the box. "This one is from him to you. It got stuck in a mailbag and then the bag got shoved back into an old desk drawer down at the post office. They didn't discover it until last week. According to the postmark, it should've been mailed sixty years ago, but it never left Happy. You might want to start with it. They brought it out to the ranch and apologized for losing it all those years ago. Gramps told me to put it with the others, and he didn't even open it. He said he remembered right well what it said."

Clarice's hands trembled. "Gramps? That would make you his granddaughter, then? He got married and had children?"

"Yes, he did and he is—was—my grandfather. He's only been gone four days and I'm still not used to the idea of saying 'was.' It sounds so final."

"I understand. When my husband died, it took me a long time to use the past tense too. So Marvin had a granddaughter and I have a grandson," Clarice whispered.

Dotty shook her head slowly. "Marvin Cooper! When I first met Clarice she told me all about Marvin, but we never thought we'd hear that name again. And you drove all the way across the state to bring those letters? You are talking about Happy, Texas, right?"

"Yes, ma'am."

"You aren't plannin' on drivin' all the way back tonight, are you?" Clarice asked.

"I'm staying at a hotel in Sherman," Emily said.

"Please stay with us for supper. I've got to hear all about Marvin and how his life went." Clarice's eyes misted over and Emily couldn't have refused her request if it had meant standing in front of a firing squad.

Besides, it was just supper and a couple of hours' worth of talking about her grandfather. It would make

Clarice feel good, and Gramps would like that. Maybe it would even give Emily the closure she needed so badly.

"And if that damned old mama cat brings up another rat, we might have to stick together to get rid of it," Dotty said.

"Thank you. I'd like to stay for supper, but Miz Dotty, if that cat brings up another one of those vicious rats, you're on your own," Emily said.

"Rat, my hind end. It was probably just a baby mouse. Every time that Dotty tells the story it'll get bigger and bigger," Clarice said.

"You didn't see it. It was only slightly smaller than a damned old 'possum," Dotty argued.

Emily giggled and wished that she could take Dotty to Florida with her. That old girl would be a real hoot to have around all the time.

Clarice's phone rang and she fished it out of her shirt pocket. "Greg, darlin', the most amazing thing has happened." She gave him the one-minute shortened form of Emily bringing the box of letters and told him that she'd tell him the rest of the story when he got home.

Emily looked at the blaze in the fireplace, at the ceiling, and finally settled back on the picture of Clarice's grandson. She locked gazes with him, wondering what he would be like in the flesh. Was he really that handsome or just very, very photogenic?

"That's her grandson, Greg," Dotty whispered.

"She told me." Emily nodded.

"He's gone right now, but he'll be home tomorrow night. We miss him," Dotty said.

"I bet he misses being home," Emily said.

"Emily," Clarice said.

She whipped around when she heard her name, and an instant flash lit up her face.

Clarice giggled like a little girl. "I'm so sorry. He asked me what your name was again and I told him. It's a good picture of you. You have your grandpa's eyes. This is a new phone and I keep taking pictures of things rather than hanging up. I miss the old corded phones that we used to have and cameras that used a flashbulb. This new technology is enough to drive a person crazy."

Dotty picked up her cup of coffee and sipped at it. "Ain't that the truth. Us old dogs havin' to learn all these new tricks is frustratin' as hell, and that damned computer shit is the worst thing of all. Y'all best drink that coffee before it gets cold. Want some cookies to go with it? It's a while till supper."

"No, this is fine." Emily covered a yawn with her hand. "I'm sorry. I drove all day, stopped at the hotel, and then got lost twice trying to find this place."

"How did you find me?" Clarice asked.

"I stopped at the post office and the lady there said that there wasn't a Clarice Barton around. The only Clarice she knew was Clarice Adams and I might check to see if that was you."

"She's new in town. Ain't been here but ten years or she would have known the Bartons helped to build Ravenna." Dotty pointed to the door. "I know Clarice is just dyin' to dig into those letters. And I've got things to do in the kitchen. Would you like to take a nap until suppertime? You can rest in the first room on the left upstairs."

"I wouldn't want to be a bother," Emily said.

"No bother at all. You go on up there and rest. If you aren't awake by supper, I'll holler for you," Dotty said.

Clarice reached across the space separating them and patted her arm. "And thank you so much for bringing these letters."

"I promised Gramps I would do it. Is it all right if I take this upstairs with me?" Emily picked up her cup of coffee.

"Of course it is," Clarice said.

Dotty stood up at the same time Emily did. "Clarice was right about Marvin. She said that she thought he was about to ask her to marry him. She's the only one of us four that isn't a mail-order bride. That's the way I come to live in these parts. I was from Kentucky and he lived here. I thought any place was better than Harlan County, Kentucky, so I climbed on a bus and come out here. Married Johnny and loved him to his dying day, but the best thing that come out of me bein' a mail-order bride is that I met Clarice and we become best friends."

"Four of you?"

"Yep." Dotty nodded. "Me and Rose and Madge all come to Texas right after the war was over more than sixty years ago. I got here first in January and the other two came on later that spring. It's a long story how it all happened. Rose and Madge are cousins. Madge was writing to a soldier that she met through the church pen pal group. So she came out here to meet him, and then Rose came to visit and wound up married to a local guy too. Our husbands are all gone now and we are widows."

"You were all kind of like mail-order brides?"

"Mainly me and Madge were, and Rose kind of got in on the deal like shirttail kin. Clarice is the only one of us that was raised right here in Ravenna," Dotty said. "Now get on up there and get some rest."

"Supper is at six?" Emily checked the clock and glanced at that picture one more time.

"Yes, it is." Dotty smiled.

A two-hour nap, supper, some talk about her grandfather, and then back to the hotel. Tomorrow she would be on her way to Florida for a whole month on the beach.

"Oh, my!" Emily gasped when she opened the door into the bedroom.

Back when she was in high school she would have hocked her tomcat, Spurs, to have her own room like the one before her. A queen-sized four-poster bed covered with a pretty quilt and lacy bed ruffle sat on one side of the room. A big, deep recliner and a vanity with a three-way mirror were located over beside the door into the bathroom, which sported a deep claw-footed tub. She'd always shared the one bathroom in the small three-bedroom ranch house with two men who did not understand why one girl needed so much hairspray, lotion, bath oil, and her own pink razors to shave her legs.

She washed her hands, dried them, and then rubbed lotion into them—sweet-smelling lavender lotion that reminded her of Great-Aunt Molly, grandmother to her favorite cousin, Taylor.

Her grandfather's words the day that he and Molly went to the courthouse together came back to her as she looked in the bathroom mirror. Molly had deeded her ranch to Taylor, and Marvin had given what was left of his adjoining ranch to Emily. On the way home he had said, "I'm not real sure your future is on Shine Canyon Ranch, Em."

When she'd asked him why he'd say a thing like that, he'd just smiled and tapped his heart. "Ranchin' is in your heart and you'll always love it, but something in my soul tells me your future is not on Shine Canyon. When I'm gone, I want you to take a month and think things through before you commit to this land for the rest of your life. You'll have a hard row to hoe even with family to help with just a hundred acres. I'm not sure in today's economy that you'll ever make it without taking a job in town, and that means ranchin' at night after you work your ass off all day at your job."

She blinked away the tears and turned away from the mirror. "A hundred acres might not be much, but it's mine, Gramps. And I love the land as much as you did. I'm not afraid of hard work, and piece by piece I'll buy our land back from Taylor. He promised he'd sell it to me when I could buy it, remember. That was the rule when you sold it to him."

Lacy curtains covered the narrow window overlooking the backyard. She drew a corner back and peeked out. She dropped the curtain and took a step back, stumbled over a small footstool, and went down on one knee.

She wanted to cry, to curl up in a ball and weep, but she couldn't. She limped over to the recliner, flipped the handle on the side, and leaned back as far as it would let her, looked up, and right there on top of the chest of drawers was another picture of Greg. A bust shot of him in his high school graduation robe and mortarboard hat with a tassel hanging to the side. The gold charm told her that he'd graduated two years before she did and that his school colors were orange and black. A sticky note attached to the side of the frame held the message, "I'll bring home the best bull. Miss you!"

He was younger, but the eyes were the same and they

still looked right into her soul like the picture down in the living room. She threw her arm over her face and forced herself to think about the beach, to hear the seagulls and the slapping of the waves against the sand-bar. The soft smell of the lotion on her hands sparked a deep memory of her mother in her dreams. They were playing in the wildflowers like the ones in the picture of Greg Adams. She was a little girl with dark braids and a cotton dress. The grass was soft on her bare feet but cool, so it had to be spring. They'd sung the "Ring around the Rosy" song, then fallen back in the flowers. Her mother touched her cheek and said, "Don't ever give up your wings. Always know that you can fly, my child."

Then out of nowhere there was a door right in the middle of the pasture of wild colorful flowers, and there was a yellow cat peeking around the corner. A mouse darted through the cat's front legs and was coming right at her when she sat straight up in bed and her eyes popped wide open.

"Damn it! I don't get to dream about Mama very often. Why'd you bring that thing into my dreams?" she asked.

Someone rapped gently on the door, but she thought it was part of the dream until it happened again. She cocked her head to one side and said, "Come in."

Clarice pushed inside and sat down on the vanity bench. "Thank you. It's been more than an hour and I was hoping you were awake. Would you please tell me more about Marvin? I read the letter and it said what I thought it would. Strange, that something sixty years old can still be so bittersweet."

"Is it all right if I sit on the bed?" Emily asked. "This chair would be a lot more comfortable for you than that bench."

"Honey, this is your room right now. Make yourself at home."

"Is that your grandson in that picture too?" Emily asked.

Clarice nodded. "When he graduated from high school. He leaves me little notes when he has to be gone. It's to convince me that he's coming back. I have a fear that he'll change his mind about ranchin'. Now please tell me about Marvin."

Emily kicked off her boots and crawled up in the middle of the bed. She crossed her legs Indian-style, kept her gaze on Clarice and off the picture on the chest, and said, "He fought cancer for five years and last week the battle ended. It won. I thought he'd kick it for sure right up until that last week. He was diagnosed the week I graduated from college five years ago. I had planned on coming back to the ranch anyway, so it didn't change my life drastically. I took care of him. He was always too stubborn to hire a foreman, so I took care of that too. As the ranch dwindled to pay for his bills, there was less ranchin' and more caretakin'."

"How many children did he have?" Clarice asked.

Emily held up one finger. "Just one son, my father. But Nana's family lived on the next farm over. She came from a family that had five girls, so I had lots of family around me and lots of cousins to play with when I was growing up. My father died nine years ago in a horse accident. I was a senior in high school and the shock was horrible. Even worse than when Mama died, but I was just barely four that year and too little to really understand what an aneurism was. He was fine that morning at breakfast and that evening he was gone. I thought it was the worst thing I'd ever endure, but watching Gramps go by degrees was even tougher. How many children did you have, Miz Clarice?"

"Just one son, Bart. He and his wife, Nancy, only had one child—Greg. He's thirty now. And you?"

"Twenty-eight," Emily answered.

"Did Marvin ever mention me?" Clarice asked softly.

"He talked about you that last week and to you the last hours of his life. I really thought that you were probably dead and had come to help him cross over into eternity. He made me promise that I'd find out if you were alive and see to it that you got those letters and understood that he hadn't been a jackass. It all started when the mailman drove out to the ranch with that letter they found at the post office," Emily said.

"Thank you for keeping that promise. You'll never know what this means to me. Did Marvin, was he, did he suffer?" Clarice dabbed at her eye.

Emily shook her head. "He was sick for a very long time, but there at the first he was still able to be up and around. It wasn't until that last round of chemo that he wasn't able to at least sit on the porch swing with me every evening. At the end I prayed that God would take him on to a place where he wouldn't hurt anymore. That sounds ugly, doesn't it?"

Clarice shook her head. "No, it's the way life is. Why didn't he come to Ravenna all those years ago? He knew where I was."

Emily shrugged. "I asked him that, but he just smiled

and said that God must've had other plans for both of you or that letter wouldn't have gotten lost."

Clarice nodded. "Can't undo history. I was happy with Lester Adams. We had a good life, raised a good son, and he married well. Now I have Greg to help me run the ranch. I'm glad you brought the letters home to me, Emily, and I'm glad you agreed to stay for supper."

"Thank you," Emily said.

"Want to come with me to the kitchen and help Dotty get things on the table?" Clarice asked.

"I'd love to." Emily bounded off the bed, stomped her feet back into her boots, and followed Clarice on down the stairs.

About the Author

Carolyn Brown is a *New York Times* and *USA Today* bestselling author with more than sixty books published, and credits her eclectic family for her humor and writing ideas. Her books include the cowboy trilogy *Lucky in Love*, *One Lucky Cowboy*, and *Getting Lucky*; the Honky Tonk series with *I Love This Bar*; *Hell, Yeah*; *Honky Tonk Christmas*; and *My Give a Damn's Busted*; and her bestselling Spikes & Spurs series with *Love Drunk Cowboy*, *Red's Hot Cowboy*, *Darn Good Cowboy Christmas*, *One Hot Cowboy Wedding*, *Mistletoe Cowboy*, *Just a Cowboy and His Baby*, and *Cowboy Seeks Bride*. Carolyn has launched into women's fiction as well with *The Blue-Ribbon Jalapeño Society Jubilee*. She was born in Texas but grew up in southern Oklahoma where she and her husband, Charles, a retired English teacher, make their home. They have three grown children and enough grandchildren to keep them young.